Prais ...

"Foun... ... SEAL Team 6 . . . that many believe led the assault on bin Laden's compound."
—*The Washington Post*

"Richard Marcinko is a master at showing us his world. It's not a very safe place, but visiting is well worth the risk. Marcinko's stories are as vivid as they are real. He's been there, and he has the talent to take us with him."
—Larry Bond,
New York Times bestselling author of *Exit Plan*

"Marcinko is the real McCoy, a warrior who has lived it."
—Stephen Coonts,
New York Times bestselling author of *The Assassin*

"Marcinko is the real thing: combat veteran, killer SEAL, specialist in unconventional warfare."
—*The Washington Times*

"Marcinko gives new meaning to the word *tough*."
—*Publishers Weekly*

"Marcinko's Rogue Warrior yarns . . . are the purest kind of thriller around, with action, pacing, and hardware galore."
—*Booklist*

ROGUE WARRIOR®

Blood Lies

Richard Marcinko

and

Jim DeFelice

A TOM DOHERTY ASSOCIATES BOOK
NEW YORK

This is a work of fiction. All of the characters, organizations, and events portrayed in this novel are either products of the authors' imagination or are used fictitiously.

ROGUE WARRIOR®: BLOOD LIES

Copyright © 2012 by Richard Marcinko and Jim DeFelice

All rights reserved.

A Forge Book
Published by Tom Doherty Associates, LLC
175 Fifth Avenue
New York, NY 10010

www.tor-forge.com

Forge® is a registered trademark of Tom Doherty Associates, LLC.

ISBN 978-0-7653-6454-8

Forge books may be purchased for educational, business, or promotional use. For information on bulk purchases, please contact Macmillan Corporate and Premium Sales Department at 1-800-221-7945, extension 5442, or write specialmarkets@macmillan.com.

First Edition: September 2012
First Mass Market Edition: October 2013

Printed in the United States of America

0 9 8 7 6 5 4 3 2 1

Dedicated to the Brotherhood of SEALs who gave the ULTIMATE sacrifice in Afghanistan 2011, and to their families and loved ones who must live through the pain

PART ONE

In Mexico, you have death very close.

—GAEL GARCIA BERNAL,
FILM ACTOR AND DIRECTOR

[1]

IT'S NOT HARD to get mugged in Juarez, Mexico. Walk down the wrong street, flash some cash, act a little tipsy — before you know it, you've got a crowd lining up behind you, fighting over who has dibs.

Getting kidnapped is harder. First of all, it pays to be choosey. You don't want to be kidnapped by just anyone. Or let me say, you don't want to be kidnapped by the *wrong* anyone. The crime has to be seen as a business transaction, not one of passion. Passion will quickly get you killed, not just in Juarez but anywhere.

It also has to be the right kind of business transaction. You don't want it to be part of a merger and acquisition. The latter is pretty common in Juarez, where drug cartels and their various factions are constantly jostling for position. If your kidnappers grab you as part of a hostile takeover, your chances of emerging with significant limbs intact is small.

You want to be kidnapped by someone who doesn't see you as competition, who expects a good ransom, and who knows that damaged goods are bad for business. He should be fairly adept at it, too — the last thing you want is a nervous finger on the 1911 Model knockoff when it's pushed against your ribs. (Most kidnappers in general are male, and this is especially true in Mexico. I'm not sure why they gravitate toward inexpensive versions of the venerable Colt automatic; maybe they get a bulk discount. Or maybe they missed out on our ATF royally fucked-up scam—excuse me, *sting* operation—"designed" to trace U.S. illegal gun sales throughout the Southwest, Midwest, and dead West. It was your typical cocked-up brain-dead government operation, helped along by some greedy cock breaths on the U.S. side of the border.)

If you want to be grabbed by higher-end thugs, you have to position yourself just right. Attractive and available alone won't cut it. Your cover story has to fall close to the profile of people they like to snatch. You also have to present yourself as easy, but not such a patsy that lesser villains try to pick you off the street.

Becoming functional bait isn't just a difficult business, it's an art form.

MY INTEREST IN kidnapping was sincere and honorable. I wanted to be grabbed as part of a plan to free a legitimate kidnap victim, the twenty-two-year-old, tactfully blond and delicately curvaceous daughter of a fellow SEAL.

There were ulterior motives as well, the most important of which had to do with Hezbollah[1] and a reported terror camp in the border area. But that part of the story is best saved for a moment when things are a little calmer. Because at the moment this book begins, I'm east of Juarez being chased by a pair of pickup trucks filled with gun-toting banditos. My foot is to the floor

---

[1] Hezbollah is the Iranian-funded terror group that controls the Gaza Strip, hates Israel, and has sworn to do things to the U.S. that don't include giving us a birthday cake. We'll go into more detail later.

and the big Cadillac is fishtailing across a sandy Mexican road parallel to the border.

The car responded by pulling to the left, the torque steer nearly jerking her out of my hands. Careful not to overcorrect, I muscled the vehicle onto the pavement, holding the nose steady as the speedometer stretched toward triple digits.

I'm not ordinarily a Cadillac guy; if I were going to choose a car from Government Motors at all it would probably be more in the Chevy line. But this Caddy had a lot going for it—most especially the ceramic plate inserts throughout the chassis and body designed to withstand anything short of a 120 mm armor-piercing shell. The glass—front, back, and sides—had been replaced with thick bulletproof material, all of which added a shitpot of extra weight to this lead sled. In exchange, the armor could ward off slugs from a .300 Win mag.

Unfortunately, the bastards behind me opened fire with a pair of fifties—as in 50 mm machine guns. The bullets, heavier and designed to act like frickin' can openers, peppered the back of the car. A dozen shattered the window, embedding themselves in the ceramic plates in the driver's seat behind me.

I ducked as low as I could, trying to hide behind what was left of the seat as bullets splattered through the interior of the car, smashing the burled walnut interior accents and adding random vents to the automatic climate control. The front windshield spiderwebbed with bullet holes, and the radio, which had been playing an old Willie Nelson tune about cowboys, gave up the ghost.

That was pretty much the last straw. I veered right, then reached for the flasher button.

The button was preset to send a radio signal to my trail team; roughly translated, the signal meant "Get your fucking butts over here and rescue my ass." Only not as polite.

In theory, I didn't need the signal: we had a small UAV overhead watching, sending signals to a temporary command post and the trail team. But theory and reality had already separated: in *theory* the gang I was enticing as a kidnap victim didn't fire at its victims. In reality, the bastards behind me were about to fry me alive.

I swung left and right, onto the shoulders, then back to the highway. As I came up over a rise, I spotted a tractor-trailer headed in my direction and moving at a good clip. I waited until he had pulled almost even, then swerved my car, sliding off the road behind him but managing to regain the pavement in the opposite direction of my pursuers.[2]

Somewhere between the bullets and the hard turn, two of my four tires blew out. That didn't slow me down too much, since they were run-flats (or more accurately "run while shot to shit" flats), but I strongly suspect there was a connection between the blowouts and the stench of burning rubber that began filling the cabin.

At least I didn't have to worry about ventilation. I kept my foot firmly on the floor, heading in the direction of the pickup truck with the first half of my trail team,

---

[2] The lawyers suggest I add the standard disclaimer here, to the effect that you should not try this at home; I am a trained professional who has taken several counterterrorist driving classes. But I say screw the legal beagles. If you have keys and a driveway, give it a whirl.

Shotgun and Mongoose, aka Paul "Shotgun" Fox and Thomas "Mongoose" Yamya. Somewhere to the east, behind me now, was another vehicle with two more of my shooters, Trace Dahlgren and Tommy "Tex" Reeves. Both halves were undoubtedly heading at high speed to my rescue. I thought *eventually* they were going to converge and help get me the hell out of this mess.[3]

Unfortunately, it didn't look like I was going to reach *eventually*. As I approached the back of the tractor-trailer, the tailgate rolled up, revealing another machine gun.

It began peppering the pavement in front of my car with bullets. I pulled the wheel hard right, taking the car off-road. The Caddy's front end had been carefully reinforced, but even a Bradley Fighting Vehicle would have buckled under the strain. What was left of the windshield disintegrated; steam started shooting from the hood area. I lost the rest of the tires and struggled to keep the car moving, wrestling with it as it wove and bucked in a drunken, smoky swirl.

Flames flicked from the floor. I had two options:

a) get the hell out of the car or
b) start a second career as a burn-center test dummy.

---

[3] But to complete my earlier thought—if you do try this at home, I recommend using a rental car, preferably something along the lines of Rent-a-Wreck, definitely not your own wheels. And buy—what am I saying?—*steal* a set of cheap tires because you are going to burn the ones you start with down to the cords. It's all shits and giggles—shit when you fuck up and giggle when you pull off a maneuver out of your ass. Think of it this way: it's a self-taught defensive driver course. Probably deductible on your taxes as an education expense.

I chose a).

The car, against all common sense and probably the laws of physics and motion, was still moving at a very good pace; jumping would have been even more suicidal than staying. We careened back toward the road, then swirled sideways and slid down a washboard gully flanking the macadam. Sparks flew as the rims and chassis hit the asphalt, rebounded across the highway, then spun onto the soft desert sand and came to a stop.

I wish I could have said the same for my head, which was turning revolutions so fast it felt like it was trying to unscrew itself. By the time I managed to get my seat belt undone and the door open, I was engulfed in a thick, inky fog of smoke and fire. I coughed like a three-pack-a-day smoker, falling to my knees on the ground. I started crawling toward daylight.

The tractor-trailer stopped catty-corner across the road about seventy-five yards ahead. The machine-gun fire had stopped. For a moment I thought the smoke might give me enough cover so I could hide in the desert until my people arrived; surely they'd be along any second now.

Then something flew out of the back of the trailer. It looked like a fastball thrown by Nolan Ryan during his heyday, but it was even more explosive — a 40 mm grenade.

It sailed well off the mark, a good seventy yards or more over my head: right into one of the kidnappers' pickup trucks. The driver tried veering at the last moment, but all he succeeded in doing was tipping the vehicle as the grenade hit. It toppled over impressively.

I scrambled to my feet and began running to the south, trying to get behind as much of the drifting cloud of haze and smoke as I could. A second grenade flashed overhead, exploding a little closer than the other.

Murphy,[4] or his close cousin, Dumb Luck, smiled on me at that moment, sending a tourist bus down the highway. The bus driver, driving like the attentive, cautious man most are, was doing close to ninety and didn't realize the truck wasn't going to get out of the way until he was too close to stop. He hit the horn, slammed on the brakes, and then power-steered off the road, trying to swerve around it. He nearly made it . . . until the rear quarter panel of the bus came back and clipped the front fender of the truck.

The bus tumbled and the trailer slammed sideways just as the grenadier fired another round. I jumped up and ran, heading toward a wide ditch a hundred or so yards off the road. Sliding in, I took as long a breath as I dared, then started down it to the east, trying to put as much distance between me and the artillery as possible.

Unfortunately, the plan to have myself kidnapped had left me without a personal weapon; even business-like kidnappers tend to think the worst when they spot a gun. There was a small radio device in my belt transmitting my location, and I also had a special phone imbedded in the heel of my boot.[5] But aside from my fists and my wits, I was unarmed.

---

[4] I can't believe I have to explain who Murphy is, but I will: the proprietor of the famous law dictating that whatever can go wrong will go wrong, but only at the worst possible moment.

[5] Readers of a certain age and aficionados of Nickelodeon will notice the similarity to the device used by Maxwell Smart. Shunt, who designed it, swears he never heard of Don Adams, though if you've seen Shunt's apartment, you'll know he's a big fan of Chaos.

There were undoubtedly weapons in the overturned pickup. The occupants were scattered around it, mostly doing what people tend to do right after they've broken their necks: nothing.

Figuring they wouldn't mind if I borrowed their guns, I started climbing out of the ditch and heading in their direction. I got about two steps before two or three of the campesinos in the other truck, which had stopped nearby, spotted me. The ground erupted with automatic weapons fire. I slid back into the ditch.

The Mexicans started taking target practice. They weren't particularly good, nor did they seem to realize that I was in a ditch rather than a hole. I crawled about twenty yards eastward while they continued firing where I had been.

Right about then, Shotgun and Mongoose finally arrived on the scene. Assisted by instructions from Doc, who'd been studying the video feed from our overhead UAV, Mongoose pointed the Jimmy SUV straight at the tractor-trailer. Shotgun rolled down the window and hung out the side. As they closed in, he began writing his name on the trailer with his HK416.[6]

---

[6] Doc is Al "Doc" Tremblay—aka Cockbreath and other assorted terms of endearment—one of my original partners in crime; he's been with me since the invention of gunpowder. The gun Shotgun was using was built for him by Heckler & Koch, one of several my company (Red Cell International) is testing. We also have somewhat similar M4 derivatives built for us by a company owned by a former SEAL; the weapon may or may not go into general production and I've been asked to avoid publicizing it. Basically, it's an M4 on steroids; do a Google search and odds are you'll come across it. From here on out I'll just refer to it as an M4. We also had SCARs, a few Chinese AKs, and of course my trusty MP5 at our disposal during this op.

The bad guys immediately forgot about me and started firing at the Jimmy. Mongoose spun the truck to give Shotgun a chance to aim at the banditos near the pickups. Then he turned to come back around for another blast at the trailer. As he did, a grenade smacked into the Jimmy's rear quarter panel. The truck bounced upward, then settled down on all four wheels, engine dead.

The boys bailed just before another grenade hit the truck's cabin, setting it on fire. Good thing we'd opted for the optional insurance.

While all this was going on, I climbed out of the ditch and half crawled, half ran to the nearest gun, an M16 lying in the dust near one of the dead banditos.

The gun was a U.S. Army issue early model, probably given to the Mexican army under some sort of assistance plan, only to quickly fall into the hands of drug gangs. But I didn't particularly care about its provenance, just the fact that it was loaded.

Looking through the drifting black smoke, I saw a fat-ass Mexican near the trailer with a single-shot grenade launcher — probably an M79 — taking aim at the Jimmy. I sighted, shot . . . and missed. Several times.

Frustrated, I flipped the rifle off single to burst fire, and took aim again. Even so, it took three bursts before I hit him. He staggered backward, straightened, then lowered his launcher and tried loading it. NATO rounds never seem to put anyone down when you need them down.

I fired before he could get his load in the launcher, this time putting the burst into his face.

Shotgun reached me a few seconds later. He and Mongoose had already killed the three campesinos who'd been left; Mongoose walked slowly among them, making sure they were dead. Trace and Tex showed up maybe thirty seconds later.

"About time you got here," said Shotgun with a laugh as Tex hopped out of the truck. "You're tardy to the party."

"You're all goddamn late," I told them, sprinkling the usual words of endearment among my hearty congratulations that they had actually seen fit to arrive.

"Hey look," yelled Mongoose, holding up a small metal box he'd found in the cab of the tractor-trailer. "It's filled with pesos. Gotta be fifty thousand at least."

"Buy a burger at least," said Shotgun.

"Drinks are on them," I told everyone. "Let's head back to the motel."

[II]

ACTUALLY, THE HAUL amounted to just over fifty-eight thousand pesos, which computed to around a thousand dollars. I've seen plenty of bar bills higher, but it was a welcome addition to the kitty.

We'll skip over some of the boring stuff here:

—ransacking, aka searching with great dignity, the bodies of the bastards who'd tried to kill us;

—searching the trucks for clues about who these assholes were;

—retreating when Doc warned that the Mexican police were on the way. (The local police were not, as a general rule, law-abiding, let alone friendly toward Americans.)

While all of that is going on, I'll give you a brain dump and fill you in on some of the background.

OUR ADVENTURES HAD begun about a week earlier, when I was visiting Texas and New Mexico for a series of mixed martial arts competitions: the Rogue Warrior/IFC/MMA fights. While the sport is interesting in and of itself—who can resist the spectacle of grown men beating the crap out of each other—in this case there was an extra attraction: the matches were helping raise money for wounded veterans. The contests are held among active and former service members, with proceeds benefitting the Stars and Stripes Foundation, an organization I'm proud to say I support.

But let me stow my soapbox and get on with the story.

One night after a show in New Mexico I was approached by a weaselly looking fellow in a pin-striped suit. He had the clueless air of a junior diplomat, so I wasn't surprised when he said he worked for the State Department. He claimed to have been sent by the secretary of State herself and had an important matter to discuss.

"Well, why didn't you say so?" I told him. "In that case, I'm afraid I'm busy tonight. And every night for the foreseeable millennium."

"B-b-but, Mr. Marcinko. Your country is calling."

"I have a full slate right now. Meet me in the Star Hotel coffee shop tomorrow morning."

"OK, great. Thanks."

I seem to have neglected to add that I was leaving town that evening. Very forgetful of me.

While I have a general aversion to government officials, bureaucrats, and especially politicians, I had special feelings for the secretary of State, who had managed to screw up one of my company's overseas "relationships"—aka security contracts, aka how Papa gets the bread buttered—with some ill-timed remarks a few weeks before. And while there are *some* matters I agree with her on—she did, after all, raise people's awareness of the Chinese hacking of Google, et al,—she and I haven't gotten along since my adventures in Cuba, where I was hung out to dry while she had her nails done.[7]

I made my escape and went about my business, forgetting entirely about the State Department and Pinstriped Suit until the next afternoon, while doing a book signing in Odessa, Texas. Someone in a pin-striped suit stuck a book in my face and asked me to sign it, "Dear Hillary."

There was the assistant, as pimple-faced as ever.

"I missed you at breakfast," he said.

"You must have overslept."

He was holding up the line. Readers at a Rogue Warrior signing can get a bit ornery—a good portion are packing—and things would have been nasty if I didn't get rid of him. So I promised to talk to him as soon as the signing was over. Hell, I didn't have anything to do

---

[7] My interpretation. Judge for yourself by reading *Seize the Day*. Available at fine bookstores everywhere.

until the show anyway, and that was several hours away.

He waited. When I was done, we repaired to a thinking emporium down the street, where I ordered a small sarsaparilla and he got a Diet Coke. Our discussion started out badly and went from there.

"Have you ever heard of Hezbollah?"

"Gesundheit," I replied.

"No, no—the organization. *Hezbollah*. Do you know who they are?"

"Is that the Chinese company that took over the warranty claims on my truck?"

He crossed his brow. I'll give him credit: he gave an almost accurate explanation, saying that they were a "Shi'a militant group and political party with Iranian backing in command of a good portion of Lebanon and looking to expand their influence in an international dimension."

"That so?" I signaled the waiter for more sarsaparilla. If the secretary of State insisted I listen to this sort of drivel, I was going to make it worth my while. "Haven't heard of them."

"I think you're pulling my leg," said Pin-striped Suit. "I think."

That was the smartest thing he'd said since I met him, and I rewarded him by tipping my glass. He got to the point: the State Department had heard rumors that Hezbollah was working with Venezuela and trying to set up camps in Mexico.

"A few weeks ago, we heard additional rumors that Hezbollah was working with a Mexican drug cartel south of the border," he told me. "The rumors are bullshit, I'm sure, but—"

"Hold on just a second there. How do you know they're bullshit?"

"Do you really think terrorists would be working with Mexican drug cartels? Not going to happen."

Such is the caliber of the people going to work at the Foggy Bottom these days. Though I suppose I should take this more as an indication of what his boss thought than what he thought—in his defense, I doubt he was capable of thought.

I ordered another round of drinks.

"We want to hire you to check out the rumors," he told me.

"You can't check them out yourself?"

"We have. So has the CIA. Everyone has said they're unfounded. But no one believes us."

The rest of the conversation was just as inane. I did mention the Customs and Border Protection Service, which I believe had issued some of those "rumors"—known as intelligence briefs in some circles.

I'll spare you the blah-blah-blah: the bottom line was that State wanted to hire me to say that there were no terror camps in Mexico.

Not that my drinking companion said that in so many words. His tongue twisted into a square knot trying to find ways to avoid saying it quite that clearly.

"What if I find out there are camps?" I asked finally. "Would you do anything about them?"

"Well, of course, if, of course, in that case, that possibility, if there were evidence of activity backing up the potential of the hypothesis, then we would take it under advisement."

Pretty much what I figured he'd say.

"Well then I'll take this under advisement myself," I told him, getting up.

He frowned, probably realizing that was a fancy way of saying go shit on a stick. Getting involved with the State Department was about as winning a proposition as being Lindsay Lohan's parole officer.

I will say one thing, though—Pin-striped Suit promised a good payday. An appropriately prepared report would net Red Cell International $250,000, plus expenses.

That's a lot of food for the hounds. It's more than a few coats of paint for Rogue Manor. The work would truly not be onerous, even if I actually did it right: truck across the border, check for falafel sales, get a GPS position, and come home with a nice tan.

But let's face it: what the secretary was really trying to buy here was Yours Truly's seal of approval. She didn't *want* me to find anything. I could hear her in Congress now: "If Dick Marcinko says there are no terror camps down there, then damn it, who am I to disagree?"

As far as I'm concerned, my imprimatur on serious matters like counterterror is not for sale. Let me be clear: I don't mind endorsing beer or helping put a video game together; those things are good for you in the first place, and fun in the second. (And vice versa.) Knives? Watches? Necessary equipment.

But you can't screw around with national security. And for all the fun and games I have in my books, Red Cell International itself is very serious business.

I definitely believed the rumors, even if I had no evidence to back them up. But more importantly, I knew that if I actually *spotted* a terror camp, I would feel obliged to do something about it. While I'd be happy to do that if authorized (and compensated), I had no plans to go south of the border on a raiding mission. I'd also been recently lectured by both my lawyers and my accountants not to look for trouble unless it paid very well.[8]

OUR TEA OVER, I went about my business, preparing myself in mind and body for the MMA event, at which a good brawl was had by all. It was so absorbing that I had completely forgotten about the State Department and terror camps when a long black limo drove past me after the event. The rear window rolled down, and a man in a cowboy hat leaned out.

"Y'all need a lift?"

"Just going for my cab," I told the man. "I have some business to attend to. Thanks."

"Well now," he said. "I know you SEALs always get down to business after hours. But I would venture to say that my business may just prove worth your while—even better than whatever business you have in mind. And look here: plenty of Sapphire Bombay sitting right in the ice bucket—no need to water it down with ice."

Ah, the siren song of Dr. Bombay. No gin sweeter, no elixir more potent. The cure for all that ails you.

"I have my own supply, thanks," I replied.

The limo kept pace as I walked to the cab. I lost

---

[8] For the record, I feel that striking terror camps is a *government* military function, as opposed to something the likes of yours truly ought to be retained for. Hell, that's why I set up SEAL Team 6. Not that I won't do it if asked.

track of it in the jumble of vehicles leaving the civic center and promptly forgot about him, checking the BlackBerry for messages and the next day's schedule. So I was a little startled when I arrived at the hotel and found Cowboy Hat standing between me and the door.

"Y'all took your time getting here," he said.

"I didn't realize it was a race," I said.

My first thought was that he was another State Department official, but a closer examination showed that couldn't be the case. It wasn't just the ten-gallon hat or the custom handmade cowboy boots that would have taken a lifetime of tuna-fish lunches to afford on a government salary, even these days. He had a confident, lean-toward-you stance, exactly the opposite of the stay-back diplomatic posture they implant in the spine of every diplomat-to-be. He was tall, though with a bit of a paunch that his bespoke suit couldn't quite conceal.

"Maybe you'll let me buy you a drink in the bar," he said. "Name's Jordan Macleish. And I have a business proposition for you."

"If you're buying," I told him, "I'm listening."

And so I did, for the next half hour, in a private room off the bar. Macleish gave me his whole life story, which included wildcat oil drilling and assorted misadventures in the home building trades, all of which led to a position as board president and CEO of several corporations. There was a large ranch, and a private plane. Companies in Michigan, partnerships in Oregon: all mentioned to indicate that he was more than a little rich.

But no hint of what it was he wanted with me.

"Well, it's been very nice to meet you," I said finally, draining the last of my drink.

"We haven't discussed business," he said.

"Was there business?"

Macleish gave me a little squint, as if he were looking through a glass at a diamond, then smiled. "They told me you were particular," he said. "But things might change if I mentioned Bill Reynolds."

I drew a blank at the name—Reynolds is not exactly uncommon, and it didn't bring any special association to mind.

"You know him?" Macleish asked.

"I'm afraid I don't recall."

"Hmmm." Macleish reached into the pocket of his jacket. "Take a look at this gal and tell me you've seen one more beautiful."

He laid down an eight-by-ten computer image. I *have* seen more beautiful women—Karen Fairchild came immediately to mind—but the woman in the photo would have won ninety-nine of one hundred beauty contests she entered. The picture was just a head shot, but the blond hair, the perfectly spaced blue eyes, the million-watt smile—this was a girl who could get your attention. And other things.

"She has a body to match," said Macleish. He took out another photo, this time of her in a short skirt with a clinging top. Think Angela Jolie as a blonde, only a little prettier.

And younger. The woman in the picture was in her very early twenties.

"Ms. Reynolds and I have a special relationship," Macleish told me. He didn't wink, but he might just as well have—and at the same time, he nervously turned the wedding ring on his finger. "I'm very concerned about her welfare."

I could see where this was going: middle-aged rich guy plays sugar daddy; girl takes him for a ride. She gets tired and hops off the train. It was sad in a way, pathetic even, though looking at Macleish I couldn't help but think he was getting what he deserved.

"I was wondering . . ." His voice trailed off as he glanced down at his hands. Belatedly, he seemed to recognize the tacky symbolism fiddling with his wedding ring implied. He folded his hands together. "I wonder if your company, Red Cell International—"

"I'm sorry, but we don't do missing persons cases," I told him. "We're not a detective agency."

"She's not missing, actually. She's been kidnapped. When I told Bill Reynolds, he suggested you might be able to help. I think you know him better as Greenie. Bill is her father."

Greenie—ah, now I knew who he was talking about: a stout, balding retired SEAL whom I met at a reunion a few years past. He'd served in the teams after I left, and our paths had never crossed in the service. Still, the fact that he was a SEAL meant that he was part of the brotherhood, and had a certain call on my loyalties. If his daughter was in trouble, then I had to help.

I glanced at the photo. If this was his daughter, she took after her mother. As I recalled, Greenie had a thicker, far uglier face, with brown eyes and black hair, what was left of it.

I sat back down and listened as Macleish told me the rest of the story. There wasn't all that much: the kidnappers had made contact with Ms. Reynolds's boss, who hadn't actually realized she was missing because she had a no-show job, supplied of course by Macleish, who was duly informed.

According to Macleish, Reynolds was bent out of shape, naturally, and vowed vengeance not just on the kidnappers but on all mankind if his daughter was harmed. He was, unfortunately, working as a security guard aboard a ship in the Arabian Sea, part of a force hired to protect against pirates. Macleish had arranged for him to be picked up as soon as the ship made port, and planned on flying him home.

"In the meantime, he mentioned you. I must confess," added Macleish, "I hadn't realized the extent of your post-navy accomplishments. I'm not much of a reader. I don't think I've read a book in the past twenty years."

I'm never sure why people brag about that, but I let it pass.

Macleish told me a few other things, the most important of which was an offer to pay Red Cell International twenty-five percent of the three-million-dollar ransom if Ms. Reynolds was recovered unharmed.

"Or, if you advise that a ransom be paid, expenses and one hundred thousand dollars. Plus whatever you can recover from the kidnappers yourself," added Macleish.

I know what you're thinking. From a purely business point of view, it would have made sense to advise that the ransom be paid, get the girl back, then go and get the money. But if the operation was fairly sophisticated—and with a ransom that high it ought to be—the money would undoubtedly be difficult to trace.

Not that we couldn't take a good shot at it. Between Junior and Shunt, I have two of the best hackers on the planet on my team. Excuse me. The term they prefer is "computer security analysts."

Slackers has been proposed as well, though it has yet to stick.

(Junior is Matthew Loring, called Junior because he is literally a chip off the old block, that block being me. And Shunt is Paul Guido Falcone, our number one geek and all-around weird egg. He's called Shunt because he has some metal in his head. He's also from New York—enough said.)

But I had a serious problem with that approach. Bluntly, paying off kidnappers and blackmailers is an invitation to get screwed again, and again and again. Look at the pirate situation off Somalia. Has paying ransoms to the pirates there decreased or increased piracy? It's now the biggest industry in northeastern Africa— maybe the *only* industry in northeastern Africa.

Of course, the real way to deal with that is to cut off the piracy at its source. Yes, that means attacking the pirates before they get out to sea. But it also means attacking the financiers who are bankrolling them from Europe: the Russian, Ukrainian, and, dare I mention, Western individuals who put up money to fund the syndicates in the first place.

But I digress.

Our meeting broke up without me making a firm commitment one way or the other. Upstairs, I called Doc and asked him about Greenie. He verified the basic facts of Greenie's existence and the fact that he had a daughter. By morning, he had confirmed that he was aboard a ship and incommunicado.

And so I agreed to work for Macleish. And since it was obvious that I was now going to be spending at least some time in Mexico, I had Doc call up the secretary of State and work out an arrangement for her little assignment, making sure to include a provision stating that we would be paid "no matter what evidence was produced."

Adding the words "whether you like it or not" would have just been rubbing it in.

I'LL SKIP THE grunt work of setting up surveillance, bugging phones, and doing various background research—all critical, but frankly not exactly exciting. There are only so many ways to tap into a phone line, so many ways to check case histories, so many ways to find a halfway decent restaurant on the Mexican side of the border.

Our research led us to believe that Ms. Reynolds had been snatched by the Archuleta group, named after the man who ran the operation. They were a small subset of criminals working for the Tabasco cartel, with Archuleta himself a midranking slime bag in the organization.

The cartel had no relation to the sauce of the same name, but there was a definite historical connection to the area of Mexico where the sauce comes from. It was there that the cartel's early leaders formed their syndicate to smuggle drugs from places like Colombia north to the U.S. Drugs were still the cartel's number one commodity, but like any international conglomerate, it had recently decided to branch out in search of greater profits. Among its big moneymakers were a people smuggling business—in other words, transporting illegals to and from the U.S. for various purposes—and a number of semilegal interests, including exporting flowers. Kidnapping Americans and well-off Mexican-Americans was a recent sideline, and small burritos as far as their profit margins were concerned.

But let me not get too far ahead. Background finished. Let's return to our normally scheduled mayhem.

FOLLOWING MY ATTEMPTED kidnapping, we debriefed at a small bar named *Negra*, a place as dumpy as it was politically incorrect. We filtered into the place one at a time, trying not to look too suspicious, though since we were the only gringos we undoubtedly stood out. I had to assume that my cover story about being a rich hippie-gringo looking to set up a pottery business was probably now blown, since hippies rarely do well against machine guns and grenades. But we kept up the pretenses for inquisitive ears.

I'll spare you the recriminations that accompanied the debrief, not so much because they were pointed and bitter, but because I made a personal pledge to my publisher to cut down on the number of curse words used in my books. I felt pretty bad about the whole situation and frankly had to shoulder the blame. We'd had our asses kicked by a bunch of Mexican gangsters and none of us was very happy about it.

True, they paid a pretty good price for screwing up my plans. But that wasn't the idea of the operation. The whole reason I'd tried to get myself kidnapped in the first place was our lack of intel on where she was being kept; without that information, I couldn't protect her.

"Best thing now is to pay the ransom," suggested

Doc. "Kick the negotiations into high gear. Tell Macleish to stop stalling."

I couldn't disagree. Nor could I answer Trace's question, which as usual was exact and to the point.

"Why did they change their business model?" she asked. "Why come after you with guns and grenades, rather than just grabbing you? Assuming they didn't know who you were."

"Maybe we're too close to figuring it out," suggested Mongoose. As a retired SEAL, he tends to be relatively quiet, but to the point. "But we're too stupid to realize that."

"The second half of that is possible," said Doc. "But I think we'd have more information if the first was."

There was some more general discussion. Eventually things settled down into a heated debate on the merits of tequila versus vodka—the default discussion topic when the team was done talking business for the night. We all recognized we needed to take a fresh approach in the A.M. There was no use talking the problem to death.

Somewhere around there I decided to head back to my hotel down the block to get some rest. Doc had pretty much convinced me that paying the ransom was the only logical next step, but before we did that I'd have to get Shunt to infiltrate the banks the cartel used. After hacking his way past their security—easier than you think—he would insert a handy little program he called "Tell Me Your Secrets," which would allow him to easily trace the wired payment and then divert it to one of our accounts. (He has threatened to make it commercially available if I don't give him a raise next fall; watch the iPad ap store for the latest version.)

I was in such deep thought contemplating how we would proceed that I barely noticed the two sawed-off runts lurking near the exterior door to my room. In fact, I might have ignored them completely had I not caught sight of the suspicious bulges at their waists.

The sawed-off shotgun they brandished would have been difficult to ignore, though.

"What is this about?" I asked as one of the men pointed it at my face.

"You will come with us, senor," said the nearest runt. His English was heavily accented, but no worse than the average lawn care worker's in the States. "You will be quiet or your family will never hear from you again."

"You didn't have enough this afternoon?" I growled. I took a side step to the right, angling close enough to grab the other goon.

He made a strange face. "What do you mean?"

"You want what your boys got?"

"Who are you talking about?" said the man closest to me.

"You are mixing us up with someone else, senor," said the runt with the shotgun. "But it is of no consequence. You will come with us now."

"And if I don't?"

He pointed the shotgun at my face.

At that, I threw up my hands and said, "Oh my, oh my. Please don't hurt me. Oh, my."

HONEST, I DID.

I recognized the man from some of our background material IDing the possible kidnappers. In fact, he appeared to be one of the men who had been following Ms. Reynolds in the marketplace the day she was kidnapped. The surveillance footage we pulled from one of the town video cameras was grainy as hell, but the ID was cinched by a large scar that ran down the man's right cheek. His name was Hector Lopez, the ostensible number two of the Archuleta group.

"Take my wallet here," I told him. "It's yours."

"We will take your wallet and your passport," said the runt. "But it's your friends who will pay. You'll see."

"You're kidnapping me?" I said with mock surprise and horror. "I'm not worth your while."

"You had better hope you are, senor," said the other man. "Or it will not go well for you."

"Now, now, do not worry. We do these things all the time," said Lopez. "You will cooperate and it will not be very bad. It will be like a vacation for you. You'll see."

They took me down the stairs. At this point, Trace came out of the bar and saw me down the street. I had to make an instant decision. Were these guys really from a different organization—the one that we had been hoping to get kidnapped by? Or was there only one organization, and did it want to kill me?

Surely, the odds favored the latter: how many people in the world hate my guts enough to want to kill me?

Don't answer that.

I decided that if they had been part of the gang from earlier in the day, they surely would have shot me by now. And their whole approach now jibed well with the modus operandi we had sussed out for the Archuleta group, certainly much more closely than the bozos from the afternoon.

My gut said take a chance. My head said something else.

I went with my gut. I reached my hand up to my face and gave Trace the high sign indicating I was OK. She backed off; as soon as we passed, she went and alerted the others and they began tracking me. I still had my tracking device and the hidden phone, which made things a little easier.

My abductors led me down to a VW van parked around the back. They didn't bother tying my hands, and once we were in the truck they became even more friendly, telling me to call them Juan and Geraldo. Juan was actually Hector Lopez; Geraldo was probably a fake name as well, though I never actually found out what the right one was. But I was already thinking of them as Garlic Mouth and Fish Breath, respectively, for the obvious reasons.

Garlic and Fish were clearly in no hurry. They asked for my wallet and I handed it over; then they decided they wanted my watch as well. I told them it had great emotional value: it was a $15 job that I got on sale at Target for $13.99, and you don't get deals like that every day. They chuckled when I offered them my pocketknife instead.

"Oh, you keep that," said Fish Breath, laughing. "Maybe you need it for food."

I was beginning to think that I'd done a little too good a job prepping my cover as a wimp when Garlic produced a black hood.

"You'll put this on while we travel," he told me.

"And if I don't?"

"That would be very bad for you," he said. "I will

leave you untied, but if you give us any trouble, you will be beaten. And worse."

I complied. I spend half my life in the dark any-way — another half hour wasn't going to hurt.

WE DROVE INTO Juarez — pretty obvious from the turns and traffic congestion — then farther west. Neither Garlic nor Fish Breath said anything; they were too busy listening to insipid Mexican hip-hop, the sort of stuff you wouldn't let your daughter listen to even if she didn't know a word of Spanish. We eventually stopped out in the countryside, a good twenty miles southeast of Juarez according to Doc, who by now was back at our base camp watching my movements thanks to the tracking device. I was taken into a ranch build-ing with two rooms; Garlic brought me into the back room, sat me on a chair, and told me I could take off my hood once I heard the door close.

"Remember, if you give us trouble, there will be pain," he said. "No trouble, no pain. Very easy to under-stand this is, no?"

"Sure."

The rest of the night passed without incident or conflict. Garlic Mouth and Fish Breath sat in the front room drinking beer and watching Mexican wrestling. I amused myself in the back room by using my pen-knife to fend off rats. They were fast little buggers; I only managed to get three.

I nodded out for a short while, then woke when Fish Breath brought me some greasy eggs for breakfast.

"Morning already?" I asked.

"Yes, yes, morning. Here is your food."

"So, what happens next?"

"Next, your friends get money and everything's happy. Eat. You must keep your strength."

He put the plate down on the floor. The eggs were the color of dried nicotine stains on year-old cement. I'd rather have skinned the rats and swallowed them whole.

"Have you kidnapped many people?" I asked.

Fish Breath gave me a quizzical look, as if he didn't understand.

"I'm interested in it as a business model," I told him.

"Your English is hard to understand."

Ordinarily I would have annunciated a little more clearly by using my fists, but the need to display my passive side harmed my pronunciation. Fish Breath left without saying anything else; possibly he wouldn't have known the answers to my questions anyway. I thought I might have better luck with Garlic—he had a slightly less retarded look in his eyes.

But I never got to ask. Fish returned a short while later with a black hood.

"We're going for another ride," he told me, holding it up. "You come?"

How generous—it almost sounded like I could opt out. His grin, though, indicated that wasn't an option.

Over the course of the next few hours I found myself transported in the back of a van. We moved from point A to point B, D, and F, stopping briefly each time to pick up a passenger. The procedure was extremely businesslike, given the circumstances. We sat on the floor, each silent except for an initial grunt in greeting and the occasional curse as the truck bottomed out on a pothole.

There were five of us by the time we stopped for good. The rear doors of the van flew open. A pair of thuggish Mexicans leaned in and began roughly grabbing us, one by one. Someone started to object; he was quickly thrown to the ground.

"You will obeys, or you will be sorries," said one of the men. His pronunciation was clear, but obviously he hadn't mastered noun-verb agreement.

I kept my reaction in check—barely—and moved along with the others, shuffling my feet as one of the guards tugged me into a large building. I was the next to last inside; the door closed a few seconds later.

"It's OK," whispered someone several feet away. "They're gone."

I took that as my cue and pulled off my mask.

I was at the front of a large, dimly lit warehouse. The people I'd been in the van with, all still wearing their hoods, were standing in a clump around me. Another half-dozen people stood near blocks of hay about fifteen feet away at the side of the building.

I helped a few of the others take off their hoods, then started playing Mr. Congeniality, introducing myself using my cover story of course. Most of my fellow prisoners were white Americans; there were a few Mexican-Americans, all citizens, mixed in. While everyone's background was varied, their stories all had a common thread: they had been in Juarez or the nearby area, were on their own, and while far from rich had enough wherewithal in the family to afford a modest five-figure ransom. There was an older couple from Green Bay, Wisconsin, who had decided to spend a few days in Juarez sampling tourist trinkets for their small shop

back home, and a born-again Christian thinking of
starting a church who had been viewing possible loca-
tions. I knew immediately which real estate agent had
been "helping" him: the same one as mine, whom I'd
already flagged as a scout for the gang.

I worked my way around the building, introducing
myself and nodding in sympathy when they said they
weren't sure if they could hold out much longer. They
were all pretty calm, given the circumstances. Most
had been held for a few days though two had been prisoners for nearly a month. Their kidnappers had kept
them in a variety of places; a few had been beaten, but
most had been treated relatively benignly. Not that any
of them were likely to buy roses for their guards or cap-
tors anytime soon.

The longer the prisoners had been detained, the more
resigned and even philosophical they seemed about the
situation. A middle-aged woman stood with her fingers
against her temple, talking about all the work she had
to do for her daughter's wedding, interrupting herself
every few minutes to say that maybe it was good she
was missing some of the confusion. A man said he'd
been exercising and if he stayed in captivity another
week or so, he'd be in the best shape of his life.

In two or three cases, trembling lips and shaking
hands betrayed dim hopes of being ransomed. "I don't
know what's going to happen," said a man who had
worked as a fishing guide in Colorado. "If you get sprung
before me, could you go to my brother-in-law and ask
for a loan to get me out?"

While in theory any of them could have been a
plant, their body language and the way they talked
convinced me otherwise. Victims hold themselves a

certain way—shoulders down, head slightly bent. Not one of them looked me in the eye when I spoke to them.

With one exception.

"I know exactly who you are," said Melissa Reynolds when I finally found her toward the back of the warehouse. "Don't give me a bullshit story like you're giving the others."

She folded her arms and twisted her mouth in an expression that said don't mess with me.

It was a pretty mouth. The arms weren't bad either, though my eyes were drawn to the chest behind them. She was wearing a pair of khaki pants and a Texas Longhorns shirt—I know there's a lewd pun in there somewhere, though I can't seem to find it. She was a little too short to be a model at five-four, but her body was classically proportioned. Her curves were definitely curves, without being top or bottom heavy.

Her face?

A shimmering white opal.

Her hair?

Blond. Probably natural, though I wasn't at liberty to check.

"I assume my father sent you," she said with a sneer.

"Something along those lines."

She displayed her gratitude, both for her father and for me, by screwing her face into a deeper scowl.

"How do you know who I am?" I asked.

"My father is your biggest fan. I should have known you'd come. Where's Trace Dag-her?"

"You mean Trace Dahlgren."

"Right. And what's his name, the big guy who's always eating?"

"Shotgun?"

"How fat is he in real life?" she asked, leaning over to look around me.

"He's big, not fat. And he's not here."

"Just as well. For your information, I don't need to be rescued." She folded her arms a little tighter. "Thank you very much."

"You think your sugar daddy's going to pay your ransom?"

That earned me a slap. It had been a while since I'd been slapped by a pretty woman; it did my heart good to know I can still rouse emotion.

"I don't need your help," she said. "I don't want it. You're nothing but a conceited SEAL."

The word "SEAL" was definitely a four-letter word in her mouth.

"Your daddy was a SEAL."

"Don't remind me."

"You don't love your dad?"

"I love my dad—it's SEALs I can't stand. They're two-timing, loudmouthed know-it-alls, and you're the king of the bunch."

"Just because you had a bad love affair—"

"Two bad love affairs. And you're not going to be the third. Believe me."

There was absolutely no possibility of that. My inclination at that point was to put her over my knee and give her a good spanking, something that surely would have benefited both of us. But at that moment the door opened and two large scruffy Mexican toughs came into the warehouse. Each carried a Styrofoam chest. They put them down about twenty feet from the door, snarled in our direction, then strolled back the way they had come, bodies rocking nonchalantly as if they were bankers taking their evening constitutionals after counting the day's profits.

A crowd of prisoners ran to the chests. They dropped to their knees and began scooping out the contents — rice and beans, mixed together, a hodgepodge. There were no utensils; they used their hands.

"Better feed your face while you can," said Ms. Reynolds derisively. "You'll be hungry later."

"What about you?"

"I'd rather starve than eat that shit. I'm sure it's been pissed in. Or worse."

"Now I'm sure you're your father's daughter," I said. "You talk just like him."

"Shove it."

She walked away from me, heading toward the corner of the building.

I got the distinct impression that she was playing hard to get and wanted me to follow, but I had other things to do. I went over behind the bales of hay, made sure I was alone, then pretended I was Judy Garland at the end of *The Wizard of Oz* — I clicked my heels three times, activating the signal in the phone that told the team I had located our target.

Now all I had to do was wait to be rescued, right?

Sure. That sounds exactly like me.

Rescue could take hours; Doc would have to assess the situation and come up with a plan. In the meantime, more intel of the target site would be extremely useful, and guess who was perfectly positioned for a recce?

I started with a quick inspection of the interior.

There were only two doors—the one that the food patrol had just used and a massive, garage-doorlike panel, both on the north side of the building. The floor was poured cement, relatively new and from appearances thick enough that it would take a jackhammer to get through. The walls were another story: these were thin steel panels strapped to the girders; they would be easy to cut through. A QuikSaw would take no more than a minute to slice a hole. Hell, I could probably use the can opener on my pocketknife if I wanted to take the time.

There were two dozen vents along the roof. These were raised the way you see on some barns in the States; they looked like little rooflets standing on a pole at each corner. They appeared just big enough to squeeze through—a fact I took under advisement as I continued my survey.

There was no furniture, aside from the hay bales. There were a few rags and some old Mexican newspapers, stained with oil, scattered on the floor, but otherwise the place was empty.

You're wondering where people relieve themselves?

Pails behind the hay. There was a stack of newspapers near the pails, but otherwise it was as wretched an arrangement as it sounds. The building was pretty warm, and the smell . . .

I went back and looked at the roof vents. If I could get through one, I might be able to poke out and have a look around. The problem was getting up there. I considered stacking the hay into a stairway, but the bales were damn heavy and I'd need a lot of them; I'd be exhausted by the time I got them in place. Even if I managed it, the stairway would obviously be noticed by the guards if they returned.

The idea was good; it just needed to be altered. I stacked one bale on top of another pair, making a three-story stack. That gave me about nine or ten feet toward the roof. The rafters remained twelve feet away. But that wasn't insurmountable. I took some of the rags and the rope holding the bale together—my trusty pocketknife helped again—until I had a line a little more than two dozen feet long. I tossed it up, missed, tossed it up again, then got enough of it over the rafter to tie it off. I started to climb.

The line broke about halfway up. Luckily I landed on the hay.

Melissa Reynolds was standing nearby, smirking.

"Help me up?" I asked, extending my hand.

She reached for the broken strands instead. Lashing them together, she spun the rope up over the rafter, tied both ends together, then began climbing hand over hand to the top.

I have to confess that when I first took this assignment, I began with an entirely different mental image of the woman. I thought I was rescuing a well-spoiled princess, one of those girlie girls who dresses in pink and wears pearls to afternoon tea. Her personality would be somewhat similar to Pearl White's (the damsel of distress in Perils of Pauline). Here instead was Lara Croft, the ball-busting heroine of Tomb Raider, come to earth not only climbing up the rope but scrambling across the thin rafter beams to the skylight and wedging it open with her back.

She reminded me a lot of Trace, with blond hair and

more Nordic features.[9] They both certainly have nice butts.

I grabbed the line and began following. Doubled, the rope held almost to the top.

Almost.

It snapped just as I reached for the beam. I swung my arms out as I began to fall, getting just close enough to the wood to grab it with one hand. I hung there with one hand for a moment, Tarzan of the Apes style, then pulled the rest of my body onto the upward beam.

The space between the rafter and the roof was damn hot, but that was nothing compared to the temperature of the metal roof as I put my hands up to pull myself out. I pulled off my shirt and used it as a makeshift glove, spreading it out so I could put my hands down without burning them. But then I faced another problem. Ms. Reynolds was svelte. I was anything but. I struggled to get through the space, twisting my shoulders back and forth through the opening, finally angling them just right to scrape halfway out.

Then I got stuck. I pushed, I pulled—still stuck. I squeezed, prodded, and poked, and then was finally through.[10]

I looked around on the roof. Melissa was nowhere to be found. Cursing to myself, I crawled out to the edge. The warehouse was at the edge of a large complex of similar buildings built to take advantage of NAFTA— the Nuke American jobs and Fuck The public Act.

---

[9] I might mention something about an alleged difference in age, but I value my body parts too much.

[10] Sounds like my editor's love life, I know.

(Someone's going to have to explain to me how opening our borders to dirt cheap labor, nonexistent safety standards, and 1900s-style industrial pollution is good for America. Not that you should think I'm not open-minded.)

NAFTA hasn't worked out quite as well as planned, even on this side of the border: a lot of the cheap crap envisioned for Mexico was now being manufactured even more cheaply in China. There were roughly two dozen buildings scattered around the area. A few had definitely seen better days—the closest one was missing a roof, and the one next to it, about half the size and lower than the one I was on, had large gashes in the walls.

A chain-link fence ten or twelve feet high circled the entire area, setting it off from scrubland and the occasional cactus. At the south, an old and very battered metal rail fence about four feet tall separated the glass-strewn parking lot from another field pockmarked by a dozen small piles of debris and gravel.

Needless to say, there were no signs of sentient life inside the compound, assuming you don't count the two thugs who were sitting in the shade on the eastern side of the building. They had their backs against the wall and were talking loudly in Spanish, complaining about money they were owed, and how neither one of them could find a good girlfriend who would give them what their wives wouldn't.

Two thugs, one of me—those were much better odds than I was used to. They were so good, in fact, that I didn't trust them; surely there must be more guards around somewhere. I slipped over to the other side of the roof, continuing my survey and wondering where the hell Melissa had gotten to. While the roof's gentle slope made it easy to climb, I was afraid I could be seen easily from the distance, and so I kept low, sliding along the hot steel like an egg slipping down the griddle.

The buildings to the west were empty as well. There was another complex a half mile to the southwest; the buildings there seemed a little higher and blockier, but looked just as empty.

Our lovely Ms. Reynolds, meanwhile, was nowhere to be seen, no matter how hard I squinted. I was just starting to wonder if she had had a stealth helicopter waiting when I heard the loud hum of trucks in the distance. I strained my eyes toward a brown cloud in the distance to the east. A truck emerged ahead of it. It had a familiar shape and form: boxy front, rectangular rear, attractively oversized tires. It was a U.S. issue military vehicle known as an M-3582, aka a deuce and a half. Two more followed, half consumed by the dust from the first.

The Mexican army had decided to pay its respects.

I stood up to get a better view of the nearby area. When I did, I spotted another complication: a pickup filled with armed thugs was driving toward the side gate of the complex, approaching from the opposite direction the army was taking.

They were still some distance away, but it's safe to say they saw me on the roof: why else would the two assholes standing in the truck bed aim their rifles at me and start shooting?

If the gunfire had been less accurate, I might have stopped to contemplate the discrepancies: the Mexican army was driving three vintage U.S. hand-me-downs, serviceable vehicles to be sure, but all older than their occupants. The thugs had a gleaming, brand-new Ram 3500, with chromed running boards and fuzzy dice hanging off the mirror.

And consider the weaponry. The thugs were armed with the Belgian FN SCAR MK. 17S, or more likely reasonable copycat versions—7.62 mm assault rifles that could be configured for a number of tasks including highly accurate sniping.

How accurate?

Let's just say one of the rounds put an unsightly hole in the back of my shirt as I dove onto the hot roof. Sliding and burning at the same time, I let myself fall onto the ground. By some miracle I managed to land on my feet and roll down the way I had been taught way back in Army Basic Airborne Training at Fort Benning, Georgia.

And just like lo so many years ago, I fell sideways on my ass.

Adrenaline is a wonderful painkiller, though. I stumbled to my feet and staggered to the eastern side of the building, around the corner from the guards I'd spotted earlier. Alerted either by radio or the gunfire that I was on the roof, they were looking up at it when I peeked around the bottom corner of the building.

No way was I getting a better chance than this. I tucked my arms down and lowered my head. I hit the nearest Mexican like a linebacker laying out a quarterback. He went down; I kept going. Goon number two was wearing an armored vest, which damn near split my elbow when I hit him. Both he and his rifle flew to the ground. I scooped up the gun, but then tripped somehow and hit the dirt. Curling around, I leveled the muzzle at him and fired. The bullets went through the top of his head. I got up to my knee and riddled the other man's neck and back, dispatching him as well.

The goons had only five mags between them. That was disappointing: with those guns, you could empty the boxes after only a few presses of the trigger.

I pulled the vest off the second man, then grabbed his sunglasses. Half the battle of being cool is looking cool.

But I wasn't here to look cool.

"Melissa?" I yelled. "Ms. Reynolds — Melissa Reynolds! I know you're around here somewhere. Show yourself!"

No answer. I tried again.

"Melissa! We have company coming! Time to go!"

I guess I knew yelling to her would do as much good as my calling the dogs to stop chasing a rabbit at Rogue Manor, but I had to give it the old school try. I trotted around the nearby building, not really expecting to hear her answer, let alone see her. I wasn't disappointed.

Threading my way through the complex, I ran until I came to a building a little lower than the others. With the help of an oil drum, I hopped onto the roof.

The truck with the Mexican banditos had entered the complex and was speeding toward the building with the hostages. I had a decent shot of the front of the truck as it emerged from behind a building, and took it.

People think that the best way to stop a vehicle quickly is to put a round into an engine block. While I won't deny that that works, it does so primarily in movies and military novels. Blowing an engine block *does* disable an engine; steam will fly out from the water jacket, a piston or two will sheer, etc., etc. But the vehicle the engine is pulling still has considerable momentum, and a skilled driver can use that momentum to get relatively far, or at least to cover.

Shooting the driver is different: dead men not only don't tell tales, they don't drive very well either.

Of course, shooting the driver doesn't rob all the momentum from the vehicle any more than killing the engine does. The truck continued to move, passing behind a building before I could get another shot. But the loud crash as it hit into the side of one of the buildings made it clear it was no longer going to be operating.

Taking out the truck was not the same as taking out the goons. Within seconds, three came out from around the corner, heading in my general direction. I laid him out with a shot to the top of his head. Blood splattered all over the place; it was the sort of thing that really has to be seen in slo-mo to be properly appreciated.

Not that I would have been in a position to admire it. The other two peppered my roof with gunfire, and so I decided it was time for a tactical maneuver: in other words, I ran for my life.

Hopping back down onto the barrel, I scrambled to the ground and ran behind a nearby building, hoping I had enough distance between them and myself to circle around and flank them. But I was surprised as I turned the first corner of the building to find two different goons, guns in hand, coming right at me.

They got off the first shots. But the key in a gunfight is not to get off the first shot, it is to fire the *final* shot. Their bullets missed high; mine caught both in the chest, pushing them back in a jumble. Since they were wearing bulletproof vests, I didn't kill them, but at that range the slugs must have felt like a heart attack.

I know because a bullet fired by yet another campesino caught me from behind, kicking me face-first into the dirt.

My life flashed before my eyes. Unfortunately, I couldn't stay for the whole show. I folded my elbow under my chest and levered myself up, turning back toward my assailant. Between the vest and the sunglasses, I'm guessing he thought he'd shot one of his own men, because his gun was lowered and he had a pained expression on his face.

I gave him some physical anguish to go with whatever pangs of guilt he was feeling, cutting him across the shins with 7.62 mm slugs. He tripped into a crazy pirouette, tumbling down a few feet away. A head shot took care of the rest.

My back felt as if someone had put it under a drill press. I fell back against the side of the building, trying to catch my breath.

Several ancient religions have mental techniques for willing away pain, developed in the era before morphine and Novocain. While Bombay Sapphire is my painkiller of choice, I am open-minded on the subject of alternative healing, and at that moment would've tried the secret chant of Tibetan garbagemen if I thought it would relieve the pain. The best I could do was slow my breathing and put my head down. My field of vision began shrinking, and I nearly lost consciousness. Then something moved on the periphery of what I could see. Fear kicked away the pain.

Turning to the right, I saw a shadow cast by someone moving down the road between the buildings. I started to point my gun in that direction but a surge of pain sent me to my knees.

Very possibly I blacked out for a second or two. The next thing I knew, someone was shouting in Spanish that I should get the hell up. I groaned and raised my head.

"Up you lazy sack of shit," said the voice. (The actual words, in Spanish of course, began *¡que va!* and got a hell of a lot more vulgar from there.)

Groaning, I got to my feet. A sudden wave of nausea hit me, and for a moment there I thought I was going to puke. Instead, I got my rifle up and fired off a burst.

Nothing happened. I tried again, then realized the problem: I was out of bullets.

Doom on Dickie.

I had two choices: I could throw a nothing-is-fair, Murphy sucks, life's a bitch hissy fit. Or I could rely on my many years of training, my skills as a warrior, and my deep and well-tested knowledge of martial arts.

I went with the hissy fit.

I pushed off the wall in the direction of the voice, raising the rifle to use it as a battering ram. I hit into something substantial, then fell down to the ground. I rolled over, then tried to get up. I had gotten as far as my knees when I heard the sharp crack of a pistol a few feet away.

I blinked until my eyes focused on a Mexican army captain standing a few yards away. He had his pistol out, and was just lowering it; he'd fired it into the air to get my attention. Four or five privates were nearby, covering me. I hadn't bounced into a man; I'd hit the barrel I'd used to get on the roof earlier.

Maybe the pain made me silly, but for a moment there I thought the Mexican army was there to rescue us.

"There are prisoners in the building across the way," I told him. "I've been tracking a kidnapping ring."

"You'll raise your hands," said the officer in perfect English.

"You don't understand. I'm Dick Marcinko." I coughed.

"And who is that?"

"Doc didn't call you?"

"Don't worry, we'll found out who you are," said the captain. "And then we will be sure to set the ransom at twice the normal rate."

[III]

NOT EVERY UNIT or officer of the Mexican army is corrupt. On the contrary, I'd venture to say that the majority are honest.

It's a slim majority though. Many supplement their meager incomes with graft from the drug cartels. And then there are the units that are so tight with cartels that it's hard to know exactly what the difference is.

This unit represented yet another variation: an army group that was in competition with the cartel, or at least one small segment of it. Apparently acting on intelligence he'd gathered, the captain was here to rescue the captives—and put them into his own protective custody. They would be released when their paperwork was in order. Which meant when their ransoms were paid.

I can't say I was surprised, exactly. Disappointed maybe?

Butt-kicked, definitely.

Pulled to my feet, I was pushed toward one of the army trucks parked at the front of the building. I found the others inside—all but Ms. Reynolds.

A problem to be solved at a future date.

I KNOW WHAT you're thinking: Dick, you're a prisoner of the Mexican army. How hard can it be to escape?

Good point.

THE KIDNAP VICTIMS were confined to the middle vehicle in a three-truck line. The army detail, roughly a dozen soldiers, was divided among the other two trucks. There was no effort to blindfold anyone or tie them up. In fact, the prisoners came along willingly; they were under the impression at first that they were being rescued.

It wasn't until one of the women asked if she could go to the bathroom that their real purpose became obvious: the soldier pointed his gun at her and told her to shut up, or she would never have to go to the bathroom again. One of the men started to protest; he was silenced by a muzzle strike to the knee that laid him down.

As we passed out of the complex gate, the convoy began to spread out. The driver of the truck behind us was clearly paying more attention to his friend in the front seat than the road. He gestured and waved his hands as he drove, moving them so emphatically he looked like he was practicing karate moves. He was so absorbed that he didn't see the man leaping from our truck until it was too late — he swerved at the last moment but still managed to run over the escapee's leg.

A good thing, because I was worried that he would miss him entirely.

Horns sounded. Our vehicle pulled off the road to the right. Soldiers leapt from the truck behind us. Our driver and his escort hustled from the cab and ran to the back, unsure what was going on but determined not to let any of us escape.

They got out so quickly, in fact, that they left the truck running. This was highly convenient — when I crawled out from under the chassis and climbed up into the cab, all I had to do was throw it into gear and step on the gas. The truck lurched back onto the highway, leaning a bit with the acceleration.

Yes, you're correct: I had slipped down under the truck before the "escapee" leapt out. And not to keep you in further suspense: said escapee was a dummy constructed from various items of clothing.

The lead truck had started a three-point turn back in our direction. In a better world I would've given them a twenty-one-gun salute as I roared past. Not being armed, I settled for the bird.

If you're starting to wonder where Doc and the rest of my esteemed group of Red Cell International shooters, assistants, and underlings were, you're not alone. Without delving too deeply into methods and tactics here, some sort of overhead surveillance of the warehouse should have started shortly after I clicked the magic heels. Some sort of surveillance team should have been rushed to the scene to cover any contingency, including the situation I faced now.

In other words, the friggin' cavalry should have been nearby.

I clicked my heels a few times, frantically trying to make sure Doc knew I was in trouble. I thought about pulling off my shoe and talking to him directly, but I didn't have that luxury — shortly after I passed the other vehicle, bullets started flying past my window.

Glancing in the rearview mirror, I saw that the truck that had been right behind us was speeding up. There was a soldier on its passenger side running board. He was firing a light machine gun.

His aim was surprisingly good, too: bullets chattered against the truck, splintering the mirror.

The road before me was straight and narrow, which made us easy pickings. I decided it was time to work on my off-road skills.

Cranking the wheel to the left, I skidded off into the desert sand. The truck wobbled slightly, hitting a soft patch on the shoulder, but most of the ground was hard-packed, and I was able to keep us upright as I headed north of the road.

The machine-gun fire either stopped or became so inaccurate that I lost track of it. But we were far from home free: a rifle round cracked through the side window, putting a hole in the glass a few inches from my head.

I ducked instinctively, which saved me from the second and third rounds. The shots came from cartel snipers, who happened to be posted nearby. Their usual purpose is to pick off Customs agents interfering with drug shipments. We seem to have been some sort of bonus round; either they were alerted by radio or saw what was going on and decided to try to help.[11]

In a way, this was actually good news—it meant I was a hell of a lot closer to the border than I thought. Extremely close—less than a thousand yards in fact. But I wasn't in a position to celebrate.

Between the snipers and the machine-gunning soldiers, I was having a hell of a time driving the truck. I cranked right to get away from the snipers, only to be hit by a barrage of automatic weapons fire from the trucks. One or two of the back tires went out, and I felt the truck pulling to the left.

There's nothing better than the pitter-patter of bullets to contract the sphincter and focus the mind. But what really came into focus as I raised my head just barely above the dashboard was the large fence ahead.

The border.

I decided that's where I was going. Foot pressed to the floor, I held on to the steering wheel as the truck bounced over the washboardlike terrain. Suddenly, the front end dipped beneath me like a horse trying to buck a rider. Before I could react, the front bumper hit hard against the steep incline of the ditch and the wheel wrenched out of my grip. We hit the fence sideways, wire mesh draping across the truck as it swerved to a stop after twenty or thirty yards.

---

[11] I'm tempted to take a timeout here and expound on the idiocy of allowing criminals to operate freely a few hundred yards from American soil, or maybe berate the idiotic government rules that prevent Border Patrol members from properly defending themselves from these thugs even when it's clear their motive is murder.

The people in the back piled out, funneling around the broken chain-link sections and running to the north. The Mexican army trucks stopped about fifty yards away; the troops piled out and began taking potshots at the escaped prisoners.

The fence blocked the door and most of the windshield; the only way out was on the side nearest the Mexican army. I crawled over to the door, kicked it open, and fell down to the ground, crawling beneath the truck and scrambling to my feet on the other side. Fortunately, the Mexicans couldn't hit the broadside of a barn, which is what my butt felt like as I pushed it under the truck.

Eventually, one of them did hit the vehicle in exactly the right place with a tracer and it caught fire. By then, though, I was back with the rest of the escaped kidnap victims, saved by the reluctance of the Mexican army commander to cross the border.

This was somewhat less than characteristic, and I wasn't sure what we owed our good fortune to until my head started vibrating. I was so banged up that it took a few moments before I realized it wasn't some new and esoteric form of pain—a helicopter was overhead.

The cavalry had finally arrived.

[IV]

THE HELO BELONGED to an Air National Guard unit assigned to help Customs stem the flow of drugs over the border. They had been scrambled by a call from Doc, who decided the proceedings were getting a little out of hand. It had taken the National Guard unit less than five minutes to get their bird in the air and down to our site. I criticize Air Farcers all the time, so let me now give them a big wet kiss for saving my ass. Whether they can live that down or not remains to be seen.

The Mexicans stopped shooting as soon as the helicopter tucked toward them. I heard later that he said over the radio that he had been pursuing a drug ring, and was requesting permission from his headquarters to round up the criminals who had escaped across the border—very likely a first. He didn't push things when the National Guard pilot told him he had things under control. On the contrary: the Mexicans double-timed back to their trucks and vamoosed.

Shotgun and Mongoose showed up a few minutes later, barreling across the desert as if they were in the Baja 500.

They were coming from the Mexican side, obviously, and as it happened, they spotted the wedge of the sniper blind as they approached.

While they didn't know the sniper had shot at us earlier, they had seen the hides earlier in the week and developed a certain attitude about them.

"Looks like a road hazard to me," said Shotgun, pointing out the position. It was a squat, long triangle, barely aboveground.

"Yeah." Mongoose snapped the wheel, aiming the truck. "I'm betting it'll squish."

"I got a bag of Doritos says the sides are built up and we just fly right over it. No squish."

"A big bag or a little bag?"

"Who would bet a small bag of Doritos on something important like this?"

Mongoose barreled into the wedge, which was a canvas tent piece folded down over a very shallow ditch. Something thumped beneath the truck.

"You cheated," protested Shotgun. "You slowed down."

"Didn't want to miss it. That's allowed."

"I don't think that qualifies as squished," said Shotgun, leaning out the side window. "It just looks run over."

"I ain't done," said Mongoose, putting the truck into reverse.

He backed over the hide four or five times before he was satisfied that it had, in fact, been squished.

No LONGER IN danger, the freed hostages gathered in a knot about a hundred yards into the U.S., huddling away from the black smoke curling from the truck. I began interviewing them, looking for information on Melissa, along with anything else that might be useful. I was soon joined by Trace, Tex, and Stoneman; done with their joy riding, Shotgun and Mongoose rolled up a few minutes later. The freed victims were all grateful for being rescued, but they didn't seem to know much that I hadn't already figured out. They answered our questions as best they could, between gulps of water from our thermoses and whatever snacks Shotgun passed out.

It took a while for the Border Patrol to reach us. There were only two agents on duty in the vicinity, and they were both handling a more conventional mess several miles away. Border agents catch a lot of crap for the country's messed-up immigration policies and especially our lax border security, if "security" is ever the right word to use. I'm sure there are lousy Border Patrol agents, just as there are lousy everything, but the men and women I met during my Mexican holiday were professional and motivated to do their job, as impossible as it sometimes seems.

The Border Patrol is part of the Homeland Insecurity Department. Because of that, their first responsibility is to stop terrorism. Now while that's a good idea, you have (a very few) border agents who'll occasionally tell you that illegal immigrants and drugs aren't even their responsibility. That's ridiculous: the problems are absolutely connected.

And besides check 8 U.S.C. 1103, 1182, 1225, 1226, 1251, 1252, 1357; Homeland Security Act of 2002, Pub. L. 107–296 (6 U.S.C. 1, et seq.); 8 CFR part 2; all lay out tasks that are a lot more extensive than watching for men with towels wrapped around their heads.

Excuse me? You in the back of the room?

Sure, go ahead and read the section. We'll wait.

For various reasons, morale among Border Patrol agents was very low at the time I was there. That's not just my opinion. The service was considered the least desirable of thirty-six government agencies to work for during a survey in July 2006. Manpower shortages, crappy training, bitchy work conditions, and mandatory overtime were all cited as factors.

Then there's the case of Ignacio Ramos and Jose Alonso Compean, two Border Patrol officers who were railroaded to jail for shooting a pot-smuggling scumbag in the butt to keep him from escaping after they caught him trying to smuggle a few hundred pounds of pot across the border into Texas in a cargo van. The numb nut *American* prosecutor claimed that they could not *absolutely* conclude that he had a weapon, and therefore had no right to shoot him. Because everybody knows that drug smugglers are peaceful, law-abiding citizens who always comply with the orders of Border Patrol officers, and would *never* think of harming them.

The two officers were actually *convicted* in 2005. (Clearly, none of my readers were on the jury.) After considerable publicity and teeth gnashing, they were pardoned by George Bush when he left the presidency.

Myself, I'm curious about who's going to give them their reputations back, but I suppose that's an impertinent question. What is pertinent is that the Border Patrol is undermanned and shit on from above and below. I don't doubt that it could be doing a much better job, but I think the bulk of the problem is the bureaucracy around them and the government decisions that handcuff them, not the people themselves.

But you knew that, I'm sure.

THE AGENTS WEREN'T surprised that the Mexican army had gotten involved.

"There are good units and bad units," one of the officers told me. "We have yet to see one of the good ones around these parts."

The officer unleashed a litany of problems, including a few I've just mentioned. He did make one point that I hadn't heard from a fed before: if the federal government wouldn't take care of the problem, he said, then they should get out of the way and let the States do it.

"I don't think it's entirely practical," he added. "The federal level is where the coordination belongs. Hell,

I'm a federal employee myself. But someone has to do the job."

In case you're wondering, I haven't included his name because a federal employee making such statements has no right of free speech, according to the Supreme Court. That's right: he could be bounced for criticizing his dumb-as-shit bosses.

"Say, you know there's a ditch under the fence deep enough that you barely have to duck to get under?" asked Shotgun, pointing about a half mile away. The desert was worn out with the tracks of people sneaking through there.

"We know about it," said the officer. "We've asked it be closed up. They say they'll get to it eventually. Like maybe next century."

"To be honest, having the ditch there helps a little," added the other officer. "Kind of funnels them into us."

He had a point—the ditch was not only an obvious place for illegals to come across, it was an obvious place to catch them. Which didn't bother the coyotes, or people responsible for guiding the illegals—they would send a few people across there as decoys and then bring the rest across a mile or so away.

"There's only so many we can catch," said the first officer when I pointed this out. He held out his hands. "It's not like we don't know all their tricks."

We talked a little more, this time about Hezbollah and the potentials for a camp on the other side of the border. Both officers thought it was very much a possibility, though they admitted that they hadn't seen any direct evidence of it.

I won't mention their opinion of the State Department.

I WENT BACK to questioning my fellow captives, getting nowhere until I came to a thin, white-haired woman
named Mrs. Snowpeck who was eating a Drake's fruit
pocket Shotgun had given her. They shared a common
affection for flakey yet sugary crust.

"I know the girl you're talking about," she told me.
"We talked, but she never gave me her name. Melissa?
It fits her."

I wasn't sure about that—Attila the Hun would have
been more appropriate from what I'd seen. But I nodded
anyway.

"She was chained inside some ruins out in the
countryside somewhere," continued Mrs. Snowpeck.
"An old couple looked in on her every day. They brought
her food. She swore she'd go back as soon as she got
out."

"Go back and do what?" Trace asked.

"Thank them, I guess."

"More like kill them," I said. "Tell me everything
you know."

Everything wasn't much. Melissa had described her
jail as a ruined stone building; there must be thousands
if not millions in Mexico. But she seemed to know at
least the general vicinity of where she had been kept:
near a place called DeLucas. There was an old church
not far from her makeshift jail, but very few houses.

"She tried to escape one night to the church but was
caught. That's why she was brought here."

"Did they beat her?" Shotgun asked.

"A little," said Mrs. Snowpeck. "She didn't seem to
want to talk about it."

That sounded even more ominous than if they'd broken her bones. But while I believed her guards deserved whatever reward Ms. Reynolds might bestow, I also realized that if she killed them, things could get immensely complicated. The Mexican government wasn't much on catching Mexican criminals, but give them an American suspect — even one who was a victim herself of a crime — and they would undoubtedly throw the book at her.

"No Deluca," said Doc after I filled him in. "No town with that name. Got a Lucadia, a Fugado, a . . ."

Look for a little town with a Catholic church, I told him.

"Dick, the country is wall to wall with Catholic churches." Doc cleared his throat. He was so loud I had to hold the phone away from my ear.

"It would be a tiny town, with some ruins and that church, maybe a little house or a few houses," I told him. "It should be no more than a couple of hours from where we are now."

"Oh, that narrows it way down," griped Doc.

"Somebody didn't have his happy pills this morning," said Shotgun, who was nearby and couldn't help overhearing.

But Doc does some of his best work when he's grumpy. With Junior's help, and the mapping system provided by our satellite imagery contractor,[12] he quickly located two likely candidates, a place called Mesa las Dos and Ojo de la Casa. They were both spits of towns, and both roughly thirty minutes from where

---

[12] We occasionally supplement them with Google. But there are a number of advantages of using a commercial provider; you do get what you pay for.

we had been brought in the warehouse. They weren't particularly close to one another—Ojo de la Casa was due south of El Paso, while Mesa las Dos—or a Mess of Twos as I called it—was much farther west, above la Ascension.

When I'd last seen Ms. Reynolds, she'd been on foot. Thirty miles was a good distance in the desert. It wasn't killer hot, but it wasn't particularly cold either.

"Probably stole a car," offered Mongoose.

"I wouldn't put anything past her," I said.

"She could just as easily have headed north," said Trace. "She could be across the border by now."

"Yeah, but then she's not our problem anymore is she?" said Mongoose.

"It is if she doesn't make it back alive," she answered.

[V]

THE SCRUBLAND AROUND the border area was filled with coyotes, banditos, and various species of snakes, most of them warm-blooded. I saw quite a lot of them over the next few hours, touring the environs trying to make sure that Ms. Reynolds had not, in fact, gone north.

I was flying with a friend who flew helicopters out of El Paso. Chester "Chet" Arthur—no relation to the president of the same name—flew for the army back in the day, and played an extremely minor role in the Panama invasion. We reached an understanding soon after meeting back in the late 1990s: I don't hold his service affiliation against him, and he doesn't tell people how we met.

Chet and I were in a Robinson R22, also known as the Beta II. I don't know if you're familiar with the R22. You've undoubtedly seen it. The helicopter has been around for years and is considered one of the best light helos in the world. It's cheap to operate, and so stable and dependable that a lot of flight schools use them to train newbies.

But it is *small*. I've seen phone booths — remember those? — with more elbow room. My svelte, girlish figure just barely fit in the seat. Chet's pretty much overwhelmed his.

It was a close encounter of the personal kind. Fortunately, he had showered in the recent past.

The helicopter was the only one he could spring on short notice. He assured me that there was enough room for Melissa if we found her.

"Where?" I asked.

"She'll sit on your lap. Any objection?"

Not in the least.

We flew a series of boxes ten miles deep on the north side of the border, covering about twice as much ground as I figured she could walk in the time since she'd escaped.

Nada.

"Let's try south," I told him after we'd gone over the boxes several times.

"Roger that." He was a big guy, but he had a high voice, almost like a girl's. It was very loud in the headset, and something in it rattled the hard shell of the earphones. "You know, Dick, anybody who's on foot out here is either loco or nuts."

"What's the difference?"

"Someone who's nuts has a skewed view of the world; they don't look at reality the same way you and I do. But they do see it. Someone who's loco has no clue what the world is.

"Of course, odds are now that we're over the border, anyone we see down there is going to be illegal. Or nuts," added Chet, considering. "Or most likely both."

We had only been over Mexican territory for a few minutes when something *binged* behind us. I'd heard that kind of *bing* before. So had Chet.

"Somebody's shooting at us," he said nonchalantly.

"Who?"

He tilted the aircraft and pointed to the right, beyond his side window. By the time I spotted the pickup tucked down in the ditch, two more bullets had hit the fuselage.

"Better shot than most." Chet gunned the engine, skittering away. "I thought maybe that might be your girl, but I don't think she'd be shooting at us, right?"

"I can't really say."

"Same old Rogue," Chet said with a laugh. "Always in trouble with the ladies."

I picked up a pair of binoculars as Chet took another pass, this time at low altitude. He skittered back and forth to make it difficult for the shooter to aim.

"Probably a cartel goon, thinking we're honing in on his territory. I doubt he thinks we're Border Patrol."

"You sure?"

"Oh, yeah. He'd be firing a lot more bullets if he did. They get a good bounty for every officer they take." Chet banked hard to avoid yet another shot. "You like being shot at, Dick?"

"I think you know the answer to that."

He reached to the holster on the side of his door and handed over a Smith & Wesson Model 28 .356 Magnum. The Model 28, known as the "Highway patrolman gun," was very old school, a no-monkey-business weapon. Based on the Model 27—itself a classic—it lacked the fancy polish but none of the precision of the earlier Magnum. (The Model 27, with a three-and-a-half-inch barrel and an ivory handle, was Georgie Patton's weapon of choice.) I'm told it came in four, six, and eight 3/8 inch models; the one Chet gave me was six.

A good gun, but not the sort of weapon you fire from a moving helicopter with much hope of hitting anything.

"How close can you get?" I asked Chet.

"I can get you right on top of him," he said. "The question is, how close can we get without getting shot?"

The answer was some twelve feet away. Chet ran a straight line as slow as he dared, roughly fifty knots, twisting in from the southeast. I leaned out of the cockpit, holding on to the frame with my left hand while aiming the gun with the right. I missed my first shot, and my second.

The third time was a charm. The bullet took out part of his skull.

Such a shame. I'd been aiming for his heart.

ABOUT AN HOUR and a half later, with the sun going down, we gave up the search. There was no sign of Ms. Reynolds, on foot or otherwise, north or south of the border.

Chet set me down on a dirt road outside of Estacion Samalayuca, where the rest of the team was waiting.

Our first target, Oja de la Casa, was about four miles away.

A herd of wild horses looked over at us as we touched down. They seemed not to care about us at all, until one gave some secret signal and they all thundered off, running toward the yellow-red sun as it lipped the horizon.

It would have made a great beer commercial.

I considered splitting up and hitting both places simultaneously, but we had a relatively small force to begin with, and I didn't want to get too overextended. We made up for that somewhat by launching two UAVs, so we could watch each spot. If we saw something happening at the other location, we could change gears and head there. It wasn't the perfect solution, but it would have to do.

I've mentioned our UAV a few times now without giving you many details. The "Bird" is very similar to the Israeli Skylark—not a coincidence, since ours was made by the same company. It looks like a broomstick with wings. Beneath the center fuselage hangs what looks like a miniature torpedo. The "torpedo" is a configurable sensor pod; depending on what we need, we can hang different equipment on the rails.

To watch over the houses during the day, the UAVs had been equipped with optical sensors—a fancy-ass name for a video camera, which beamed its signal back to the command center, an oversized laptop with hand controller attached via a USB port. When I arrived, these were just being replaced by aircraft with a night-vision sensor. This pod held your basic infrared camera, though according to the manufacturer it's anything but basic; unlike most infrared, the Bird's can see through a light rain. (Interference from raindrops, whether falling or in a cloud, is one of the main deficiencies of most IR gear.) How well this works depends on your definition of light rain, but we weren't likely to encounter that problem here: there was a cloudless sky above.

The Bird runs on an electric motor and can stay aloft for about three and a half hours before the batteries poop out and it has to land. Or in actual practice, crash, since I've never found one operator on my team who can actually get the damn thing down in one piece. They're designed to come apart, however, so as long as the crash is at relatively slow speed, it's not a big deal.

Launching can be even harder than landing. Junior is our best operator, but even he has trouble getting the damn thing up. (Yes, that was a pun. Sick but unavoidable.) The procedure is something of a cross between boosting a kite and flying a paper airplane, except that it involves considerably more cursing, at least when Junior is at the controls.

"Sonofabitchingstinkingsuckasspieceofcrap" appears to be his command for takeoff.

This is usually followed by a nose dive to the ground.

His first attempt to launch an IR-equipped aircraft to take over the watch on the first house we were to hit was true to form. The plane loped upward, then dove straight to the ground. Junior retrieved the various parts, pushed them back together, then started running.

"SonofabitchingF-ingstinkingsuckasspieceofshitting crap," he yelled before letting go.

Obviously the extra curses gave more power to the plane. It headed upward, climbing a good twelve or sixteen feet before once more diving into a crash.

Trace stifled a laugh. Junior tried again with roughly

the same results—this time, the wing hit the ground before the nose. After the fifth or sixth unsuccessful attempt, Mongoose went over and took the plane from him.

"You're not cursing right," he said. And with a stream of foul-mouth expletives and other tender encouragements, he hoisted the Bird into the air.

The aircraft found a current overhead. Its wings fluttered left and right. Then it began to climb into the darkening night sky, following a preprogrammed flight pattern. Junior went over to the control unit and began flying it toward the target buildings. When it was on-station, he commanded the original aircraft to return. We recovered that—as in, picked up the pieces after the hard landing—then mounted up for the op.

The target building was a one-story, ranch-style house, similar to something you'd see in the States. It was big for the area, but simple even so—maybe twelve hundred square feet, all told. It was less than fifty yards from the old ruins on the other side of the street, a good match for what Mrs. Snowpeck had told us.

The infrared sensors on the aircraft were sensitive enough to give us readings on three people in the house. Who they were, of course, couldn't be determined.

"She's not there yet, if this is the right place," said Junior. "They're too calm."

"Unless they're dead."

"Hmmm . . ."

"Only one way to find out," I told him. "Let's get up close and personal."

TEN MINUTES LATER, Shotgun and I drove past the house. The lights were on in the front room—exactly the spot where the three figures were, according to the Bird. We continued down the road, passing a ruined building where we thought Ms. Reynolds had been kept. Made of stone, the structure was one story high. Part of the roof had caved in, but there was ample space to lock someone up.

"Church is up there to the left," said Shotgun, pointing down the road.

"Find a place to park and let's check the ruins," I told him. "Let's make sure there's nobody there. Then we'll go to the house."

"You think this is the place?"

As a matter of fact, I didn't. But I couldn't explain why, and even though my batting average on hunches is pretty good, now that we were here it didn't make any sense to simply blow it off.

Shotgun pulled into a field on the right side of the road about thirty yards west of the ruins. He went in a ways, far enough from the road so a casual passerby would likely miss the vehicle.

One thing you can't control on ops in enemy territory — in any territory, but especially places you don't "own" — is the casual passerby, the shepherd who happens to get lost on the way home and turns up in a place you never expected him to be. Little accidents and incidents that perforate even the best laid plans — the iceberg that just happens to zig when it should have zagged — can end up sinking you.

Some call things like that bad luck, but you and I both know it's really Murphy, playing his tricks. You plan for contingencies as best you can — we both knew what we would do if someone wandered across us, for example — but there is always a point beyond which no one can plan: a spaceship full of aliens arriving would have forced us to punt.

Neither Murph nor a UFO joined us in the field; there were no shepherds and no cars. Neither Shotgun nor I saw anything as we approached the ramshackle building. I had a new toy with me—what I'm calling Gen 5 night vision. These glasses were the next-*next* generation of night goggles, still under development by some friends at a company I've been asked not to name. They were very light, and where most night gear has lens bodies similar in length to binoculars, these were compact, more along the lines of very thick glasses: the barrels were just over an inch.

One big problem with night gear in the field is weight. Currently the best units weigh in the range of a pound and a half; that doesn't sound like much, but it can feel like a bowling ball after a few hours. (Straps can be another problem—but now I'm getting picky.)

These glasses weigh about four ounces. They sacrifice a small amount of range compared to standard units, but we could see to roughly twenty yards with excellent detail. The developers still have some bugs they want to work out, but when these finally come on the market they'll change everything you know about night vision.

We approached the ruins from the rear, moving quickly but quietly. Junior was watching via the Bird's feed and gave us occasional updates; according to his screen there weren't even ghosts nearby.

Part of the building's back wall had fallen at some point in the distant past, making it the obvious place to enter. So naturally, we didn't go that way. Instead, I took a quick look eastward—the side facing the house—then moved back around to the west. I poked my head through an empty window.

Nada.

"Place is empty," groused Shotgun.

"Keep looking."

"I'm getting hungry," whispered Shotgun.

"Keep your mind on your work," I told him.

"My mind's there. It's my stomach I'm talking about."

I ignored him. Getting into a discussion about food with Shotgun is like talking about water with Neptune; the conversation will never end.

The stones that made up the building had been cut at least a hundred years before, maybe two or even three. Whatever had filled the windows was long gone; there wasn't even a hint of glass, let alone wooden frames. After poking my head in to make sure the room was empty, I eased myself through one of the openings. I'd recovered fairly well from the bumps and bruises inflicted earlier in the day; my body has been battered so much over the years that it starts to think I don't love it if it's not taking serious abuse every twelve hours or so.

I was in a room about thirty feet by twenty. The roof was intact overhead. The floor, hard-packed dirt, was littered with bits of stone and rubble from a wall that ran about two-thirds of the way through. It had obviously been knocked down at some point, though it was impossible to tell when, or even if it had been done on purpose.

I examined the walls, looking for some sign that the place had been used to hold prisoners. Suddenly I heard Shotgun curse.

I looked over in his direction just in time to see

something scurrying into a pile of rocks at the far side of the room.

"A rat," he said. "I'm jumpy. I almost shot the damn thing."

He reached for something to calm his nerves—a fresh stick of red licorice.

I went to the wall at the far end of the room, and worked around it and through the doorway into an adjoining room. My MP5 was in my hand. By now I realized the odds were almost infinitesimal that there was anyone else inside, but that's exactly what Murphy wants you to think right before he bends you over and butt-slaps you back to reality.

I hugged the walls and worked around the room, scanning for booby traps and any sign of habitation. I found neither.

There were two more rooms. They were both empty. There were no chains or ropes or anything on the walls that might have made it easier to keep a prisoner here. No furniture. No chairs. Nothing but dust.

Once we were sure the place was clear, we went back through the rooms again, looking for a trapdoor or some other indication that there was a basement. We didn't find any. I don't think anything bigger than a rodent had been in the building in years.

Wrong place.

I was considering whether it was even worth going to the house when Junior warned us that there was a pickup coming down the road.

I moved up to the front of the building, watching from one of the window openings as the pickup sped down the road. Just as it drew parallel to us, the driver hit the brakes.

"Shit," I cursed.

"See us?" asked Shotgun.

"Worse," I said as the pickup pulled into the ranch's driveway. "Come on."

The driver was out of the truck before we reached the road.

"Junior, what do you see?"

"Driver's got something—damn."

"Man or a woman?" Shotgun asked Junior.

"Could be either."

"Everybody move in!" I yelled. "And we want that driver alive. Don't fuck that up."

[VI]

EVEN IN MY younger days, I would never have been able to sprint the thirty or forty yards from the ruins to the house in the two seconds it took for the driver to get inside.

I didn't admit that to my legs or my lungs. I pushed my head down and ignored the stitch in my side, grinding it out with everything I was worth. I left Shotgun in the dust, I'll tell you that.

Still, the door was closed well before I got close.

"We're going in," I yelled over the radio between pants for breath. "Shotgun?"

"Behind you, boss," he huffed. "Ain't heard a shot yet. Maybe she's gonna torture them first."

I could only hope.

Barging through a door without proper backup and preparation is a damn good way to get yourself killed. Hell, even *with* backup and preparation, door bangers have it rough. But I figured if I was going to save Ms. Reynolds from herself, I had to take a chance.

What followed wasn't the carefully choreographed ballet perfected by SEAL Team 6. It did, however, get the job done.

The door splintered as soon as my foot hit it. I sprang inside, then pushed back against the wall and screamed in English and then Spanish.

"Hands in the air! Hands in the air! *¡Ahora!*"

I kept shouting. Turning twice, I made sure I had everyone in the room covered.

I did. The only sound came from the flickering of the birthday candles on the cake in the center of the room.

We had just busted into a four-year-old's birthday celebration; the late arrival was mom, just home from work.

THE FAMILY WAS exceptionally understanding; they even offered us some cake.

I made Shotgun refuse; one bite and the cake would be history.

Nonstop ball-busting was the order of the day as we headed into position for House Number 2. Most of it was mild:

Gonna be a five-year-old's birthday this time, Dick?
Maybe someone'll pop out of the cake?

Even the tough stuff didn't really bother me, though. I always get the last laugh: I sign their paychecks.

The team snapped back into business posture when we reached House Number 2. We went through the same routine, with Shotgun and I driving by first and checking the ruins.

These proved more substantial than they had looked from above. The roof material itself was in bad shape, but the broken rafters and truss beams were still substantial. There was also flooring material for an attic, keeping the top of the structure covered. The front door had a pair of thick metal straps for reinforcement, and the few windows were all covered by boards or metal.

Once again we checked out the area, made sure there was no one nearby, then found a place to park the truck. Tire tracks rutted the field, obscured by weeds. This looked like the place.

The material over the ruined building was so thick the Bird's sensors couldn't see through it. Junior, controlling the aircraft, had better luck with the house. He told us there were two people inside.

"What are they doing?" I asked.

"Could be sleeping," said Junior.

"Sleeping or dead?"

"Can't tell. I'm looking through a roof. The heat signature is kind of fuzzy."

"All right. Keep watching. We're going to check the ruins."

Shotgun and I made a wide arc behind the building before approaching from the rear. It was a quiet night, peaceful, almost silent.

So quiet, in fact, that I heard the same sickening click Shotgun did when we were about five yards from the ruins.

"Oh, shit," he muttered. "I think I just stepped on a fucking mine."

THE MILITARY USES a high-tech airborne system to scout minefields. The devices—officially known as the ASTAMIDS, for Airborne Standoff Minefield Detection System—can be mounted on helicopters, UAVs, and standard aircraft. They work by scanning an area with infrared gear. Because mines are made from different material than the ground around them (duh), they cool down (or heat up) at a different rate, and very sensitive infrared can show them. Under the right circumstances, the mines stand out like sore, uh, thumbs.

The IR pod on the Bird was not quite as sensitive as the military system, unfortunately. Even so, I had Junior bring the Bird over the area.

"I can't see anything, Dick," he told us.

"I know what I heard," said Shotgun. "There's definitely a mine under my foot."

"Did you bend down and look?" asked Junior.

"I ain't shifting my weight. Damn."

"Relax and stay where you are," I told Shotgun. "I'll get you out."

"In one piece, right?"

"There'll be at least one piece."

"Ha. Well, I'm just going to eat while I wait."

The next ten minutes passed the way time always does when you're having a real blast . . . or are one wrong step away from one. I worked myself over to Shotgun, retracing my own footsteps and then coming back up in his. I got down on my hands and knees and crawled the last yard or so.

The ground seemed hard-packed and undisturbed. I took out my knife and gently probed—very, very gently.

"You're sure you heard something?" I asked Shotgun.

"I heard it," he said between chews. He'd taken his emergency can of Pringles from his pants to calm his nerves.

I looked around for something to replace Shotgun's weight with. A direct replacement would have been difficult—the boy weighs three hundred pounds if he weighs an ounce—but all I needed was enough weight to keep the trigger from lifting. Most mines are set to trigger at five kilograms, or roughly eleven pounds; put at least that much weight on them, and you're OK.

Usually. Often. Sometimes. Occasionally never. Depends on the mine. But I wasn't about to share that information with Shotgun.

To be safe, I decided I had to put about forty pounds on the mine plate.[13] There were plenty of stones, but they were all near the building—which would have meant going across the minefield to get them. Instead, I worked my way back to the car, and found three heavy rocks there. I carried them one by one over to Shotgun.

"I don't think it's enough weight," said Shotgun after I put down the last one.

"No shit. Maybe if you'd stop eating for a minute, I could catch up."

"Gees, you're in a bad mood."

Trace and Mongoose came up the road to help. They grabbed a couple of water jugs and brought them to the edge of the path I'd marked. I took them and balanced

---

[13] I'm not sure how technical to get here, and I don't want every tango asshole playing with mines. Basically, I made an assumption about the type of mine likely to be used, and how to fail-safe it. You can probably work out what the alternatives are on your own, but then you're also probably smarter than the average terrorist.

them on the rocks against Shotgun's boot. We still looked a little light.

"What about the gas can?" suggested Mongoose. "It's full."

It was a five-gallon jerry can—about thirty pounds on its own.

"You're going to put a can of gas on a mine?" said Trace.

"What the hell?" said Mongoose. "If it blows up he's dead anyway."

I lugged the can out there and slid it into place on top of the rocks between his feet.

"Unlace your boots," I told him. "And step back with me."

He took his left foot out, wiggling his toes and angling his ankle to keep the rocks and everything else in place.

The smell almost knocked me over.

Whether because of nerves or maybe the sweat from his fingers, he had trouble unlacing his right boot. Then he couldn't get his foot out without starting to lift it. I stopped him, then bent down with my knife to cut the material away.

I swear the gases from his socks started melting the edge of the blade.

"From now on, you change your socks more than once a year," I told him as I folded the leather upper out of the way. "On the count of three. One . . . two . . ."

Shotgun obviously failed kindergarten, because he pulled back his foot on two. I held the stones and everything in place as he jerked backward. Off-balance, I felt him slip and fall.

I closed my eyes. Nothing happened.

Now it was my turn. I took a deep breath, then pulled my hands upright quickly.

"Either heaven looks a heck of a lot like earth, or we're still alive," said Shotgun, sitting on his butt a few inches away.

"You're not going to heaven," yelled Mongoose from back by the truck.

"Well, this *could* be hell," said Shotgun, getting up.

We retraced our way to the truck. Once there, Shotgun celebrated by grabbing a full bag of Oreo cookies he'd stashed and inhaling them.

"I don't think there's mines out there at all," said Mongoose, smirking. "Shotgun was just hearing some of his candy rattle."

"Nah." Shotgun took out his pistol and shot at the ground below the gas can. The mine beneath it exploded. Dirt and grit flew everywhere, and the gasoline flared. The reverberation set off two other mines, which started a chain reaction—half the field had been sprinkled with the damn things.

"Told you," said Shotgun, reaching for another bag of Oreos as the explosions continued. "Anyone want a cookie?"

JUST AS JUNIOR had thought, the people in the house had been sleeping.

The explosions took care of that. The door popped open and an old man came out, peering over in our direction.

"Hola," I yelled, deciding there was no sense waiting. "Hello."

I walked over. He was short, stocky but not over-weight. His gray, close-cropped hair put him in his early sixties, but he was in good shape, a laborer unbent by his labors.

"Excuse me, senor," I said as I approached. "I'm lost and was wondering if I could use your phone."

"There was an explosion," he said in Spanish.

"Yes, yes, I know — a mine. We are all OK — we threw something into the field and it went off."

He leaned his head to one side, as if he was trying to see the back of mine.

"You are American." He wrinkled his nose, as if smelling the air. He was still speaking Spanish. "DEA?" he asked, giving the initials for the Drug Enforcement Agency.

"No. Not at all." I put my arm on his shoulder. "I'm here about a mutual friend. A Melissa Reynolds. Do you know her?"

He didn't say anything, which was answer enough.

"Let's talk about it inside," I told him.

"Yes," he said, this time in English.

Trace and Mongoose followed me inside. It was a tight fit — the house was maybe fifteen by twenty feet, and just one room. A bed was pushed against the far wall. A wooden armchair sat catty-corner from it. A gray-haired woman a few inches shorter but just as solid as the old man stood in front of the chair, arms folded in front of her chest. She lifted her head when I came in, the sort of gesture that says I'm not sure who you are, but don't try pushing me around.

The old man started talking to her in rapid-fire Spanish. It was so quick that I couldn't quite make it all out; something along the lines of *Melissa*.

The old woman made the sign of the cross.

Generally when people do that, they're praying for my soul, the same way the saintly if ferocious Sisters of Perpetual Mercy and Everlasting Torment did when I was a wee lad in New *Joisey*. I was going to inquire what the cause of prayer was here, when I was interrupted by a beep in my headset.

"Goldilocks has landed," said Junior.

There was a commotion outside. I raised my machine gun and told the old man and his wife to stay on the bed behind me.

"¡Rápido!" I added. "Get down and stay down!"

I stepped in front of them just as the door opened.

I will give Melissa Reynolds one thing — she is a feisty little package. She entered the small little house kicking and screaming, much to the amusement of Shotgun, who was carrying her.

He stopped smiling when she connected with the family jewels. He let go and reared back, but Trace caught his arm before he could connect.

"Ms. Reynolds, it's very nice to see you again," I told her.

Her eyes flashed, and she started to pull her arm back to hit me. Trace grabbed her before she could.

"Why are you here?" Melissa demanded.

"We're here to take you home," I told her.

"Who told you I'd come here?"

"I thought it was a pretty good bet that you'd come to get a little revenge on your jailers. Not that I blame you," I added.

"I'm not here for revenge."

"Then why are you here?" asked Trace. As strong as she was, she was still straining to keep her grip.

"To thank them. They're the whole reason I'm alive."

THAT WASN'T AN exaggeration. The first night of her captivity, Melissa had been chained to the wall in one of the rooms of the ruined building across the street. She managed to slip out of the chains within seconds and made her way to the road—she didn't know there was a minefield, and was as lucky as I'd been. She managed to get to the hamlet, another sixty or seventy yards down the road.

Unfortunately for her, the men who had brought her had only gone across the street to talk to the Garcias. When they went back, they saw she was gone and quickly found her near the church at the center of the hamlet. They dragged her all the way back down the road.

At that point, Mr. and Mrs. Garcia interceded. They were themselves prisoners of the cartel, brought here to work off their debts by providing food for the prisoners kept in the ruins across the way. The guards wanted to kill her, but Mrs. Garcia threatened to tell the guards' boss if anything happened. The thugs might have simply killed them as well, except then they would have been responsible for the Garcias' debt. They decided it was easier and cheaper just to leave her with tightened chains.

"I promised that I would help them escape the cartel," Melissa told us. "They're coming with me."

"Just what America needs," said Trace. "Two more illegal aliens."

"I'll help them get citizenship."

"Excuse me," said Mr. Garcia. His English was very

good, when he chose to use it. "We don't want to go to America. It's no offense to you. America is a beautiful country. But we are Mexican and want to live in our own home back west. We do not need to be crossing north."

Mrs. Garcia sprang to life, insisting that we have something to drink.

"Got any beer?" asked Mongoose.

"No alcohol," said Mr. Garcia. He waved his hand with the vigor of a temperance leader.

We settled on coffee. Truly, these people didn't have much. There was no running water; Mrs. Garcia filled a small steel percolator pot from a large plastic jug. The cups looked like they had been around during the Inquisition. But the coffee was amazingly sweet.

The Garcias told us some of their story as we drank. They were respectable people who had nothing to do with the drugs or anything else illegal. But like many Mexicans, they had inadvertently found themselves wrapped up in the cartel's web. And once that happened, they were trapped.

Their problems had begun two years before, when a bad storm had damaged their house. When no bank would lend them money, they borrowed from the local loan shark.

You can see how that's going to end, and I suspect Mr. Garcia did as well. But he was able to keep up his payments for quite a while. He repaired his house, and with the few pesos he had left over, rented a small patch of land next to his to grow more corn.

If the corn had come in, he would have done well enough to pay off the remainder of the loan. He also would have been able to enter a contract to lease the property for seven years; it was owned by a widow who couldn't take care of it herself. But a few nights before he was to harvest it, catastrophe struck in the form of a half-dozen large trucks. The vehicles ran wild through the field, smashing down the corn. Mr. Garcia heard the commotion around midnight and ran to protect his investment; when he got to the door, he was hit over the head by a person or persons unknown.

Mrs. Garcia found him a half hour or more later. By then, the perpetrators and vehicles were gone. So was any hope of repaying the loan shark. The loan shark foreclosed, taking the only collateral the cartel considered worthwhile — their lives.

Even that was heavily discounted. At the time, the loan and its interest was worth a total of eight thousand dollars. But in a place where a decent job paid eighty dollars a week, the Garcias had about as much chance of paying it off as I have of becoming the next president of the United States.

A work "arrangement" was "proposed," and the Garcias were moved north to work off their debt directly for the cartel. They had been working for nearly two years, with no end in sight.

As sad as their story sounds, I have to say that they might not have fared much better even if they had had a legitimate loan. The Mexican banking system and the laws surrounding it are not particularly friendly to small businessmen and farmers, let alone the common man. The bankruptcy laws are very much in the creditors' favor. Banks can't get away with murder, but they can get away with just about everything but.

And you thought *that* was only true in America.

Freeing the Garcias would not be an easy matter,

certainly not if they were going to stay in Mexico. It was even worse than that: they wanted to go back to their own hometown.

The cartel didn't hand out coupon books and stamp each sheet to show that you were paying off your debt. I wasn't sure at all that they would *let* the Garcias pay off their debt, even if we found the money for them.

THERE WAS A lot to admire about the Garcias: the fact that they had risked their lives to protect Ms. Reynolds, their determination to stay in Mexico. I wasn't necessarily opposed to helping them if we could arrange that somehow. But I did have priorities.

"Look, Melissa, I don't care what you do tomorrow," I told her. "But tonight we're going to Texas. Your father is on his way back home to see you."

A small white lie, or maybe just wishful thinking—Doc hadn't actually managed to talk to him yet.

"I'm not leaving without helping them. We can buy their freedom."

"And how exactly would that work?" Trace asked.

"I'm sure Dick can figure it out," said Melissa. "He does stuff like that all the time in his books."

[VII]

I'M NOT EXACTLY sure how or why I became such a goddamn bleeding heart that I agreed to help the Garcias. Maybe it was because Melissa Reynolds made it clear she'd fight us every step of the way back to the

States if I didn't. Maybe it was the look Trace gave me as the Garcias told their heartrending tale.

Maybe it was the looks Junior and Shotgun and even Doc gave me after Melissa asked them for help convincing me. Put a good set of lungs on a girl and she can rule the universe.

Then again, the idea of kicking a drug kingpin in the balls had a certain appeal. And I still had the State Department gig to consider: nothing like going straight to the top to find out about the terrorist connections.

And who knows? Maybe all those rosaries Sister Mary Elephant has been saying have had an effect.[14]

THE QUESTION WAS how to proceed. Should we go, hat in hand, to the cartel leader and plead for mercy?

Hahahahahaha.

I thought you might need a laugh.

THE GARCIAS BELIEVED that the leader of the cartel, Pedro de Sarcena, was a man of his word and would honor an agreement to free them if the debt was paid off. Personally, I thought this was probably a bit of bull. Cartel leaders, mafia dons, and criminal masterminds in general are often said to be "honorable men" living by a "code of honor." Supposedly, when they give their word, it sticks.

That's mostly hooey. De Sarcena's word was probably about as good as Muammar Gaddafi's. Still, if he gave his word in the right way, it might work.

---

[14] The good sister was one of my former teachers. She now leads the Rogue Warrior Book Club at the Holy Rollers Home for Lost Causes and Retired Nuns.

The right way being at the point of a gun.

We'd definitely pay him off, though. Not, as Melissa suggested, with the reward for her, but with his own money. He undoubtedly had so much lying around that he'd never miss it.

While I needed time to work out the details, the first order of business was to get the Garcias out of town. I decided the best thing to do was to send them home, and so I detailed Trace, Tex, and Stoneman to get them there. I told Trace to stay with them until I had things under control from my end, and in the meantime to do whatever she could to make sure the arrangement was permanent.

"No shit," she said.

I told Doc to take Melissa north and out of danger.

She refused to go.

"How do I know you're going to carry out your promises?" she asked.

"I always do."

"Not from what I've read."

"You're going to trust a drug lord and not me?"

Melissa began reciting a litany of misreadings of my various books, starting with *Rogue Warrior*.

I hate it when people use my words against me. I might have simply taped her mouth shut and shipped her home to daddy, but logistics intervened. The nearest city was Nuevo Casas Grande. It had a municipal airport, according to Shunt, who was acting as our on-line resource officer back in the States. (The resource officer handles arrangements like booking flights, wiring money, shipping Shotgun's snacks, arranging lawyers and bail money, etc.)

We headed to the airport, only to discover that a)

calling the wavy line of macadam that ran along the desert an airport is like saying I'm ten feet tall, and b) the next flight north was three days away.

My friend with the helicopter company was booked solid, and while he offered to free up an aircraft on an emergency basis, I decided to hold off calling in that favor until I really needed it. I suppose I could have had Doc rent a car and take Melissa north in the trunk; lord knows a hell of a lot of drugs are smuggled that way. But they were both tired and cranky, and I figured it was better to let them rest for a few hours.

Not that I intended to rest myself.

MY NEXT ORDER of business was to touch base with one of my main sources of information and background on the cartel, a man I'll call Narco since he's still living and working south of the border. (It'll also piss him off, an added benefit.) As the nickname indicates, he's an agent working for the DEA—officially, the Drug Enforcement Agency, though probably better thought of as Dicks, Eraserheads, and Assholes.

I first met Narco through some friends of Danny Barrett, my main man stateside when it comes to handling Red Cell International's police accounts. We do a number of different things for law enforcement agencies, mostly in the area of training though we have occasionally been asked to "supplement" in areas like investigation and retrieval. The work isn't glamorous, but it does keep a steady trickle of shekels flowing into the coffers. It also provides an array of useful connections, including the one that led to Narco.

Leaving Doc to organize the others, I headed east to a small village about three miles outside of Nuevo Casas Grande. When I say the village was small, I mean almost nonexistent. There were a total of three houses, one of which hadn't been occupied in four or five years. The only other building was a combination general store, restaurant, bar, barbershop, and shoe repair place.

The cobbler doubled as the bartender and barber. I declined a polish—battered sneakers don't shine up well—and walked past the barber chair to the bar, where Narco was sitting alone. I hadn't called ahead, nor was there a need to: Narco spent most of his mornings at that table.

"Join me, stranger?" he said in Spanish-accented English.

"What are you drinking?"

"Tequila. Elixir of life and nectar of the gods."

"I was looking for a gin myself," I told the owner as he walked over.

The bartender nodded. Unfortunately, he didn't carry any version of Bombay; the gin was a local brand undoubtedly made in a basement a few miles away. Nor was it likely to taste very different than the lighter fluid Narco was drinking: gin, tequila, vodka, whiskey, it was all a matter of which food dye you added.

Since he's still working south of the border, I won't describe Narco too closely, but I will mention one accessory that was rather prominent in his wardrobe: an old-school .44 Magnum tucked into the waistband of his tie-died dashiki.

I don't know why I saw so many revolvers south of the border this trip. The Mexican cartels can certainly afford the best: they import literally thousands of American guns every year. In fact, the Bureau of Alcohol, Tobacco and Firearms has even helped them get weapons, in a rather notorious sting operation that went sour. But I guess we'd expect that given the players.

(If you want the details, Google: John Dodson, ATF, Phoenix, and "Fast and Furious." Dodson, maybe one of the few people in the agency with any sort of sense, was ordered by his superiors to let weapons go south in an "operation" dubbed Fast and Furious, allegedly designed to trace the flow of guns to the cartels. The orders were given even though upward of a thousand Mexicans were being killed each month in the area just south of Phoenix. And we're not talking peashooters: the weapons included fifty-caliber machine guns and just about every assault rifle you can name. Now I'm a firm believer in the Right to Bear Arms, but that doesn't mean we should be arming the cartels.)

In any event, I complimented Narco on his belt-wear after my drink came.

"Love the old-school iron," he said. "Some things can't be improved on."

"One thing about automatics, though. You don't have to reload as often."

"Something to be said for that."

We drank a toast, then had another. I was careful not to spill any of my drink, lest it burn a hole in the floor.

Narco gave me some more background on de Sarcena. While the cartel honcho was clearly a thug and a murderer, he was not without an education or some refinement. He had gone to college in Spain, where he majored in accounting and business administration.

After graduating, and a year or so of slumming around Europe, de Sarcena went back to Mexico and drifted into working for a small cartel. He seems to have started by working a legitimate job at a bank as a loan officer—yes, I know, that's not really a legitimate job, even in Mexico, but humor me for theory's sense. Within a year, he was helping the local banditos launder money; another year after that, he was moving up the chain at both the bank and the gang.

He was so well regarded, in fact, that he was offered a job by an American bank looking to expand into Mexico. He apparently turned it down, but only because it didn't offer as much money as he wanted.

Think about that. A major American bank almost employed the man who later became the head of one of Mexico's most notorious cartels.

Another thing that intrigued me about de Sarcena was the fact that he had come from a solidly middle-class family. They weren't rich, but they had enough money to send him to school in Spain, which was an achievement and dream far beyond the reach of most Mexicans.

A lot of Americans as well, I might add.

So why did he go bad?

If you come up with an answer, let me know. It will tell us a lot about why the cartels run things in Mexico, and why the country is so screwed up.

IF YOU'VE EVER seen Versailles—the extravagant waste of sous that led to King Louie and his cake-eating wife to lose their heads during the French Revolution—then you have an excellent idea of what Pedro de Sarcena's house looks like. Though a bit smaller and without the elaborate grounds and outbuildings (to say nothing of the tourists), de Sarcena constructed his mansion to match Versailles's most famous halls mirror by mirror.

Apparently he had taken a liking to *le France* following his college graduation. He'd become obsessed with the fancy palace, and a few other accoutrements of ridiculous wealth. He did need a big house — he not only lived there but used it as an office building as well. He had literally dozens of people working in the mansion, handling the cartel's business.

Marble aside, a house is still a house. And every house needs a sewer connection or a septic tank to handle its waste. In this case, de Sarcena had opted for a septic tank — a reasonable choice, given that there were no sewer systems within a hundred miles or so.

The only drawback to a septic tank is that it had to be pumped on a fairly regular basis. That's a lousy, dirty job that most people would greatly prefer someone else do. In fact, few people even want to watch. Between the stench and the potential for a fatal splash, the entire operation is always given a wide berth.

Perfect for us.

The honey wagon and excavator were stopped briefly at the side gate later that morning when we showed up. We looked and smelled the part: Mongoose, Shotgun, and I were wearing the universal uniform of working septic pumpers the world over — oversized jumpsuits and woolen caps pulled down over our ears for protection. (It was a tad hot for the ski caps, but the integrated earphones and mike sewn into the brim made up for the sweat. Hands off Jawbone; we've already made the patent submission.) They were stained with a variety of bodily fluids and one or two solids, having been thoroughly prepared en route. We had prepared our trucks well, rolling through a muddy farmyard oozing with cow manure before heading to de Sarcena's mansion.

The smell was really all we needed to clear the gate. We were quickly empowered to proceed, and trundled on over to the greenest part of the back lawn, the tell-tale sign of the septic field's leach system.

Bring an excavator onto a criminal's property and you are sure to attract attention. Half a dozen thugs surrounded us soon after we pulled around to the back. I let Mongoose deal with them while Shotgun and I unloaded the excavator.

Mongoose's Spanish may have been a little hard for them to understand, especially given the fact that he was chomping on a big wad of chewing tobacco or "dip," a disgusting habit that he had picked up en route to the job. It not only provided cover for his slight Filipino accent, but gave his inquisitors another reason to back off—he sprayed tobacco juice with every sentence.

More important than anything he said was the clipboard in his hands. Mongoose thumped that thing back and forth like a true pro, fanning out work orders and rapping his knuckles with the staccato of a project manager two weeks behind schedule. Even the security supervisor gave way before Mongoose's clipboard—though in all fairness, a timely shift in the prevailing winds may have had something to do with it as well.

Shotgun climbed up and took the controls of the excavator. You can judge for yourself what sort of damage he was capable of by the fact that he was making motor noises as he got into the cab.

Me, I headed for the house to find out where the clog was.

"What clog?" asked the security thug who met me near the door to the basement.

"The one holding the shit back," I responded, leaning toward him.

His face blanched at the whiff of eau du toilette.

"You stink," he said, holding up his hand.

"This nothing," I told him. "This is our first job of the day. Tonight—that is when I'll smell really bad."

The guard made a U-turn and disappeared.

The back wing of the house was graced by a stone porch topped by large doors and windows, massive things that made for a great view and even bigger AC bill. For further particulars, I refer you to the butt end of Versailles, which these duplicated in every way. To the very left of this platform was a simple set of steps leading to a more modest door. This opened to the basement. I trotted down the steps, grinning at the security camera recording my progress.

The basement door was unlocked; I didn't even need the key gun in my pocket. It opened onto a shallow landing, with steps up to the right and down to the left. I chose down.

A single video camera covered the basement hallway from the stairs. De Sarcena's security people were overconfident about security. Among other things, the man who met me should have stayed with me at all times, even if that meant wearing a gas mask. I'm guessing he may have thought the video cameras would suffice. I was counting on that, actually—I wanted them to know exactly where I was at all times. This way it would be much easier to disappear.

I proceeded nonchalantly, turning into the first room I came to on the right. This was a large basement kitchen, indifferently stocked and apparently used only for special occasions. A long prep table split the room in half; the sinks and stove were on the wall to my right, just below narrow glass block windows that sat at the base of the outside porch. Cabinets stacked the wall opposite them. Dead ahead as I came in were some large refrigerators and freezers.

I stood near the table for a moment, sizing the place up. I spotted one video camera in the corner; it was a large, boxy unit, about twice the size of the one I'd already seen outside and in the hall.

Which I suspected meant that it was for show, meant to be detected. So where was the real one?

I went over to the sink and leaned down, placing my ear right next to the drain and listening. Then I straightened, ran the water a bit, and repeated the process.

The pipes didn't talk to me, but I did manage to spot a video camera similar to the one in the hall. It was in the corner, hidden in a braid of garlic.

There was another in the opposite corner, this one behind some onions. You may think that the fact that there were at least two video cameras covering a relatively small amount of real estate is a bad thing. On the contrary, I was happy to see so many, and would have been ecstatic to see even more.

Why? Because the more cameras there are, the greater the odds that no one is really paying attention. And in-attention is always your friend when you're somewhere you don't belong.

Not that you could plan on having it, of course. But it was always useful as a counterweight to Murphy.

Narco had never been inside the mansion himself, but he had talked to several people who had, and he theorized that de Sarcena kept his money somewhere on the opulent second level of the mansion. It seemed like a reasonable guess, and it was my ultimate destination. But I wasn't going to rely on a simple treasure hunt. If I didn't find the money during my visit, the bugs I intended to leave along the way would surely give me a clue.

And if they didn't, then my tap into the video system would. Shunt, our resident high-tech guru, had supplied a handy-dandy little device that would pump their signal out to us. But for it to work, I had to tap in at a camera. And of course I had to do that without being seen. Both the bugs and the video system feeder were activated by an external signal; this way we would be safely away if they were discovered.

I only had four bugs left after looking for Melissa and setting up the fake kidnapping operation. I wasn't going to waste one of the bugs down here, and given the fact that both cameras were covering each other, this wasn't a great place to tap in. But what better place than a kitchen to establish your bona fides? I worked deliberately, a man on intimate terms with effluent.

The sink seemed to drain a little sluggishly. I filled it up again, then poured a small bottle of food dye inside.

Yes, definitely slow. I took out my pipe wrench and went to work below.

I had just started to clank around when a security guard came in.

"What are you doing?" he demanded, pointing his M4 in my direction.

"Clog," I told him. I leaned back out and showed him the monkey wrench.

He nodded solemnly. There is something about a

good-sized pipe wrench that convinces people you are an honest worker.

"I don't know where the clog is," I told him. "I will have to keep looking until I find it."

He frowned. His expression turned grave as I told him I would check the bathrooms next, but then would have to start looking at the pipes if that failed.

"You are here to clean the septic," he asked. "Why are you looking for clogs?"

"Good question. I should not have to do this." I nodded vigorously. "Your boss tells my boss to do this, then he kicks it to me. Always the man on the bottom gets the shit job, yes?"

I can't say he appreciated the pun, but he was someone who was undoubtedly on the downhill side himself. He nodded in sympathy, and stopped asking questions.

"Where are the bathrooms?" I asked. "Can you show me?"

"Just down the hall." He waved his arm. "Hurry and do your job. There is a party tonight. They need to get ready."

I fiddled with the pipe below the sink for another few seconds, then straightened. I could see the shadow of the excavator through the window. The guard was right; I'd better hurry. If I left Shotgun with that digging machine too long, he'd have a tunnel dug clear to the border.

I took my tool kit and went down the hall to the restrooms. *Chicos* and *chicas* were side by side.

I've always believed in ladies first, and so I knocked as loudly as I could, yelled *¡hola!* And went in.

A word of warning, girls—if you ever find yourself answering a call of nature in this bathroom, be careful of the miniature cameras embedded in the floors of the second and third stalls. They're perfectly positioned for that up-skirt porn Web site your boyfriend has been looking at when you're not around.

The camera in the upper corner near the door is somewhat less dangerous, unless you decide to do a striptease near the sinks.

I did my nonchalant, check-for-the-gummed-up-drain thing a little more quickly this time, throwing in some pipe banging for no charge. I was even quicker in the men's room. Not only were there no hidden cameras there, but the small monitor was discreetly placed so as to avoid catching anyone at the urinal.

Out of the bathroom, I walked down to the end of the hall, a dark expression on my face—there's nothing gloomier than a sewage worker who has not been able to find the lump of crap he's been sent for.

A stairway sat at the end of the hall. There was a camera above it, but from the way it was positioned, I could tell there was a blind spot beneath it, right along the wall.

I thought it was an oversight. It certainly seemed that way.

Until I went over and saw that there was a set of steps leading farther downward. And these steps were not covered by a video camera at all.

Interesting.

The basement I'd been in was cool and dully lit, but it was definitely the basement of a well-appointed mansion. The floors were made of nice tile, and the stucco walls would have seemed elegant in a lot of houses.

The level I descended to was a lot more like a dungeon than a finished space. Except for a small patch of cement near the stairs, the floor was entirely dirt. Massive spiderwebs hung from the rafters, and the place smelled as damp as any place I'd smelled in Mexico.

It was also dark. I had to close my eyes and wait for a moment while they adjusted. Even then, it was so dim that I resorted to my flashlight.

I moved away from the steps and began sweeping the space in front of me. It was open and empty. There was no furniture, no rats, nothing.

You were expecting a safe, maybe?

I was. Loose piles of money would have been even better. The Mexican cartels are so flush with dough that they have been known to keep pallets of hundred-dollar bills in various places, moving them around by forklift. But there were no such easy pickings here.

I scuttled around, looking for signs that something had been buried recently. Most likely it would be a body, though you never knew. Halfway through, my cap buzzed. I tapped the side of my head and activated the link.

(The communications system is designed to work only over short distances; the discrete burst signal it uses — "low probability intercept" is the technical term — has a limited range. I could talk to Mongoose and Shotgun; calling Junior or Doc would require using my sat phone, which of course was relatively easy to intercept.)

"How's it going?" asked Mongoose.

"Slow."

"You get upstairs to the library rooms yet?"

"I'm still downstairs," I told him.

"I don't know how much longer we can keep them out here. Shotgun is really making a mess."

"All right. Stick with it. I'm on my way upstairs right now."

This was exactly the sort of op where Trace was invaluable. If the guards started getting antsy, she would have just lowered the zipper on her jumpsuit a half inch and they would be begging her to take her time. That wasn't going to work for Mongoose.

I quickly scanned the rest of the floor without finding anything, then went back to the stairs. I slipped back around, and reemerged from the blind spot to walk up the stairs.

The first floor was filled with offices of the cartel. It was a regular little corporate operation, with its own store of bureaucrats and pencil pushers. Apparently it takes a lot to keep thugs on the street.

A set of high heels clicked across the floor as I climbed up the steps. They belonged to a young woman in a miniskirt who was just crossing the hall. She disappeared into an office; a moment later she and two other young ladies came out, and all three began walking down the hall away from me. My view was limited, but sometimes less is more — and that is definitely the case when it comes to skirts.

I like a well-sculptured thigh on a woman. There's nothing like it, really, except for a calf, or a derriere, or a breast, or a neck, or . . .

It's easy to lose focus when you start noticing the scenery. I was brought back to the problem at hand by a loud and angry growl.

"You again!" snapped the guard I'd met below. "What are you and your filthy nose[15] doing up here?"

I explained that I was still looking for the clog. He frowned, waved his hand, then ducked back into the room just to the right of the stairs. This was the security center.

As I passed, I noticed that my boot was untied. I stooped to tie it—and slipped my first bug next to the door molding before taking a peek inside.

The guard was too busy playing Spider Solitaire on the computer to pay much attention, either to me or the bank of TV screens above his station. He was the only person in the small room, though there were two other chairs behind him.

My next stop was the men's room at the far end of the hall. It was a hell of a lot fancier than the one downstairs. I thought of putting one of my bugs here—you can learn a lot through toilet talk—but with only three left, I decided to hold off. I rapped on the pipes a few times, then started to leave.

"Something's up," said Mongoose over the radio. "Security just sent a bunch of people around from their little building in the front to the side entrance we used."

"Someone coming in?"

"Could be. I don't know."

"How are things going out there?"

"Shotgun's complaining about being hungry. Other than that, we're looking all right. With all this activity, they're paying less attention."

---

[15] The words he used were *nariz mugrienta*—an interesting insult, and I assume some sort of perverted pun, though no one has been able to untangle it for me.

"Excellent."

"Can I hook up the hose?"

"Give me another ten minutes if you can. Anybody ask about me?"

"They're staying pretty far away," said Mongoose. "Not that I blame them. We smell worse than Shotgun after he does a chili run."

"That's a matter of opinion."

"Now here we go," added Mongoose. "Truck pulling up. Going right up to the house. Two of the security dudes are riding the boards."

"Delivery?"

"Looks like it."

I went back into the hall, walking deliberately toward the back of the building. I was nearly to the end when a burly guard stepped out from a connecting passage to the right and blocked my path. He took one whiff and nearly fell over.

"Back," he told me, waving with his arm. A wire coiled up from beneath his jacket to his ear. "Whew—way back."

I shuffled backward to the wall, then watched a pair of guards come out of the passage. They were followed by two more men, who were pushing what turned out to be a safe.

Talk about hitting the jackpot. Now if only they weren't all holding shotguns.

The safe was wheeled into the center of the hall, then in my direction. And what a buffoon I was—I got so close as they came that they actually ran over my foot.

Almost. I certainly reacted as if they had, collapsing to the ground and muttering every Spanish curse I could think of. I struggled to get my balance—and managed to slip one of the bugs on the very bottom of the safe.

The guards were not particularly nurturing. They pushed me out of the way with a few kicks. One of them gave me a good swat across the back of my head with the barrel of his shotgun. Fortunately, it caught my skull.

"You idiot," said the guard I'd encountered earlier, who ran down the hall from his station. "Get to the shit hole where you belong."

There were a few other choice phrases. Meanwhile, the men with the safe continued to an office a few doors away.

I stumbled to the men's room to tend to my wounds.

And to tell Junior to activate the bugs.

"Are you sure?" he said over the sat phone. "You're still inside."

"We may get the combination, and in the meantime you'll be tracking where it is, right?"

"Yeah, but it's a risk."

"Go for it."

I put the sat phone back in my pocket and waited. I didn't have long—maybe three seconds after turning off the phone, an alarm began sounding through the building.

The bug had been detected.

[VIII]

THERE'S A MAJOR advantage to being a peon, unworthy even of contempt. People don't think you're capable of pulling off a clever stunt like bugging the mansion of one of Mexico's biggest criminals.

I walked out of the restroom, hand in pocket, fist wrapped around my PK. I contemplated how many shots I would have to take until I reached the office suite at the back of the hall, where I could go out through one of the massive glass windows and join Mongoose and Shotgun. But I was completely ignored. Security had already decided who must have done the deed—the two men wheeling in the safe.

Or more likely their boss, but he was unknown and inaccessible. They were there for the pummeling.

Apparently the detection device was limited to the room the safe had just entered. Since the bug was turned on shortly after it went inside, the guard monitoring the system assumed that the bug had been transmitting all along, and was only detected once it went past the threshold. That made sense, given the capabilities of the bugs they were familiar with.

As soon as they heard the alarm, the men bringing the safe went for their weapons: another natural reaction. This proved to be a mistake as well, since it incriminated them in the eyes of the others. The security people began screaming at them; they screamed back. A pair of shotguns went off in the little room.

I didn't catch the rest of the chaos—it seemed like a perfect time to walk calmly to the stairs and go up another flight, to the main floor of the mansion—the second floor, where Narco believed the cash was kept.

If the building actually was the palace at Versailles, this would have been the level with the fabulous Hall of Mirrors, a supremely ornate room big enough to line three bowling alleys up and still have space for a sports bar or two. What de Sarcena's version lacked in gold, it made up in silver. The metal twisted around the windows, topped off the molding, and held the massive mirrors at the side in place. The glare was so intense I wished I had sunglasses.

De Sarcena had taken a few other liberties in creating his version—I'm guessing the chandeliers were from China, and I wouldn't be surprised if he skimped on the floor tiles, which appeared ceramic rather than marble. But the place wasn't going to be mistaken for the living room of a double-wide anytime soon.

The discovery of the bugging device led to a full-scale alert and a lockdown of the estate. But as usual, everyone focused on the *threat*—the safe and its transporters. Everyone and everything else faded into the woodwork, or plumbing, as the case may be.

The faux Hall of Mirrors was covered by four video cameras, which gave reasonably good coverage throughout the entire eight thousand or whatever square feet of space. I made note of them, but didn't bother trying to hide where I was going. Instead, I put on an act, shambling and looking around with a pipe wrench in my hand: the errant sewer expert, lost in a jungle of riches. If anyone was watching, they were getting an Academy Award performance, and would see no reason to intervene.

The *real* Hall of Mirrors has two large rooms at either side, the *Salon de la Paix* and the *Salon de la Guerre,* aka Salon of Peace and Salon of War. De Sarcena's house was laid out the same way, except that the room where the Salon de la Paix would have been was used as an office.

That was my destination. I was mildly surprised but definitely pleased when I found the door unlocked.

I shambled inside, ignoring the half-dozen safes in

front of the bookcases on the far wall as I went to the bathroom, which was located on the wall right of the door. (Another de Sarcena alteration from the original, I might add.) I went to the commode, took off the top, then arranged the water feed hose so that it was just about to come loose; a stray vibration would do it. If I needed a diversion, I could simply stomp my foot and the hose would detach, sending a spray of water upward.

The next order of business was to locate the video cameras, which surely were watching the room. That wasn't particularly hard—they were stuffed into the chandelier, an obvious if utilitarian choice.

The cameras focused on the desk—actually an ornate table—and the safes behind them. While that left plenty of blind spots, it almost meant the coverage on the safes was pretty good. We'd have to beat the video system to get at the safes.

In the meantime, the video might help. The locks were digital; it would be easy to watch someone open them and get the combination.

I was almost ready to pack up when I realized that getting into the safes was unnecessary: the bookcases that covered the wall behind the safes as well as most of the two flanking walls were stacked with money.

The cash wasn't right out in the open, but it might just as well have been. Starting about the sixth shelf from the bottom, packets of cash were tucked behind the books. Three-quarters of the room was literally lined with hundred-dollar bills.

I retreated to the bathroom to formulate a plan. We could, of course, take over the video system and make a second trip. But why take the risk when the money was crying out to be stolen? All I had to do was get around the video cameras.

The table and a single, leather-upholstered chair were the only pieces of furniture, not counting the safes, in the room. I admire a man who has an uncluttered office. I also admire a man whose office has extremely high ceilings. Not only does this keep the circulating air fresh, but it makes it difficult for video cameras to capture the upper areas of the room. The cameras not only missed the side of the room where the bathroom was, but missed everything over roughly twelve feet high. Which meant they would miss me if I climbed up the bookcases.

I arranged my toolbox so that it could be seen at the edge of the door, then fiddled with the toilet so the water would run without overflowing. After that, I de-shoed—easier to climb these walls barefoot. I got up on the sink, then with the help of a curtain on the high window, worked my way up the interior corner and around to the first bookcase. Once there, I had a difficult decision to make: euros or dollars.

I went with the greenbacks. Much more solid currency, especially considering how much of it is owed to China—they'll never let us default.

The next big question was how much to take. It didn't pay to be too greedy in a situation like this; on the other hand, money is money. I settled for five stacks of hundred-dollar bills. Five stacks = fifty thousand smackers.

Being of a literary bent, naturally I couldn't help but notice the titles of some of the works around me. A surprising number were in English. Most of these were classics: *Gun Bible Digest, Best Shotguns of the*

Nineteenth Century, How to Rip-off People Without Even Trying.

But wouldn't you know, down on the shelf closest to the door, at eye level when you came in, was a familiar black-spined book with white and baby-blue type.

Rogue Warrior: Domino Theory.

And my publisher claims my demographics don't include the world's important people.

There were a few other Rogue titles as well. It almost made me feel bad that I was ripping the poor guy off. Then again, the spines looked a little worn. He'd probably bought those suckers used.

I filed the information away; maybe my editor could hit de Sarcena up for a blurb on the back of the next Mexican edition.

Clinging carefully to the shelves, I worked my way back to the bathroom and shimmied to the floor. I got my sneakers on, fixed the toilet, and prepared to move out. I still had work to do: retrieve the first bug I'd planted so it wouldn't be accidentally discovered, and tap into the video system, which I planned to do in the men's restroom in the basement.

I was maybe two steps from the door between the office and the hall when I nearly bowled over a tall, dark-haired woman. She flashed her eyelashes in my direction, wrinkled her nose, then took two steps back.

Maybe three, actually. The last thing I was doing at the moment was counting.

I've already told you how pretty Melissa Reynolds was. This woman was just as beautiful. And then some. Her hair was brown where Melissa's was blond. Her neck was ever so slightly slimmer, and her hips just a smidgeon wider. She was taller and older, in the same way that a few years makes wine richer. She had an elegant but businesslike air, which is what happens when you wear a silk suit. Her skirt, not quite as short as those of the women I'd seen on the floor below, was tactfully draped in a way that magnified the gams below it.

Gams — sometimes the old-fashioned words are best.

"¿Por qué?" she asked. "Why are you up here?"

"The pipes were clogged," I told her, starting past.

"Halt, you!" shouted someone from down at the other end of the Hall of Mirrors.

I did what any self-respected septic worker would do at that point; I pretended he wasn't speaking to me, and started down the hall. This neither fooled him nor impressed him. He put his hands on his hips and stretched out his elbows, a human roadblock. He spread his shoulders to make his unbuttoned coat splay open, revealing the gun in his belt.

"Phew," he said loudly. "You stink."

"Yes, senor," I told him. "The sewers always stink."

"You are the sewer rat," he said, as if he were Columbus discovering Cuba. "Why are you up here?"

"The clog in the line," I mumbled. "It was a big problem. I think I have it fixed now. The water, she needs to flow downward to push the crap out."

He scowled, eyeing me suspiciously. Then he glanced toward the office, no doubt aware that it was filled with money.

The woman I'd nearly bumped into was standing there.

"He does stink, doesn't he?" she told him. "This sewer man — he's ruining the whole house. It all stinks."

The guard nodded, then turned at me and made as if he were going to swat my head.

"You—get out—go back to the sewage where you belong. Out!"

I headed for the stairs. I was nearly there when the guard yelled at me again.

"Wait!" he said. "I will inspect your toolbox."

I held it out.

"Open it," he demanded. "And show me what is inside."

I started pulling my tools out. The money was at the very bottom, and if the guard had been diligent—or interested in anything beyond showing off his power for the beautiful bystander—he would have been able to spot it. But he was only interested in flexing his authority, and after I removed two screwdrivers and a ballpeen hammer—which would have been convenient to hit him with—he waved his hand and told me to leave the tools be.

But he wasn't quite done.

"What do you have in your pockets?" he demanded.

I had a gun in one pocket, and the video bugging device in the other. Actually, they were the pockets beneath the overalls, but a good pat down would undoubtedly discover them.

I put my hands inside the shallow exterior pockets and pulled them inside out.

"Why are you bothering this poor man?" said the woman. "He is just a stupid sewer man. Get rid of him and his smell. Come help me here. I need to get something from the office."

The guard didn't need to be asked twice.

"Get out of here," he told me. "Go back to your pit of shit."

THE REST OF my op went by quickly and without complications. I recovered the bug, then with the help of a quick diversion in the men's lavatory—something the idiot sewer man did caused the water to spurt wildly, temporarily blocking the camera's view—I tapped into the security system. I fixed the water, dried off, and exited the building just as Shotgun and Mongoose were loading back up.

As you may imagine, Shotgun had made quite a mess of the backyard. Not only had he driven the excavator back and forth over the wide, pebble-strewn walkway (see Versailles), but he'd messed up a good part of the sodded lawn. The security people were preoccupied, but his handiwork did not go completely unappreciated. As we were getting ready to leave, a short, red-faced man came running at our trucks from the back of the property, swinging a rake.

It was the head gardener.

"Doesn't sound like he thinks you did a good job," said Mongoose over the radio.

"I can take the excavator off the truck and fix it," he offered.

"Maybe next time," I said.

I put the truck in gear and started out. As Mongoose followed with the honey wagon, the gardener began banging his rake on the back of the truck.

Talk about living dangerously.

About a half mile from the gate, Mongoose and Shotgun started laughing hysterically.

"Pull over," said Mongoose over the radio. "Pull over."

"What's up?" I asked.

I rolled down my window and stuck my head out,

looking back at the pumper. Mongoose pointed toward the estate.

"Three-two-one," he said, counting down.

A second later, there was an explosion at the rear of the cartel leader's estate. Mongoose had left a charge of plastic explosive in the middle of the septic tank.

He had also pumped all the crap he'd collected back into the tank before sealing it.

I don't think I've laughed so hard since I got a look at the homemade porn SEAL Team 6 snatched from Osama's lair.

[IH]

WE WERE STILL laughing when we met with Doc and Melissa in Nuevo Casas Grande a few hours later. We'd gotten rid of the trucks, burned all our clothes, and taken about twenty showers apiece.

We still smelled, judging from the reaction of the bartender when we walked into the bar.

Doc and Melissa didn't exactly welcome us with open arms either. We ordered some beers and moved over to a corner of the room. Our smell had one salutary effect—it kept other patrons away. Not that there were more than a dozen people in the rest of the place. They were all foreigners, Americans, and a pair of men from Scotland, judging from their accents.

Given the local tourist highlights, they must have all been there on business. And that meant they were doing something with the cartel.

"I swept the place when I came in," said Doc, turning over his hand to reveal a bug detector a little smaller than a smart phone. "We can talk."

We filled each other in. We were now getting live feeds from de Sarcena's faux Versailles; Junior was in fact upstairs watching what was going on. De Sarcena was shooting hoops alone in his private gym, part of a massive suite on the north wing of the building that included a bedroom, den, and poolroom.

"He needs to work on his jump shot," said Doc.

Our video surveillance had also picked up a more useful tidbit: de Sarcena was planning a party that evening.

"Great," I told Doc.

"You can't just walk in there and pretend you're an invited guest," said Doc, who knew me well enough to know immediately what I would do. "They'll have all sorts of questions for you, starting with who the hell you are."

"I'll tell them."

"You won't get through the front door," he said.

"I'm not going through the front door."

NIGHT PARACHUTE JUMPS have always been among my favorite ops. What's not to like about hurtling into a screaming black void, unsure where the ground is and shaky on which way is up?

Ouuu-rah!

Mongoose and I stepped out of Chet Arthur's rented Cessna at somewhere around ten thousand feet. Stepped out may be a slightly optimistic way of putting it: the aircraft was not designed for skydiving, and squeezing through the door and onto the wing spar with a full pack of gear and a parachute was a pain in the butt, or in my case the pinkie, which got smashed as the door flew back because of the slipstream. It wouldn't have hurt so bad, but it was one of the fingers I mangled last year when I was chopping wood and accidentally got too friendly with the rail splitter.

I was still trying to stifle my curses when Mongoose squeezed out behind me. We gave each other a thumbs-up and plunged away, heads up, bodies into the wind.

There's a point during skydiving—and this occurs whether it's daytime or night—when you feel free as a bird. You let go and the world is just insanely beautiful, where everything is just perfect and you feel very much like you are a master of the universe.

I've never felt any of that myself. What I feel is a sharp tug in the area of my family jewels as the parachute deploys.

And I thank God for it. It hurts like hell, but it's much better than the alternative.

When we train, we usually steer down to a box target on a large field. For some reason, I never have any trouble doing that—push here, lean there, and nine times out of ten I hit the mark precisely.

Put me on an actual mission, though, and I have a hell of a time. Murphy is always doing something to my chute.

I started having problems almost as soon as I pulled the ripcord. The wind was negligible, but I couldn't seem to get myself pointed in the right direction toward the roof where I was supposed to land. Then I lost sight of the roof, and for a few moments I had no idea where the hell I was even going. Finally my eyes focused—maybe Murphy took his hand away—and I realized I had to angle just a tiny bit to my right to get on my target.

The problem was, I had twisted around completely in the other direction. And Mongoose, below me, assumed I was following him as planned.

Did I spell that right? Ass-u-me?

He looked up and saw me at the last minute. He tried to avoid coming directly below me, which would steal my air and make me fall. He was only partly successful—my chute half deflated, and by the time I yanked back and started to recover I hit the roof.

At least it made me forget about the pain in my finger.

"Sorry, Dick," said Mongoose, helping me after he'd secured his chute.

I gave him an appropriately profane response, and secured my chute. We'd hit above the basketball court—empty—for this very contingency; any sound we made was lost below.

We stowed the chutes together near one of the ventilation shafts. I radioed Junior, who was monitoring the video security system.

"No reaction from the guards," he told me. "You're looking good."

Pulling off our jumpsuits, we worked a few of the wrinkles out of our evening wear. We'd managed to do a little more research on the evening soiree, determining that it was one of de Sarcena's regular get-togethers and would feature a wide swath of local government officials, drug dealers, and other mass murderers.

The life of a cartel grandee is not an easy one. A man in de Sarcena's position has to constantly entertain his minions, handing out trinkets and favors to the rabble or risk losing their approbation. When that happens, of course, he has to shoot them, which can get very expensive, given the rising price of lead.

De Sarcena held regular parties to keep his various lords and ladies happy. Judges on the take, elected officials on the payroll, corrupt businessmen—all were invited each month to mix with high-ranking members of his organization and the occasional vendor.

I was coming as myself. If anyone asked, I'd say I was there to autograph my books.

Us *auteurs*, you know—doors open for us.

Skylights as well. Mongoose and I undid one of the frames over the hoop court, threw down a line, and zipped onto the hard wood. Now that we were inside their security system via our tap, we no longer had to worry too much about being spotted on video—Shunt had rigged a handy little override that re-looped sixty-four seconds of video feed from any selected camera on demand. (Why sixty-four seconds? Damned if I know. It either had something to do with how much memory he could use in the system, or was his lucky lottery number for the day.)

We did a quick makeup check—that would be the makeup of our ammo and other gear—and then headed for the hallway.

WE'LL PAUSE THE action here for a moment to mention that my dinner companion and I were wearing very lightweight body armor constructed especially for us by Tactical Protection Solutions, a company owned by some former SEALs. This isn't a commercial, so I'll leave you to find the brochure yourself, but the vest was extremely lightweight and fit under my clothes without making me look like I was wearing armor.

Man does not protect himself with armor alone, and naturally we were armed. My PK was tucked into a holster halfway under my arm beneath my sport coat— there's nothing worse than unsightly VHLs (visible holster lines) when you're bellying up to the chocolate fountain. In my rucksack was an MP5 and twelve magazines of ammo—if things turned sour and we had to leave in a hurry, I figured I'd have to leave a lot of bodies behind.

I had the money with me as well, inside a number five manila envelope that was taped beneath my sport coat. There was a slight bulge at my pelvis, but I've always thought a money bump somewhat cute.

Mongoose has been studying Krav Maga, an Israeli self-defense martial art. Probably because of that, he'd taken a recent interest in Israeli weapons. Thus, he sported a pair of Jericho B's outfitted to fire .45 ACP rounds, nice big slugs that could stop a bull in its tracks. He had an MP5 in his backpack (making it possible for us to share ammo in a pinch), along with a few other goodies we could use if we needed to make a quick escape.

"How are we looking?" I asked Junior once we were ready.

"Hall's clear. Same with the stairs."

"Ready to re-loop the video?"

"On my mark."

I glanced at Mongoose. He was very downtown: like me, he wore a black sports coat with a black shirt and pants, but it was the wraparound sunglasses that made the outfit. Like my identical pair, they had tiny speakers and mikes built in.

Junior gave us the signal and we moved out. Having studied the layout of the mansion with the help of the video security system and an old guide to Versailles, we had worked out a pair of routes that would take us down to the Hall of Mirrors with a minimal chance of running into anyone. He had also spotted a place where we could stash the backpacks just inside the room.

We were halfway down one of the servant staircases when Junior squawked a warning — a pair of de Sarcena's people had just shot down the hall and were on their way up in our direction.

Inconvenient.

We backed up the steps and turned the corner, waiting along the wall. The video coverage on the upper floors of the mansion was fairly sparse, but there was only a few square feet to hide where we were. We needed to stay inside them and save the replay trick for when it was truly needed.

As I leaned against the wall, I reached into my back pocket and took out my trusty sap or slapjack. The sap is a handy, underrated weapon. The leather, socklike exterior holds a fair amount of lead; properly applied to the back of the head or neck, it never fails to induce a sleeplike trance in the subject.

The trick, of course, is to properly apply it. This is most easily done when the subject is unaware of you — when say, you're behind him, and he's presently involved in something that requires a large amount of attention, such as kissing the girl he's snuck away from the party with.

Slapppp. Kerplunk.

Slappppppppppp. Ouuuuuffff.

Mongoose and I hit our targets at roughly the same

time, felling them together in the middle of the landing. It was romantic, like a scene out of *Romeo and Juliet*, or maybe the uncut version of *Caligula*. Unfortunately, my partner either misjudged the amount of space we had to work with or doesn't know his own strength. The girl flew out of the man's arms, rebounded against the wall, and then tumbled into the middle of the passage, unfortunately right in the camera's view.

Junior hit replay. We pulled her limp body back into the blind spot. But she'd made a lot of noise, apparently enough to be heard; Junior spotted a pair of guards being sent up to investigate.

We posed the bodies together to make them look as if they were necking, then made our way to the floor below the Hall of Mirrors via an alternate route. We worked through one of the offices and out to the hall where I'd had my close encounter with the safe.

There were a dozen guards, but they were all watching the main staircase, which guests were using to go up to the Hall of Mirrors.

Outside, a row of black Hummers and Mercedes S600 sedans were lined up all the way to the gate and the road with arriving guests.

I don't mean to criticize Mongoose, but he didn't have quite the savoir faire that Trace, my usual dinner partner on these sorts of occasions, would have. For one thing, Trace would never have worn combat boots with a black jacket—the eyelets definitely clashed. In fact, Trace would never have worn boots at all. She's more a stiletto girl—as in the knife as well as the heel.

Mongoose, by contrast, is more combat KA-BAR, which is what he slipped from his boot when a guard met us in the back hallway.

The guard pointed his finger at me and started asking annoying questions like "Why are you here?" and "Why do you look familiar?" and "Where is your invitation?"

The last one sounded more like "Wheregurgurgur . . . ugh?" Mongoose had slipped behind him while he confronted me and slit his throat with the knife.

The blood spurting from his severed artery made quite a mess on the floor. Being considerate guests — and concerned that the puddle would attract attention before we wanted it — Mongoose grabbed the man's black sports coat and used it as a mop while I pulled his still quivering body into the room where he'd been sitting.

But they say that no good deed goes unpunished, and that was certainly true in this case. My decision to tidy up the place brought me face-to-face with two other cartel thugs, sitting in the room watching a Mexican *telenovela* or soap opera. The thugs were sitting on a couch opposite a large screen TV, tongues hanging out of their mouths as the show's star did a little shimmy with her bootie.

I must take the blame for what happened next. Because surely if I had been a more highly evolved creature, I would have been able to handle the situation in a more civilized manner. I might have struck up a meaningful conversation with them, perhaps on the shameful decline in broadcast standards.

But being a rogue, I did what rogues do best in such situations: I dropped the dead man's legs, reached under my jacket, and grabbed my pistol. I shot both men in the forehead as they reached for their guns.

Actually I missed the forehead on the second, drilling him in the nose. Next time I'll wear my reading glasses.

Mongoose met me at the door.

"What happened?" he asked, tossing the blood-soaked jacket inside.

"FUBAR,"[16] I told him. "Let's get upstairs quick."

FUBAR was a bit of an exaggeration. Because really, the outlines of the mission were clearly recognizable, and our goal was well within reach. In fact, it was only a short staircase away. We double-timed up the stairs, huffing and puffing our way to top.

Junior, meanwhile, was asking what was going on. "What the hell?"

"What the hell yourself. Why didn't you tell me about that guard?"

"You turned into the wrong hall. That one's not covered."

"What about the room?"

"Same. I can't see you right now. I told you—the back hall isn't covered."

"When did you tell me that?"

"Twelve times during the brief."

"You should have told me thirteen."

"They're scrambling people," he warned. "They must have heard your gun."

"No shit." We paused at the top of the steps. "Just keep watching."

There were large panels between a few of the mirrors at either side of the room. Two panels on each side

---

[16] FUBAR: Fucked Up Beyond All Recognition. Probably an exaggeration here; a more appropriate term probably would been goat fuck. It was definitely beyond SNAFU (situation normal, all fucked up).

were actually hidden doors to the stairs, designed so that servants could make their entrances and exits without using the main stairway. We were behind the panel closest to the Salon of Peace, the room I had stolen the money from earlier in the day. Mongoose tapped me on the shoulder, indicating he was ready. I turned the little knob that worked the latch and pushed the door open slowly. The panel was semihidden by large vases with frondy fake flowers and a pair of pretend lemon trees. We stepped in quickly, as nonchalantly as we could. The backpacks fit nicely behind one of the large vases, hidden there from the cameras and the view of most of the people in the room.

The room was immense, but the crowd de Sarcena had invited filled it nicely. There had to be close to five hundred guests. About a quarter were wearing uniforms, either of the army or the police. Chicago during Prohibition had nothing on this corner of Mexico. Money didn't just talk here, it sang and sashayed, seducing everything and everyone in sight.

"There," said Mongoose, pointing across the room toward the Salon of Peace. "De Sarcena's gotta be in the middle of that knot."

Mongoose pointed toward a pack of women in brightly colored dresses, all giggling and laughing. We headed in that direction, fighting through a thick cloud of perfume.

Junior gave us a blow-by-blow of the security team's response to my gunshots. They had closed the front door and started a sector by sector search, methodically moving from bottom to top in the mansion. Junior had no audio, so he could only guess that they were in the process of calling each man on his radio unit and having him check in. If that was the case, he figured they would discover the dead men within the next two minutes; if not, then it might take another thirty seconds or so.

Plenty of time to party.

A waiter with a tray of champagne flutes passed nearby as I headed toward de Sarcena. I reached over and grabbed a pair of glasses—one doesn't want to greet a despicable scumbag empty-handed.

I'm sure you've all formed a mental image of the cartel leader. No doubt you see him as a blond-haired, blue-eyed Nordic semi-cowboy, a handsome stand-in for the Marlboro Man.

Not quite the image you conjured?

How about your typical bean-eater then, with gross oily hair, a wispy mustache, and a belly protruding over his belt?

For shame, imagining a stereotype. His mustache was hardly wispy at all.

His goatee—now *that* was wispy.

As we'd guessed, de Sarcena stood in the middle of the bevy of women, basking in their glow and cologne. He was wearing a diamond-stud earring in his right ear; the diamond was a stud all by itself, big enough to choke a horse. His suit was tailored well enough to hide most of his paunch, though not quite so generous that it obscured the gun in his shoulder holster—intentional, I'd guess, from the way the rest of his clothes draped. He was wearing one of those pretentious string ties, which set off the four or five gold chains he had around his neck. The women around him swayed and nodded as he spoke, as if they were a doo-wop chorus.

I paused for a moment, admiring the scene. The grand staircase up from the downstairs was directly behind him, and the light from below provided a perverse halo around the criminal leader.

And that's when I saw her:

Melissa Reynolds, sweeping up the main staircase like a debutante at a ball.

[H]

DOC HAD SENT Ms. Reynolds to her room some hours before, then checked on her shortly thereafter, cracking the motel-room door open and peeking in. She appeared to be sleeping. Being a gentleman, he didn't disturb her any further, instead retreating across the hall to his own room, where he cracked open a cold one and began flipping through the television channels.

With Junior's help, he had set up a video camera for surveillance in the hallway; every few seconds he glanced at the monitor, which was positioned strategically so he could see it from anywhere in the room. While his primary concern was to make sure no one was coming to resnatch Melissa, he was also watching in case she tried to leave as well. Frankly, Doc didn't think that was a possibility, and so he didn't bother to guard her window, which is how she got out.

The killer dress?

Well, after striking out at the airport, Doc had taken her into town to get some clothes. The dress she chose, a little silky number with a plunging neckline and a strategic slit, was hardly suitable for travel, but Doc did what most guys do when they accompany a woman clothes shopping—he sat in the most comfortable chair in the store and tried not to fall asleep.

So why had our darling Melissa decided to attend de Sarcena's castle?

A good question. One I intended to ask immediately— after administering a good spanking.

"Dick, Doc needs to talk to you," said Junior over the radio. "We have a problem."

"I'm looking at her," I mumbled, changing course.

I met her a few steps from the stairs. She smiled so sweetly I almost forgot that I was mad.

Not.

"What the hell are you doing here?" I took hold of her elbow and tugged her toward the wall.

"That hurts," she complained.

"It's supposed to."

"I'll scream if you don't let go."

"I wish you would scream," I told her.

"Couple of guards coming in the back way," Junior warned.

"Time to talk business then," I told him. I pushed Melissa toward him. "Watch her."

"Why are you here?" Mongoose asked.

"I wanted to see the great Rogue Warrior in action," she said. "I can take care of myself. I got in without you. I can get out anytime I want."

"How'd you get in?" Mongoose asked.

She rolled her eyes and leaned over just enough to make her tactics obvious.

While that might work to get past a guard or two when things were running smoothly, with the mansion on lockdown mode it could no longer be counted on.

"If it goes to shit, take her out with you," I told Mongoose. "In one piece if you can. Bullet holes are optional."

"Dick, stop treating me like a child," protested Melissa.

"Stop acting like one."

"I can twist any of these men around my pinkie."

There was no sense debating the point; she was undoubtedly correct. I nodded at Mongoose, then turned and walked over to de Sarcena.

The cartel boss had already spotted Melissa and was making a beeline toward her. He blinked when I stepped in front of him. Then he pointed at me.

"Y-you—" he stuttered. "You."

I held out my hand. "I understand you're a fan of my work," I told him. "I came to sign some books."

The mobster regained his composure quickly and stroked his little goatee.

"Well, this is an honor," he said. He laughed a little. "The Rogue Warrior. A guest at my party! Ladies, do you know this man? He is a Yankee hero—the inventor of SEAL Team 6."

I bowed my head in modesty.

Two security thugs had come through the panel and were heading toward us. Two more were making their way up the steps. Besides these four, there were four more scattered nearby, pretending to be discreet.

"I have some business that may interest you," I told de Sarcena. "So let's sign some books."

"You must have a drink first," said de Sarcena. "A gin—a Dr. Sapphire Bombay."

"Bombay Sapphire would be perfect," I told him. I don't like to correct my host, but it's important to get the name of the drink right.

"Yes, yes. You know, I read the books in English." He switched from Spanish midsentence. Though heavily accented, his English was not bad. "I have read all your books, starting with the first. The first is my favorite. And which is yours?"

"It's hard to pick," I told him. "They're all my children."

"Ah yes, the diplomatic Rogue Warrior. People do not remember how diplomatic you can be. Yes, into my office down the hall. Please."

He took a step, then stopped, reaching for Ms. Reynolds's hand.

"And this lovely lady — she must be with you. Is this the famous Trace Dahlgren?"

"No," I said quickly. But before I could add anything else, Melissa interjected.

"I'm Melissa Reynolds. You had me kidnapped."

"Oh no, no," he chortled — it really *was* a chortle — "I am a businessman, not a kidnapper. And who would kidnap you? You are too beautiful. Too, too beautiful. A lovely creature."

One of the security people was making a high sign a few feet away. De Sarcena nodded, almost imperceptibly.

Not good.

"Let's step into the other room," I told him. "That way over there."

As I pointed, my coat came open, and my gun became visible. This may have been a bit theatrical, but I needed to move things along.

"Yes, yes," said de Sarcena. "Business before pleasure, eh, Rogue?"

We started toward the Salon of War. Ms. Reynolds

followed. Mongoose grabbed for her, but she was too quick, sliding between de Sarcena and myself.

I gave her a dose of dagger eyes. Clearly, though, she had SEAL blood in her veins—she shot them right back.

By now, de Sarcena's security people had closed in and were only a few feet away.

"We're going into the room alone," I told the mobster. "You won't be harmed. But it's better if we don't have witnesses when we talk."

"This is always what I say," he agreed. "Truly, you are a man after my own heart. I have learned much from your books."

There's an angle the marketing people haven't thought of: *Rogue Warrior, a favorite guide of Mexican cartels and scumbags world over.*[17]

De Sarcena gestured with his fingers and the guards backed off. I looked at Mongoose and glanced at Melissa, indicating that he should keep her out. But de Sarcena protested.

"Please, bring your lovely assistant with you. Is she replacing Ms. Dahlgren?"

"She's more a party girl," I told him. "Very undependable. She better stay outside."

Mongoose grabbed her around the waist, and despite her protests, held on tight enough to keep her out.

"So, to what do I owe the pleasure of your visit?" asked the cartel leader when we were alone. The room was as ornate as the Hall itself, with marble walls and a large chandelier. A hammered metal table sat in the

---

[17] The publisher informs me that, in fact, they are readying a special Twitter campaign just for drug dealers and other miscreants in the near future. I'll let you know how it goes.

exact middle of the floor. Unlike the real thing, de Sarcena's Salon of War had doors fitted into the marble walls. They were not quite twenty feet high, which left a good gap between them and the thirty-foot ceiling.

"A pair of peasants owe you money," I told him. "I'm here to pay their debt."

"Peasants? Hired you? I did not know you did this kind of work."

"Only as a favor."

"Hmmmph." De Sarcena played with his peach-fuzz goatee again. "And how much do they owe me?"

"Is that really important?"

"Regrettably, no."

"It started as a few hundred," I told him. "Now it is in the thousands."

I reached below my jacket, grabbed the envelope, and tossed it on the table.

"That's enough to cover their debt several times over," I said.

Now, you would think that someone who has a room stacked with bills just down the hall would not really care that much about money, even fifty thousand dollars of it. But de Sarcena did not become rich not caring about money. He grabbed the envelope greedily and tore open the top even though it wasn't sealed. He dumped the packets of money onto the table, grabbed one and fanned it.

"Fifty thousand," he said.

"More or less."

"And for this, I do what?"

"You don't bother the Garcias," I told him.

"Hmmmph."

There was something in the way he looked at the

money that convinced me things weren't going to go the way I had planned. I guess I'd realized that from the start; it was only now that I admitted it.

I took a slight step backward, aligning myself toward the door.

"You know, having read your books, I believe there may be more to this transaction than meets the eye," said de Sarcena. "That is the expression, yes, more than meets the eye?"

"I try not to use clichés," I told him.

He picked up one of the bundles of money. "You wouldn't try to pay me with my own money."

"I might," I admitted.

"It would be a very Rogue thing to do. There was trouble in the yard this afternoon. A septic system. You don't have any knowledge of this, do you?"

"I try to keep my distance from sewage."

He reached into the right pocket of his sports coat and took out a piece of paper. When he unfolded it, I saw it was an image of yours truly taken from one of the security cameras in the hall when I'd come in. The print quality wasn't all that good—the cyan had run into the magenta. And it wasn't my good side.

"Did you find the clog you looked for?" de Sarcena asked.

"As a matter of fact, I did."

Clearly, it was time to take my leave. De Sarcena was no more than three feet from me; I took a half step and leaned toward him, my head barely an inch from his.

"If the Garcias are ever harmed, by anyone," I said, emphasizing the last phrase, "I will come back and extract revenge. Remember today."

"Who says you're leaving?" De Sarcena took a half step back. "We haven't concluded our business."

There were any number of responses I might have made, but I never got to choose any of them, for at that moment the room exploded.

EXPLODED MAY BE too strong a term. It seemed like it exploded, but to someone with experience in the black arts of special operations, hostage rescue, and general ass-kicking, what really happened was obvious: someone had tossed a flash-bang grenade into the room.

Painfully obvious, because the explosion of the grenade was so loud that my ears popped and I could no longer hear.

The flash blinded me as well, though given the fact that I spend half my life being blind to inconvenient facts that wasn't much of a handicap.

I relieved de Sarcena of his handgun — a Beretta 9mm — then hooked my arm around his neck. He started to resist, or at least that's how I interpreted his kicking and elbowing, so I pushed my other arm up and choked him out.

It generally takes about three very long seconds to get someone to lose consciousness in that hold. Every so often you run into someone with a neck like a bull, and no matter how hard you press or how you maneuver your arms, they won't go down.

De Sarcena was just the opposite. His eyes rolled back so quickly I wasn't sure I had him at first. But his limp arms and legs quickly convinced me. He was out.

Which was slightly inconvenient, to be honest. He was heavy, well over two-fifty.

I grabbed the money — no use leaving it behind — and

pushed open the door, not quite sure what I would find. Mongoose was standing nearby, MP5 in hand, holding on to two of de Sarcena's guards. Another two were on the floor nearby, ugly holes in their foreheads.

And where was Ms. Reynolds?

A few feet away, my MP5 in her hands.

"Time to go!" I yelled to them. At least I think it was a yell—I was still unable to hear, even myself.

I dragged de Sarcena to one of the windows at the back wall. Only a select few window panels would open, and I wasn't in the mood to try each one. I decided to break them, and did so with the first thing that came to hand—de Sarcena's head.

He didn't seem to mind. Maybe he groaned a little, but my ears were still out and I couldn't hear it.

The blood that trickled down his forehead was inconsequential.

The guests had thrown themselves to the floor as soon as the grenade went off. They stayed there now; I'm sure they would have climbed under the tiles if they thought it possible.

We ran out to the narrow balcony that ran across the back. It was only about three feet wide, a bit smaller than the original I believe, though I haven't been back to measure. Mongoose took a rope from the rucksack and quickly tied it off on the railing.

Under the best of circumstances, the next thing that would have happened would have been this: we would have rappelled from the Hall of Mirrors to the back of the mansion grounds. There an MH-60 would be waiting to pick us up. As we ran to the helicopter, a pair of Apache gunships would have swooped in and obliterated any of de Sarcena's men foolish enough to follow us.

I can dream, can't I?

"Go first!" I yelled at Mongoose. "Secure the rope."

He leapt to the window, grabbed hold of the line—he'd pulled on gloves—and began sliding downward, using his feet as a brake. I now had to make a decision: should I take de Sarcena, or should I leave him?

Kidnapping the leader of the most dangerous cartel in this half of Mexico had not been in the original game plan. I hadn't even considered it, frankly. But now that I had him, it seemed a shame to let him go. So I hauled him up onto my shoulder and got ready to go down.

"Ladies first!" I yelled to Melissa.

She yelled something back. My hearing was starting to return, but I couldn't quite get it. I assumed that she was being her usual difficult self and refusing to take directions.

"No, you go," I insisted.

She answered by spraying the MP5 a few inches from my head.

I started to curse, then stopped as she pointed across the room. Two more guards were lying dead near the staircase. Apparently they had decided to rush in and save their boss; Ms. Reynolds's work with the submachine gun had dissuaded them.

SEAL genes at work once more.

"Go!" I yelled at her. "Go, so we can get out of here."

This time she didn't hesitate. She kicked off her heels, then climbed onto the ledge.

"Use the gloves!"

She reached into the backpack, then looked up, a worried look on her face. I turned and saw what she was worried about—two more thugs had appeared from the far side of the hall, both carrying automatic rifles. I dropped to my knees, then using de Sarcena as a shield began firing my pistol in their direction. I don't think I hit either one, but I scared them enough that they hit the floor.

When I turned back, Melissa was gone. I pulled de Sarcena a little tighter against my shoulder, hooked my arm around the rope, and started down.

He was frigging heavy. I had trouble right away.

The reason you wear gloves when you go down a rope is that the rope hurts like hell. That's obvious when you're rappelling, but even going down hand over hand you can do some serious damage to your palms and fingers.

Of course, you could just suck it up and burn the crap out of your hands, which I'm sure you're expecting me to do. But I'm not that masochistic. I hooked my left arm around the rope, put my feet on the line as a brake, and used my jacket as a glove as I went down to the ground.

Unfortunately, this made for a pretty awkward arrangement with de Sarcena on my back. I got maybe fifteen or twenty feet before my fingers started to slip. I tried scrunching my shoulder up to shift his weight but it was too late—he fell off to the ground.

Fortunately for him, he landed on his feet rather than his head. Unfortunately for him, the ground was cement rather than dirt, and he ended up breaking one of his ankles.

I was appropriately sympathetic when I reached the ground a few seconds later.

"On your feet, asshole," I barked, pulling him up.

He whined something, adding a few choice words

about my parentage, all in English. I corrected his pronunciation with a quick chop to the nose.

I'll say this for him — he bled easily. He now had
blood on every piece of clothing as well as his face and
hands.

And mine. I made a mental note to send him a laun-
dry bill.

I hoisted him over my shoulder and began running
along the pool toward the back of the property. Floodlights lit the way, making it easy to see. But this was
bad — the lights also made it easy for de Sarcena's thugs
to see us, and a few began taking potshots as we ran.
Apparently the possibility that they might hit their boss
was not enough of a deterrent to keep them from
shooting. For all I know, it may have been an added
incentive.

The outer perimeter of the estate was oriented to
prevent an attack from the outside. In theory, this should
have made it easier for us to escape; we didn't have guns
pointing in our face. But the reality was more complicated. The high walls and fences were formidable bar-
riers no matter which side you climbed them from, and
once we were out of the building, de Sarcena's minions
began coming at us from every direction.

Doc, watching along with Junior, anticipated this
and put our emergency extraction plan into operation.
A series of rockets began landing on the northern end
of the property. These were actually little more than
bottle rockets, slightly modified so that their show arrived on their downward trajectory. This had the effect
of confusing the response by the security forces. Their
confusion was increased by a timely power failure, ini-
tiated by a remote-controlled explosion that took out

two of the main transformers feeding the mansion property.

Shotgun had placed the charges earlier. He had then moved into position to cover our retreat in the case of an emergency—which clearly we were in now. As we ran toward the back of the estate, there was a massive explosion in front of us: Shotgun had fired a Carl Gustav into the wall.

I'm sure you're all interested in the weapon—your basic 84mm recoilless rifle. Unfortunately, we're all a little pressed for time at this point in the narrative, so I'll give you the abbreviated version: the Carl Gustav is made by a division of Bofors. The name comes from an alternative name for the town where the state armament factory was once located. (The factory, or more correctly its descendants, are now part of the Swedish gun company.) You can think of the weapon as a rifled bazooka—a very large shell spins down the barrel like a bullet would, then emerges and flies toward its target. While intended as an antitank gun—and a damn good one at that—the Gustav or "Goose" is nondiscriminatory; it will pulverize concrete and stone just as readily as metal.

And so it did here, blowing a four-foot-wide hole in the wall at the back of the property.

Naturally, de Sarcena's goons reacted with outrage at this, and immediately rushed to plug the gap. Which was why instead of going through the hole, we headed to the western side of the property, where Shotgun had carefully placed a chain metal ladder over the top of the wall.

There was one remaining complication—the video surveillance system had a camera covering the area we wanted to escape through. The camera was located so close to the house that it didn't make sense to detour around it, and killing the video there would be as good as drawing a big arrow and saying *Here we are!* Shunt's looping trick wouldn't last enough for us all to get across and over the wall, and rather than risk someone noticing that the feed was acting funny, I told Junior to kill the entire system.

"Got it," he said. "Cameras are off."

My butt was dragging badly by now, and so was de Sarcena, who was pushing me so low his legs made skid marks in the ground. Mongoose came over and grabbed him, hoisting him onto his shoulder like a light ragdoll. He climbed the metal ladder quickly, and when he got to the top he heaved the Mexican over, sending him to the other side in a tumble.

"Ooops," he said, climbing over. "How clumsy."

"Where are we going?" asked Ms. Reynolds.

"Just go over," I told her. "You'll see."

"They'll catch us out here," she insisted. "There's no cover."

"With everything you've seen so far, you don't think I'm prepared?"

She probably made a face, or maybe she gave me the finger—it was too dark to see. In any event, she grabbed hold of the ladder and started upward.

As I said, it was too dark to see, or I would have thoroughly enjoyed the view.

I hustled after her. The others had jumped from the top, but I'd sustained enough bruises for the day—I twisted around and hung down, narrowing some of the distance to the ground. It was still a hell of a fall, and I probably would have rebounded into the wall if Shotgun hadn't materialized to grab me.

He had his usual big grin on his face and automatic weapon in hand. The Carl Gustav was on a strap across his back.

"They're sending a Jeep to run around the perimeter," said Junior over the radio. "Coming at you from the north."

"That's mine!" shouted Shotgun. "Hot shit."

He sprinted in the direction of the perimeter road. I told Tex to go cover him.

"Junior, where's our ride?" I asked.

"Less than two minutes away," he said. "You should hear him soon."

The next thing I heard was the roar of a missile shredding through steel — Shotgun had launched the Gustav at the Jeep, incinerating it. There was a short burst of automatic weapons fire, obviously from Shotgun and clearly meant only for show — no way anyone in the vehicle could have survived the initial blast.

A moment later, I heard the sound of a helicopter sweeping in from the northwest. Chester was back with our ride.

REMEMBER THAT OLD saying about how no battle plan survives contact with the enemy? It's actually a bit of an exaggeration, since most plans *do* survive, they're just ignored.

Still, planning is critical, since it tells you what to do if the situation goes well, and if it goes to hell.

Plus, if you didn't have a plan to begin with, you wouldn't know when you were completely screwed.

Our main plan in this case had been to go out the

front door, unless things got crazy. In that case, we would move swiftly to Plan B, which we were more or less following from the moment the flash bang exploded. Plan B called for us to effect our retreat with the help of my pal Chet Arthur, who was now skimming over the ground toward us in a Robinson R44 helicopter.

The R44 is a bigger helicopter than the R22 or Beta II he'd flown me around in the day before. But it's not that much bigger: it has four places rather than two, and that includes the pilot's seat. Aware that it was the biggest helicopter he could access, I'd studied the weight requirements and obstacles where he had to land, determining that we could just squeeze aboard.

The problem with that plan was that we now had two more bodies to stuff into the helicopter—Melissa's and de Sarcena's. And while I'm sure I could have gotten either Shotgun or Mongoose to let Melissa Reynolds sit on his lap, there was no way the helicopter could lift even her extra weight.

Chet informed me of this with his pilot's calm drawl.

"There are too freaking many of you, goddamnit!" he yelled, exuding the patient professionalism that has long endeared him to me. "I told you this afternoon, this is a small helicopter and the engine's already downrated. I can't take off with anything more than nine hundred freaking pounds."

There may have been a few more terms of endearment and colorful adjectives in his pronouncement, but you get the message.

"It's OK," I started to tell him, but Chet cut me off.

"We gotta go. There are a hundred guys on their way here. I saw them on the infrared coming in."

"Chet, you're exaggerating. I doubt there's more than fifty or sixty."

"I can't clear the freaking second fence with all of you," he shouted. "Someone's gonna have to stay behind."

"I'll put a slug in the dipshit's brain and leave him," yelled Mongoose, taking out his gun and pointing it at de Sarcena.

It was a possible solution, but having come so far with de Sarcena I was loath to leave him. And even if I did dump him, the weight calculations had been pretty close; as light as Melissa was, she still might tip the balance.

"Put him in the helo," I told Mongoose. I started backing away before he or the others could object. "Make sure he stays out of it. But keep him alive. We may be able to use him. Melissa, get in the front with Chet. Shotgun, you're with me! Keep that gun loaded."

PART TWO

Perfect order is the forerunner of perfect horror.

— CARLOS FUENTES,
NOVELIST

[1]

A FLARE SHOT up from the north side of the compound and ignited as we ran. The burning magnesium and sodium nitrate illuminated everything before us.

I was about two feet from the torso of a body that had been thrown out of the Jeep Shotgun had blown up earlier. It was a gruesome sight, even in the dark, yet somehow I couldn't muster any sympathy.

"Come on, keep moving," I told Shotgun. "Keep that big head of yours down."

An M16 lay on the ground behind the Jeep. I grabbed it. The gun was loaded, with a second mag taped to the engaged magazine.

We were on the west side of the mansion, on a gravel road that ran between the wall surrounding the inner yard and the perimeter fences. The latter were closely spaced, and topped with razor wire. I suspected that there were mines beyond them, if not in the four or five feet sandwiched in the middle.

We were easy pickings where we were. Either we had to go through the outer fence, or back into the heart of de Sarcena's stronghold.

I always go for the heart.

"We need to get back over the wall," I told Shotgun.

"We're going back?"

"Temporarily. I'll give you a boost."

"You're going to boost me?"

"I won't be able to pull you up," I told him, taking a knee near the wall. "So you go first."

Shotgun paused, went down in a three-point stance, then ran at me like a high jumper eyeing a new Olympic record. He put his Size XXX boot in my back and launched himself upward, snagging the wall with his fingers and pulling himself to the top of the stones.

Let the record show that Shotgun is one heavy SOB. Every vertebrae in my back cracked; I won't need to go to the chiropractor for quite a while.

Rising, I backed to the fence and then sprinted toward the wall. I managed to get just high enough to grab Shotgun's outstretched hands. He jerked me topside, scraping the crap out of my face in the process: exfoliation on the cheap.

We hopped down on the other side of the wall and began running. The flare was still burning, throwing long, flickering fingers of white light on the ground. Some sort of truck pulled up near the front of the mansion to my right. Figures with guns ran in front of its headlights, throwing ominous shadows in our direction.

With everything that had happened, the guests would be in a panic and trying to escape. If the security people let them—unlikely, admittedly—our best chance would be to join the flood and run out across the road with them. Otherwise, we would have to scurry around the grounds long enough for Chet to drop off a few passengers and return.

As we ran toward the building, I saw a figure coming down the set of stone stairs to our immediate right. The figure was slim, with legs that flowed.

I grabbed Shotgun before he could fire at her.

"Wait here for me," I told him, pushing him to the ground.

I trotted toward the figure, who stepped into a sliver of light—it was more gray than white, but there was enough illumination that I could see she had a set of night-vision binoculars held to her face. She walked toward me with a quick pace, raising her arm.

I froze. I thought she must be waving to one of de Sarcena's goons, telling them where I was. By the time I realized she was signaling me, she was only a few yards away.

It was the woman I'd seen in the Salon of Peace after stealing the money.

"What are you doing?" I asked.

"Come. There's no time—hurry."

"Why?" I asked.

"I'll explain when there's time. Quickly—before the dogs."

Did she say dogs? On cue, I heard the baying and barking of a dozen rottweilers charging from the back of the property.

I whistled to Shotgun. He trotted from his hiding spot, joining us as we headed for the stairs.

"Where exactly are we going?" he asked.

Our guide shushed him.

"Be quiet now. I'll explain. There is a passage. I'll help you. Then you will help me."

MAYBE MY COMPANY'S new motto ought to be: send us your damsels in distress.

I will say one thing—the quality of distressed damsels is definitely on the upswing.

148 Richard Marcinko and Jim DeFelice

As she pulled open the door, I had to make an instant decision—trust her, or not?

I took the Ronald Reagan option: trust, but verify. As she started to take a step inside, I gently pushed her out of the way, moving to my right, gun ready. Shotgun came right behind me—together we could have wasted half of de Sarcena's crew.

It wasn't necessary. The hall, lit by dim emergency lights, was empty.

"Just making sure," I told our guide.

"It's all right." She clutched a small bit of her evening gown and held it up to make it easier to walk. Her high heels clicked as she strode ahead. "Come on. The passage is this way."

We followed down a narrow hall. This was another of the servant passages, and while it wasn't exactly narrow or dank, it was nowhere near as fancy as the ones in the main part of the building. The stucco walls were painted a neutral white, and the floor was serviceable ceramic. No doubt they washed up quickly—a plus for the cleaning crew if we needed to shoot someone.

Our guide paused when she came to a steel panel door. She motioned with her hand for us to stay back, then opened it. Raising the night binos to her eyes again—they looked like Yukon Night Rangers, but don't hold me to it—she peered down the passage, scanning it before stepping back and waving us forward.

We entered another hallway, this one unlit and so dark that we had to stay close behind our guide. I put my hand on her shoulder and let her lead me to a staircase at the far end of the passage.

"Watch your step," she told me as we started to descend.

This was easier said than done in the dark. Once or twice I stumbled as we walked down what seemed to be one of the longest staircases in the western hemisphere. The stairs were narrow and rickety, made of wood or some reasonable facsimile. Shotgun was a few treads behind me. If he lost his balance, we'd all tumble like bowling pins.

Suddenly the passage filled with light. The string of overhead bulbs had just come on; power had been restored to the mansion.

"Must have an emergency generator," mumbled Shotgun as we continued downward.

"Or maybe somebody didn't use enough explosive," I told him.

"Impossible."

We reached the bottom after another fifty or sixty steps. The cellar around us smelled of cement dust and mold.

"This way, quickly," said our guide, pointing across the open floor.

She took us through a door on the near wall. This led to a passage with a dirt floor. We were in some sort of tunnel that ran beneath the grounds; the sides were made of stone and unglazed bricks. Timbers lined the ceiling. Another string of small lightbulbs ran along the right side of the passage. There was a gentle but definite slope upward.

We went about two hundred yards, maybe a little more, before reaching a set of concrete steps upward. At the top was a wooden trapdoor.

"They may be waiting for you there," said our guide, stopping.

"Fine time to tell me that."

"I'll look if you want."

I grabbed her arm and gently tugged her back down the steps.

"It's all right," I told her. "I'm going first. Shotgun, kill a few of the lights—I don't want to leak any light when I crack the panel. And don't shoot it," I added, not sure that he wouldn't take it as a challenge.

"Gotcha, boss."

"What's your name?" I asked the woman. "And why are you helping us?"

"I'll give you the details later. There's no sense telling you now."

"You expect us to be caught?"

"I'm not sure what to expect."

"Your English is pretty good," I told her.

"It should be. I was born in Michigan."

Actually, those two facts didn't necessarily correlate, but I let it pass.

"What's your name?" I asked.

"Veronica."

"I'm Dick."

"I know who you are. I recognized you yesterday." She didn't sound like much of a fan, exactly.

As soon as Shotgun dimmed the lights, I pushed the trapdoor open. The area around us was pitch-black.

I took Veronica's night glasses and looked around. We had come up in a small building with machinery. It appeared empty, so I squeezed out onto the floor, crawling snake-style away from the trapdoor.

Further inspection revealed that the building was a

pump house, with large machinery for increasing the pressure of well water before sending it up to the house. The squat, rectangular building featured a roof only a little taller than shoulder high.

"We're just outside the razor wire," Veronica whispered behind me. "But the garage for the vehicles is about twenty yards away. I'm not sure which way it is," she added. "I'm a little turned around."

I poked my head out the door. I spotted part of the garage to the left of us. I also saw the shadows of at least half a dozen men, most with rifles, walking in the headlights and floods in front of the building.

"Dick, can you talk?" whispered Junior over the radio.

"Yes. Can you see where we are?"

"I have your location but I don't have video," he told me. "Their system doesn't go out that far. Chet just dropped Mongoose and the others off. He's heading back. Where should I have him meet you?"

"Beyond the razor fence."

"Between the wall and the fence?"

"No, the far side of the wire. There are too many goons running around back here. If they see the helicopter, they're likely to shoot it down."

"That minefield is close to a hundred yards deep. How the hell are you going to get through it?"

"Walking wasn't what I had in mind."

MOST OF US don't give a lot of thought to mines as a military weapon. When we do, we tend to think of them as defensive weapons, and underhanded ones at that—it's really no fair getting blown up by something below snake level, is it?

But mines have played an important role in many battles. If you're into some heavy thinking, study the Battle of El Alamein (the August 1942 contest, though mines played a role in the first battle as well) and consider how that might have gone without strategically placed mines.

And really, if you're fighting fair in a war, you're fighting stupid. What was it Patton said? The object of war isn't to die for your country. It's to make the other dumb bastard die for his country.

I wasn't intending to die myself. I have a healthy respect for mines, and I hoped de Sarcena's men would as well. And if they didn't—well, the mines might settle that score on their own.

Minefields are generally only a problem if you don't know where the mines are. I figured that if we knew where the mines were here, we could tiptoe between them and grab our helicopter ride.

When they're laid out by hand, minefields come in a discernible pattern. The reason is simple: the person who put them down wants to be able to recover them in a reasonable amount of time without risking his neck. He also wants to be able to guide someone across the mines without them risking their neck. Or feet, as the case may be.

During our earlier adventure, I recognized that the jailers had used a simple grid pattern where the mines were laid out in rows seemingly different distances apart, but all in parallel. (I say seemingly, because they would have actually been measured from a specific landmark, and then sited along the row according to a predetermined set of angles. But without doing a bunch of mental trigonometry, the mines would seem random to anyone walking through the field. And frankly, while

I love tangents, I was never very good with sines and cosines.) So all I had to do here was find four mines, establishing the rows, and proceed.

My first hope was that the glasses were powerful enough to pick up the mines at close range. They weren't, not completely. They worked for the first mine, which I spotted a few feet from me on the right. I marked it with a handkerchief. The next was considerably harder; I literally nosed along on the ground, hunting with the glasses and my knife before spotting the slight mound at last.

That should have tipped me off that it was going to be harder than I thought, but I'm nothing if not stubborn. After a couple of false positives, I finally detected the mine that formed the parallel line with the first one. It took a little less time, though at least as much sweat to find the fourth.

I stood up and mentally marked out the rest of the lane. It ran northeast from the house at about twenty-five degrees.

I went back to Veronica and told her how much I appreciated her help and wished her luck in the future. I did this with a heartfelt kiss on the lips.

"I'm going to hold on to the glasses if you don't mind," I told her. "Thanks for everything. If I can ever do anything for you, let me know."

"That's OK," she said.

We were about three steps into the minefield when I looked back and saw that she was behind Shotgun.

"Where are you going?" I asked her.

"I'm leaving with you. They'll kill me if they find out that I helped you. And you just said you would help me. I plan to collect."

The security goons at the front of the building were so busy doing whatever they were doing that they didn't take any notice of us as we slowly made our way through the minefield. Things were proceeding swimmingly until, maybe twenty yards deep, I spotted what I thought was a mine just in front of my foot.

I stopped, bent down, and examined it.

Definitely a mine. I'd misread the pattern.

Worse, as I stared through the glasses, trying to get my bearings, I realized I had missed at least two other mines. It was a Rogue-sized miracle that we hadn't blown ourselves up.

Goatfuck city.

THE WORST THING you can do in a minefield is lose your head. Objectively speaking, we were no worse off now than we had been a minute or so before. But ignorance is bliss, and while I wasn't feeling particularly intelligent at the moment, I wasn't feeling blissful either.

There was really only one solution—Chet had to pick us up where we were.

"Will do," he said over the radio after I switched over to his frequency. "Where are you?"

"Minefield on the east side. About twenty or thirty yards north of the guardhouse and garage."

"Repeat that? You're *in* the minefield?"

"That's right. We're in the minefield."

"On purpose?"

"Don't get existential on me. We are where we are."

"Well, try not to breathe too hard. I'm about five miles away."

Even if Chet was quick about it, he'd be an easy target when he came in to pick us up. We'd have to divert the bad guys' attention somehow.

"When the helo comes," I told Shotgun, "throw Veronica in, grab the rungs, and get the hell out."

"Where are you going?"

"I'm going to double back, go behind these guys, and get their attention before Chet comes in."

"What happens then?"

"I'll shoot them all, and you'll pick me up."

"Let me go with you."

"No. Stick with her."

The helicopter's Lycoming engine and its attached rotors were pounding the air by the time I made it back to the low building where we'd come out. I went spread-eagle on the roof and raised my gun. As the helo bore in, de Sarcena's men started coming around the corner of the garage building. It was a turkey shoot: I squeezed the trigger and started gobbling them up.

Within seconds, I was the target. I emptied the M16, slapped out the empty mag, and jammed in a fresh one. They had me outnumbered, but de Sarcena's goons were too used to attacking people who couldn't fight back, and the sheer weight of my fire forced them back around the garage — the few that weren't shot up, that is.

I started to hop down, thinking I would follow, picking up ammo on the way, when I found myself in the middle of a windstorm: Chet and his helo were bearing down on me.

A few of the goons refound their courage as the helicopter swooped in. Emptying the M16, I chased them back, then threw down the gun and grabbed the helicopter's skid as it came within reach. As I did, something exploded above me—Shotgun had "found" a Carl Gustav in the helo cabin and fired it at the garage.

The missile hit something flammable, and the next thing I knew I was treated to a preview of the afterlife: fire and brimstone surrounded me. The R44 thundered through the turmoil.

We cleared through the flames and a large cloud of smoke. The razor-wire perimeter fence was dead ahead.

"Up! Up!" I yelled.

I tucked up my legs and closed my eyes. I may have cleared the fence by inches, maybe by miles; when you're not looking, it's all the same.

A minute or two later, we settled down over a field a mile away. My arms and hands had locked around the skid strut, and I actually needed help from Shotgun, leaning out of the interior, to get them undone. I fell to the ground—fortunately just a foot or so away—then climbed into the helicopter.

[II]

FUN LIKE THAT is hard to top, and I decided that we would call at least a temporary halt to our Mexican sojourn. Chester ferried us north, first getting us far enough away from the goons that we didn't have to worry about being ambushed, then finally taking us to a ranch owned by a friend of Doc's in New Mexico. The most strenuous thing we did for the next few hours involved elbow exercise and adult beverages.

Our guest of honor, Pedro de Sarcena, snored in the back room. Doc had seen to his comfort with an espe-

cially generous dose of Percocet, a mixture of acetaminophen and oxycodone often administered to patients
after surgery. Acetaminophen you know; it's Tylenol
by another name. Oxycodone is an extremely effective
substitute for morphine; it has gained unwanted fame
as a favorite of drug abusers in its time release form of
OxyContin.

Deciding what to do with de Sarcena was an important problem, and it occupied a good portion of the
business meeting that Doc and I conducted once he
arrived. But there were other problems as well, starting
with the beautiful Ms. Reynolds, who believed that her
arrival at the mansion had led directly to our escape.
Her head had swelled to the point where it was larger
than the other portions of her anatomy—an incredible
accomplishment.

And then there was Veronica, who had still not told
me who she was, or what she wanted.

She did both, with the help of a few longneck bottles
of Corona.

VERONICA DI FILIPO was the daughter of a state police officer from Arrowsmith, Illinois, a very small
town in the rural center of the state. (One of the highlights is the annual Labor Day parade; most years the
Illinois State University Marching Band comes over
and plays its heart out.) Unfortunately, Veronica's father had been killed in the line of duty when she was
very young; her mother died of cancer not long afterward, and she was raised by her maternal grandparents, Joseph and Marianna Cortina, who lived in a
similarly small town in Michigan.

Probably strongly influenced by the memory of her

father, Veronica had gone to college and studied pre-law, then joined the Michigan State Police upon graduation. She became a detective, working undercover. Among other things, she helped bust a pair of drug rings before being promoted to a job investigating porn. The job included a promotion, but after the excitement of her undercover stint, it was understandably a lot less exciting.

In the meantime, Veronica's grandparents decided to retire. They started looking around, and eventually decided to move to Mexico.

Retiring to Mexico was not as crazy as it sounds. With housing and other prices skyrocketing in the States, a good number of Americans have moved across the borders over the past decade or two. Even after the housing bust, they took advantage of the low cost of living and the weather, which in general is a lot balmier than Michigan's.

Roughly two years before I met her, Veronica's grandparents found Angel Hills, which was just south of the New Mexico border. They'd visited a number of other luxury retirement communities, almost all of them on the coast. They liked Angel Hills because of its location, relatively close to the border and out of the path of most hurricanes. Like most other retirement communities, it advertised all the usual amenities: a swimming pool, clubhouse, and bingo three nights a week.

"The brochure was one thing, the actual buildings another," Veronica told me between sips from her beer. "I guess they weren't *that* bad. They were decently constructed. But plain. Bottom line, they're a bunch of buildings in the middle of the desert, surrounded by people whose language they don't understand. Why move away from home in the first place? That's where all their friends were. That's where I was."

Progress on the construction of the development was frustratingly slow. Eventually their unit was finished and they moved in. There was still a lot of work to do: the grass wasn't growing, the pool wasn't finished. The housing market's downturn in the States hampered sales, which slowed construction on the overall complex.

Still, Veronica had to admit that it didn't look any worse than many developments she'd seen in the States. Her grandparents were thrilled about it. Their Spanish had improved to the point where, while they were still clearly Anglos, they could keep up with most of the locals and with Veronica, who had minored in the language in college and honed her skills as an undercover agent.

Things seemed to be fine for the first year or so. Veronica was too busy to visit again, but they spoke regularly over the phone and Skype, and used e-mail to exchange photos and the like.

Gradually, the communications lessened. The calls stopped. The e-mails became terse. Worried that her grandparents were having health problems they wouldn't admit, Veronica took a vacation and went to Mexico. She found her grandparents quiet and depressed. Work on the condo development had now completely stopped. At least half of the units that had been built were empty. That included several that had been occupied when she had last visited.

There were other disturbing signs. The sales office

had been closed. There seemed to be only one grounds-keeper left; he was noncommunicative and smelled of booze. The people in the small Mexican town nearby were particularly standoffish and wary.

Since they were clearly unhappy, Veronica asked her grandparents to come back north with her. Spend a few weeks visiting, she suggested. See a few old friends.

They made excuses. When she pushed, they refused. She suspected something was wrong, but couldn't decipher what it was in the two days she was with them. She left baffled and worried that one of them had some sort of medical problem they weren't sharing.

She got an e-mail from them a few days after she returned, telling her how much they enjoyed her visit. That was their last communication.

E-mails weren't returned. Their phone—they only had a land line—went unanswered. Within a few weeks, Veronica discovered that their Skype account had been closed. Eventually she got a message on a return e-mail that their in-box was full and not accepting any more e-mails.

Worried to the point of almost becoming frantic, Veronica flew down to New Mexico, rented a car, and traveled over the border. There was no one home at her grandparents' house. When she went to let herself in with her key, she found it didn't work. That wasn't much of a barrier for a practiced detective—she got the lock open easily enough by slipping a credit card through the jamb slot and work the bolt back.

Her grandparents' unit was completely empty—"broom clean" as a real estate agent would say.

There was no trace of the pair. The sales office was still closed. Veronica couldn't find a maintenance person, nor was there anyone at the pool or other community buildings. There was supposed to be a volunteer neighborhood patrol and a development police force; Veronica saw a pair of vehicles but couldn't find anyone manning them. The security offices were in the community center, which was itself closed.

The units near her grandparents' were unoccupied, and the neighbors Veronica approached claimed to have just moved in and didn't know them. One thing struck Veronica as odd—while the development had been marketed to Americans, the only two residents she met were Mexican. Neither seemed to have much time for her.

She went to the police in the nearest city, about a half hour away.

She suspected this would be useless. She was right. Frustrated, she identified herself as a fellow police officer, which had exactly the opposite effect than what she intended: rather than getting increased attention and a modicum of sympathy, the officer she'd been talking to turned almost mute. His boss was worse.

The American embassy was no help. Various and slight connections she knew through her job were equally useless. Her grandparents had disappeared with no trace, and no one seemed concerned enough or capable enough of figuring out what had happened. Veronica finally decided to take a leave of absence from her job and investigate on her own.

She discovered that the company that had developed the condos had gone bankrupt almost on the very day that her grandparents moved into their house. Bankruptcy is a complicated business in Mexico. There's the legal tangle, which is as convoluted as any tangled rope you've ever seen. (Nautically speaking, we call them ASSHOLES in the running line.) And then there's the overlay of corruption, a shadow system that almost always dictates what really happens.

I'll cut through some of the knots, skipping about two beers' worth of the story in the process, and simply say that the Tabasco cartel ended up owning Angel Hills. They also ended up owning the bank that had financed much of the project, and the construction company that did most of the building.

Still unable to get any real information about her grandparents, Veronica decided to do what she did best—she went undercover. Posing as an accountant who could speak good English but was a Mexican national, she got a job in the crooked bank, which had a large office in the city a half hour from Angel Hills. She began as a liaison to American customers, and was soon promoted to work directly with American banks.

Much of the business came from borderline legal companies under the cartel's control. It was only then that she began to realize just how extensive the cartel's holdings were. It had tremendous cash flow on both sides of the border.

The cartels rely on American banks to help them "wash" their profits and conduct their business. As the cartels have grown, they've sunk their fingers deeper into the pies of what were once legitimate businesses, shades of the Mafia decades ago. And so in some cases the banks have no reason to suspect that the cash going into their safes comes from illegal sources. But there's also a good deal of what you might call willful ignorance. Gee, big Mexican customer, where did you get all that money? Wait, wait, don't tell me—I don't have a right to know.

And more importantly, I don't *want* to know.

Once you see the numbers, you begin to understand why. A few years back, investigators found that Wachovia Bank[18] had taken $378 billion from Mexican "casas de cambio"—currency exchanges, very often little more than fronts used by cartels to launder money—and put it into U.S. accounts.

The fees and interest generated to the bank on $378 billion will buy you more than a Big Mac at the local Mickey D's, I guarantee.

Weeks turned into months as Veronica sorted through the tentacles of the crime organization. She was learning a lot about the cartel's finances and its connections with supposedly legitimate businesses and politicians, but none of it was getting her any closer to finding her grandparents. She was considering leaving the bank with evidence she had gathered when one of the cartel underbosses named Heriberto took an interest in her.

"Heriberto was actually very nice, in a slimy, criminal way," Veronica told me after taking a long, suggestive pull on her beer. She'd changed into a plain sweatshirt the ranch owner leant her; I've never seen a sweatshirt worn so well. "These guys are so used to getting their way that most of them are basically slap and grab apes. He wasn't. Not that I was actually attracted to him."

---

[18] Wachovia is now part of Wells Fargo, and I hope the new regime has cleaned up the act. To keep the lawyers happy, I should also note that while the bank paid a $160 million fine, there were never any criminal prosecutions.

Dates with Heriberto primarily meant going to parties as eye candy. Heriberto's main job for the cartel was importing stolen cars from the U.S. and selling them in Mexico, and vice versa. While the car business was definitely a moneymaker, it was more a sideline for the cartel, and Heriberto didn't have access to the top people Veronica suspected were involved in whatever had happened at Angel Hills. But one afternoon he took her to a party at de Sarcena's pseudo-Versailles mansion. De Sarcena was debuting some rap music videos he had commissioned, a common pastime among cartel honchos. The songs portrayed him as a tragic Caesar figure, betrayed by a number of underlings; those underlings, no surprise, were next seen on a flatbed truck at the front of the estate, heads on one side, bodies on the other.

It was a pretty powerful message, even without the music. The entire crowd was forced to pass by the truck; de Sarcena wanted to make sure everyone understood the lesson. Heriberto's stomach turned. Veronica was unsure if it was because of the general gore or because he had been considering throwing in with some of the men. In any event, he immediately made a beeline for the grass beyond the gravel, where he joined most of the other partygoers emptying their stomachs.

Veronica, who had seen sights even worse during her undercover days, stood on the gravel alone. At some point, de Sarcena came up to her.

"These bodies do not bother you?" he asked.

She shrugged. "They are traitors. One doesn't waste emotion on traitors. They deserve worse."

A beautiful woman good with numbers and English who could withstand such sights — this was a very rare

commodity. A few days later, two of de Sarcena's thugs
showed up at the bank and told her that she was to come
with them for a job interview. She was naturally suspicious. Sure that her background had been uncovered,
she let them lead her outside to a waiting Cadillac
Escalade. Veronica fingered her purse as she approached
the truck, waiting for the right moment to pull out the
pistol she had hidden inside.

Just as her fingers unsnapped the clasp, the rear
window of the SUV rolled down. De Sarcena leaned
through it.

"I am in need of someone in my accounting department," he said. "Perhaps you will have lunch with me."

Veronica reasoned that if the cartel leader had decided to have her killed, he wouldn't have made the trip
himself. The gun stayed in her purse. She went along to
lunch, and had what she described as a rather routine
job interview. She had memorized all the phony facts
she'd fed the bank, which was a good thing — de Sarcena had already raided the personnel department and
had a copy of her résumé for reference.

The next day, she started at the mansion.

She had been there for roughly three months when
I nearly bumped into her in the Salon of Peace. She
claims to have guessed what I was up to, but decided
not to say anything. No one in the cartel had the guts to
steal from the boss, and she was both fascinated and
perplexed by my boldness. She also knew that the cash
would not be missed — bundles of money were stashed
all around the mansion, relics of de Sarcena's rise and
accompanying paranoia.

"He always wants cash nearby, in case he has to flee,"
said Veronica. "He has accounts in a dozen countries,

South America, Europe, Russia, Hong Kong, and of course the U.S. The financial side of the operation is as sophisticated as a London bank. But in his head, he's still the kid who had to scrape to make ends meet when he was going to school."

"I heard the security people talking about some of the workers after the septic tank exploded," Veronica continued. "They talked to de Sarcena. I thought they mentioned you, but I wasn't sure who you were until the party. Then it all came together for me. I realized who you were and decided to help you."

"Thanks."

"My grandmother reads your books," she added. "You have more women readers than you think."

I bowed my head.

"You *are* a bit full of yourself," she added. "And sometimes you overwrite."

Everybody's a critic.

I got up and went over to the refrigerator to salve my ego with another beer. Veronica had done a great deal of work at huge personal risk. Her information would no doubt help put de Sarcena away for years—assuming she could find a prosecutor who was willing to take on the cartel. But unfortunately for her, the information she had would be fairly useless when it came to finding her grandparents.

Frankly, it wasn't hard to guess what had happened to her grandparents. They had crossed the cartel somehow, and were dead. If they had been kidnapped for ransom—the only other logical possibility—Veronica would have gotten some sort of communication by now.

There was no way of helping her. I felt bad, but that was the way it was.

Besides, I was up to my eyeballs in damsels in distress.

"You're not going to help, are you?" Veronica asked as I studied the different brands inside the fridge. I'd had my fill of Mexican beer. In fact, I didn't feel like drinking anything foreign, including the Budweiser at the front of the shelf. I stared into the back of the fridge, trying to will a few bottles of Rogue Ale into existence.

When none appeared, I settled for a Coors Lite.

"Look. This is them," said Veronica, unfolding a piece of paper for me to look at.

A kindly looking, white-haired grandma and a portly though distinguished grandpa grimaced for the camera on the main drag of the Mexican town next to Angel Hills. But it was the figure in the background, passing on the street maybe twenty yards behind them, that caught my attention.

He had a long shirt on, an extremely long shirt. The kind you see a lot on the streets of Lahore, Karachi, and practically every other city in Pakistan. It's also extremely common in Afghanistan. In fact, you can see the long-sleeved, loose-fitting *kameez* in many Muslim countries.

"Man dress" is the politically incorrect term. Not that we would *ever* be politically incorrect in the Rogue universe.

[III]

WHEN LAST WE saw them, Trace, Tex, and Stoneman were escorting the Garcias to their home in south-central Mexico.[19] The trip was long and hot, and took the better part of the day. The countryside was beautiful, but poverty was just as plentiful and nearly as obvious. Many of the houses they passed on the less-traveled roads were hovels; there were more than a few lean-tos. There were farms, but most were pretty primitive; the few tractors they saw dated from the early 1980s.

After several hours, they began climbing up the gentle slope of a mountain. Everything around them became deep green. Bushes edged against the road; trees hung down. Suddenly the branches parted and they were in the Garcias' hometown, a village cut into the sides of a mountain.

While the buildings were mostly old, they seemed uniformly in good repair. Many had been painted within the last year or two in a warm rose color or a light wash of yellow. The small main street was a hodgepodge of buildings — garage spaces jostled vegetable stands in a large one-story structure, a motel that could have been right out of the 1950s stood next to a courthouse that could have dated from just after the Spanish Conquest.

The Garcias' house was a small stucco building tucked into the hillside at the southeastern corner of

---

[19] In the interests of keeping them below the radar, we'll neglect to mention the name here. I hope you understand. And if not — tough turds.

town. There were chickens in the front yard . . . and a twenty-something man with no shirt in the back room.

The man turned out to be a squatter, easily dealt with — Tex took his arm, Stoneman his legs, and together they dumped him unceremoniously with the chickens.

They camped out against the front door that night, just in case he or his friends had any thoughts of coming back. Trace took the couch, sleeping as comfortably as she had in weeks.

The Garcias paid a visit to the local police station just as the sun was rising the next morning to make sure everything was in order. Trace tried to talk them out of bribing the police chief with what they euphemistically called a "thank you fee," but Mr. Garcia assured her that was the way it had to be done.

"He is a poor man besides," said Mrs. Garcia. "The government salary is very little."

The chief's office made exactly the opposite impression: it was at least the size of the Garcias' entire house, furnished in finely polished wooden furniture, with thick leather chairs and various mementos and photos scattered around the room. Trace bit her tongue, remaining silent as the chief and the Garcias engaged in small talk about the village and things that had happened in their absence. The squatter was not mentioned, and the trouble with the cartel waited until the very end of the meeting.

"We have paid our debt to the boss," said Mr. Garcia, sliding an envelope across the desk. "We expect no more trouble."

"I'm sure there will be none," said the chief pleasantly. He tucked the money into the top of his desk.

The Garcias got up to leave. Trace got up as well, and walked over to the chief. She bent over his desk. He gave her a quizzical look—until she grabbed his shirt and pulled his face into hers.

"These are my relatives," she said in Spanish. "Anything happens to them for any reason—you will personally bear the consequences."

Tex, who'd carried his rifle into the office, glared at the chief. Trace is part Indian and her accent is very Mexican, but Tex couldn't pass for Hispanic in a roomful of white Russians. The combination unnerved the chief of police, who must have thought they were representatives of a rival cartel. He reached into his desk to give the money back.

"Keep it," said Trace, letting him go. "Make sure you earn it."

[IV]

RIGHT ABOUT THAT time I was assigning Doc to escort Ms. Reynolds back to Austin, Texas, where she would wait for her father and they would collect our reward from her paramour. There was a surprising bit of teeth gnashing, not from Melissa—having heard Veronica's story, I think at this point she had decided that she was lucky to have escaped the cartel without real damage—but from Junior.

Junior had apparently fallen in love with the comely Ms. Reynolds, and wanted very much to be part of the escort.

"Totally unnecessary," I replied when he asked.

"Dad, please."

I gave him a cross-eyed look. Clearly, he was thinking with an organ other than his brain.

"I think Doc can handle it just fine," I told him.

He sulked away, head down and spirits lower. I felt bad, really—I don't like to get between a man and his hormones. But I needed him to help watch over de Sarcena.

By all appearances, our honored guest was still feeling no pain, sleeping peacefully in the back room thanks to the continued administration of Doc's Percocet. He had to be turned over to the authorities, but which ones? I knew the Mexican government would never prosecute him. Could New Mexico or some other state, armed with Veronica's information, build a case? It was possible, but their track records were not the best.

As for the feds, their record was even worse. Not being a big believer in catch and release, I decided we'd hold on to him for a while. If we could find the right prosecutor or agency, then we'd hand him over. If not . . . Rogue justice might be the better way to go.

"Nothing happens to him, you understand," I told Mongoose, who along with Junior was tasked to look after him. "You understand? No blindfolded walks down steps, no midnight swims."

He gave me a sour-milk look. "You really take the fun out of life, you know that?"

IF YOU LOOK at the southern border of the U.S., you'll notice that the straight line that extends from El Paso makes a ninety-degree cut south once it reaches western New Mexico. The rectangle that results is because of the Gadsden Purchase; completed in 1854, it was the last big real estate buy Uncle Sam made before realizing it's better to rent than own.

Some thirty-two miles east of that sharp line south is a small New Mexico town called Columbus. Columbus is a fine little city, that's been very hospitable to me the few times I've had occasion to visit. It's packed with history, not all of it the remembering kind. It played a major role in the undeclared border war with Mexico in 1916–17, first by being victimized by Pancho Villa, and then by hosting the so-called Punitive Expedition led by Black Jack Pershing afterward.

I'm a history buff myself, but its interest to me at this point in my Mexican sojourn was its location, directly north of a small border crossing that was about ten miles east of Angel Hills. This is fairly rugged terrain and, with the exception of Puerto Palomas on the border, relatively empty of people.

Not a great place for a retirement community, I thought as I drove out there with Shotgun and Veronica early in the afternoon after sequestering de Sarcena. But it would be perfect for a drug-running operation.

Not to mention a terror camp, to get hysterical now that I've been historical.

We stopped briefly in Columbus to pick up supplies— Shotgun just about bought out the grocery—then ambled over in a pair of rented Chevies, Veronica and I in the lead. I let Veronica drive; it was easier to observe the scenery from the passenger side.

I looked out the window, too. Occasionally.

The surrounding area was breathtakingly beautiful, though on the dry side. Once over the border and approaching Angel Hills, green became more plentiful, first in little pockets, then as the crown ringing the hills. It's easy to forget, living in places where you can regularly curse the rain, how critical water is for development. Underground springs percolated in the rolling rifts where the condos were nestled; without them, the land would have been haunted by tumbleweed rather than bulldozers.

Not knowing what to expect, I had Shotgun pull off the road a few miles from the development, parking in the shade of a battered old billboard. The tattered remains of three different cigarette ads clung to the splintered wood. Shotgun sat in his car, munching Cheese Doodles. He was determined to answer what for him was a burning question: how many doodles are there in an average bag?

The road to Angel Hills ran through the small Mexican village of Villa Angela. More a hamlet than a village, Villa Angela was a collection of maybe three dozen buildings nestled around a short main street that zigged through a narrow pass in the hills. When I say that the main street was short, I mean it was no more than thirty yards long. The buildings were mostly whitewashed adobe, with two exceptions, both in the exact middle of town: the hardware store was painted pink, and the bank was constructed of red brick and what looked like limestone to my untrained eye. At two stories high, the bank was also the tallest and most substantial building in town.

"Owned by the cartel, lock, stock, and barrel," said Veronica as we drove toward it. "Opens only on Friday."

"Why Friday?" I asked.

"Payday. They bring two employees in, and an armored car with cash."

"Big payroll?"

"As far as I could tell, just the security and maintenance workers over in Angel Hills. The townies are too poor for the most part to bank. Or too smart."

"They don't work for the cartel?"

"Not directly," said Veronica. "But it doesn't matter. The cartel owns them, whether they know it or not."

Main Street ran roughly west to east. The road was paved and in fairly good shape—not potholes or ruts, no trash or even piles of sand littering the sides. A hill jutted up sharply behind the buildings on the south, but to the north there was a small grid of houses. These were small and mostly made of stone or stucco, though I did see one with what looked like vinyl siding—rare in this part of Mexico.

We drove in slowly, eyes scanning the street. A pair of older men were sitting on a bench outside the barbershop, which announced with blue and red diagonal stripes on the whitewashed exterior. There was a little step up to the interior of the building, where the barber was cutting a customer's hair. There was no one else on the street.

"Let's get something to eat," I told Veronica. "Get a better look at the place before we go up to the condos."

"There's only one place to eat in town," she said. "A café. It's a bit of a dump."

"Sounds like my kind of place."

The words *"Cocina Juanita"* were written across the plate-glass window, announcing the place as Juanita's kitchen. Juanita herself greeted us as we walked in. We were the only customers: not surprising given the size of the town and the fact that it was around ten-thirty in the morning.

"You sit where you please," she declared in English.

We did. The dining room was small, maybe twenty feet by thirty. It had a collection of small tables of different sizes and shapes — round, square, rectangular — with an equally mismatched set of chairs. A counter area separated us from the kitchen, which was a long galley with a stove wide enough to grill a hundred eggs.

Juanita remained behind the counter as we sat, working a dishrag around a drinking glass.

"You having?" she asked.

"Coffee for me," I said.

"I would like a menu," said Veronica in Spanish.

"No menus," said Juanita, sticking to English. "Tell me you want, I'll make it."

Stubbornly sticking to Spanish, Veronica said she would have an egg sunny-side up.

Veronica had changed her hair, dying and cutting it, since she'd been here last, and she didn't think she'd been recognized. Juanita cracked open a pair of eggs, got them sizzling on the griddle, then came over with two cups of coffee even though Veronica hadn't ordered any.

"Maybe I'll have some eggs," I told the cook.

"How you like? Scramble?"

"I'm in your hands."

Juanita smiled, then swaggered back to the stove, happy that her abilities were being trusted. Behind the counter, she fell to work, frying up some bits of onion and vegetables, swirling yolks, and furiously shaking a peppermill. A few minutes later, she came over with

Veronica's eggs—two bright suns, smiling up at her—and a plate of what turned out to be some of the best scrambled eggs I've had in a long time.

"Good?" the cook asked as I took my first bite.

"Very good," I told her.

She folded her arms and smiled. I doubt Michelangelo looked more satisfied when he finished painting the Sistine Chapel.

"How are the condos at the other end of town?" I asked. "Nice place to retire?"

As soon as I mentioned condos, her face clouded.

"Angel Hills," I added when she didn't answer. "I was thinking I might look to see if one of them was for sale."

Juanita remained silent.

"It's only that I'm looking for a place to move to that's inexpensive," I added.

Still no answer.

"It's only that I heard the place was pretty cheap," I repeated. "So I asked my daughter here—"

Juanita bent her head toward the table.

"Never mind what you heard, senor. This is not a good place for gringos. Go to Cancun or somewhere else. Some nice place. Here—not very good."

She took the towel off her shoulder, pretended to wipe something off the table next to us, then went back to the grill.

"THAT WAS THE sales office, right there," said Veronica, pointing out a corner condo as we drove into the development.

"Looks closed."

"Exactly."

There was no sales sign, or anything else that would indicate it was an office—or that there were even units for sale, for that matter.

A pair of children's bikes were parked on the lawn of the next unit over.

"I thought this was a retirement community," I said to Veronica.

"It was."

I followed the road as it crested, then started down a hill to the south. The place looked very much like any of a million condo developments in the States, with two-story, pseudo-colonial units featuring peaked roofs, porches, and large bay windows—perfect in New England, I'd say, though about as appropriate in this landscape as a diving board. But the grass was well tended, and the small pond shimmered in front of immaculately white sand.

We drove down a hill and turned up the street. There were porches, but no people on them.

"Up there," she said, pointing to a corner unit. "That's theirs."

We pulled into the driveway. There were curtains on the windows, and a quartet of flowers on the porch. Veronica, puzzled, yanked at the door and got out of the car. She strode briskly up the walk, putting a good crease in the new chinos she'd picked up across the border.

I got out of the car but hung back for a moment, scanning the development. There wasn't anything overtly suspicious about the place.

Veronica stepped onto the small porch and rang the bell. She swung her head back and forth, glancing at the windows, then reached for the button again. As she did, the front door opened. A short, squat man in a button-down white shirt opened the door.

"*¿Sí?*" he asked quizzically, greeting her in Spanish.

"I'm looking for my grandparents," said Veronica, also speaking Spanish.

"Where do they live?"

"They live in this house."

"This house?"

"Yes, this house."

Veronica took a step toward the door. The man glanced at me.

"Your grandparents do not live here, miss," said the man. "I think you are mistaken."

"They bought this condo. I was here when they moved in."

The man shook his head. Someone inside said something. He answered with a "no."

"I want to see for myself," said Veronica.

"See what?"

"That they are not here?"

"You want to come in?" asked the man. He stepped back. "Come. Come then. Have a drink with us. You, too, sir."

I followed inside, still wary. The door opened into a short hallway that ran alongside a small kitchen. Beyond the hall was a combination dining and living room, with a master bedroom to the right. Upstairs there was a single room being used as a guest room. The man led Veronica through them all. After a quick peek downstairs, I went into the kitchen, where the man's wife was setting out four glasses for *Agua de Limón,* a kind of lemonade that in this case was made with limes.

"You have a very nice house," I told her.

"Your wife, is she crazy?"

"No more than most women," I said.

The woman's eyes knotted into a scowl. "Why does she think her grandparents live here?"

"How long have you been here?"

"Two years. Almost since it was built."

"Very expensive?"

She gestured with her hands that she didn't know. "My husband handles the money. Here, drink."

It was a little sweet for my taste, but otherwise good. Veronica came back into the kitchen with her guide, a perplexed look on her face. The man had introduced himself as Senor Torrez.

"This is a very nice place," I said. "I wonder if there are others for sale."

"Why would you live in Mexico?" said Torrez. "You are from the States."

"I was thinking that I would find a place to retire to. The taxes are very low in Mexico. Compared to the U.S."

"It's true," said Torrez. "But this would not be a good place for you."

"Why not?"

"All sold."

"Really? I thought I saw some empty units up the street. In fact, most of them look empty."

Torrez shook his head.

"Maybe they'll build more," I said.

"You speak Spanish very well. Are you from Mexico originally?"

"My wife is," I said, gesturing toward Veronica. She had the tiniest of frowns—I could tell she was going to ask for a divorce as soon as we got outside.

"Are there a lot of people from the States?" I took a sip of my drink. It was one of those rare, nonalcoholic beverages that got better as you drank it.

"At one time," said Mr. Torrez. "But there have been changes. Not a good place for tourists."

He didn't explain, just shook his head. I tried a few more questions but our hosts were now well on their guard and determined not to say anything. When I finished my drink, Mrs. Torrez took the glass and immediately put it in the dishwasher. We left a few minutes later.

"YOU DON'T BELIEVE me," said Veronica as I backed out of the driveway. "You think I'm crazy."

Danny Barrett had checked Veronica's bona fides for me that morning, confirming that she was a detective on leave from her department. He'd also tracked down a lieutenant in her department, who confirmed the grandparent story and said she was a good investigator. But that didn't mean she wasn't nuts.

I grunted noncommittally and drove slowly back up the hill. There hadn't been a car in the driveway.

"Did you go in the garage?" I asked.

"I looked in. Their car wasn't there."

"Any car?"

"No."

"Hmmmmph."

"My grandparents did live there," she insisted.

"I believe you," I said. "I also believe we're being followed."

Veronica reached into her purse and redid her lipstick—strategically maneuvering the makeup mirror to get a look at the battered green pickup I'd spotted.

"Just a driver," said Veronica as we passed. "Back is empty."

I kept going, nonchalantly rolling down the windows and putting on the music, tapping my hand out as if I were having a good time.

Which I was.

"How good are you with a gun?" I asked Veronica as I started down the hill toward the Mexican hamlet.

"I can handle myself."

"There's a Walther under your seat," I said. "It's a P99. You'll have to undo the tape. Shotgun has a thing for duct tape, and usually goes overboard."

Veronica leaned down, fishing for it. She pulled it out, rubbing off a bit of sticky adhesive from the handle.

"Am I going to need this?" she asked, sliding it into her lap.

"Maybe. We're going to get a flat tire on the way out of town. Assuming he's still following us. He may not."

"You think he's going to tell you anything?"

"If he wants to live."

I kept my foot steady on the gas pedal. The pickup was fairly far back, but given the nonexistent traffic, obviously following us. I slowed as I reached Villa Angela's business district, trying to give him a chance to catch up, but he was savvy enough to keep his distance.

"Hold on," I told Veronica as we approached the first curve west of the hamlet. I stepped on the gas as I turned the wheel, accelerating for a few seconds as we went through the short z in the road. Then I took my foot off the gas, slowing down without hitting the brakes. I didn't want him to think I was trying to get away.

He remained behind us, content with the gap.

About a mile and a half out of town, we came to a

second set of switchback curves that limited the view down the highway. I put the gas all the way to the floor this time, went another quarter mile or so, clearing the curves, then jammed the brakes and pulled over.

"You stay in the car," I told her, reaching down to pop the trunk with the remote button. "If things go bad, use the gun."

"I intend to."

I tapped on my sunglasses. The embedded radio woke up, sounding a little beep in my ear.

"Shotgun, where are you?"

"Halfway through the Cheetos."

"Get your ass over here. We're on the main road out of town."

"Comin', boss."

The truck was just coming around the bend as I ducked my head into the trunk to grab the jack and spare.

I'm not sure what I was expecting when the pickup pulled up alongside me. I know what I wanted—an Arab in man-jammies offering to confess to having plotted heinous crimes against America, but willing to tell all just for the honor of having been apprehended by *the* Richard Marcinko.

I can dream, can't I?

What I did *not* want was what I got: a double-barrel staring me in the face.

[V]

HAVING BEEN STARED down by a wide variety of weapons over my career, I think I can say with some confidence that I am a connoisseur of the business end of a gun. And in that light, I must say that there is definitely something about the round circles of a double-barreled twelve-guage that gets your attention.

The gun was pointed out the passenger window of the pickup. The man holding it was leaning toward me from the driver's seat. His face was in the shadows.

"Is this a robbery?" I asked in Spanish.

"What?" came the reply.

He was speaking English.

"You're going to hurt someone with that shotgun," I said, taking a step toward the truck.

"You just hold on there a second, mister," said the man in the truck. "I'm the one with the gun."

"I can see that."

"I have some questions for you."

"Come on out and ask them."

"I like where I'm at just fine."

He no sooner said that than he yelped, falling backward and out the driver's side of the truck.

While we'd been talking, Veronica had opened her car door and slipped out to the ground. Scrambling around the car, she circled across the road and approached the driver's side of the truck. Easing her thumb onto the handle of the door, she'd slipped it open, then grabbed him by the collar and pulled.

The man dropped the gun as she dragged him from the truck. I retrieved it—an Ansley H. Fox model, in case you're keeping track — and went over to join them on the highway shoulder.

"Don't hit me, don't hit me," he told Veronica, his hands in front of his face.

"Why shouldn't she hit you?" I unloaded the shotgun, letting the bullets fall to the ground. "What the hell were you doing, pointing a shotgun in my face?"

"I was just trying to find out who you are," he said. "I didn't mean no harm."

A horn tooted down the road. It was Shotgun, coming hard in his rented Impala.

"Go on up into town and see what you can see," I told him over the radio. "We have this under control."

"Any place good to eat?" he asked as he whipped by in the car.

"Concentrate on your job," I told him.

"I can eat and shoot at the same time, no sweat."

"Don't shoot — just look."

"You got it, boss."

Veronica pulled the man who'd accosted us to his feet. He was an older man, short and fairly rotund. He had thick, wire-rimmed glasses that magnified his eyes when you looked directly at them.

"Who are you?" Veronica asked.

"Please, don't hurt me. I wanted to talk to you. That's all."

"What about?"

"The house you went to — the people who used to live there are gone. The folks that are in there now — they don't really live there."

"Why are they there?" Veronica asked. The emotions she'd been keeping in check rose with her voice.

"I need to talk to you."

"So go ahead," I told him.

"They'll come for me." He glanced upward, back in the direction of the development and the Mexican town. "They'll be watching."

"Who?"

"They have a telescope in the last building in town and they'll watch what's happening."

"They can't see here." The curve in the hills blocked the town from view.

"They will."

"Are they going to come out and check on you?"

"They might."

"Put the shotgun in the truck," I told him, handing it over. Then I raised my shirt so he could see the pistol. "Then come over and help us change the tire. This way if they come out, it'll look natural."

The man nodded. I walked back over to the rental, got out the tire jack and the spare.

I will say one thing: I hate those damn donut tires they give you instead of real rubber.

THE MAN'S NAME was Saul Freeman. He had come to Angel Hills around the time Veronica's grandparents had, for basically the same reasons. He had been a heating and cooling contractor in North Carolina, didn't have much savings, and had lost his house in a divorce, having to sell it at the height of the 2007 housing bust. His ex had then died, which he somehow found heavily ironic. She was his second wife; he'd lost contact with his first long ago. Both marriages had been childless, a fact that still baffled him.

"The place seemed like heaven in the brochures," he said. For someone worried about being discovered, he was awful lackadaisical about getting to the point. "And it wasn't that bad. At first. Except for the air-conditioning. Cheaped out on that. Supply was way undersized and some of the connections were so loose they came apart the first time I turned it on. Fixed those."

"So what happened here?" I asked.

"Right after I moved in, the company that built the place started having a lot of issues—problems with finances, I guess. I don't know exactly what the story was. Cash flow, they said. That might have been true. For a while, we stopped seeing most of the maintenance staff. They were laid off, I guess. Most of them. Everything stopped. Couldn't find no one to cut the grass or fix the dishwasher. Then, one day, things changed. The lawns started getting watered and cut again. Some of the streets that hadn't been paved were paved. They brought some trucks and what-not in."

Less than a quarter of the units had sold when the problems began, and Saul estimated that a dozen families left, at least some because they couldn't pay their mortgages. So he was surprised to see new buildings going up. Nor was there a sudden rush of potential buyers. Still, work continued. A few more residents left, generally without announcing their departure. He assumed it was due to personal money problems.

"Only families I saw move in were Mexicans. Which was kind of odd," said Saul. "There were only two, though. Well, three I think. They came, stayed a couple of months, then moved out. New people came in. Always claimed to own the place, but I don't know—buy it for a few months, then sell? You never see a for-sale sign. And like I say, these were Mexicans, not Anglos like me."

They were in Mexico, of course, and Saul prided himself on being open-minded and accepting of all nationalities. But until now the place had been marketed exclusively to ex-pats, and it just seemed strange when the Mexican nationals moved in. They were much younger than the Americans; a few had small kids.

Saul wanted to talk to the salespeople about this, but there was no one to ask. The sales office was closed permanently. The maintenance supervisor claimed not to understand either his English or his Spanish. There had been a community manager with an office at the community center, but the office was closed. Calls to the management company, headquartered in Mexico City, went unanswered.

"About the only people related to the company were the security police," said Saul. "That was going strong. They didn't patrol much in the day, but they were out in force at night. Two cars."

"You have a lot of crime here?" asked Veronica.

"No."

"Two cars to patrol that little development?" I asked.

"They always want backup."

Veronica seemed skeptical, but didn't say anything else as Saul continued.

"I started talking to people at the pool, when they'd come. A couple, two or three, were talking about moving out. Others."

He shrugged. Most of the people who'd moved here kept to themselves, not wanting to be bothered. It was one reason they'd left the States—they weren't too sociable.

One day Saul went to the pool and discovered that it had been closed, supposedly for repairs.

"It looked fine to me," he said.

Now suspicious, Saul began poking around. He was especially interested in the newcomers and went out of his way to be friendly. But they generally didn't do more than wave or say hello. One evening after he'd been talking to some of the kids who had moved in on his block, a pair of Mexican policemen showed up at his door. They asked why he had been talking to the children.

"I like kids," he said, taken by surprise.

"You like them in what way?" asked one of the cops.

They stayed for more than an hour. Their questions implied that Saul had had evil intentions, as he put it, though they never actually accused him outright. When they left, they warned him to make sure he was careful in the future.

He kept to himself for a few weeks after that.

"I thought about leaving," he told me. "But I'd sunk every penny I had into the condo. Plus, without a sales office, I didn't know how to arrange it. I was afraid of talking to people about it—certainly not the Mexicans. I thought one of them had called the police on me."

One night, Saul decided that even though he would lose everything, he would leave. He packed his things into two suitcases and threw them in the back of the truck. Then he headed out of town. A mile past the Mexican village, he found the highway blocked by a pair of police cars, red lights flashing. There were two large trucks just beyond them. He slowed, thinking it was an accident investigation. One of the cops brandished an M16 and told him to turn his truck around and go home.

"What is going on?" Saul asked.

"Police emergency."

A few days later, a piece of paper was slipped beneath his door. There was going to be a meeting that night at the community center. A few minutes before the meeting, Saul was still trying to decide whether to attend. There was a knock on his door. When he opened it, he found two thugs standing there, inviting him to go.

There were about a dozen and a half white residents left. All were at the meeting.

"A Mexican lady lawyer type got up to speak just after I got there," said Saul. "She had good English. Better than mine."

The woman told the crowd that there had been a bankruptcy, and that earlier developers had sold to another development company. That company in turn had hired a management firm—she was its representative—that would now see to all of the needs of the residents. She was sorry that it had taken so long for them to explain, but the bankruptcy procedures were extremely complicated in Mexico, and her firm had to follow very specific rules so as not to upset the process. Those rules, she added, had prevented them from speaking up until now.

There were now going to be very strict rules for security. Security, she said, was becoming an important issue in northern Mexico. Additionally, the residents would have to comply with new laws passed by the Mexican government requiring that they have Mexican driver's licenses and IDs. She was happy to announce that American drivers would not have to retake their driver's license tests, and if they handed over their documentation this evening, she would arrange to have their licenses processed in the morning.

There was other paperwork involved—a blizzard of it, in fact, with so many papers passing back and forth that Saul couldn't keep track. They were also in Spanish, a language that he couldn't read very well.

"Well you just sign the papers," said the woman. "You don't need to read them."

"But what are they for?"

"Different things—to keep you from being taxed, to make sure you own your property, to say your car is insured—all different things."

One of the two other Americans in the audience raised her hand and asked what was going on with the phones. She hadn't been able to call the U.S. for the past few days. Not even her cell phone worked properly.

"The workers at Telmex are on strike," answered the rep. Telmex was the telephone company. "It is regrettable. They will solve it soon, I'm sure."

"Cell phones, too?"

"The area has never had good coverage," said the rep apologetically. She changed the subject, asking if there were any volunteers for a neighborhood watch program. Saul's hand shot up almost involuntarily.

"Very good, very good," said the lawyer.

"I don't know how good a lawyer she was, but she had a hell of a smile," said Saul. "I felt things I hadn't felt in twenty years."

"You got a couple of guys heading your way out of town in a charger all duded up like a police car," warned Shotgun over the radio.

"Are they police?" I asked.

"That's what I said."

"No. You said they looked like police."

"Well, there's no Dunkin' Donuts in town, so how can I tell?"

"They're private security," said Saul, listening in on my side of the conversation. "They work for the company. They're coming out to check on me."

"Shotgun, get ready to get out here if I need you."

"You got it. By the way, this little café is a hell of a place. You know the lady who owns it cooks up these tiny little honey ball things that are even better than Drake's pies."

I put a knife through the tire and slid it out on the ground where it would be visible. Veronica went to the car and pushed back her seat, making it look as if she were taking a nap. Saul leaned against his front fender, watching me work.

The police car—you had to stare closely at the insignia to realize it was private security—rounded the corner and came up slowly. As it slowed to a halt, Saul went over and spoke to the officers. They laughed, then drove on.

"They may be back," he said. "I told them you have trouble with the nuts."

"Story of my life."

SAUL WAS THE only member of the neighborhood watch program. The security people mostly just humored him, letting him fill the truck up with gas whenever he wanted.

"What do they think about your shotgun?" I asked.

"They don't know about it. I don't tell them."

I suspected they did know about it but chose not to make an issue.

"You know who bought the development?" I asked.

"No. But I have a good suspicion."

"What's that?"

"Drug dealers. Cartel. Trying to go legit. They probably see it as an investment. Shelter their money. Like the mafia did. Take over everything, then pretend they're legal."

"Did you know my grandparents?" Veronica asked.

"To nod at, sure. But they moved away months ago."

"Where to?"

"Just left, as far as I know."

"What about Arabs?" I asked.

"Arabs? Like with turbans and camels?"

"I doubt there'd be camels. People from Pakistan, Afghanistan, Yemen maybe. Egyptians?" I named a few more countries in the Middle East.

"The only place you might find foreigners like that," said Saul, "is out at the chicken farm. They produce Halal food, and sometimes the imams come out. I've seen one or two in town, on their way out."

"Where's that?"

"Other side of the hills, that way." He pointed southeast. "I haven't been there myself."

"How do you know about it?"

"You hear about it. Every so often. In town. The Mexicans know everything, but they're scared. They never talk to whites, not even me."

I was done with the tire, and pretty much done with Saul as well. If the Mexicans were letting him roam around pretending to be the neighborhood watch, they must have him pegged as inept, harmless, or both. I put the tire I'd punctured in the trunk, slammed it closed, and got ready to leave.

"Thanks for the help," I told him.

"Wait—don't you want to know why I stopped you?" asked Saul.

"We stopped you," I said.

"I need your help. I want to organize the rest of the citizens. We want to kick the cartel out."

"That's a pipe dream," said Veronica. "You're better off just getting out."

"It sounds to me like you can leave anytime you want," I added, opening the car door. "Just get in your truck and keep driving."

"I can't. They never gave my ID back. I can't get across the border."

"Frankly, I don't think that's much of a problem," I told him.

[VI]

NEITHER I NOR Veronica spoke as we headed toward Mexico Federal Highway 2, the main road to the south. We'd reserved some rooms at a small motel about ten miles away; we could rest there while I decided what to do next.

Frankly, it didn't look good for her grandparents, though she didn't need to hear that from me.

"I last checked with Social Security two weeks ago," said Veronica after we got on the highway. "They're still depositing checks."

"Are there withdrawals from the account?"

"I don't have access to it, so I can't tell."

"We can fix that."

"That will raise suspicions at the bank. You'd need a subpoena . . ."

"I don't need a subpoena. I have Shunt."

I got on the sat phone and told our resident geek to get into the accounts. Veronica volunteered their Social Security numbers, but Shunt, being Shunt, found them online before she finished. Then he went to work.

"Deposited and withdrawn the next day," he told us a few minutes later.

"In cash?" Veronica asked. "Where?"

"Not cash—transferred. I'm running it down. Couple of different banks involved."

Shunt tracked the withdrawals to three different *cambios*, where it disappeared as a series of cash disbursements.

"I'll look and see what I can find," he told us. "This thing is like a tangle of yarn though. I don't know what I'll see."

"Concentrate on the grandparents," I told him. "Go from there."

Shunt used the information from the first account to find other accounts, starting with their credit cards. He tracked credit card activity—none in the past six months—and looked at bills that had been paid to see if he could cross-reference to other accounts.

More importantly, he looked for parallel accounts, trying to track the cartel's money flow. He would be especially interested in anything terrorist-related.

"While you're at it, I need some other stuff," I told

him. "Sat images of the area near Angel Hills. Most recent you can get."

"No sweat. I'll download them to your phone."

"Run a series," I added. "Go back as far as you can."

"I'm looking at the most recent one now. Kind of a dinky farm thing."

"See any people?"

"Nada. This is the camp?"

"Could be."

"Maybe. You know, if they're halfway intelligent, they could figure out when the satellite passes and avoid it."

"Check anyway."

THE MOTEL WAS a low-slung, one-story building with eight units on one side and another ten on the back. Take the lowest-rung American discount chain and divide by ten, and that's what *Peso de Jesus* looked like. Built in the fifties or maybe the early sixties, the outside walls looked like they had been sandblasted to a fine dull gray. The interior walls hadn't seen a coat of paint in twenty years at least.

Veronica's face reddened when I told the clerk we only needed one room. I could feel her eyes burning through the back of my head as I took the key.

"Dick," she hissed as I headed down the hall.

"We're supposed to be married," I told her. "That was the cover story."

"For a cover, yes. Not for sleeping."

"We won't be sleeping here, don't worry."

Somehow, that didn't quite calm her fears. But she relaxed when she saw there were two beds in the room.

While it smelled more than a little stale, the sheets were crisp and clean.

"I wouldn't mind taking a shower," she said, going into the bathroom.

The next thing I knew, she was screaming. I drew my pistol and ran in.

A large iguana stood guard near the bathtub. It blinked its eyes lazily, unsure what humans were doing in its room.

I took a step toward it. The lizard whipped its spiny tail back and forth.

"I don't think it likes you," said Veronica.

"The feeling is mutual," I said.

"Watch out!" Veronica yelled, jumping out of the way as the lizard darted for the door. I stepped aside and watched as it moved faster than a jackrabbit out into the room.

"Close the bathroom door," I told her.

"Gladly."

It slammed behind me as I went out. The iguana was standing in the space between the beds, glowering at me.

I opened the door to the room. There was barely enough time to get out of the way as it bolted out into the hall.

"Oh, senor, senorita, I am so sorry," said the motel clerk from down the hall. "I forget that Senor Fred is in the room. Sorry, sorry."

Senor Fred was the iguana.

"He will not bother you anymore, I promise," said the clerk. "But you can think of this—he will have killed all the insects."

"If I knew we were getting the lizard suite," I told

Veronica when he left, "I would have asked for a discount."

Veronica still wanted to take a shower, but that didn't work out—the water that spilled from the spout was orange and hot besides. And "spill" is not a metaphor: it would have taken a good three minutes to fill an average-sized coffee cup.

Seeking a different sort of refreshment, we ambled across the street to a combination café and bar. The only person inside was a girl maybe twelve or thirteen years old, who served as the waitress and bartender.

The odds of the place being bugged were pretty slim, but I checked anyway, running my little handy detector all around the place. The girl came out with our beers as I was finishing up.

"Your best luck is near the window," she told me, thinking I was fishing around with my phone for a signal. "But the reception will not be too good there either."

I smiled and thanked her. The place was clean—electronically, if not in terms of actual dirt.

Shotgun came in a short time later and proceeded to order everything on the menu. While the girl was in the kitchen preparing it, I downloaded the satellite images to my sat phone.

There was a farm in the shadow of the hills on the other side of the development, but it was very difficult to see because of the way it was situated. When we think of satellite images, we think of them as being shot directly overhead. But that's not true much of the time. Depending on the location and the time of the day, a considerable part of any given area may not be visible. (There are ways around this, most notably by using multiple satellites or cameras. But that wasn't possible here.)

I could see all of the buildings and a perimeter fence; objects on the south side of the buildings and a good part of the hill were in heavy shadow and essentially invisible. Still, the place didn't look like a booming terrorist training camp. It didn't even look like much of a farm. There were only six decent-sized buildings. Of these, one was missing a roof, and the other looked as if it had caved in. There were animals in a small pen, and a cultivated plot of land about the size my aunt uses to plant green beans.

Shunt had helpfully annotated the images, IDing the animals.

"PIGS," he'd typed in big red letters, circling three creatures in the lower left-hand corner of one of the images.

Not the best evidence that this was a halal farm, actually.

A SINGLE ROAD ran to the farm from the highway. It was long and narrow, easily seen from the property. But there was a back entrance: a dirt trail started a hundred yards or so from the southern border of Angel Hills, ran up through the hills, and then down to a trail that led to the northern edge of the farm. While it was hard to judge from the images, it looked as if you could get vehicles across from the back end of the development, though the road was much easier.

The west side of the farm was in full view of the road, across a patchy desert that offered little cover. The area to the immediate east of the farm had been quarried for some sort of rock; there were sharp crags and a sheer cliff between them, a natural barrier to anyone who dared to go that way.

Obviously, that was my best choice.[20]

A half hour after sunset, Shotgun and I set out from the café to see if it really was possible for pigs to be raised on a Muslim farm. We traveled light: rucks, submachine guns, and for Shotgun only enough snack food for a month's survival.

Our route to the camp began on an old mining road about three miles southeast of the farm. Veronica dropped us off near a dry gully that led to the old quarry. The route was actually five miles long, counting all the twists and turns: a leisurely stroll on a moonlit night.

Shotgun kept up a running patter as we walked.

"Hey, Dick, you want some of these spearmint leaf jellies? They're really good.

"Feel like a sugar donut, Dick?

"How about a Slim Jim?"

Finally, I had enough. "Shotgun, if you don't shut your mouth, you're going to be eating shoe leather in a minute."

From that point on, he munched in silence.

We reached the quarry a short time later. The moon, which had started out so full I didn't need my night vision, was now playing hide and seek in the clouds. What had looked like a fairly easy climb on the satellite image now looked damn tricky, a hand-over-hand scramble the higher we went. The side of the hill had been chiseled into large squares of uneven depth. Some

---

[20] You understand why this is, right? If the route seems impassable, defenders will more than likely forget about it. And as I like to remind my minions, if it hurts you're doing it right!

held my entire foot; I could barely get a toehold in others. The rock poked out in places, adding a touch of vertigo to the ambience.

I was about thirty feet from the peak when it started to rain. If you're wondering how often it rains in the desert, join the club. I wasn't sure whether to blame Murphy or global warming.

Practically crawling before, I barely moved at all as the water made the rocks more slippery than a West Texas politician. Before, the sweat in my hands had turned the grit to a pasty glue. Now it was as if I were trying to climb on Vaseline.

The rain seemed to help Shotgun somehow, and within minutes he had passed me as if I were standing still. I finally found him at the top, a good half hour later. His feet dangled off a rock and he was munching on a Tootsie Roll.

"Checked for lookouts," he told me. "Nothing."

"Tell Veronica where we are," I said, sliding off the rock onto a narrow but substantial-looking shelf. "I need to get a short rest."

"Already gave her the dope," said Shotgun. "Junior launched a Bird from the ranch. It oughta be overhead in twenty minutes or so."

"Great."

I sat down on a ledge overlooking the farm property. Between the darkness and the run of trees ahead, I couldn't see anything.

The next thing I knew, I was on my butt heading downward. Murphy had kicked away the shelf I was sitting on.

Fortunately for me, the slope was smooth and not all that steep. Even so, I skidded a good 150 feet, plunging like a kid who lost his sleigh on the town's best hill. I hit a few rocks on the way down, but the main injury was to my dignity and my lungs, which filled with dust from the rock slide that accompanied me. I was still coughing and trying to clear them when Shotgun came down to me.

"I thought we were waiting," he said.

"I got impatient. Come on."

Tacking to the south, I found a gentler slope and began working my way across the face of the hill. My boots slipped on a few of the rocks, but I managed to remain upright and reach a wide though shallow creek that fed into the back of the farm. A trickle of water ran through the rocks at the center.

The rain made the Bird's IR sketchy, and Junior warned us that he wasn't sure he'd have an image even when it arrived on station above. I didn't mind, though. If we didn't have IR, neither did they. The rain would also make it more likely that anyone inside the buildings would stay there.

I reached into my rucksack and pulled out my poncho. Shotgun did the same. His was the size of a parachute; if the wind kicked up I was sure he'd be blown away.

The farm was surrounded by a tall fence of very thin wire similar to a deer fence. Beyond that was a chain-link fence about eight feet high, but topped by barbed wire. We used a small pair of wire snips to cut through the outer fence, then made our way between the scrub brush to the second one. Here Murph decided to give me another little tickle—the jaw of the wire cutters snapped as I cut through the second link.

"Betcha those snips were made in China," said Shotgun, handing over his.

I went back to work, faring much better this time — I got three pieces cut before the replacement snips fell apart as well.

"I think it's the fence," said Shotgun.

I'm allergic to barbed wire, and if possible I prefer to avoid it. But the fence was buried in the dirt; I kicked at it in a few places but it had been put in so deeply that it didn't budge.

Shotgun pulled out his Teflon blanket, fanned it, then lay it out over the top of the fence.

Teflon is an amazing substance. You can fry an egg on it; you can sleep in it when you go to the moon. We like it for covering barbed wire because it's incredibly tough but not as heavy as some other choices. (If you're in the market, don't buy the cheap knockoff stuff from China unless you really trust your supplier.)

The Bird came overhead, and Junior gave us a sitrep. The place looked empty, except for the two-story house near the road at the front of the farm. There were lights on inside, and while he couldn't pick up a heat signature on the second floor, he assumed there was someone on the first.

"Back end of the property looks pretty clear," Junior told us. "I'm going to swing around west and run up that road, see if I can get a look at the house. You OK? Or you want me to wait until you're over the fence?"

"No, go ahead," I told him, leaning against the chain links while Shotgun scrambled upward.

Once Shotgun was over the top, I kicked my sneakers into the fence and followed. I slipped over the blanket, and was just about to hop down onto the ground when I heard something moving between the nearby trees.

"Shit!" cursed Shotgun.

The next thing I knew, he had hopped up next to me. Then something hit the fence so hard at first I thought it was a missile or an rpg.

It was something even more deadly: a rottweiler from hell.

People talk about how ferocious pit bulls are. Believe me, they have nothing on a well-trained rot.

Rottweilers are intelligent and *can* be gentle dogs, if properly nurtured and trained. Teach them to be nasty, though, and you have one mean mf. Not even my ex-mother-in-law could stand up to one of them.

The rot below us was the meanest thing I've ever seen on four legs. (My first drill instructor walked on two. At least around us.) He rebounded off the fence with a snarl, and began snapping at our shoes. Shotgun and I scrambled back up to the top as the dog threw himself against the links.

This was no dog, this was a demon. After another lunge brought its teeth to within a few inches of my shoes, I decided the only way to deal with it was to shoot it. But as I reached to my holster for my pistol, Shotgun called me off.

"I'll get him, Dick," he said. And with that, he leapt off the fence, holding the Teflon blanket out in front of him. He caught the dog from the side, whirling the blanket over its head and scooping it over, twisting the material in the same motion. The dog flipped over on its back, whining as Shotgun pinned its back legs to the ground with his knee. The maneuver was a thing of beauty, really, an impressive ballet of man versus animal, proving why we are so much higher on the evolutionary chain.

Then the dog's fangs ripped through the Teflon. Before Shotgun could react, the animal had obliterated the material, and expanded its jaws wide enough to swallow Shotgun's head whole.

I put five bullets between its eyes before the damn beast dropped off dead.

Did Shotgun thank me for saving his life? Did he say he would be eternally grateful, or offer to name his firstborn after me?

Heh.

"Aw, why'd you have to go and shoot it for, Dick?" he asked, getting up. "It wouldn't have hurt me none."

We hauled the dog to a spot behind the trees. We pulled off our ponchos—the rain was letting up—and used them to camouflage him. I reloaded my pistol, then took my MP5 out of the ruck.

"Junior, what are you seeing?" I asked over the radio.

"Nothing, Dick."

"A dog just came out of nowhere and attacked us."

"Shit."

"It's all right. Get the Bird back overhead."

"It's on its way."

Next I called Veronica. When I told her what had happened, she was extremely concerned.

But not about us.

"You shot a dog?" she asked.

"The damn thing was the size of a bear."

"You had to shoot it, though?"

I felt like I was at an ASPCA meeting. I told her to keep watching the road.

"What kind of trees are these?" Shotgun asked, gesturing at the grove we were hiding in.

"Do I look like a botanist?" I was not in a pleasant mood.

"Shunt says they're dates. You think they're dates?"

"If Shunt told you what they were, why you asking me?"

"I don't think Shunt knows all that much about trees," said Shotgun. "He lives in New York City. I don't think he knows what a tree is."

"They have trees in New York, Shotgun."

"If these are dates, then I could try one of them."

"They're probably poisoned."

"You think?"

I didn't, but it was enough to get Shotgun's mind off of the food and focus on where it belonged — watching our six . . . and our seven, our one and our eight, and every number around the clock.

Sifting through the trees, we came up a gentle rise. A large cultivated field and a smaller one sat between us and a long building. In the darkness it looked more like a shadow blending into the hill behind it.

I took my night binos out and focused on the building. There was still a light drizzle blurring my vision, but I didn't see anything that looked like a guard or another dog.

The PK was not a silent weapon, and with that many shots I would expect to get some response. Gunfire, even out in this part of Mexico, couldn't be too common. But there was nothing.

"Might not have heard us inside the house," said Shotgun, reading my mind as I stared at the building. The house was nearly a half mile away from the building, beyond another grove of trees and up a hill.

I moved along the tree line until I could no longer see the building. Then I started to trot through the field, hanging in the shadow at the edge. The land had been plowed up but was fallow, or at least there wasn't anything growing in it yet.

The rain had made the topsoil wet, and a light layer of mud stuck to the sides of my shoes. There was a chemical scent to the field that mixed with the rain; it smelled a bit like a deodorant commercial that had gone horribly wrong. But at least it didn't smell like cow manure.

Once more the clouds parted; the sky lightened as the moon was revealed. I reached the end of the field and found a ditch running between them rather than the road I had expected. This was a plus rather than a problem; it wended its way around to the right, and would give us cover all the way to the first building.

"Follow me," I told Shotgun, starting along it. "Don't get lost."

Back at the ranch, Junior was running into some sort of communications problem with the Bird. The infrared video feed went offline, though he could still see somewhat with a backup low-light camera. (I'm sorry to say, this has happened a few times.) He tried resetting—basically turning it on and off—but that didn't work.[21]

"The plane seems to be flying fine," he told me. "It's circling almost directly over your position. But I still can't see for shit."

"Just keep at it," I told him.

"No shit."

---

[21] Blame Shunt, not Murphy on that one.

I might have told him to call Shunt and try and troubleshoot it, but it didn't seem worth the effort. Shotgun and I were already well inside the compound, and there wasn't much Junior could tell me that I couldn't figure out on my own. There's a tendency to depend too much on high-tech gadgets once you have them. I'm not saying I'm exempt—like most guys, stick something with a battery in my hand and I can keep myself occupied for hours. But I started out in the era when the idea of real-time satellite imagery was sci-fi fantasy, and we still found a way to get the job done.

The building we were heading toward looked like a two-story barn made out of prefab steel panels. A concrete apron ran around the base. I guesstimated the side walls were about sixty or seventy feet, twice as long as the front and back.

I was roughly ten yards from the building when the night flooded with light; I'd stupidly tripped a motion detector planted in the ground somewhere to my left. It was completely my fault—I'd scanned the roofline of the building and examined the wall without seeing anything, but hadn't bothered to look anywhere else, including the field where it was planted. Maybe I would have missed it there—the detector was on a stake, positioned very low to the ground—but it was certainly a dumbshit moment.

I dropped into the dirt, expecting to come under fire. But nothing happened.

"Dick, there's a motion detector out there," called Shotgun, who was about ten or fifteen yards behind.

"No shit. Can you take care of it?"

"Yeah."

He backed around and circled behind the light. I

stayed motionless until the light flicked off. A minute or two later, Shotgun reached the detector and slid a small piece of thick glass over it, blinding it. He then took the stake it was mounted on and angled it into the ground. The detector was still working, but all it would find now were earthworms.

Shotgun moved up in the field, looking for other detectors. I watched the building until he said it was clear.

I rose and started toward the building again, this time more cautiously.

I spotted a set of floodlights at the front of the building that had motion detectors attached to the bottom. But they were angled in a way that made it clear there was a wide blind spot along the front wall. All I had to do was hug the exterior of the building to avoid detection.

The far side of the building was partly exposed to the rest of the farm. I slipped back to a pair of empty oil drums sitting against the side of the building. Apparently used as burn barrels, there was nothing inside but a few pieces of charred cardboard and firewood. I worked around to the back, where I found a set of floodlights similar to the ones in the front. I slid beneath them without setting off the detectors and continued around to the side I'd started on. From there, I walked back to the front of the building, having completed a full circle.

The only opening was a large door on a rail at the front. It was padlocked in two places — Yale locks, relatively easy to pick.

"Somebody moving up near the house," said Shotgun over the radio. "Rifles — two guys."

The warning was a relief — I'd been starting to think the night was a complete waste of time.

"Truck," warned Shotgun. "Two maybe — hear them?"

Just barely. I got on the radio and asked Junior if he saw anything.

"Still trying to reset."

"Keep working on it."

"Here they come," said Shotgun, breaking in. "Two troop trucks, canvas off."

"Mexican army?"

"I don't know, Dick. I think they're all ragheads."[22]

"You sure?"

"They got AKs." Shotgun used the slang for AK47s, the rifle of choice for terrorists and other miscreants the world over.

"Doesn't mean anything," I told him.

"All of them have beards. I see some of those Saudi scarves. They have khakis."

Definitely not army. But were they cartel members? Or tangos?

There was only one way to find out, really. Ask them.

ONE OF THE popular misconceptions about SEALs is that we like to get into fights where we're outnumbered. Nothing can be further from the truth.

Now, it is correct that we often *find* ourselves outnumbered — after all, who in their right mind would take on SEALs on a one-to-one basis? And of course, if you succeed in getting surrounded, any decision you make will lead naturally to an attack — you have no option for a tactical withdrawal.

---

[22] I'm sure he meant to say something more politically correct. There's no one more PC than Shotgun.

My intention at the moment was not to actually fight the two dozen or so assholes who were riding toward us in the trucks. I was here on a recce or reconnaissance mission; the word "suicide" did not appear anywhere in the op description. But I didn't intend on leaving until I was sure who they were.

"Get over to this side of the barn with me," I told Shotgun. "Before the trucks come down the road."

"Too late," he said as a pair of headlights swung across the field. The truck made a turn on the road above and the lights focused ahead, illuminating the narrow dirt road down from the house. The lights on the barn flashed on, apparently worked by remote control since the trucks were too far away to set them off. Another set of lights, back up near the house, flashed on as well.

"Wow, definitely Arabs," said Shotgun.

"You're sure they're not Mexican?"

"A couple got those long coat things and the Afghan hats. I'll get a picture with the camera."

"Make sure it doesn't flash."

Yeah, I know, only an idiot would leave the flash on.

You'd be surprised.

"Got it," said Shotgun.

"I have the visual," said Junior over the radio. "I can see the farm—there are two trucks coming down the road toward you."

"Stand by," I told him. "Shotgun, can you move back in the field without being detected?"

"I think so."

"OK, let's do it. We have what we need for now."

"Right."

I started trotting in a half crouch through the field

toward the shallow ditch. I had just reached it when I heard heavy breathing over my shoulder.

It wasn't Shotgun in heat. I twisted around just in time to see a rottweiler launch herself at me, teeth flashing in the moonlight.

[VII]

IF THE FIRST dog we'd encountered was the hound from hell, this was its mistress. She was meaner, and probably had twenty pounds on her mate, all of it muscle and fangs.

I got my left arm up in front of my face, knocking against the bottom of her jaw. She snapped the air, then rolled down over me. Her momentum carried her into the rocks beyond my head. She tumbled over, then leapt to her feet for another try. I fumbled with my knife, unable to yank it from the scabbard before she dove at my side. I ducked; two of her teeth caught my shirt and pulled me around, bending me against her snout as she fell down. Fortunately, my armored vest kept her teeth from reaching my chest. She clawed at me with her legs, scratching my cheek with claws that felt like ice picks.

I managed to elbow her as we rolled over. I finally freed my knife, but just as I swung it around she rolled onto my arm. The weight of her body against my arm made it go numb. The knife fell, and I swear for a moment I thought she had bit my hand off. In a rage, I bowled forward, pushing the mutt off and sending her head over heels backward.

Blood rushed back into my hand and I grabbed the knife, then leapt at her, blade first. I put the dagger into her throat and held it as she twisted her body, snapping back and forth, trying to bite. Blood spurt everywhere, and the hot spit of her breath torched my face. Finally she fell back, exhausted and drained.

That made two of us.

"Dick! Dick!" hissed Shotgun. "Hey! Are you OK?"

"Where are you?" I growled.

"Up near the barn. I can't get down any farther without being seen? What's going on?"

"Stay where you are." I scrambled up out of the ditch. The headlights from one of the trucks illuminated the road and the field all the way to the grove.

Sure that whoever was in the trucks was looking for us now, I realized our path to the fence would be cut off. The only place to hide, I thought, was up—the roof to the barn. So I leapt out of the ditch and ran to the barn, retreating to the back of the building.

"They're getting out of the trucks," said Shotgun.

"Where did that dog come from?"

"It leapt out of the truck. They're calling for it. They ain't using Spanish, Dick."

Shotgun wasn't the best judge—he didn't speak Spanish. In any event, the problem now was to avoid detection. Except for the floodlights above me, I had a clear path to the hills that wedged the building in and separated the farm from the condo development to the north. I slid beneath the detectors, eyeing them. Shooting them or the floodlights out from where I stood would be easy, but my gunshots would be heard. I reached down and scooped up some rocks, tossing them at the light.

I broke glass on the third try. Two more rocks and the second flood was down.

As soon as the glass shattered, I leapt out across toward the sharp incline. As I reached it, I saw a faint orange glow out of the corner of my eye. I had broken the glass on the right bulb but not the entire light; the filament was still intact.

Fortunately, the glow couldn't be seen on the other side of the building. I went up the embankment, clawing my way up the pitch with the help of the brush.

Moving to my left, I looked across the way and saw the tangos milling around the trucks. A pair of men had gone down after the dog.

It was only a matter of time before they organized a search. I could escape simply by climbing the hill. Shotgun, though, was trapped, unable to move without being seen.

"Run when I tell you," I told him over the radio. "Go back the way we came. You'll have a clear path. But don't stop."

"Where are you?"

"I'm up on the embankment at the north. I'll go out this way."

"Kind of far."

"Get ready." I raised the MP5 and aimed at the man who was giving orders. A squeeze of the trigger, and he fell to the ground.

No one moved for a second or two. Caught unawares, the tangos' brains undoubtedly needed time to process what had happened. I used that time to reduce their numbers, dropping three or four before a tracer told me I was coming to the end of my mag. I shot the last rounds, dropped the mag and reloaded. As I did, I realized someone else was firing—not the tangos, but Shotgun, who'd risen in the field and was dousing the area near the trucks with bullets.

"I told you to get the hell out of there," I growled.

"What, and let you have all the fun?"

I swear to God, Shotgun laughed as he said that.

We'd caught the tangos completely by surprise, and with a little bit of luck we could have wiped them all out before they had a chance to organize themselves. But the two men who'd gone down to look at the dog managed to scramble into a position where they could fire at me, and I had to duck; sliding four or five feet out of the line of fire, I lost my shot at the main ground of tangos. Shotgun had to pause and reload at roughly the same time. That reprieve gave the tangos enough time to run between the trucks and the barn for cover, neutralizing our initial advantage.

Between us, Shotgun and I had killed or wounded eight or ten men. That changed the odds considerably; there was no sense retreating now.

Right?

I went a little farther up the hill, trying to recover my shooting angle, if only on the two guys who'd fired at me from the area near the ditch. But they had already taken cover. With no one to aim at, I moved across the slope to the west, intending to find a spot where I could cross over and join Shotgun.

I'd only gone a few yards when the filament on the spotlights flared. I dropped to one knee and turned toward the building. Two men with AKs stood a few yards from the corner, looking up in my direction. They seemed to be looking right at me, but must have missed me in the shadows and the brush. As soon as they turned around to go, I rose and told them where I was with three bursts, back and forth across the head, neck, and shoulders. Both men crumpled to the ground.

"There's another troop truck coming down the main entrance," warned Junior.

I ran up the hill, intending to spray the back of the truck as it passed. But I was a little too late; the vehicle started past as I began trotting up the hill. It was a canvas-backed troop truck, a military-type vehicle though it had no markings.

I raised my submachine gun and began running toward the truck, intending to get as close as possible before firing. When I was less than ten yards away, I realized that the back of the vehicle was empty. Instead of firing, I kept running, catching up to it as it made the last turn toward the barn. Hopping up and over the rear tailgate, I slid on the metal floor, crashing into a pair of large metal ammo boxes at the side of the truck as the driver hit the brakes.

Nowadays, everything is plastic or some fancy high-tech alloy that will last for a billion years, weighs nothing, and in a pinch can make dinner for you. But for my money, there's nothing like an old-fashioned painted steel ammo box, the thirty- or fifty-caliber variety that served our forebears from World War II forward. Basic, rugged, and dependable, it's a design that can't be improved upon.

Especially when it holds grenades.

The truck pulled in behind the other two. The driver and his companion got out, joining the men who were mustered in a semicircle around the front of the building.

"Shotgun, I'm in the truck that just pulled up," I told him. "I'm coming for you."

"Better not. All sorts of people over by the barn."

"I'll take care of them. Anybody between you and me?"

"Just one guy in the field that I can tell. I can take him if you get the people by the barn. I have to move to my right."

"All right. That's the plan. Stand by."

The grenades were old, with a rounded belly and a lever at the side. They looked like Chinese Type 541s, an old but steady design.

I stuffed a couple in my pockets, then took a pair and ran to the back of the truck. Slinging my MP5 over my shoulder, I held both grenades firmly, one in each hand, then hooked out their respective pins with my forefingers.

It would have been cooler to use my teeth, I know.

"Fire in the hole!" I yelled to Shotgun, tossing a pair at the cluster of soldiers at the front of the truck. Then I turned and bounded across the field in two steps, diving headfirst to the ground to avoid the shock of the explosion.

The grenades exploded in a loud double bang. The pops were loud, but a little hollow, and I realized instantly they were practice grenades, "bangers" designed to scare people into paying attention, but without a fatal payload.

I gave myself another kick in the rump for not inspecting them more closely as the air filled with lead.

Shotgun, meanwhile, had risen a half second after the grenades went off and shot the man in front of him. He quickly ducked back down as the fusillade continued, the gunners happily aiming in his direction as well as mine.

"We got them right where we want them, Dick," he said over the radio. "L-shaped assault."

He was calling for a standard small unit maneuver, where an enemy is engaged on two fronts; looked at from above, it appears as if the attacking forces form an L, with the enemy locked in the middle between them.

I swung back around, moving parallel to the road. Trotting some twenty yards, I hunkered as low as possible, held my breath, and sprinted back across. Concentrating solely on Shotgun, the thugs didn't see me as I crawled into position to ambush them. I waited until four or five of them paused to reload. Then I rose and got off a mag's worth of bullets before dropping again to reload.

One of the lights above the barn in the front had been shot out, but there was more than enough light to see the bodies scattered on the ground. A few were moving around, but we'd clearly taken down between two-thirds and three-quarters of the group.

I don't care who you are: seeing that many of your friends and comrades cut down puts a crimp in your confidence. The boys who were left alive were just looking for a way to get the hell out of there. The shots they'd been pouring into the field near Shotgun hadn't been particularly accurate; they were aiming with their fear, not their eyes.

As a lull set in, Shotgun worked his way forward on his elbows, dragging his body forward in the field and waiting for a clear shot.

Looking for a target myself, I fantasized about grabbing one or two of these bozos and presenting them to the secretary of State. In fact, I might not even deliver him to her—better to deposit him in the middle of the

Senate rotunda, just in time for a tasty committee hearing on border issues or terrorism.

There's nothing like a little overconfidence to set you up for a good swift kick in the rear, which was promptly administered in the form of a large caliber machine gun. The gun began chewing up the ground behind me a second before I could yell at them to surrender.

The shots came from a Browning M2 fifty-caliber, an old but remarkably effective weapon that was being fired across the roof of a pickup truck that had come down the road behind me.

The pickup bounced up and down, making the machine gun particularly difficult to aim—a good thing as far as I was concerned. I scrambled back toward the truck, temporarily routed.

About five yards from the rear, I tripped and fell. My MP5 clattered away in the dirt. Some of the men by the barn, courage rallied by the arrival of reinforcements, rose and began firing in earnest. The pickup truck pulled sideways across the road. The man with the machine gun swung it around. The weapon made an awful sound as it fired, clunking and vibrating while its bullets sprayed in a wide and unfocused arc.

The gunner paused, undoubtedly to rearrange his gun. I scrambled forward, grabbed the MP5, and fired in his direction.

Actually, that's what I wanted to do. I definitely pressed the trigger, but nothing came out. I'd apparently shot myself empty and not realized it in the heat of the battle.

Now it was a race—which one of us would get his gun loaded and set first?

As I fumbled for a fresh magazine, a black shadow

appeared behind the truck. It was a car, but it looked like a dive bomber come to earth, cruising toward its target. A second later it hit the truck broadside, tossing the machine gunner and his assistant out as the vehicle spun wildly to the side.

I pushed the magazine home. Pumping bullets into the two men who'd been tossed from the back of the pickup, I started running toward the car. The door to the pickup opened; I put a couple of bursts into it, and the man behind it slumped down to the ground.

The driver already lay lifeless against the steering wheel.

A few yards away, Veronica stumbled out of the rental, which she had just used to upend the machine gunner by crashing into the pickup. The air bags had deployed; her face had been burned from the bag as it went off, and her right knee was bruised, but otherwise she seemed intact.

Dazed, but intact.

"Dick?" she said. "Dick?"

"It's all right. I'm right here," I told her.

"Did I get them?"

"You got them. Good work," I said. I grabbed hold of her and pulled her to the ground behind the car.

"Dick?"

"How many fingers?" I asked, holding up my hand.

"Two?"

"Close enough. Stay here until I come back for you. It won't be long."

By the time I got back to the big two-and-a-half-ton trucks, Shotgun had come up through the field and taken out the rest of the tangos. He stood in front of the barn, gun dangling at his side, surveying his handiwork.

He looked a little sad. Depressed even.

"I think we got them all," he muttered. "But my bag of potato chips got crushed."

"I'll buy you a case as soon as we reach the States," I told him.

[VIII]

WE HAD KILLED a lot of people—twenty-six to be exact. But two men had apparently managed to escape over the hills in the direction of the condo development; Junior could see them clearly on the Bird's feed. A third figure was on the road heading away from the house. He too had probably been with the tangos, maybe in the house, and was now making a getaway.

There wasn't a lot to be done about any of them. Calling the Mexicans would have been a waste of time. And while we were close to the border, no U.S. agency was going to cross it on my say-so.

The two men heading toward the development were my main concern. I estimated it would take the two men a good half hour to reach the development; at that point we might have another ten minutes to get the hell out of there before cartel members or whoever was helping these bastards sent someone to find out what had happened.

"Twenty minutes," I told Shotgun. "We have twenty minutes to look for anything useful. Don't waste your time figuring out what it is—just pile it in the back of the truck."

"Anything?"

"Anything nonedible."

"Man, you are in a bad mood."

Veronica was still a little woozy from the crash. I helped her into the cab of the third truck, the one I had found the grenades in.

"You're a gentleman," she said. "You know you're a lot nicer than you let on at first."

"Don't let it get around," I told her, going over to check on Shotgun.

All of our guys take a special lock-picking course taught by a former Christian In Action agent in New Orleans. Generally, the first or second lock they learn to pick is a Yale lock similar to the ones that were securing the building—not because they're particularly easy to pick (they're not hard), but because they're ubiquitous. I would say that a good three-quarters of the padlocks I've encountered in my travels have been made by Yale.

Nice lock. But when you get so much practice picking it . . .

Shotgun has been through the course three times—they serve a wicked po'boy in the bar next to the building where class is held. I would venture to say he could have picked it in five seconds flat if he wanted.

Instead, he got it open in about two, counting the time it took him to retrieve his gun from his holster.

Blammm. Blammm.

"They're making these better and better," he said, pulling the broken lock away. "Took me two shots."

"It helps if you hit the metal."

We rolled the door to the side and found the light switch on the wall to the left.

The interior of the building was set up like a cheap movie studio or soundstage, with canvas and sheetrock walls mounted on two-by-four frames and arranged to form the outlines of a building.

"Practicing a D.A.," said Shotgun. "What were they going for?"

(A D.A. is a "direct action," a term used for a strike against a house or some other small target. It's slightly more generic than, say, "snatch and grab," which would be an operation to, duh, retrieve a particular individual. A snatch is a D.A.; a D.A. is not necessarily a snatch. And then you have operations like the bin Laden raid, which are BFWs for the good guys—*big fucking wins!*—and damn good work too, I might add.)

I looked at the layout. It was pretty generic—it could have been a large house, it could have been a small office building. It could have been an office suite. Whatever the target, they had been quite serious about what they were doing—there were bullet holes and scorch marks on the walls.

There were some weapons and uniforms hanging on a rack at the back. Besides a range of Mexican army trousers and shirts, there were several uniforms of Arizona and New Mexico state troopers. There were even Smokey the Bear-style trooper hats on a rack next to them.

"Hey, who wears a blue uniform?" asked Shotgun, pulling out a jacket from a nearby box.

"About half the police agencies in the hemisphere," I told him.

There were a dozen jackets, and a similar number of shirts and pants in the boxes next to it. Another box held an assortment of hats and caps. The guys who were working here had the raw material to disguise themselves as just about any police agency they wanted.

They had a decent amount of arms, too, stacked in a row of lockers against the wall behind the area that was used for mock attacks. The men who'd been in the trucks outside had all had AK47s. There were a few more inside, but they were in the minority. There were a handful of FX-05 Xiuhcoatls recently introduced to the Mexican army. There were M16s similar to those we'd encountered earlier. More plentiful than either were AR15s—updated civilian versions of the M16 often used by police departments—and a surprisingly large stock of what were either Strum Ruger MP9 submachine guns or very good knockoffs.

Very compact, the MP9 can be thought of as an improved Uzi. With a thirty-two-bullet magazine, it fires 9mm bullets from a closed bolt. It has a telescoping, paratrooper-type stock and is very small, adding to its utility.

There were other weapons as well, a veritable smorgasbord that included shotguns and grenade launchers.

So were these guys Hezbollah?

They were definitely Arab, but there was no way to know their actual affiliation. They hadn't posted any large flags or pictures of their leaders on the wall—how very inconsiderate of them.

We ran upstairs but the loft was empty.[23]

"Put one more load of guns in the truck, then grab some pictures on your cell phone," I told Shotgun. "Get

---

[23] For my fans who make the annual Rogue Warrior Musters at Fort A.P. Hill: it looked like a cheaper, plainer version of the lodge we use there.

pictures of all the people outside. I'm going up to the house."

"All of them?"

"As many as you can. Get moving. We have maybe ten minutes to finish up."

THE MAIN HOUSE was set up as a dormitory, with a great room and a large, country-style kitchen downstairs, then a number of bedrooms behind them and upstairs. Bunks were stacked tightly in the rooms, four units high; you had to squeeze in to fit, and God help you if you sneezed in the middle of the night.

Or I should say, Allah help you.

There were plenty of signs that the majority if not all of the men who'd been staying here were Muslim, starting with the Korans that we found in nearly every bunk.

Most of the Korans were stamped on the inside cover with an insignia showing where they had come from. The marks had a green gun raised by a fist — Hezbollah's flag.

Pay dirt.

There were videotapes as well. I grabbed a pillowcase and threw in a bunch, then continued searching through the house. The front room upstairs had been set up as an office; there were two computers and a bunch of CDs. I threw the CDs into my makeshift bag and started ransacking the drawers. I found stacks of forms — driver license applications, various substitute IDs. There was a folder with Social Security numbers and related information. There were also credit cards.

When the bag was stuffed, I ran downstairs. Shotgun had just pulled up with the truck.

"I got some grenade launchers," he said, hopping out. "Couldn't resist the heavy artillery."

"Two computers upstairs," I told him. "Grab the CPUs."

I glanced at my watch. Twenty minutes had passed since we'd begun searching the building.

Veronica was sitting in the cab, still a little winded. She nodded when I asked if she was OK, but her eyes were unfocused.

A shot of Dr. Bombay would have straightened her right out, but there was none nearby.

"Junior, what's going on?" I asked over the radio.

"The two guys are just about at the condo development."

"What about the other guy?"

"Lost him. I couldn't cover both."

"All right. Follow the other two and see where they go. We'll hit that tomorrow. I want to get some of this stuff back. Yell at me if they rally their troops."

"You got it."

I met Shotgun in the front room. He had both computers in his arms—and a twelve-pack of Coors on top of them.

"Found these in the fridge," he said cheerfully. "I thought Muslims weren't supposed to drink."

"They're not supposed to blow people up either. Doesn't seem to stop them."

Upstairs, I pulled open a file cabinet and saw a bunch of papers. The writing was all in Arabic. I piled them on the desk.

"How we doing on time?" called Shotgun, trotting up the stairs.

"We're leaving. I need something to put all these papers in. Look around for a box or something."

"Will a briefcase do?" he yelled.

"Great."

"Whole bunch of them in this closet," he said from the other room. He came in with two. When he opened it, we saw there was a laptop inside.

"Bonus!" said Shotgun. He reached for it. "Hey, you think we can get the Internet?"

"There's no time to screw around. Grab whatever you can and let's get the hell out of here."

"Roger that. Man, I'm hungry."

I stuffed the papers in the cases, piled more on top, then ran down the stairs. Shotgun followed, four more briefcases in his arms.

We threw everything in the back, then ran up to the cab.

"Anybody coming for us?" I asked Junior over the radio.

"Not that I see."

"Good. Where are they?"

"They ran into the development. But they didn't go into any of the units, or the community center. They went into the sewer."

"The sewer?"

"Yeah. Down a manhole."

"Can you download the image to my sat phone?"

"Uh, stand by."

I fiddled with the phone. Unlike in the cellular world, there are no cool Apple iSatPhones — yet. The interface on my phone was clunky, and the screen was fairly small. The keyboard on the front—the phone looks a bit like a RIM BlackBerry on steroids—was convenient, but not particularly accommodating for thick fingers like mine.

"Doesn't look like much," I told Junior. "This manhole cover?"

"Yeah. They put it back on."

I zoomed out. The manhole was in the street a block south of Veronica's grandparents' home, a block from the southern end of the development. It didn't seem to make sense, though—it was an odd place to put a hideout.

"Shit," said Junior.

"What's that?"

"You got two police trucks heading your way on the main road. They'll be there in four or five minutes, max."

"All right, we'll go the other way," I said, laying on the horn. Shotgun ran out of the building, his arms full. "Let's go. Get in the back."

He jumped in and I threw the truck in reverse, backing up the hill to the path that ran from the north side of the compound. The first hundred feet or so were rough; I lost the road, rumbling through a shallow ravine before finally regaining the path.

I'd started climbing the hill in earnest, gaining speed, when I heard Junior curse again.

"Shit, shit—I moved the Bird south to see the police. Damn."

"What's up?" I asked.

"You got two security SUVs coming up that dirt road you're on. They're maybe two minutes away."

As always, Junior was being ridiculously optimistic: headlights were already streaking up the hillside.

[IX]

I'VE ALWAYS BELIEVED that the best defense is a good offense.

There's a corollary to that—you can never actually have too much of a good offense.

Or too many grenades. Especially when Shotgun is handling the launcher.

He cut a hole in the canvas back of the M35 two-and-a-half-ton truck (aka deuce and a half to us old-timers) and set himself up in the back, turning the troop truck into something like a medium tank, sans armor. He rigged an M249 submachine gun in place, threading it with one of the ammo belts we'd found in the house. The grenade launcher—an M79 stand-alone, truly a classic—had to be held by hand. Shotgun saw this as an asset—he armed himself with seven launchers, strapping three over each shoulder and holding a seventh in his hands.

The launcher has a safety, but I was damn sure to avoid as many potholes as possible as we drove out the front gate and started to accelerate. I had the lights off, which added a bit of difficulty to the navigation. Veronica, leaning forward against the windshield, tried helping.

"Curve to the right coming up," she said. "Watch the fence—big boulders on your left. Oh, shit."

We glanced off the boulders as I took the turn a bit too fast. "Just tell me how far they are from us," I said.

"A thousand meters. Seven hundred. They're moving pretty fast."

"Shotgun, you ready?"

"Born ready, boss."

The SUVs had their lights on, and I could see the advancing halos as we started down a particularly steep part of the road.

Something thumped above me. Shotgun had fired the grenade launcher.

The missile hit a rock outcropping just ahead of us to the left, spraying shards of rock in the air. As they splattered across the windshield and hood I involuntarily flinched, pushing the truck to the right and sending my back wheels half off the road. By the time I corrected, the SUVs were only about a hundred yards away.

Thump-thump! FRUUUU-KKKKK. Poooooghhhhh.

Shotgun's next grenade flew into the windshield of the lead SUV. It exploded with a flash and the front end burst immediately into flames.[24] The grenade that followed sailed over the second vehicle, exploding harmlessly to the right. The next hit the road, lifting the front end of its target a foot or so before blowing out its tires.

I'm not sure where the other grenades went, since I was too busy trying to steer around the flaming SUV while staying more or less on the road. The M35 is many things, but I would never compare its handling to a sports car. I grazed the front bumper of the SUV as I struggled to keep the truck on the road. I didn't think much of that until I heard Shotgun say over the radio that we were on fire.

The next thing I heard was the gentle pitter-patter of

---

[24] The grenade seems to have ignited something flammable; either one of the men in the front had whiskey breath, or they used a cheap ten-minute-lube place that left the engine streaked with oil.

bullets ripping the crap out of the passenger side of the truck. A few seconds of wild confusion followed, as I tried simultaneously to hunker down, steer, and push Veronica below the dash. The result was that I didn't see the second SUV until its side loomed a few yards in front of me. At that point, I had only two choices:

a) hit the brakes and very possibly roll the truck, or
b) nail the accelerator and push the SUV out of the way.

Easy decision.

Head-butted off the side of the road, the SUV shot over the sharp drop at the side of the road and began rolling sideways down the hill. Our truck, meanwhile, continued straight down the road at what now seemed like a ridiculously fast speed. I slapped at the brakes with little success, trying to slow our momentum in time to take yet another sharp turn in the hills. Once again I couldn't hold the road; my front right tire went off into the ditch and as I jerked to pull it back, the rear of the truck flew out behind me. The wheels sailed over a bump and for a long moment I thought we were going to flip. But the truck managed to find its feet, and glided, more or less, to a stop as the hard-pack ended in a broad, pockmarked field just beyond the edge of the development.

Did I mention we had caught fire?

"Out! Out!" I yelled at Veronica, before realizing she was already on her way. I grabbed at the door handle and jumped out as flames started shooting by the side window. I'm not sure whether they treat the canvas of those trucks with fireproof material or if it just burns funny, but the flames on back of the truck were a strange orange that I'd never seen before. Rather than forming your classic tongues and triangles, they looked like furled towels, flapping slightly on the side of the vehicle.

I ran to the back. Shotgun was busy firing at some of the tangos who'd managed to get out of the second SUV before we hit it.

"Get out!" I shouted.

"We got one more," he answered.

Something tinged nearby. It wasn't until then that I realized we were under fire.

A long burst from Shotgun put an end to that. I reached up to pull him out, when there was a loud *swoosh* and a fog enveloped me. Heptafluoropropane or some other environmentally proper alternative to Halon whooshed over the back and side of the truck, beating the crap out of the flames.

Veronica wielded the hose on the extinguisher like a pro, attacking the flames at their base and snuffing the strange orange curls into black and green knots of smoke. She got me and Shotgun for good measure, and we coughed our way over to the side of the road.

The front end of the truck had been mangled so badly that it was undrivable, even by me.

"We're going to have to set up another ambush," I told Shotgun between coughs. I was hacking like a three-pack-a-day smoker. "We can get above them on this hill as they come over it, fire down. We'll take out their trucks."

When I went to call Junior on the radio, I realized my radio had come undone somewhere along the way. I fished around for it, and found the wires dangling apart.

I reconnected them, and Junior's voice practically exploded in my ear.

"They're turning around, they're turning around," he said.

"What are you talking about?"

"Dick, do you hear me?"

"Yeah, I hear you."

"I've been trying to tell you—the two police cars backed up as soon as they saw the bodies on the ground. They got the hell out of there."

"All right. Good."

"Are you all right? I saw you guys get out of the truck, but then the radios started fuzzing out."

"Yeah, yeah, we're good. See if you can get Shunt to tap into the police network and find out what's going on."

"Uh, OK. You already gave him a lot of stuff to do."

"Tell him to close out one of his chat-room feeds and he'll have plenty of time."

Shunt is brilliant when it comes to computers, but he's probably the only human being alive who believes those pop-up windows saying LonelyHeartXXXX is looking for love in his hometown. He routinely keeps a dozen chats going, claiming it's his way of giving back.

"Slide the Bird back over the condos and find out what's going on," I told Junior. "We'll go out that way—I'll steal a car."

"On it."

Between the computers and everything else we'd taken, we had far too much to carry down with us. We left the guns and ammo, but took everything else over to a nook on the hillside about fifty yards off the road. I stacked a bunch of guns and ammo there as well.

"Don't call attention to yourself," I told Shotgun. "If somebody comes, you stay down and be quiet. Firing at them is only a last resort."

"Got it."

"Swear to it."

I'm not saying he has an itchy trigger finger, but . . . he has an itchy trigger finger.

"I swear," said Shotgun. "On my last bag of Cheetos."

"I'll be back with a car as soon as I can. If something goes wrong with the radio, I'll pull up in front of the truck and blink twice. Wait for me to come to you."

I turned to go back down the hill. Veronica started walking with me.

"No, no," I told her. "You stay with Shotgun. It'll be a lot safer."

"I know this place better than you," she told me, continuing ahead.

"I'm only going to steal a car."

"That's fine. I can do that."

"Listen—"

"At a minimum, you need a lookout. Besides, I'm better with my hands than you."

I never argue with a woman who says that.

THE BEST CAR to steal is the easiest car to steal. We climbed the hill overlooking the condos and headed toward the dead end at the east, where I had seen two cars parked outside. The street was parallel and one over to the one where Veronica's grandparents had lived. It was also, by coincidence, the one where the two tangos had disappeared into the sewer.

Since we were going there anyway, it made sense to take advantage of the opportunity and scout the manhole. I could do that while Veronica stole the car—assuming her bragging was backed up by facts.

"I wasn't kidding," she said as we entered a backyard near the street. "I can steal cars. I learned from the best."

"The FBI antitheft ring?"

"Hell no. When I was undercover I met Candyman Lopez, the Detroit junkyard king."

The Candyman had a hefty procurement chain to supply his salvaged parts business. Veronica immediately ticked off the procedures for jumping the two pickups on the street.

"Which one do you want, white or brown?"

"White. Brown's never done much for me."

I waited until she got close to the truck. Then I slipped out to the middle of the street and had a look at the manhole.

Why exactly would a condo development that covered far less than a square mile need a storm sewer system so large that it required manholes?

Answer: it wouldn't. Especially in the desert.

So to my mind, the hole had to be the entrance to some sort of underground hiding place, or maybe a way of getting into one of the nearby houses without being seen from above. Unfortunately, the only way to find out was to look.

I got down on my knees, and using the barrel of my submachine—heresy, I know—I pried the cover up and slid it to the side.

The tunnel was dark. I stuck my head down, but couldn't hear anything.

Obviously, more research was needed.

"Veronica, how are we doing?" I asked over the radio.

"I just got to the truck," she said.

"I'm going to go down the sewer hole here and see what I see."

"Do you think that's wise?"

"No. Bring the truck around and wait for me near the hole, OK? I'm not sure how the reception will be once I'm down there."

"Well, don't get lost."

"I'm not planning on it."

I found a metal rung ladder on the side and went down a few steps, pausing and listening. The hole was dark, and smelled about the way you would expect a drainage tunnel to smell. I took the night-vision binos from the pack and cinched the MP5 tight against my shoulder.

Starting down, I realized I'd been spending a lot of time in sewers since coming to Mexico. There was something appropriate in that.

Every time you descend into the darkness, you're one unlucky kiss of Murphy away from getting your head shot off. But Murph must have gone to bed, exhausted from his various hijinks back at the farm. No one grabbed my leg as I stepped down off the ladder into the large tunnel beneath the street. No one came at me from behind with an ax, and no bullets whizzed past my face. Nothing, in fact, happened.

What a letdown.

The tunnel I descended into ended a few yards to my right in a thick block wall. It extended to the north, bending downward and then twisting to the left. It looked exactly like a storm sewer, right down to the slime-green liquid—I won't call it water—coating the bottom and the red eyes of sewer rats, or other suitably disgusting vermin, near the curve.

I held my breath so I could hear any faint echo in the distance. Lingering runoff from the earlier rain dripped somewhere nearby; the only other sound was the light scratch of a rodent looking for food.

Holding the MP5 ready, I started walking as quietly as I could. The floor of the tunnel, constructed of cement bricks, was pitched so that the crown was dry. I turned my feet sideways to get slightly better traction and lessen the chance of landing on my butt, which had already taken more than enough abuse for the week. I used the night binos to see, which slowed me down some and made it a little harder to keep my balance.

As I came to the curve, I noticed that there was a bulkhead door to the right. This was not unlike the sort of full height hatchway you would find in, say, a submarine. It had a large wheel in the middle, which turned a set of arms that latched into the top, bottom, and sides of the frame. It had a chain lock on it, the sort you might use to keep a bike secure (well, almost secure) in a city.

By my reckoning, the portal was about where Veronica's grandparents' house would be. The fact that it was locked from this side meant that the two tangos who'd run from us hadn't gone there.

I continued down the tunnel, walking another thirty or forty yards. I passed two more locked portals before the tunnel angled sharply to the left.

Until now the tunnel had been empty, except for the slimy water and the rodents. The floor was solid brick, the walls concrete block. While the width varied a bit, I would say it was always in the area of six feet, just wide enough so that I could barely touch or barely miss the sides. After this turn, the tunnel straightened and widened to roughly eight feet. There were grooves in the center of the floor. My first thought was that they were for drainage, but as I studied the area ahead I saw what looked like a low-rise coal car in the tunnel. The wheels beneath it fit into the grooves. I walked toward it slowly, not exactly sure what I'd stumbled on: an ancient Inca subway system?

More like a tunnel to the border.

But that was a mile away. Would they really burrow that far?

I looked at the car doubtfully. It was made of wood, sturdy two-by-eight planks fitted as the floor and sides. There was no engine, and the tunnel didn't smell of diesel or gasoline.

A metal panel about the size of a garage door was hung on rails at the side. It had a chain lock like the hatchways I'd seen earlier, fastened to a set of thick steel loops top and bottom. I went over and put my ear against the panel, thinking maybe I'd hear something. But all I could hear was my own heart, pounding away in my chest.

I'd been down for a long while — too long, really. I tried checking in with Veronica but couldn't reach her. I turned and began making my way back as quickly as I could.

Moonlight streamed down from the two small pry holes as I approached, dust drifting in the shaft of yellow-silver light. I stopped, suddenly wary.

"Veronica, are you there?" I asked over the radio.

There was no answer.

The rungs felt cold to the touch. I went up slowly, keeping the gun ready. I pushed the edge of the cover up tentatively, looking around. The moon was strong enough that I didn't need the glasses. Not seeing anything, I lowered the cover and tried on the other side.

Nothing. But it would be easy enough to stand across the street in the shadows.

I climbed up a rung, put my shoulder to the cover, then jerked it upward, ready and yet not really ready at the same time. That one last instant before something happens is a mix of anticipation and adrenaline, with a sprinkling of fear. It comes, it hits you; you push through it.

Nothing.

I took a breath of fresh air and looked around. There was no one there: no Veronica, no phony Mujahedeen, no cartel slugs, no development security people.

Climbing up out of the sewer, I saw the nearby houses were all dark, the street deserted. I slid the sewer cover back into place and ran over to the side of the nearest unit.

"Veronica?" I said over the radio.

This time, Shotgun came on the circuit. "Dick, what's going on?"

"I'm looking for my ride," I told him. "Did she drive up to you?"

"Negative."

"She say anything?"

"Hasn't been on the air that I heard. You need me?"

"Stay with the stuff," I told him.

A rock or something was kicked nearby.

I raised my gun and took a step back, staring at the edge of the building. When nothing appeared, I backed around the side of the condo, turned the corner, then ran as fast as I could to the other side. I came up to the front, where I saw a figure crouched on the lawn, head swiveling slowly as he looked toward the side of the building where I'd been.

His back was turned.

My first two steps were slow and stealthy. The next two were quicker, and probably not as quiet. I took another but my foot hit a soft piece of turf; off balance, my other foot fell harder and louder than I wanted.

From that point on I just ran as fast as I could. The man started to rise and turn. I pulled up my gun to give him a muzzle strike in the skull. Just before I hit him, his hands flew out to his sides.

"Mr. Marcinko!" the man yelled. "Don't hit me! It's—"

That was about all Saul got out of his mouth before I clocked him. I'm sorry to say that I got him pretty hard, even though I pulled back at the last moment and managed to get him with my forearm rather than the gun. That was a good thing: the muzzle would have split his skull; my arm only knocked him unconscious.

"I KNOW WHERE the lady is," were the first words out of Saul's mouth when he came to in his truck a few minutes later. He'd parked down the street; I'd hauled him there over my back after making sure we were alone.

"Tell me."

"If I help you find her, will you help us?"

"I won't kill you. How's that?"

He gulped, the way villains do in old-fashioned movies. But he stuck with his agenda.

"A deal's a deal," he said. "I help you and you help me."

"We don't have a deal," I told him. "You tell me where Veronica is, and I won't kill you. That's the deal."

"W-w-we want the same thing," stammered Saul. "To get rid of the cartel."

"That's not my goal here, Saul. I just want Veronica."

"She's in the community building. Will you help me now?"

"How many people are in there?"

"Four."

"Four? You're sure?"

"Yes."

"How do you know?"

"I . . ."

He didn't, not really. He was guessing. But it wasn't a bad guess. He'd seen the two SUVs leave and not return, and knew from experience they drove around in pairs. With eight men on, that left four at the security post.

There was a police-style scanner and radio under his dash. He turned up the volume and hit some buttons to make it scan, but there was no traffic.

"What happened to those SUVs?" I asked, not telling him that I knew very well what had happened to them. "Did they radio back?"

"Not that I heard. In the hills the radio has trouble

transmitting. So maybe they did call back and I didn't hear."

I drove around the development. The lights were on in the security station on the first floor of the community center. There was a single SUV parked in front of the door; three more were in the back, lined up side by side.

"Call them on the radio and tell them you found an intruder," I told Saul.

He reached for the mike.

"Wait—let me get into position first." I put my finger in his face. "Give me ten minutes. On the dot. You double-cross me, Saul, and I'll get you. Even if I have to come back as a ghost."

"I'm, I'm, I'm not going to double-cross you. We have a deal."

I slipped out of the truck and ran through the backyards of the units until I got to the community center. Sneaking to the patrol SUVs in the back of the building, I knifed the front and rear tires of each. Serenaded by the satisfying hiss and gentle thud as they settled onto their rims, I trotted over to the building, peering into a lit basement window.

Veronica was sitting at a table, arms crossed, a scowl on her face. Two thugs were with her, Mexican rent-a-cop types, in this case rented, bought, and wholly owned by the cartel.

Before I could crouch down and get a better view, I heard a sound from around the corner. I went over and saw one of the security types walking out toward the SUVs. Sizing him up—skinny little runt, easily handled—the door opened again.

Unsheathing my knife, I waited as a second officer gathered his gear, pulling a large duffel bag and a soft-sided tool kit out from the vestibule. He shouldered the duffel on his left side and picked up the tool kit with his right, then began slowly walking from the building.

I caught him after a few feet. He was as tall as the other man was short, and I actually had to reach up quite a bit as I got my knife into his throat. This had the unfortunate effect of making the blood spurt even more wildly; I hate an untidy execution.

The other guard remained stubbornly oblivious, not only of what was happening to his partner, but of the fact that the SUV had four flats. He got in, started the vehicle, adjusted his seat belt, and fiddled with the gear. By the time he glanced into his rearview mirror, I had already dropped his partner and run up to the side of the truck.

I rapped on the window. Surprised, he rolled it down.

Two fists to the face stunned him. I reached in, pulled his head through the opening, and gave him two more for good measure. I hauled him out of the truck, pulled him around an electric utility box a few yards away, and slit his throat. While he bled out, I retrieved his partner, dragging him across the yard and dumping him behind the box as well.

By the time I got back to the window of the room where Veronica was, the two guards had changed position. They were talking to her, but whatever they were saying didn't make much of an impression. She sat stone-faced, staring at the table.

Finally, one of the thugs got up and left the room.

Twenty or thirty seconds passed before Veronica rose. Her hands went to her hips, and she thrust her boobs out — from where I was squatting, it looked like she was propositioning her guard.

Maybe it looked that way inside, too. The man started to rise, reaching his hand out toward her.

The next thing I knew, she had flipped him over the table and given his head two quick heel kicks. She grabbed his pistol, then ran to the door in time to bash the other guard as he ran inside.

Pretty stupid of them to bring their weapons in while interrogating a prisoner, but these guys weren't exactly the sharpest tools in the shed.

I tapped on the window. Veronica twirled around, pistol in two hands, braced to fire.

"Just me," I said. "Good work."

She couldn't hear me through the glass, but pointed to the side, mouthing the words "Meet me."

MAYBE IT TOOK ninety seconds for me to get there. I was still feeling a little winded; carving my name into veins takes a bit out of me. But I didn't dally. Still, by the time I got there, not only had Veronica caught the other rent-a-slime, but she'd trussed him and the other man with their own zip ties. There was a holding cell at the far end of the basement; we carried them there and tossed them in. (The second guard woke about halfway down the hall; a kick on the side of the head put him back to sleep. I may market it as a replacement for Ambien.)

"You have blood on you, you know," said Veronica, pulling the cell door closed and making sure it was locked.

"I cut someone shaving."

"Shame."

I went out in the hall and looked around. The offices

were new and clean, but mostly empty. There were no computers in the main dispatching center; the only thing there was the radio, a simple affair that looked about twenty years old at least. The underground garage was empty.

The walls flanking the ramp entrance were made of large cement blocks. Where had I seen those before?

Duh — down in the tunnel.

I walked to the wall opposite the entry ramp to the garage and examined it. Unlike the other walls, this was a veneer panel, the sort of thing your great-uncle installed in his basement "man cave" back in the 1970s to lend a little "class" to the joint.

Since when did garages need class?

I pushed on it. It gave a little. I fiddled some more, gently pushing.

"I found the cell keys," said Veronica, coming over after searching the main security office. "Are you sure we shouldn't take one of the goons with us and question him?"

I was too engrossed in the wall to answer.

"What are you doing to the wall, Dick?"

"Lifting it." I spread my fingers like a wide receiver trying to grab an errant pass, then pushed upward. The wood panel moved, revealing . . . not the wall, but a panel of metal slats similar to the panels used by merchants to protect their storefronts on city streets.

"What's in there?" asked Veronica.

"Probably the tunnel I was in." I worked out the direction. "It comes up the road, angles over here. It would go right past your grandparents' house."

"Can we get out that way?"

"It's locked on the other side."

The radio cackled. Saul was making a call, trying to be cool, I think, but warn us at the same time.

"Unit Patrol to Base. Base, do you read Unit Patrol? Base?"

I went up to the dispatcher's area and picked up the microphone.

"We're in control, Saul. You can relax."

"Did you hear that last transmission on channel ninety-eight-seven?"

"I didn't hear anything."

"They're trying to get the security headquarters—it's the Mexican police. The real police."

The phone started to ring.

"Say you're the dispatcher," I told Veronica. "Find out what's up."

I left Veronica to handle the call while I went back to the cells and considered her suggestion that we take one of the lugs to interrogate. Both were sleeping soundly. Which was more likely to talk?

More importantly, which was less likely to lie?

I did a quick eenie-meenie, then chose the bigger of the two. In my experience, the old cliché—*the bigger they are, the harder they fall*—speaks true.

I dragged him out of the cell and relocked it. There was a restroom next door; I figured a good dunk or two in the toilet would revive him.

"Dick—we have to go," said Veronica.

"What's up?"

"The local police unit says there's been reports of shooting at the farm. They're sending people there."

"They've been there already," I told her.

"They say they're sending people now. They're calling in the army, too. I tried to find out what else they knew, but they started asking questions about who I was. I told them I was new. I don't know if they believed me."

I HATE LEAVING a jigsaw puzzle half finished on the table. To me, once you have the four corners figured out, there's no sense not putting the rest of the damn thing together.

Here, an immense jigsaw puzzle was staring us in the face. There were all sorts of pieces out, little clusters of answers and half-answered riddles scattered. I just needed a little more time—a few dunks with my friend here and I was sure to get the sides worked out.

But it was clearly time to go.

"ALL RIGHT," I said. "Here, take my gun."

I gave her the MP5, and repositioned my pistol so it couldn't be easily grabbed by anyone other than me, and even then I'd have to unsnap the tie-down. Then I went into the cell and scooped up our prisoner.

I bent about four or five inches straight down under his weight as I walked out. "Damn, he's heavy."

"You should take the other one. He barely weighed anything."

"It's my penance for using clichés," I told her, staggering toward the front of the building.

[H]

WHILE I'M GROANING my way out of the building, let's catch up with Trace and the boys.

The morning after they arrived, some relatives of the Garcias came over. After talking to them for a while, Trace decided that the Garcias would probably be about as safe as anyone in the village — not exactly the sort of ringing endorsement an insurance company would like to hear, but good enough. Sometime after mid-afternoon, she bid farewell and started northward with Tex and Stoneman. The plan was to go across the border and meet us at the ranch. At that point, we hadn't yet had any of the real fun and games that made my evening so memorable.

Trace was behind the wheel a short time later when a large tractor-trailer swerved in front of the car, nearly throwing her off the road. Once she recovered, she stepped on the gas and caught up. She was probably thinking about how she would extract some revenge from the driver when the truck swerved again, this time into the other lane. It narrowly missed another car, then pulled back in, once again cutting off another car.

Trace followed along for a few miles, her anger gradually diminishing. It seemed to her the truck driver was probably drunk, but that wasn't her concern. And while one of the final provisions of NAFTA had just been approved to allow Mexican truck drivers to drive as far through the U.S. as they wanted, Trace has never been much for political issues. "Screw them all, before they screw us," is about the extent of her political beliefs.

Gradually the distance between her and the truck increased until she couldn't see it anymore. Not too long afterward, she decided to find a place to stop to powder her nose.

Cars and trucks clustered at the side of the road ahead, spread in disorganized fashion near a large tent pavilion and a food stand. Trace parked at the very back of the line.

Leaving Stoneman sleeping in the back, she and Tex got out and stretched their legs. There was an outhouse beyond the tent; holding her nose, she went inside to inspect the facilities.

Tex, meanwhile, ambled over to the parked vehicles. There at the lead was the truck that had nearly run them off the road. Deciding to give the driver some friendly instructions on road etiquette, Tex's pace became somewhat more deliberate. But as he passed the back of the trailer, the sound of banging caught his attention. He stopped and listened. It sounded very much like someone was pounding on the inside of the trailer.

He went to the rear door and found it padlocked. Before he could satisfy his curiosity, the truck started moving.

"There you are," said Trace, coming up behind him. "What are you staring at?"

"I think there's people in the back of that trailer."

She rolled her eyes.

"I guess it's none of our business, huh?" added Tex.

The comment poked at Trace's conscience, but probably she would have simply dropped it had they not seen the truck stopped at a police roadblock a half hour later. By now, it was dusk, and the red lights of the police car threw strange shadows across the back of the vehicle and the road.

"That's that same truck," said Tex. "We oughta tell them to search the back."

"Yeah."

There were two policemen. One was talking to the truck driver; the other eyed the line of cars.

"You want me to try my Spanish?" asked Tex.

"I'll deal with it," said Trace. She left the car in park and got out.

"You should check the back of that truck," she told the policeman who was dealing with the traffic. He frowned at her and waved her back to her vehicle.

"Really, you should look in the back," insisted Trace.

The officer waved the other cars around the side of the roadblock, sending them on their way. The drivers happily ignored the rocks and ruts and sped off.

"There's something in the back of that truck," she told the policeman. "You should look into it."

"You are a Yankee," said the man. "Let me see your license."

"Are you going to check that trailer out or not?"

The cop whistled to his partner—then pulled his gun on Trace.

"You will show me your license, and pay a fine, or you will spend the next year in Mexico."

[41]

VERONICA RETRIEVED THE vehicle she had been stealing when surprised by the security thugs, returning with it while I bound our guest with a few more zip ties and gave him a gag for good measure: the last thing we needed was a backseat driver.

I appropriated some riot guns, tear gas, and tactical equipment from one of the security vehicles, sticking them in the pickup truck. I also found a mobile radio, charging in a cradle on the console between the front seats. All of this took time, and when I finally got into the pickup and closed the door, I could see the dim outline of a revolving red and blue bubblegum top coming up the hill from the Mexican village.

"Let's show them the way," I told Veronica.

My head flew backward as she stepped on the gas. I picked up the police radio and, holding my hand around the mike to add a little distortion to the ambience, announced that a patrol was en route to the camp via the off-road route.

The police closed in on us as Veronica found the trail. I had my MP5 on my lap, ready to use it, but they hung back, no doubt believing we were who we said we were. They slowed down when we slowed down — which was a little disappointing, as I was itching to show the MP5's effectiveness when used as a turn signal.

"Shotgun, we're coming up the road toward you," I told him over the team radio.

"Yeah, I can see the lights. How come you get to have all the fun?"

"We're in the pickup. We're the first car through.

Take out the second. They're the ones with the bubble-gum lights."

"Gotcha."

We took the last switchback and started uphill. The troop truck sat off the side of the road to our left, its rear end off the road in the ditch, the front crushed and low against some rocks. It occurred to me that the police might stop and inspect the wreck; that would mess up my plan.

There was no need to worry with Shotgun on the trigger. A second later, a grenade swooshed overhead, exploding just in front of the vehicle behind us. The driver jerked off the side of the road, rolling the vehicle across the slope.

"One down, one to go," said Shotgun.

"Wait," I said. "Two vehicles? *Wait!*"

"Fire in the hole," he said, launching grenade number two.

"Stop! Stop!" I yelled, this time to Veronica. She slammed on the brakes and I bolted from the truck, running back to the second vehicle.

Saul's.

I found him barely conscious, about ten yards from the side of the road. The pickup was obliterated.

The police SUV was in better shape, its front end and cabin pretty much intact. The same could not be said for its two occupants. The grenade had exploded at the base of the windshield, and between that and the force of the rollover, the results were gruesome.

The word "mutilation" comes to mind. "Decapitation" as well. That's all I'll say.

Veronica helped me get Saul back to the pickup. He started moaning as we lifted him into the passenger seat.

"You're alive," said Veronica. "Don't try to move."

"I'm OK," he said. "I jumped."

"When?"

"As soon as that grenade hit the police truck, I knew I'd be next."

"Good guess," I told him.

"I wasn't guessing," he said. "I've read some of your books."

UNDER PERFECT CIRCUMSTANCES, we would have headed over to the border crossing, and there contacted the Border Patrol, Immigration, Customs, the National Guard, the U.S. Army, the FBI, and anybody else I could think of who might be interested in busting open a major case that tied terrorism and Mexico's biggest cartel together.

But perfect is a world we don't live in. And given the strength and financial resources of the cartel, I wasn't entirely sure who I could trust. So instead, we went to the motel where we'd faced down the iguana earlier, where I would have a little more leisure to consider my next moves. Instead of the iguana suite, we appropriated a pair of rooms on the back wing. The doors opened directly on a narrow concrete veranda, giving their occupants a lovely panorama of the glass-strewn parking lot.

I realize I've hurt the feelings of a whole lot of hardworking Border Patrol types, insulted half the Homeland Insecurity Department, and made mortal enemies of a union hall's worth of federal employees. Let me admit my remarks are not entirely fair: the *majority* of people who work on the border, in immigration, on counterterror, etc., etc., are honest and hardworking, and want to do the right thing. A good portion put their lives on the line every day to do just that.

But at that particular moment, I couldn't afford to take a chance on coming across the one or two bad apples I knew would be lingering in the barrel.

Besides, my guest had an appointment with a toilet bowl, and if I tried taking him across the border, he'd never be able to keep it.

"Nada!" he gurgled the second time I dunked him, headfirst into the fetid water in the motel bathroom's skanky toilet. "Nothing."

"I'm sure you're not that dumb," I told him in Spanish. I dunked him again. The water was clean, by the way—you have to leave some room for escalation.

"Nada! Nada! Nada!"

Again. This time I flushed. He gurgled a few curses, but we got nowhere.

He had taught me a few choice phrases relating ancestors and goats before finally agreeing to talk. I pulled him upright, threw a towel on his head, then dragged him back into the room. Shotgun and Veronica were both outside with Saul, keeping watch. It was roughly four in the morning.

"Tell me about the tunnel," I told him.

"A cigarette. I want a cigarette."

"You tell me about the tunnel, and I'll get you a cigarette." If he wanted to die an early death of lung cancer, who was I to argue?

He told me what I had already deduced—the tunnel had been built to get under the U.S. border. He wasn't sure how far it went, and claimed never to have been through to the other side himself. I prodded him a bit, satisfied myself that he was telling the truth, then changed the subject to the ragheads training at the farm.

"The foreigners we do not talk to," he told me. "Off-limits."

"Two of them came into town and went into the tunnel. Where did they go?"

"When did they come?"

"Tonight."

He shook his head. "I don't know. When did they go in the tunnel? We heard explosions at the camp. But we are never to go there. That is a strict order. Always."

We went back and forth like that, me probing, him denying. He was adamant that the camp was off-limits, and that even asking about it was dangerous. I believed him, more or less; clearly whoever had set up the camp wouldn't want some cartel rent-a-thug to be looking over his shoulder. The cartel leaders would only be too happy to pass along such orders — secrecy was in their best interests as well.

"What about my cigarette?" he said finally.

"Will it improve your memory?"

"I am telling you everything I know," he said, almost crying.

Nicotine addiction is a terrible thing.

I took some parachute cord and tied his feet to the chair. I secured the chair to the metal bed frame before going out and getting Shotgun to come in and watch him.

"Stand near the door," I told Shotgun. "With your gun on him. He moves out of line, shoot him. No questions, no second chance. Grin while I tell him what I just said in Spanish."

Shotgun beamed a thousand-watt shit-eater as I repeated the instructions. The Mexican nodded grimly before I was done.

Back outside, Veronica was sitting next to Saul on a pair of time-worn metal rocking chairs, gently extracting information from him. It seemed like a casual conversation on the surface, but as I listened I realized she had an agenda, doubling back to fill in holes and then giving the occasional poke when there was a discrepancy.

"You have a second?" I asked, signaling that I wanted to be alone.

She got up and we walked a few yards away.

"Get anything useful about your grandparents?" I asked her.

"Not really. He gave me the first names of the security staff he knows, including Paolo inside. Some information about how they staff and whatnot. But he doesn't know much. They were pretty good about shutting him off. He was the token white man."

"Sure." I mentioned before how pretty Veronica was. She was smart as well—you could hear the confidence in her voice, and tell from the way her eyes darted that she was curious about things. Those two traits don't make a person smart, but they lay the groundwork.

Are smarter women more attractive? Damned if I know—I love all women.

In a theoretical sense, of course.

"You're a pretty good interrogator," I told her.

"He's easy. He doesn't even know he's being questioned."

"You want to try with our friend inside? He claims he doesn't know anything about the camp. He's probably telling the truth, but maybe you'll have better luck."

"Sure."

"I told him I'd get him some cigarettes." I glanced across the street at the café. The place was closed, of course. "Think they have a computer in there?"

"Assuming they're owned by the cartel, they will," Veronica told me. "Everyone has to keep their records electronically."

"Aren't they afraid of the government getting a hold of them?"

It was a stupid question, and Veronica didn't even dignify it with an answer.

"WAIT UNTIL YOU get flashing green on the sat phone," Shunt told me over the cell phone. "Then hook the USB cord into the computer at the front. Be careful with the cover off. Don't touch anything metal."

"Like your head?" Shunt was walking me through the procedure to hook one of the terrorist CPU units into my sat phone so it could be used as a modem. I'd already connected the monitor and keyboard from the café's computer.

"My head is nonconducting," answered Shunt. "It's thick, too."

"Amen."

"Oh, good—here we go—I have the connection," said Shunt. "Go ahead and boot up the tango CPU."

It took a few seconds for the computer to do its thing.

"All right, I have you," Shunt told me finally. "You see the Windows splash?"

"It's asking for a password."

"Hang on."

The screen blanked. Back in New York, Shunt used one of his private-label software tools to take the pass-

word from the protected sector of the hard drive—or
at least that's what I think he was doing. I can't understand half of what he says.

The screen came up. There was an error message on
it, indicating the disc had a bad sector.

"These guys are decent," said Shunt. "*I* need you to
reboot, then press the F12 key as it comes up. If that
doesn't work, we'll get more complicated."

We went through the process three times, changing
small things until finally the regular screen came up.
But from that point, Shunt had the computer completely
under his control.

"Military-level encryption," he said. "They spent a
bundle."

"They have a bundle. Can you decode it?"

"Not a problem. That's why I get the big bucks. By
the way, would this be a good time to talk about my
raise?"

"It'd be an even better time to talk about kicking
your butt."

"Come to think of it, I'm pretty well paid for what
I do."

He is, actually.

THE ENCRYPTION GAVE Shunt a lot more trouble than
he was willing to admit. Used to having their networks
probed and compromised by the Israelis as well as U.S.
intelligence, the terrorists had employed several layers
of protection, and Shunt finally decided to mirror everything on the CPUs' hard drives into his system so he
could analyze it and attack it properly. While the data
was uploading, he had me reconnect the monitor and
keyboard to the computer in the bar. He took it over, and

within a few minutes used it to get inside the cartel's system.

"This is more like it. Tell me what you want."

"E-mail. Financial records. Connections with the terrorists. Payoffs to American officials — everything you can get."

"How about their instant messaging service? They use two."

"No Twitter account?"

"Haven't found one yet. Give me a few minutes."

While Shunt went to work, I went over to the cigarette machine. I didn't have the right change, but the machine didn't seem to mind once I broke the glass: it gave me all the cigarettes for free.

Our guest practically leapt out of his tie-downs when he saw the cigarette pack in my hand.

"Careful," I told him, glancing at Shotgun across the room. I put my hand on the Mexican's shoulder and pushed him back down. "You want to die of lung cancer, not lead poisoning."

I took out a cigarette and lit it for him. With his hands tied behind his back, he needed help smoking. I called Saul in and had him do the honors.

"He's not acting," she told me outside. "He doesn't know anything about the camp. They were told never to interfere. That's why they didn't go over in the first place."

"What about the tunnel?"

"The cartel uses it to move people and drugs over the border, but not too often. Dick, I think my grandparents are alive."

"Why?" I tried to keep my voice neutral, but her frown said I hadn't succeeded.

"They carted some residents away when they got nosy about the tunnel. I think my grandparents were among them."

"Where did they send them?"

"I don't know yet. I'm not sure he knows. But they were alive when they left. I'm going to go push him some more."

I hate being negative, so I didn't tell Veronica what I was thinking: There was about as much chance of her grandparents being alive as there was of Santa Claus coming down from the North Pole and shaking my hand in the morning.

"So, when do we rescue Angel Hills?" Saul asked when he came out a short while later. He was so cheerful I decided he must have gotten a contact tobacco high from the secondhand smoke inside.

"You don't need to be rescued," I told him. "You can leave the town anytime you want."

"We don't want to leave. We want to kick the goons out. And besides—we can't leave. I told you what happens."

"You can leave tonight without a problem," I said. "Go through the tunnel I found."

"We don't want to leave."

I wondered. "Why didn't you tell me about the tunnel when you stopped the other day."

"I didn't know anything about it until Veronica mentioned it."

"All the earth-digging equipment didn't make you suspicious?"

"They were fixing the roads and putting more sewer lines in. It made sense."

More like wishful self-delusion, or maybe purposeful

ignorance. But then there was a huge amount of that going around where Mexico was concerned.

The Mexican authorities had been willfully ignorant about the cartels for years. Americans had been beyond obtuse on the various immigration and border issues that allowed all manner of criminals to thrive. And both countries had closed their eyes rather than deal with illegal immigration. The situation was so out of hand now that many serious people claimed it couldn't be solved.

Another reason never to be considered serious, if you can help it.

I HAD PLENTY of evidence for the secretary of State; all I had to do was get it back to her. Given what her aide had told me when I was hired, she wouldn't particularly like it—but that just added to the fun factor. I could wrap up the guard and de Sarcena with red ribbon, and deposit them and my pictures of the camp at the front door of Harry's place—aka the Harry S. Truman Building, the State Department's HQ.

The only trick was to get them across the border. I had a feeling the cartel was looking for me—a feeling Shunt confirmed when he called to update me on his progress a short time later. The acting head of the cartel had figured out who had caused all the ruckus and offered a reward of ten million dollars for my head. My body they would take for free.

Interestingly, there was no similar reward for de Sarcena. Obviously his replacement didn't really want him back.

"These IMs are going to accounts on both sides of the border," Shunt told me. "I wouldn't trust any of the crossings if I were you. A Border Patrol agent could easily figure you were his get-rich-quick plan. I'd be suspicious of anyone near the border. Hell, that's enough cash for me to think about taking you out."

No shit. For that kind of money, I was tempted to do it myself.

Dodging the overworked and undermanned Border Patrol is not exactly hard. The American-Mexican border is 1,933 miles long, and upward of half a million[25] people cross the border each year without being apprehended. Then again, they don't have a fat price tag on their heads. And the cartel would certainly make things even more difficult.

Going overland, especially around here, made no sense. But I already knew where there was an easy and direct route back: the tunnel at Angel Hills.

[XII]

IT TOOK SHUNT close to forty-five minutes to upload all the data from the two CPUs we had taken from the compound. I decided that the half-dozen laptops we'd found could wait until we got back across the border. In the meantime, we packed everything into

---

[25] All of the estimates of illegal border crossing and the like are really just guesses, since obviously no one is standing there ticking people off as they come in. The Government Accounting Office published a report in 2006 that is often referred to by others looking for reliable numbers. While the report focused on border deaths, it estimated illegal crossings averaged roughly 454,000 over the seven years ending 2004. The same report put apprehensions at 1.27 million a year in the same period. The report used U.S. Border Patrol numbers as well as GAO analysis.

the "borrowed" pickup and prepared to get the hell out of Dodge.

We blindfolded our prisoner—his name was Celereno—more for form's sake than for security; we weren't taking him anyplace he hadn't seen before. I told Mongoose and Junior to meet us near Deming, about a half hour north of the border (less if I was driving), with de Sarcena. While I relished the idea of depositing him on the secretary of State's doorstep, I was supposed to appear at some mixed martial arts events in California in a few days. Business before pleasure, I always say: we'd drop de Sarcena and the guard off at the U.S. Marshal's office in Las Cruces, New Mexico. I talked to Danny and got him working on finding an FBI agent we could trust to turn over the original evidence to. I'd talk to the State Department as well, as soon as I decided on the best way to ruin the Secretary of State's day.

Besides breaking into the cartel's instant messaging system, Shunt was monitoring the Mexican police computerized dispatching system. There had been no further mention of Angel Hills or the fracas at the terrorists' camp. It wasn't unusual for the police in the area to not bother checking in with dispatchers for hours if there was no problem; you can figure out the reasons why that would be on your own.

Of course, none of this meant that the cartel hadn't flooded into Angel Hills. I had Junior launch a new drone from the ranch and fly it south over the development. The UAV showed the place was quiet.

And so we headed out.

"How are we going to find my grandparents?" asked Veronica, who was sitting between myself and Shotgun in the front of the truck; Saul rode with the bound guard in the back. She stretched her legs—they looked good even in jeans.

"If we had more of these thugs, we could interrogate them," Veronica said. "One of them's bound to know. We can grab them when they report for work. Celereno says they come in at eight."

"I don't think we want to hang around that long," I told her. "Eventually, the police are going to wonder what happened to their unit. And then there's the Mexican village to consider. We want to get in and out as quickly as possible. Our job is done."

"Mine isn't. I want to find my grandparents."

I didn't answer.

"I want to talk to the people in the development when we get there," added Veronica. "And to the Mexicans. Now that the cartel has been kicked out, they won't be as scared. Maybe the Mexicans are the people to start with."

"They haven't been kicked out," I told her.

"Don't kid yourself," Shotgun said. "Once the cartel realizes what's going on, they'll hit that town with everything they've got."

"Are we going to just let that happen?" asked Veronica.

"It's not why we're here," I told her.

"Why are we here?"

"To rescue a kidnap victim, and to find a terror camp. We've done both."

"The people in the development have probably gone over the border by now," said Shotgun.

"Would you?" she asked.

"No."

"Then why should they? Why should they run away? Why should they give up their homes? Huh? Why should they be cowards? Would you do that? Tell me. What would you do?"

"Hell, I'd kick ass. Right, Dick?"

RIGHT, SHOTGUN.

And we'll lower the price of gas to a dollar a gallon and declare beer free on Sundays.

SARCASM ASIDE, LETTING those people get scared out of their homes—or worse—didn't sit very well with me, and I suppose I would have figured out some way to help them eventually. But it was the call I got from Shunt as we were approaching the Mexican hamlet that put juice in my battery.

"Looks like the cartel realized something's up, boss. They just broadcast an IM that had three words: *Atacar.* Angel Hills."

Attack. Angel Hills.

"My Spanish isn't very good," admitted Shunt. "I can't tell if they're ordering an attack or saying they're being attacked."

"I don't think it's going to make a difference one way or the other," I told him, stepping on the gas.

Saul started banging on the back window. The next thing I knew, he was hanging in my face, curled around the driver's side of the truck.

"What's going on? What's going on?" he shouted.

"You have to get your people out right now," I told him. "The cartel is rallying its troops."

"We'll fight! We'll fight!"

"What are you going to use? Your bare hands?"

"If we have to."

I glanced at Saul. He had a determined scowl on his face.

"We will fight them," he insisted.

I got back on the radio. "Junior, is the Bird above?"

"Roger that."

"See anything?"

"Just you, trying to set a land speed record."

"Run a wide circuit around the area, hitting the main roads. You see anything coming, yell."

"Sure."

"All right, here's what you're going to do," I said, skidding to a stop in front of the community center. "Get everybody awake. Tell them the shit is about to hit the fan. They have two choices—run like hell through the tunnel, or stay and fight."

"They'll fight! They'll fight!" yelled Saul.

"With what?" asked Veronica.

"I'm going to go take care of that right now," I said, hopping out of the truck.

Shotgun and Veronica followed as I went back to the tailgate and dragged Celerino onto the ground.

"Stick him in that railcar below," I told Shotgun. "Saul, round everybody up. Tell them I'll meet them in the community center."

Veronica was starting to have second thoughts. "Dick—"

"Take my MP5. My extra mags are in the pack."

"It might be easier if—"

"Give her your sat phone," I told Shotgun. "If it rings, get everyone into the tunnel and across the border. Both of you—if you're in doubt, retreat. You hear gunfire or even think you do, run. Get through the tunnel and get out. I'll have Shunt contact some people we trust at the Border Patrol. Shotgun, you're with me."

"Hot shit," he said. "Time to blow stuff up."

PART THREE

I would rather die standing than live on my knees.

— Emiliano Zapata,
revolutionary

[1]

THE WRECKED VEHICLES were still hulked by the side of the road as we sped up the back road to the camp. Down at the barn, bodies were slumped where we left them, most just lying peacefully, one or two with their legs and arms at weird angles. The gray light of the false dawn made everything gray. The shadows of the nearby hills threw an ominously dark hand across the landscape. With our windows closed, we couldn't smell the blood or even the burnt metal of the smoldering trucks, but there was no doubt that the air was heavy with it.

Sounds like a Thomas Kinkade painting, no?

I backed the pickup to the door of the barn.

"Rifles and ammo first," I told Shotgun. "Grab some of the grenade launchers as well."

"No machine guns?"

"I'll get the machine guns," I told him, jumping from the truck.

"Didn't we close the barn door before we left?" asked Shotgun.

"I don't think there was time."

"I swear I closed it."

We were too busy piling the weapons into the truck to worry about it. About midway through I stopped, found a seat in the back of the barn, and checked in with Junior and Shunt. The banditos had still not come out to the development, although there was considerable traffic on their IM system.

"I'm trying to find their cell phone network and see if I can listen in," said Shunt. "But it's hard by remote control from here. I have to break into the TelCel system. It's kind of a pain, because unlike—"

"I don't need the technical bullshit," I told him.

Shunt's response was drowned out by an automatic weapon firing near the front of the building.

"Shotgun, I'm on the phone!" I yelled.

"That ain't me!" He was standing a few feet away.

A burst of bullets raked the front of the building. Shotgun and I dove to the ground simultaneously.

Ordinarily I prefer flanking attacks and similar maneuvers, tactics that might come under the heading of *Hit the enemy in the balls before he realizes where you are.*

But there was no way to flank our enemy now; all the doors were in the front of the building. Not only that, but we had to get back to the condos as quickly as possible.

The solution was another favorite SEAL tactic—overwhelming force.

"You cover me," I told him, picking up one of the Mexican Xiuhcoatl FX-05s for myself. "Let's go."

"You got it," said Shotgun, picking up one of the fifty-calibers and jaunting it on his hip like a Mattel toy.

Shotgun is so big he probably *could* have held the damn thing at his side and done a reasonable job. But even he's not quite that foolhardy.

Besides, he could have just as much fun with grenades.

"Grenades?" he asked.

"We fire them from back here where they can't see

us," I told him. "Take the launcher, pump a couple, then
we move out. You take a SAW."

I pointed him to an FN Minimi, known in the U.S.
as an M249 Squad Automatic weapon, or SAW for
short. (There are some slight differences, too trivial to
get into. Yes, I used the American nickname instead of
the *proper* nomenclature. Sue me.) Then I picked up a
launcher and a pair of grenades for myself.

We fired the grenades, charging from the building
behind the second salvo. No sooner did I cross the
threshold of the barn than the gunfire stoked up; the
grenades had failed to find their mark.

I fired off a few rounds from the Xiuhcoatl as I
threw myself down into the dirt, the heavy fifty-caliber
bullets beating through the building behind me. I looked
for a muzzle flash in the direction the gunfire was coming from, but saw nothing.

Crawling along on my elbows, I dragged myself
through the dust for a good thirty feet, moving toward
the end of the dirt road and the ditch on the other side.
Shotgun held his fire, and after another second or two
the bastard who was shooting at us stopped as well.

"Junior, I need you to bring the Bird down here and
see what we're up against," I told him. "The bastards
have us pinned down in front of the barn."

"I'm coming in that direction. May take a few minutes."

I edged to my right, pulling along slowly so I didn't
make much noise. But evidently I wasn't quiet enough—
the ground began percolating with bullets. I heaved
myself toward the road, rolling across it and down into
the very shallow ditch alongside it.

Very shallow ditch. I had maybe three inches of cover.

Another burst of gunfire rang out and I got close and personal with the earthworms.

Shotgun began firing from the other side. That took the heat off me for a moment, but when I started to peek, a fresh volley streaked within inches of my head.

"Dick, we're coming overhead," said Junior.

"Tell me how many. And where."

"Hold."

I considered telling him what *he* could hold, but a burst of bullets to my right sent a shower of rocks over my head.

"I need to know where these bastards are *now!*" I snapped. I think I was loud enough that Junior could have heard me all the way back in the States even without the phone.

"One. At exactly two o'clock from your position. I can see you're on your back. He's up to your right."

One?

One mf was doing this?

One?

I lifted my gun and fired a burst.

"He's at three o'clock," said Junior.

I adjusted and fired another few rounds. Bullets spit out of the gun.

"Moving back — at four o'clock."

"Two, three, four, make up your damn mind," I said, rising to my knee. I sprayed the rest of my bullets out in an arc across the field. The weapon rattled, and not in a pleasing way — that's what I get for buying foreign.

"He's hit," said Junior. "He's down."

I reloaded and rose to my knee, looking out toward the field. Nothing moved.

"He's flat out," said Junior. "I think you're good."

Shotgun moved up from the other direction, drawing parallel with me. We waited while Junior directed the Bird to take a few more passes overhead.

"Nothing else," he told us finally. "He hasn't moved."

We went over and checked on the tango. He was lying facedown, three large bullet holes in his back.

The dead man was dressed in nondescript camis, similar to the others we'd shot earlier. He had a turban-like scarf; it seemed to be an identifier, as if all the men in charge of small teams wore them. He had a stamped Koran in his upper pocket.

Hezbollah.

I took a picture with my cell phone.

"Just a kid," said Shotgun, looking at his face. "I don't think he's twenty."

"Maybe he's older than he looks."

"Think he's Arab?"

"Middle East somewhere. Hard to tell."

"Dumb shit," said Shotgun. He turned the body back over so he wouldn't see the tango's face anymore. "What a dumb shit."

We grabbed his M16. He had several more boxes of ammo in his pockets.

"You think we missed him in the house before?" Shotgun asked as we went back to the SUV.

"Maybe. Or maybe he's the guy who ran off to get the police. Came back to see his friends."

"A real dumb shit."

Junior swung the Bird back toward the development, checking the road for us and then getting over the condos. A pickup truck was approaching, just passing the Mexican hamlet.

"Nobody in the back," said Junior. "Can't tell how

many people are in the front. It's a two-door. I tried radioing Veronica. She must be underground; I didn't get an answer."

"Any markings on the truck?" I asked.

"Nothing."

"Keep an eye on it. We're on our way."

We threw a few more boxes of ammo and rifles into the back of the pickup. Shotgun positioned himself in the front seat, gun hanging out the window, ready to fire.

"Dick, four more pickups on the way," said Junior as we started up the back road. "Loaded with goons."

BACK IN TOWN, Veronica and Saul had split up. Veronica went to the community building to look for weapons; Saul tried to gather his neighbors.

He started by waking the Friendlys, the only family on the block where the sales office was. Then, bypassing the Mexican family on the corner whom he believed were relatives of someone in the cartel, together they woke up the Kandinskis and the Engelhardts on the next block. He skipped Herman Leferd, who lived in the corner unit and never rose much before three in the afternoon. Mr. Leferd had the early stages of Alzheimer's, and wasn't to be trusted with a weapon.

Two blocks over, Saul found his good friend Paul Smith awake and seemingly ready for action. Smith had been a champion skeet shooter before retiring, and Saul decided to trust him with his shotgun, at that point the group's only firearm.

They were on their way to Marielle Hogan's house when the small white pickup truck came around the corner.

"Get him!" yelled Saul.

Smith swung his gun in the truck's direction and fired into the windshield. The truck skidded off the road onto a nearby lawn, crashing into the corner of the condo. The driver's side door opened. The driver fell out on the ground, blood spurting from his head.

For a second, no one moved. Then Mrs. Kandinski, who had been a nurse before retiring, started toward the man. She had only taken a few steps when the other truck door opened. The goon who'd been the passenger lurched out of the vehicle unsteadily, an M16 in his hands. He began firing in the air.

Smith fired a second round from his shotgun. But his hands were shaking—firing at clay pigeons and firing at people are two very different things. The shot went wide; pellets sprinkled across the truck, but if any hit the goon they had no effect.

"Take cover!" yelled Saul.

He and some of the others began retreating around the nearest condo. Smith got off another round but again his bullet had little effect. Fortunately, the Mexican missed as well, probably because he'd been dazed by the accident. Smith retreated to reload, joining the rest of the group around the corner.

The collective age of the little band of Americans easily topped six hundred. Excepting Saul's experience as a one-man neighborhood watch, none had police or military training. But they were fired up and feisty. Regrouping behind the building, Saul came up with a plan. Half of the group would lure the thug away from the pickup and his companion, while the other half circled around the buildings and made their way to the truck and the man who'd been shot. Hopefully, there would be a weapon there; once they had it, they could use it to get the drop on the bad guys.

Mrs. Kandinski and the Engelhardts trotted off to the north. Saul and Paul Smith peeked around the corner to see what the thugs were up to. The man who'd fired at them was kneeling near his fallen comrade. The wounded man was sitting near the truck. He had his hands on his forehead, where a shirt sopped up blood.

Saul told everyone who had stayed to go down the block to the Gilfeathers' house, which was a corner unit with a good view of the street. The Gilfeathers had left some months before, but Mr. Gilfeather was reputed to be a sportsman, and Saul thought there was at least a distant chance there were weapons in the house.

"Take another shot at them," Saul urged Smith, joining him back at the corner of the building after the others had left. "Then we'll retreat to the Gilfeathers'."

"I'm too far to hit them," hissed Smith, slinking near the side of the house. "I need to get close."

"It's barely twenty yards," said Saul.

"Closer to fifty!"

"You're nearsighted. Let me shoot."

"You couldn't hit the broad side of a barn at two feet," declared Smith. He steadied himself on one knee despite the bad case of arthritis he had been battling for several years, sighted his shotgun, and fired.

The distance was closer to Saul's estimate than Smith's, but it was still a good way off. And as Saul hinted, Smith's eyes weren't the best. Between that and his shaking hand, his aim once more went awry. The man who'd already been wounded took the brunt of the pellets, folding over on the grass. The other Mexican, after flinching with the shot, grabbed his gun and began returning fire.

Smith fired again. This time he definitely got a piece of the gunman, who fell or threw himself down face-first but continued to fire. Saul and Smith retreated, running across the yard between the buildings to the Gilfeathers'. The others were already inside, scouring the place for weapons. They found some two-by-fours in the garage, apparently left over from the original construction.

They tried rigging the pieces against the front door to keep it from opening, propping it against the nearby stairs. They couldn't get a snug fit and had no tools to cut it or connect two pieces together. While they were trying to solve the problem, they heard a bang from the garage—the man with the M16 was trying to get in.

"I locked it," said Mr. Friendly.

There was a loud burst of automatic weapons fire, followed by the sound of the door being rolled up.

"Now it's not locked," said Saul. He took one of the two-by-fours and wedged it in the hall against the garage door. The thug banged against the door with his shoulder once, then again.

"Back!" yelled Saul. "Into the living room."

A second later, the thug in the garage laced the door with bullets.

"I wish I had an iron pan. I'd open the door and smack him in the head," said Mrs. Friendly.

"Come on—out the back," said Saul.

"I'll get him when he comes through the door," said Smith.

Saul was about to tell him no—they weren't sure how many might be with the man—when the two-by-four gave way. The thug burst into the hall. Smith unloaded both barrels, and this time didn't miss. The Mexican fell in a pool of blood.

Saul ran forward and grabbed the rifle.

"Damn. I never killed someone before," said Smith.

"Just go! Just go!" yelled Saul. He tugged Smith and led the rest of the group to the back room, where they made their way out a window. They ran over to the Leterris' condo, about thirty yards away.

MEANWHILE, THE ENGELHARDTS and Mrs. Kandinski had circled around the block and were approaching the truck from the yard behind where it had gone off the road. The wounded thug was sitting back upright, holding the wadded shirt against his head and moaning.

He moaned even louder when Mrs. Engelhardt whacked him aside the head with a kick she had learned in tae kwon do nearly fifty years before. She'd been a much younger woman then; her knee was a little stiff now, and her thigh didn't have quite the spring it had had back then. But the blow caught the Mexican completely by surprise and he fell over.

This put him in a perfect position for Mr. Engelhardt. Mr. Engelhardt—Big Mike to his friends—had never taken tae kwon do and in fact had been somewhat suspicious of the instructor who had taught it to his wife, as he always seemed to be offering opportunities for personal instruction. Big Mike applied his own style of kicks, mostly with his heel, as he pounded the sense out of the wounded thug.

"Stop, stop," said Mrs. Kandinski. "We need to see if he has a gun."

He didn't have one on him, but there was a Beretta pistol with some extra magazines in the glove compartment.

"They're going to the Leterris'!" yelled Mrs. Kandinski, spotting the others.

"Let's go!" yelled Big Mike, leading the way.

[II]

VERONICA HADN'T HEARD Junior's radio transmission, but she had seen the first pickup truck through a window on the second floor of the community center. By the time she got outside, Saul and company had already begun their ambush. Starting toward the gunfire, she had just crossed the street when she heard the other pickup trucks coming down the road. Running to the porch of the nearest unit, she crouched down, some eighty to a hundred feet from the road as the procession came into view.

The wise thing probably would have been to retreat and assess the situation. And she thought of that—for about three seconds. Then she fired the submachine gun, lacing the back of the first pickup with lead.

The pickup veered to the right; the one behind it slammed on its brakes. The men in the second truck dove out of the bed, scattering for cover.

The MP5 is a fantastic weapon, but like any tool, you have to be somewhat familiar with it to use it well. Only a small portion of Veronica's bullets had found their marks; more importantly, she had shot through the entire magazine. Fumbling with the unfamiliar mechanism, it took her nearly a half minute to reload. That may not sound like much, but it gave the motley group of cartel thugs, some of whom were wearing old army or police uniforms, time to regroup. She started to panic a bit when she saw two running toward her, Bushmaster A4s in their hands. She raised the gun and fired, dumping bullets into them until it once more clicked empty, which doesn't take particularly long with an MP5. Her shots were true; one of the men had his neck practically sawed off by the 9 mm ammo. But once more she needed to reload, and the process went no smoother the second time. Veronica barely got the mag back in the gun when a fresh counterattack began, this one coordinated. Bullets came at her from two separate angles, and she realized she had to retreat. She rose, gave two quick bursts — she was learning — then ran to the back of the building. There she spotted two Mexicans running down the hill in her direction and managed to surprise them. One fell, the other retreated.

At that point, the math involved finally dawned on her. She had two more magazines, not counting the nearly empty one in the gun. Her only real option was to retreat and find more ammo.

Right about then she realized the radio wasn't working. Somewhere along the way, the plastic grommet where the speaker/mic wire fed into the body had cracked, and the wire pulled loose. A piece of molded plastic, probably worth less than a nickel, had failed, and killed the unit.

SHOTGUN AND I, meanwhile, were getting blow-by-blow descriptions of the battle from Junior. After failing to ambush Veronica behind the building, the Mexicans retreated and regrouped behind the community center. Junior watched as their leader organized them, posting a watch and mustering men to take down the building. It was the first sign of intelligent leadership we'd seen from them.

I didn't like it at all.

I drove the truck across the rock-strewn ditches and fields into the development, doing my best to avoid shattering the axles before finally reaching the paved street. Whether by instinct or sheer luck, Veronica managed to reach us just as we got there.

"There's forty of them, maybe more," she said between breaths, practically collapsing against the truck. "I killed a few but there are too many."

"We heard."

"I lost track of Saul," she said.

"They're in a house up that way." Junior had watched them go into the Leterris'. I opened the truck door. "Go up there and get them out of here."

"You don't want them to fight?"

"They're not going to make it. Get them to the border."

My plan had depended on using the community center as a kind of Fort Apache with an escape hatch. We could have fought a delaying action there, with the option of leaving if things got too tough. Without the ability to retreat, holding out anywhere else in the development would be suicidal, given the cartel's numbers.

"What are you going to do?" asked Veronica.

"I'm going to divert their attention. Shotgun, you go with her," I added, stopping him as he started to get out of the truck. "Make sure they get to the border."

"Dick."

"That's an order. I'll hook up with you later."

I grabbed one of the Minimis and a grenade launcher from the back, then stuffed ammo and grenades in the pack. Then I humped through the backyards and up the hill toward the community center.

It was like running an obstacle course. The fields where the units hadn't been completed were strewn with debris—bricks, rocks, pieces of metal, wood, you name it. Farther up, walls separated yards. They were mostly low, but they still took time getting over. I felt like I was running a steeplechase.

My one real advantage was that the cartel thugs were a motley crew. They were still clearing the community center when I arrived, and had left a small force outside—six men in total, according to Junior.

The first thing I wanted to do was eliminate the trucks. If I couldn't drive, why should they?

The trucks were on the north side of the building, jumbled at the side of the road. I crossed to the south, moving up behind the condos opposite the building until I got close. Then I went to an end unit and kicked the back door in.

"Where's my breakfast?" I yelled in Spanish. "I want coffee!"

No one answered. I cleared the place as quickly as I could, moving room to room, submachine gun ready to do any talking I deemed necessary. There was no furniture or curtains, but I still went room to room. The last thing I needed now was an ambush because I got lazy.

Downstairs clear, I went up the stairs. The Minimi is not a good weapon for working your way through a building. Sure, it fires a lot of bullets, but the long barrel is awkward in narrow spaces. The extra weight doesn't help either. By the time I was finished, my shirt was soaked with sweat and I was fantasizing about frosty cold ones on a well-shaded veranda.

The front room had a good view of the trucks. I swung off the ruck and lined up six grenades. I positioned the machine gun so I could grab it quickly, slid a magazine on top of the ruck for reloading, and took one last head count of the opposition.

Still six guys, still four trucks.

"Let's play Pin the Grenade on the Pickup," I said, firing the first round.

The grenade shattered the glass, hurtling toward the truck.[26] The projectile rocketed into the bed of the truck, setting off an explosion that blew hot shrapnel into the gas tank. In the next moment a small flash of fire consumed the truck.

I reloaded and fired again, this time aiming at the pickup farthest away. My shot went a little low, and the grenade hit about ten feet shy of the truck. If it damaged it, I couldn't tell from where I was.

---

[26] In retrospect, I should have opened the window first. Not only would it have been quieter, but it wouldn't have sent glass splattering all over the place. The grenades won't explode until they've gone a certain distance, so firing through the glass wasn't any more dangerous in that respect. Of course, that did assume it was working properly—and we all know what can happen when we ass-u-me.

Practice makes perfect. I got the cab on shot number two.

By now the cartel baboons had realized I was popping their pickups. Bullets flew through the window as I reloaded. I popped my head up, got my bearings, then ducked down as they peppered the sill. Turning over on my back, I held the launcher up and fired blind—not recommended, admittedly.

I doubt I hit anything, but the gunfire slackened immediately. I rammed in another grenade, rose, and fired. This one went way high over my target, slapping into the side of the security building. Concrete splinters and dust sprayed everywhere: an impressive explosion that accomplished exactly nothing.

I pumped another grenade out at the third truck, hitting it near the driver's side door. As it hit, I spotted more thugs coming out of the security building. The men who were already outside were pointing in my direction.

Time to leave. I fired one last round, then ducked without seeing where it went. Bullets began raining plaster down from the ceiling as the thugs shot up the house. I grabbed my stuff and ran.

I tripped as I reached the landing, slipping on a loose carpet. I tried grabbing the rail but it was no good. I slid down on my side, bashing the few intact bones left in my body. Fortunately, I was on an adrenaline high. I can't say I didn't feel any pain, but I didn't feel enough of it to stop.

At this point, my mission had essentially been accomplished. I'd disabled at least three if not all of their vehicles, and given them plenty to concentrate on while the others got away. I myself could go east, and either hook up with Shotgun and the others, or indulge my inner billy goat and go over the hill to the quarry. There, Chet could grab me in one of his helos.

But Murphy had other plans. And along with perfect timing, Murphy also has a wicked sense of humor.

As I RAN out the back of the unit, I glanced over my left shoulder, worried that the thugs might try and ambush me there. As I turned back, something loomed in front of me. I saw it too late to do anything but bull into it; in the next instant, I realized it was a man.

Not one of the cartel goons, but a resident of the condo next to the one I'd used to shoot at the trucks. I hit him off-balance and we tumbled over each other, sprawling on the dirt.

It was Mr. Leferd, the man with Alzheimer's.

"Margaret?" asked Mr. Leferd when we hit the ground. "Is that you, Margaret?"

I thought I'd knocked him senseless. I picked him up off the ground. He was wearing his pajamas.

"Margaret, what happened to the red slippers?" he asked. "Are they in the refrigerator?"

"I'm not Margaret," I told him. "Are you OK?"

He blinked at me. I could hear bullets pinging at the front of the building.

"They're selling weed-whackers half-price off at Sears," he said.

"Let's go check them out," I told him. "Come on."

I bent down and put him over my shoulder.

"Put me down," he protested. "What the hell has gotten into you?"

"We have to get out of here."

"We need to go to Sears."

"We're going."

I ran through two backyards, trying to figure out what to do with him. There was no way I could carry him all the way to the other end of the complex. I was already straining. I decided I'd have to leave him in one of the units. I carried him to one with a back porch, but just as I was about to kick down the door, there was a loud explosion up the street, at the unit I'd been firing from. The baboons had shot an RPG into it.

Still carrying Mr. Leferd, I ran across the street, hoping the goons wouldn't be able to see me from where they were. I crossed to the back of another set of units until I came to a clump of small trees. It wasn't exactly the White House bunker, but it was the best cover I could find. I practically collapsed there, exhausted from the run.

"Junior, what's my sit rep?" I asked over the radio.

"They're attacking that unit you were firing from. You OK? Who's that with you?"

"Murphy." Mr. Leferd gave me a look as if I were the one who was crazy—I think he thought I was talking to myself. "Did I get all their trucks?"

"Affirmative. They're on foot. Maybe a dozen of them firing on the unit. Won't be long before they assault. They don't really seem that organized, though."

Thank God for that.

"Tell me if they start coming down the street."

"OK."

I looked at Mr. Leferd. There was no way I could carry him all the way up to the other condo. We might be able to make it on foot, but we'd be going so slow the goons were bound to catch up. I needed to stash him someplace safe.

Wyoming, maybe.

"Come on," I told him. "Get on my back."

He blinked at me. "What are you saying, Margaret?"

"Get on my back," I told him—though when I said it, I added a few more words.

"No way."

Never hit your elders, right? There's a rule to be broken.

I scooped him over my shoulder and trotted to the back of a nearby unit. He seemed to have gained twenty pounds since I last put him down.

I broke the window on the back door and let us in. The place was empty and clearly vacant. I led him to the bathroom.

"You're staying in here, do you understand? Sit in the tub."

"You want me to take a bath?"

"I want you to sit in the tub. It's the safest place." I figured the porcelain would add a little protection. "Don't move until I come back."

"But, Margaret, what about Sears?"

"They're delivering," I told him. "I need you to stay here."

I grabbed the belt from his bathrobe and threaded it around the handle on the sliding door to the tub. It wasn't much, a weak leash that could be easily undone, but it was the best I could do.

"Stay here, you understand?" I said sternly. "Those are real guns."

"I want a commercial strength weed-whacker. Not electric."

Someday, I will find a way to get even with Murphy.

ON THE OTHER side of the complex, Shotgun and Veronica drove the pickup through a pair of backyards, cutting across the dead ends to get to the unit where Saul and the others had hidden themselves. Shunt had managed to track down the phone number and called the unit; unfortunately the call had gone into a voice mailbox. Shunt hung up and tried again. Once again, no one answered, and Shunt erred on what he thought was the safer side by hanging up without leaving a message.

Inside, Saul thought the phone call was some sort of trick. The gunfire and explosions sounded much closer than they were. He and the others thought, not unreasonably, that the baboons were about to lay siege to the place. They prepared to make a last stand, placing furniture in front of the doors and windows, and hunting desperately for things to use as weapons. The place was empty, and there was nothing suitable—probably a good thing, since it gave them an incentive to conserve their frugal supply of bullets when Shotgun knocked on the door.

"Yo! Saul!" yelled Shotgun, crouching near the steps to the front door. "It's me, Shotgun. Are you OK in there?"

Smith, watching guard, called to Saul.

"Saul?" yelled Shotgun again. "Hey. We came to get you out."

"Prove you're who you say you are," demanded Saul.

"Come on, Saul. We gotta get out of here."

"Prove you're Shotgun."

"How?"

"What's your favorite fast food?" asked Saul.

"God, that's a tough question."

"It's him," Saul told the others. He opened the door.

LEAVING MR. LEFERD, I crossed the road and ran up the hill toward the community center. Black smoke curled out of the condo where I'd been. There were shouts, instructions to the men pressing the attack, but I wasn't close enough to see what was going on.

What I was close enough to see, though, were two goons coming out from the back of the community center, M4 lookalikes in their hands.

Pushing my foot underneath my haunches, I tried to get into a comfortable shooting position without moving enough to attract their attention. But rather than coming toward me, they stopped after a few yards and reversed course, walking in the direction of the SUVs I'd disabled during the night.

One of the men veered right, walking toward the front; the other continued to the SUVs. Curious, I moved up along the back of the building, staying low enough that the scrub and brush between us would keep me hidden if he turned around. The baboon removed a jack from the back of the security SUV and went to work raising the vehicle off the ground. By the time he had the tire off, the second guard came from the front, rolling a tire from one of the destroyed pickups.

Not a bad idea, I thought.

"Junior, how many tires are left inflated on the trucks?"

"Oh—good idea. Stand by."

He had to swing the Bird through a wide arc, tilting it at a good angle to see. This took a while; by the time he had an answer, the goon was back for the next tire.

"Just this last one—they'll end up two tires short," he said.

Two was all right—there'd be spares in each SUV.

I put the machine gun and the grenade launcher down and pulled off my pack. Knife in hand, I snuck forward, angling to keep the vehicle between me and the baboon jacking it up.

Ideally, I might have waited for him to get all the tires on, but I figured it was easier to take the cartel goons one at a time. He was so intent on his work that I not only reached the truck without being seen, but got right next to him before he looked up. By then, it was too late. I swung my knife around the front of his body as I grabbed him from behind. The angle wasn't perfect—I was more on the side than behind him—but I'd gotten him by surprise and struck him fast enough that the only sound he made before falling into my arms was a guttural peep. I gave the knife a sharp and quick run against his throat, jerking the blade deep against his windpipe and whatever else it could cut. His right elbow smacked hard into my side as I pressed. I pushed again, rapping my left fist against the side of his skull as I cut.

He went limp. Blood spurted everywhere as I dropped him.

I ducked down and waited for the other man to appear.

"Damn tire lugs were too tight," he said, rolling the tire in front of him.

I got him across the skull with the tire iron. He fell against the other SUV, stunned. I hit him again, then used the knife to finish him.

There's a certain smell that comes from an artery or vein when you slice it. It's a terrible smell. You have to steel yourself against it, or it makes you sick.

I changed the tire myself. I'll tell you this: it looks pretty damn easy on NASCAR. Martin Truex will drive No. 56 into the pit and suddenly there's a swarm over the wall. Jack goes under, tire off, tire on — Truex is back on the track.

In real life it ain't nearly so quick. The second lug stuck. I nearly bent the tire iron getting it off. I *hate* those overtorqued air guns.

The third one was almost as bad. The fourth I could have taken off with my fingers. Go figure.

"Shotgun and the old folks are getting out of the building," Junior told me as I lifted the spare into place and began tightening the screws.

"Good. What are the rest of these goons doing?"

"Across the street, searching the buildings. They're moving real slow, Dick. Real slow."

"Don't complain. How many are there?"

"I count twelve."

"That's it?"

"There may be one or two left in the building. I haven't had a chance to count. I called the Border Patrol," Junior added. "They're sending some people to the fence area directly north of Angel Hills. I contacted the FBI, State —"

"The State Department? Why?"

"Dan Barrett told me to do that. He said it would avoid problems with Customs."

"What the hell was he thinking?"

"He said —"

"Forget it. You might as well call everybody. Get the National Guard, state police, everybody."

"I'm on it. Chet Arthur's helo should be in the air in a few minutes."

"Tell him to get close, but stay back. Then run the Bird south and make sure the terror camp is clear."

"Uh—"

"Do it."

"How are you going to get out of there?"

"I'll worry about that."

What I had in mind was this: I'd put the other tires on the SUV, drive down to the condo where Mr. Leferd was, grab him, drive down to the south end of the development and cut across the hill and get back to the terror camp, assuming it was empty. I could rendezvous with Chet there.

I signed off and went around to the other side of the truck, sliding the jack in under the chasis. I was lining up the little slot in the jack head when I heard someone approaching.

I pulled out my PK.

"Are you done?" he yelled in Spanish from the other side of the truck.

"Eughhh," I yelled noncommittally.

"What is this!"

This was one of the goons I'd killed. I jumped up, ready to shoot, but he'd already ducked behind the far side of other SUV. The last thing I wanted was a running gun battle between the SUVs, but that's what I got. He had an M4 lookalike with him; he fired it as I ducked around to the front end of the SUV. I waited until he had stopped, then went across the space between the vehicles, hoping to turn the corner on him. But he retreated to the back of the truck, leaving me without a target when I turned. I feinted as if I was going back; he saw me through the glass and fired.

Throwing myself down, I crawled until I could see him under the vehicle.

Two shots later, he sprawled out in the lot, wounded, but still alive and clinging to his gun.

By now the search of the units across the way had been completed. Somehow in the course of the search, a fire had started in the end unit. It spread to the next two houses, burning through the attic. In America, building codes generally call for fire walls between condo units, making that sort of thing difficult if not impossible. There were probably building codes here as well, but payoffs and shoddy work are routine, and there was no firewall here. Flames spread easily, and finding plenty of dry fuel, began leaping skyward, high over the nearby buildings.

Junior's estimate of how many people were left in the building was short—very, very short. For as I bent down to make sure the man I'd shot was dead, four or five more goons started coming out the door. I fired, chasing them back inside.

With only one tire to go, I got back on the jack and hoisted the SUV upward. As I went to grab the tire iron, I spotted one of the more adventurous cartel goonies trying to sneak around the corner from the back; apparently he'd come out a window or maybe the front of the building. I waited behind the SUV until he came parallel; I fired, catching him in the stomach with three or four slugs.

He dropped his rifle, then staggered back. He brought both hands into his belly, pressing in and staring down, amazed to see blood spurting through his fingers. Then he looked over at me.

It was quite a dramatic scene. I hate that.

I fired another few rounds into his face, cutting holes where his eyes had been. He fell down.

I'm a stubborn son of a bitch, and I might not have completely abandoned my plans to change the tire and take the SUV, except for the rocket-propelled grenade that flashed across the lot from the street, striking the hood of the other SUV. Even though I had two vehicles between me and the explosion, the concussion threw me to the ground and showered me with dirt and shrapnel. The SUV caught fire, and I barely scrambled away before its gas tank exploded with enough force to twirl the SUV next to it into a pretzel.

[III]

DAMN, UNDERTRAINED MEXICAN thugs. Didn't they realize that was total overkill?

I must have blacked out for a moment. When I came to, I was lying on my back and bullets were flying everywhere.

This was a good time to leave. The only problem was how to arrange it.

I still had my pistol. I started to raise it over the truck, thinking I would send the Mexicans back a few feet with a couple of quick shots. A fresh, thick swarm

of bullets disabused me of that illusion. It seemed like
I had an entire army zeroing in on my carcass.

You know the final scene in Butch Cassidy and the
Sundance Kid, where the two bank robbers decide to
rush the entire Bolivian army? That's about how I felt
at that moment, minus William Goldman's snappy dia-
logue and Conrad Hall's awesome cinematography.

There was no theme music, either.

Turning on my belly, I crawled toward the back of
the building, hoping to make it to my pack and guns.
Bullets continued to fly, shredding the trucks and the
dirt. A thick pall of black smoke rose from the truck.
After I'd gone a few yards, I realized the smoke was
covering my retreat. I pushed a little faster, and made it
to the back of the building. I got up and ran over to the
wall where I'd left the guns.

There was no rest for the wicked—two figures
emerged from the smoke, firing in my direction. I
dumped a grenade in the launcher and pumped the shell
toward them. Unfortunately, I was so hyped by adrenaline that my aim was way high; the projectile sailed
way over their heads. I plopped a second grenade in,
and corrected. As I did, one of the banditos rose from
his crouch to get a better aim on me.

My grenade hit him square in the chest.

I didn't stop to watch the gruesome result. Huffin'
and puffin', I retreated to the far side of the building. I
leaned against the wall, took two breaths, then turned
to my left just as something flew around the side at me.
Instinctually, I lowered the Minimi and fired, cutting
down the two men running at me. I didn't see them
consciously; my senses were on autopilot, somehow
directly talking to my trigger finger.

Running south, I crossed the field separating the security center from a cluster of condo units. I was vaguely aware that people were firing at me from the other side of the street, but by now my brain was badly scrambled, and ran as much to escape the mental fog as the bullets. We work our asses off in PT or physical training every day at Red Cell International, the idea being that we practice to survive heavy runs like this. But running four or five miles in training — or even ten or twelve when Trace is feeling her oats — is nothing compared to two hundred feet under fire. My heart thumped, my throat tightened. My legs were rubber. I finally reached a wall and dove over it, rolling flat on my back.

If I'd stayed there even for five seconds, I'd have never gotten up. I twisted myself around, picked up the machine gun, aimed it back in the direction of the Mexicans, and fired.

I got maybe three or four bullets out before it clanged empty.

Doom on Dickie. I had to pull off the ruck and fish in it for a fresh magazine, then fiddle to get it into place. That took ten or twenty seconds, even more, which gave the Mexicans plenty of time to rally — when I looked back up, half a dozen of them were at the head of the field, coming for me.

The gun rattled satisfyingly as I fired at the Mexicans, several of whom fell as I sprayed the field. Unfortunately, the gun goes through bullets as quickly as Shotgun can go through a cake. I emptied the magazine literally in seconds.

I grabbed for another mag, but there was none. I'd shot my proverbial wad.

MORE LIKELY, I'D dropped a few of the mags along the way, but I wasn't in a position to start crying over lost ammo. I left the gun and ran down the hill. The gunfire stoked up again when I was still a few strides from the wall. My legs were so fatigued I tripped as I went to leap over it.

I still had some grenades. Scrunching behind the wall, I pulled the launcher around and loaded. I counted off a few seconds, then rose. Just as I was about to fire, I realized the Mexicans had taken cover behind the wall north of me. I angled the launcher back and fired, plopping the grenade a few feet behind it. By the time it landed I was already skidding down the hill, using gravity to help get me to my legs.

By the time I reached the next wall, I realized no one was firing at me. I kept going, slipping past a fence and heading for the open field of the undeveloped units at the base of the hill.

My brain started to clear and I remembered Mr. Leferd. I had to cross the road and go back up another block to get to the unit where I'd stashed him.

Maybe the goons would be so busy focusing on me they'd miss him.

"Junior, how many of these bastards are following me?" I asked over the radio.

"Dick, you're breaking up," he said. "Retransmit."

"How many people are after me?"

"I thought you wanted me to check the camp."

"Come back and see who's behind me. Wait—is the camp clear?"

"Camp is clear." He said something else, but I couldn't hear—now *he* was breaking up.

I worked my way parallel to the unit across the street, half crouching, half running. I rose tentatively, made sure the path was clear, then ran across the road as fast as I could manage. The adrenaline was dissipating; at this point, my muscles were drowning in lactate. I sensed that if I stopped for too long, I'd stiffen and freeze in place.

When I made it to the front of the building, I caught my breath by walking a few steps, then trotted to the back. I paused at the corner, looked out, then scrambled across the narrow backyard to the next set of condos. I was out of view of the community center and behind the condos the goons were checking.

I could turn south and go to the camp as I'd intended. But that meant leaving the crazy Mr. Leferd to be caught by the cartel thugs.

Not an option.

Running through the side yards, I came out on the street and waited for a second, trying to get my bearings. I couldn't remember which of the damn units I'd left Leferd in.

The radio buzzed.

"Dick? Dick, are you . . . me? They're working in pairs. They . . . *Shit!*"

I glanced behind me and saw why he was cursing — one of the banditos was holding an M16 on me.

The goon motioned that I should put up my hands. It seemed like a reasonable thing to do, and so I complied. He moved toward me at a snail's pace. I thought of running, but if there was one of them here, there was bound to be several others nearby, and it made no sense to run from one man's gun into the guns of others.

I also figured that being captured would be a hell of a

lot better than being shot. Worse case, Doc could trade de Sarcena for me.

The goon said something in Spanish that I didn't quite understand. He yelled it again, with about the same results—I held my hands out and told him in Spanish I couldn't hear.

He motioned with the gun, indicating I ought to come toward him. He stepped back, making room for me to come around the back of the building.

"*No problema,*" I said, starting forward. I took a quick peek left, then right—nobody there.

If he was by himself, I thought, I could overpower him if I could get close enough. I moved forward at a slight diagonal, angling so I could make sure there was no one covering us from the other backyard.

After a few steps, my friend with the gun decided he didn't like the way I was moving. He pointed his weapon at me and started yelling in Spanish that I had better do as he said or I would bleed worse than I was already bleeding—my clothes were covered with blood and obviously he thought I'd been hit.

I spread my hands a little farther. He motioned toward the concrete patio on my right. He moved that way as well, out ahead of me, circling toward the glass doors. I started walking sideways, inching in his direction. I managed to get about six or seven feet away before he realized he had made a mistake. He jerked the rifle up and down, then turned the barrel to the left, demanding that I move in that direction.

Needless to say, pushing his aim away only made it easier for me. I lunged, grabbing the gun before he could point it back in my direction.

Not, unfortunately, before he could fire. The rifle

rattled as I pressed toward him, a three-shot burst spitting from the barrel. He fell back against the house, tripping as I pushed in. His head smacked against the glass door just right, shattering the glass. Both of us fell through, me on top, the gun in between.

The floor took care of the rest. His head slammed onto the stone. His eyes rolled back and his body went limp.

I glanced up and saw two of his comrades just coming through the door. Both wore the shocked look of recognition a person gets when he realizes he's in deep shit.

I pulled the M16 up, swung it around, and fired.

Nada. The Mexican had emptied his magazine.

Jackass.

Now I was the one in deep shit. I did the only thing I could do: I threw the gun at them and through the shattered door, bounding off the patio and scrambling as quickly as I could across the backyard of the adjoining unit. I flipped over the wall, sliding onto my butt as I went over. I lay there for a second, gathering my breath.

One of the goons came out of the house, yelling and screaming that he was going to kill me. I squeezed closer to the wall, hoping it would keep me hidden.

Not exactly a winning strategy, but my brain was not working all that well. I took out my pistol and waited, trying to listen for the goon, who undoubtedly would be coming down to look for me.

After what seemed like hours, I heard footsteps coming in my direction. I held my breath and strained my ears, sorting the sounds—it was only one of them, I thought, moving slowly if steadily as he tried to figure out where the hell I was.

My plan was simple. Pistol ready, I would wait until the Mexican put his head over the wall, then I'd give him a third eye.

The footsteps came closer and closer. My hand was steady. I aimed the gun in the direction I figured he would be coming from.

The goon must have been a foot away when Murphy intervened.

Murphy didn't intervene, exactly. He decided to call my cell phone.

Not the sat phone, which I had carefully set to silent ring long before and checked several times during the day. But the cell phone, intended for backup (and desperation) only.

I'm *positive* I set it to silent before I went out on the op. I don't believe I had even used it since coming to Mexico. I may even have turned the damn thing off. But somewhere along the way, possibly as the result of being jostled and jogged, it had not only turned itself on but put the ringer at its highest volume.

As I said earlier, Murphy has an *extreme* sense of humor.

I couldn't grab the phone to turn it off without changing hands on the pistol. I wasn't about to do that: I was sure the Mexican would leap over the wall now that my ringer was telling him where I was. As the phone continued to bleat, my heart rate doubled. Sweat gushed from every pore.

But the goon didn't appear. The fate of his friends must have sobered him. He wasn't about to do anything rash. Plus, he had seen me throw the gun away, so he knew I was unarmed.

Or *thought* he knew. An important distinction.

Some cell phones have an annoying feature that rings the phone not only when a person calls, but when the voice mail is activated. I've never actually figured out how to turn that off without turning off the caller ring as well. But my lack of technical expertise was a virtue now. I swapped my pistol into the other hand, pulled the cell phone from my pocket, and dished it down along the wall line. Then I nudged backward toward the house.

The phone rang.

The baboon stepped to the wall, gun ready. He jumped up, spraying the cell with bullets.

Mine hit him square in the temple.

As soon as he fell, I popped up, expecting to see his friends. But they had disappeared. I scrambled to my feet, grabbed the M16, then started running.

The M16 had a spare magazine taped to the one in the rifle. Both were thirty-round affairs, which angle off at the bottom. Not quite the banana-style round clip on an AK47, but the same general idea.

Once I reached the back corner of the unit block, I checked the side, then crept up along the wall of the building. There was a small cluster of goons up the street, milling around the front of the house.

As quietly as I could, I began to retreat. But there were shouts from the back. Two or three Mexicans were heading my way. I hadn't been discovered yet, but it was only a matter of time—I was trapped.

Then, just when I thought it couldn't get much worse, I heard a siren out front.

Great, I thought, the goons had finally called in reinforcements.

The siren was abruptly drowned out by the sound of

exploding grenades and machine-gun fire. The gunfire stoked up into a loud crescendo, machine-gun bullets and automatic rifle fire vying with grenade blasts. Then in an instant it stopped, as if it had been a sound track and someone hit the off switch.

I crawled to the front of the house. A truck pulled up—Shotgun was standing in the back bed, a Minimi in one hand, a grenade launcher in another.

"Thought you could use some help," said Shotgun. "Interested in a ride?"

[IV]

SHOTGUN POUNDED ON the roof of the cab as I climbed into the back of the truck. Big Mike put it in reverse and we lurched backward, spinning into a three-point turn and then zooming out around the other side of the buildings. Saul and Paul Smith were waiting for us; both hopped into the back.

"Where are the others?" I asked.

"I sent them back with Veronica," said Shotgun. "I told them just to go straight to the border."

"All right. We gotta pick up the old guy in that house over there. That unit there."

Shotgun banged on the roof again and the truck stopped. I took his gun and covered him while he ran into the condo.

I'd guessed which unit I'd left him in. And I'd guessed . . . wrong. Shotgun emerged a few seconds later, empty-handed.

"Next building, next building," I yelled.

A few seconds later, he came running out with Mr. Leferd over his shoulder. He hopped right up on the truck bed with him, as if he didn't weigh an ounce.

"Let's get out of here," I yelled to Big Mike. "Take us up the back way where the others went."

"No, Dick, the way's clear to the highway," Shotgun told me. "Didn't you hear Junior?"

"He hasn't transmitted."

Shotgun reached for my ear set. My wire had broken, just as Veronica's had.

Junior had been trying to get me to tell me Shotgun was coming. When he couldn't get me on the radio, he had resorted to the phones. He was the one who'd called earlier and almost gotten me killed.

"All right, let's get out of here," I said.

I grabbed one of the spare rifles in the back and pointed it over the roof of the cab as we drove. The thugs had taken a thorough beating, but they weren't all dead; Junior had seen several flee into the community center. The truck picked up speed and we sailed up the hill. No one came out, no one fired at us.

We slowed down as we came to the top of the hill and turned onto the main road.

"Dick, Junior says we got trucks moving through the hamlet," warned Shotgun, putting his hand over his ear. "Army trucks."

He handed me his ear set.

"What's coming at us, Junior?" I asked.

"Couple of troop trucks—Mexican army, looks like."

"Army or cartel?"

"Well, they have Mexican flags and they look official."

The truth is, it was probably immaterial. The army often did the work of the cartel here.

I could already see the dust coming up ahead. I pounded on the top of the cab to warn Big Mike. "Take us past the trucks," I yelled. "Flank speed. Get us past them."

Big Mike stepped on the gas. But as we dipped down the hill, I saw it wasn't going to work — the lead troop truck pulled across the road to block our path. Big Mike started to angle to the right, where it looked like there was just enough space to get by. Then the second truck pulled up to block it. Big Mike slammed on the brakes, jamming Shotgun and me against the back of the cab.

Soldiers hopped out of the back of the trucks, brandishing their assault rifles.

"A lot of 'em," muttered Shotgun. "I may have to re-load."

"Relax," I told him. "Let's see if we can talk our way out of this."

I got down out of the pickup. An officer jumped from the cab of the second truck and walked up behind the troops. He was a sawed-off rooster kind of guy, strutting behind a big belly. I guessed his ego would be about twice as big as his stomach.

I underestimated.

"You are under arrest," he said, using English.

"Why would you want to arrest us?"

"You are drug dealers."

"We're not drug dealers."

"We will judge this. Tell your men to surrender or they will be shot."

I took a quick glance around. Upward of fifty soldiers

were scattered in front of the vehicles. And I could hear another truck coming up in the distance.

Talk about a Butch Cassidy-Sundance Kid moment. I certainly wasn't willing to trust my bruised carcass to the Mexican justice system. On the other hand, fighting it out wasn't much of an option. My life insurance policy did not cover self-inflicted massacres.

I wracked my brain for contacts in the Mexican army I trusted. I needn't have wasted the mental power—such a contact, such an officer, doesn't exist. I thought of calling Narco, but of course he couldn't help without blowing his cover. My only option would be to call on the State Department.

Even writing that line makes me gag.

"Who's your commander?" I said, bluffing for time.

"I am in charge here," said Big Belly. "I make the decisions. You are under arrest. You will come peaceful, or you will come with duress."

This wasn't the place to explain the proper formation of adverbs from adjectives. I made a few more mental calculations. If I shot him, would his troops scatter? How many men could Shotgun shoot before needing to pop another magazine into his weapon?

There was a commotion behind the second troop truck. It sounded at first as if it was soldiers piling out of the late-arriving truck. Then I saw that the men holding on us at the front of the line were stepping aside.

Two women appeared—Juanita and Veronica. Another Mexican woman and a young man came through behind them, the leading edge of a small group of villagers.

"Where is the colonel?" shouted Juanita in Spanish. "Where is the Little Rooster?"

There are other translations for the phrase she used, but we'll accept that one as the "official" translation.

Juanita marched up to Big Belly and began haranguing him. He held his own for a few moments, shouting that she needed to show respect for a member of the military and a decorated war hero.[27] But she easily gave as good as she got, and within a few minutes Big Belly began to look like a henpecked husband.

"You allow yourself to be a tool of criminals," said Juanita. "You betray the people of Mexico. You betray yourself. You betray me, and all of your relatives. You have blood on your hands. These cartel people are the worst kind of criminals, the dirt at the bottom of the ocean. You take yourself to church on Sunday and you have the nerve to receive! To receive our holy God. You call yourself a Catholic. But you work for the devil."

Juanita's tirade went on for a good ten minutes. Big Belly seemed to shrink another inch as each minute passed. Juanita invoked religion, nationhood, humanity, common sense — I wished I had taped the speech.

Finally, she got to the point, at least as far as we were concerned.

"These people — this one here —" She jabbed her finger at me. "They are trying to do the good thing, the right thing. They fight the criminals. And you dare to arrest them? Your mother would be ashamed. I'm sure she is ashamed."

---

[27] Which war this may have been was never explained.

Juanita glanced toward heaven as she made the sign of the cross. That was just too much for Big Belly.

"You may go," he said, raising his hand. "Go. Go. Go."

[V]

IT WOULD BE tempting to think that all it took to turn a corrupt Mexican colonel into an upstanding Christian soldier-statesman was a tongue lashing by a beefy short-order cook who happened to be a second cousin.

The truth is a little more complicated. Standing aside and letting us pass didn't cost the colonel anything, since there were no cartel members around at that moment to see what was going on. In fact, it made life much simpler for him, since someone was sure to protest to the government if he took us away.

Then there was the matter of the helicopters in the air above us.

Chester Arthur had scrambled his helo from the airport. Getting the full sit rep from Junior as things unfolded, he realized that a single unarmed helicopter wasn't going to be in a position to help if the attack continued. So he decided he needed to get some backup.

As we've already discussed, the U.S. military has very strict rules when it comes to crossing the border, rules that can be summarized in two words: DO NOT.

However, in most circumstances they can engage in action against obvious drug smugglers. Realizing this, Chet crossed over the border, then dipped down low so that he disappeared from radar. Circling to the south, he flew a pattern about thirty-five feet off the ground, rising just enough to be detected by a border surveillance radar. The operator of the radar assumed that an aircraft flying that pattern was a smuggler. When Chet refused to answer queries, a DEA border task force was alerted. Planes and a helicopter were scrambled to intercept and question him.

Chet played possum, hovering and peeking up just enough to make it seem he was up to something big. As a pair of Air National Guard Blackhawks came into view, he high-tailed it for the border. The ruse might or might not have worked on its own, but in this case Chet fortunately recognized the call sign of one of the scrambled helos. It belonged to a friend of his.

He broadcast a greeting to the pilot on his squadron channel. The man was incredulous.

"Chester? You're working for the dopers?"

"No. Some friends on the ground need some help," he said. Chet briefly explained.

"We're not supposed to cross the border," said his friend finally.

"Not even in hot pursuit?"

"I'm not in hot pursuit."

"If it's Dick Marcinko, who's gotten himself in hot water with the cartels for killing some of the bastards?"

"Come to think of it," replied his friend. "Our GPS unit seems to be malfunctioning. I'm not entirely sure where the border is. I better get a little lower to see if I recognize anything."

Chester and the Air National Guard Blackhawks appeared just as Juanita ended her tirade. And just for good measure, a helicopter from the Mexican attorney general's office[28] came north as well.

Still, I'd like to think that Juanita's appeal to justice and propriety had something to do with it. For all its troubles, the Mexican military still has some good officers left in it. I'd like to think that Big Belly was one of them.

"Like to" doesn't mean I will, though.

VERONICA JOINED US in the truck. She'd taken the old folks to within sight of the border, where a pair of Customs agents alerted by Junior were waiting. As soon as she saw they were going to be OK, she raced back to the Mexican village on foot and rallied Juanita. The cook took care of the rest. The Mexicans hated the cartel as much as the Americans did.

"Two or three of their kids were watching from the hills and saw you kicking the crap out of the cartel goons," Veronica told me as we drove up toward the border. "Once they saw how weak the toughs really were, they were encouraged."

They might have shown their encouragement by joining a little earlier, I thought, but I kept my mouth shut. There is no sense ruining the mood of a beautiful woman.

Unfortunately, the Mexicans had no information that could help her find her grandparents. Saul, et al, were

---

[28] The Procuraduría General de la República (PGR), which is the Attorney General's office in México, operates a number of Bell 206L-4 LongRanger helicopters to assist in the war on drugs. These look like stretched versions of the Huey we all knew and loved in Vietnam; they're much more potent aircraft, though, as they take advantage of the improvements in technology since then.

equally stumped. Veronica painstakingly questioned each resident in turn, asking a full range of questions about the bankruptcy and the cartel's takeover, the work on the property, and a dozen other things that seemed to have little connection to their disappearance. Each time she finished, she looked at me and shook her head ever so slightly.

"I'm sorry they don't have any information on your grandparents," I told her when she was done. "If there's anything I can do to help—"

"Anything?"

All sorts of visions popped into my mind when she said that—including one of Karen Fairchild wringing my neck.

Have I mentioned that Veronica was a beautiful woman? Have I described the way she filled those khaki pants . . . or the way her chest strained the buttons on her shirt ever so slightly?

Stop slobbering. You'll get the book wet. Worse, if it's an e-reader, you could electrocute yourself.

"Would you really do anything to help?" Veronica asked.

"Within reason," I said. "And maybe a few things beyond reason."

Veronica put her hand on mine. At that point, resistance was futile.

"Anything," I told her.

"I'd like to question de Sarcena. And trade him for my grandparents."

I'm not sure how long it was before I managed to speak. "That wasn't quite what I had in mind."

"Oh?"

"Look—I don't know how to tell you this."

She put her finger to my lips. "I know they're probably dead. But if there's a chance, I have to take it."

Her lip quivered. A single tear rolled out of her right
eye.

"Let's see what he has to say," I told her.

WHILE WE'RE HEADING to the ranch, let's tie up
some loose ends.

Thanks to Junior, authorities on both sides of the
border now knew about the tunnel. More importantly,
so did the news media. Reporters and camera crews
scrambled to catch up with the police and military
units descending on the area.

On the American side, the tunnel surfaced in an
abandoned gas station on a scrub road about a hundred
yards from the border. Angel Hills was a little more
than a half mile away as the crow flies. That may not
sound like much, but for a tunnel that's pretty damn
long. In September of 2010, authorities discovered a
pair of two-thousand-foot-long tunnels in the San
Diego area used to smuggle marijuana (and surely
other things) across the border. If you add in the access
area before the security center in Angel Hills, this tunnel was a little longer. Those tunnels had a primitive
railcar arrangement just like this one, but weren't quite
as wide. In fact, of the 125 tunnels that have been discovered under the border during the last decade or so,
the Angel Hills tunnel ranks as arguably the most sophisticated.

Of course, that's only among those that have been
discovered.

Unfortunately, there were no thugs in the tunnel

when the authorities closed in. And while we can make several guesses about what the tunnel was used for, nothing was recovered when the police swarmed in. Pot is usually transported in wrapped-up bricks and other containers; the same with other drugs and contraband. That makes finding residue a little harder than scraping the side of your pipe bowl.

It's also important to note that the contraband flows two ways—I'd be more than willing to guess that a good portion of the weapons we grabbed at the terror farm came across the border through the tunnel. The same for the cartel's cash.

I wasn't surprised to find that every one of the residents who had left Angel Hills wanted to return to their homes as soon as possible. Now that they had fought for their homes, they weren't about to leave them. Various promises were made by the authorities; whether they'll be kept or not I have no idea.

AND THEN THERE'S Trace.

We last saw her and the boys by the side of the road, a policeman[29] holding a gun on her.

Anyone who has ever dealt with Trace Dahlgren knows that the *last* thing you want to do is pull a gun on her. It's just not a healthy thing to do. There's no saying how she will react—a kick to the face, a hard karate-style chop to the arm, maybe a tuck and roll into your legs.

In this case, the police officer was far enough away and the light was sufficiently dim that none of those

---

[29] I use the term loosely.

responses was particularly appropriate. Trace spread
her hands, and took a step to the side.

The police officer then made a critical mistake. He
misinterpreted her actions as a tacit surrender. And having successfully bullied her (he thought), he decided to
try for more.

"You are a good-looking one," said the officer.
"Maybe we can make a private arrangement. Unzip
your jeans."

"Trace?" Tex called from the car. *"Problemo?"*

The policeman turned his gun in Tex's direction.
The next thing the cop knew was that he was eating
dirt—Trace had launched herself in a flying leap at his
head, tumbling him down. His gun flew away, but it
wouldn't have helped him much anyway: his head and
most of his body were in the process of being stomped
by Trace, who had rebounded to her feet. She went at
him with all the gusto a would-be rapist deserves, making sure he would be in no position to try anything
similar with anyone else.

The man's partner climbed down off the cab of the
truck and began shooting. He did so as he ran, with the
usual result—his shots were wildly inaccurate. Finally
he stopped, took aim—and fell down to the ground,
three bullets in his forehead.

"I was sleeping, damn it," said Stoneman. "Waking
me up with this shit."

WHILE THERE ARE plenty of corrupt policemen in
Mexico, these two slimebags weren't among them.
They were not actual policemen at all, but cartel mem-
bers who donned uniforms and were shaking down

truck drivers and tourists, a common occurrence on just about any road in Mexico. The police car and the uniforms had been stolen from a town in the next state over the week before.

While Trace and the boys were figuring this out, the truck driver decided to get on with his journey. Having made an investment in the situation, Trace decided he wasn't going to get away without having his trailer inspected. She ran to the car and jumped back behind the wheel; Tex and Stoneman were barely able to get in as she burned rubber and launched after the tractor-trailer.

"Tell him to pull over," she yelled to Tex as she raced alongside the truck.

Before Tex could say anything, the truck driver twisted his wheel in their direction. The sudden lunge shoved their car off the other shoulder.

"Enough of this shit," said Tex.

He took his rifle and blew out the rear tires of the truck, the only ones he could get as they fell behind. The vehicle bounded off the road, then twisted and turned over.

The driver scrambled out and took off, running into the darkness.

"Let him go," said Trace, putting up her hand to stop Tex from firing. "It's not worth killing him."

"These guys may disagree," said Stoneman. "The ones who are alive, anyway."

Stoneman had shot off the lock on the truck's door. Inside he found exactly eighty-seven people, packed nearly solid. Most had broken bones or suffered other injuries when the truck turned over. Two were dead.

They were all Guatemalans. They had been heading

for the U.S. border, where they were promised they would be welcomed into the Land of Milk, Honey, and Better Things.

As SOON AS she saw people were hurt, Trace got on her sat phone and called Junior, asking him to call the legitimate police. She made some calls herself, then went to help Tex and Stoneman treat the wounded.

They waited until dawn, when finally a lone car came out to see what was going on. Deciding it didn't make much sense to hang around for what certainly would be a half-assed investigation, they left as soon as they heard the car's siren in the distance.

"Good thing he's going lights and sirens," said Tex. "Wouldn't want anyone to think he's taking his time."

[VI]

MONGOOSE GAVE US a warm SEAL greeting when we arrived at the ranch: he cursed the living crap out of us for having so much fun without him.

"You suck, you suck, you suck," he told Shotgun when we drove up.

He was only a little more civil to me. SEALs—even ones like Mongoose who have been separated from the service for a few years—don't like to miss out on the action. And I'm sure it was especially galling that he'd had to play babysitter while we were getting shot at. I'm afraid he may have taken out some of his frustrations on de Sarcena; the cartel leader looked a little worse for wear when Veronica and I went in to talk to him.

He was still doped, but not nearly as badly as earlier. The cartel boss was sitting upright in a wooden chair next to the bed when we came in. He'd been stripped to his underwear, and he had food stains on his T-shirt.

His eyes lit up when Veronica entered the room, but quickly narrowed. He called her words highly inappropriate for any woman, but especially one as beautiful as she was.

Veronica handled it very well: she slapped him across the face so hard he spit blood.

"If you want to live, you will tell me where Mr. and Mrs. Cortina are." Veronica folded her arms in front of her chest. Her Spanish was sharp and her eyes flashed with anger. "The people you had removed from Angel Hills so you could build your tunnel."

"I have no idea what you're talking about."

Veronica grabbed de Sarcena so violently I thought she was going to slam him against the wall. Instead, she pulled him up and held him a few inches from her face. The room was small, and hot, claustrophobic even if you weren't bound hands and feet as de Sarcena was.

"The Anglos," she told him. "What did you do with the Americans in the development where you built your tunnel?"

"I—I—I."

"When I worked for you, you said this was very potent." Veronica reached with her left hand to a spot of great male vulnerability. I felt a twinge myself. "It seems like the snake is only a little mouse."

De Sarcena groaned. Veronica pushed him back into the chair. He slipped as he went back, falling onto the bed.

"You're pathetic. Tell me what you did with the

Americans or you'll die the worst death imaginable. It will be very slow. Very slow. The worm will be the first to go. Then we'll seal it off with a tourniquet so you don't die from it. At first."

The mobster shook his head. His face had been pretty pale when we came in; now it was almost translucent.

"Maybe I should talk to him," I suggested. "Take a little break."

Veronica frowned, then with obvious reluctance left the room.

"She's nuts," I told him in English. "She's crazy."

"You can't trick me," he said. "I know you're as bad as she is. I've read all your books."

"I'm not trying to trick you. She *will* kill you. Slowly. And I'll let her."

He pressed his lips together.

"So where are they?" I asked.

"I don't know what you're talking about."

"The Americans who were at Angel Hills. You know where that was. You had a tunnel there."

"I don't know anything about tunnels."

"Right." I turned to go.

"James handles things like that," he blurted.

"James?"

"James Vincent — he is in charge of the crossings — I have a large enterprise. I don't see to the details. Don't let her kill me. Hand me over to the Mexican authorities."

Sure, I'll do that, I thought; you'll be out of jail inside an hour. But now that I knew what he wanted, dealing with him was child's play. "If you cooperate, I'll see what we can do."

He managed a weak smile. I doubt he truly believed me; he was only mildly drugged. Still, he must have wanted to grab at any possibility for hope.

"Who is James Vincent?" I asked. "Is he Mexican?"

"You promise to turn me over to the Mexican authorities?"

"Who is James Vincent?"

"Promise."

"I promise to turn you over to a Mexican, yes. Who is James Vincent?"

I DIDN'T BELIEVE what de Sarcena told me, even after I had Junior do more research.

"He's definitely the mayor," said Junior, pointing to the Web site he'd pulled of a small town about ten miles away.

"You're sure that's him?"

"I had Shunt cross-check his bank accounts against the cartel accounts he's been looking into. We've got him nailed. It's the same guy. He gets fifty grand wired into this account in Kenya. From there—*whoosh*."

Kenya as in Africa, by the way. In case you were wondering. The banking system there had several things to recommend itself to illegal activities, starting with bank officials desperate to build reserves at any cost.

The amazing thing wasn't that a politician was on the take—*ha!*—or that a government official was actually a member of the cartel payroll—*double ha!* It was the fact that the town James Vincent was mayor of—Rabbit Hole, Arizona—was in the U.S.

And did I mention that Mr. James Vincent—*the* Mr.

James Vincent—was in the primary for U.S. Senate?
And ahead in the polls?

Oh, and one of his biggest supporters was Jordan
Macleish, the man who had hired me to find Melissa
Reynolds and free her from her kidnappers.

[VII]

MELISSA REYNOLDS AND Doc had set out the day
before for Austin, Texas, to meet Macleish and her dad.
Even before they arrived, Ms. Reynolds got cold feet.
She didn't want to see Macleish, she told Doc. She didn't
care for him anymore.

Very understandable, he told her. But as a business
matter, I would greatly appreciate it if you would at
least come with me to show him that you're all right.

I will, she said, but only after I meet with my dad.

That seemed fair enough to Doc. Not only was Greenie
her father, but he was also a fellow SEAL, and therefore should come first by any measure. Greenie was
supposed to be flying in from Somalia the next day,
and so waiting didn't seem like that big a deal.

But when Doc tried getting information about where
he might meet Reynolds, he ran into a brick wall. The
number Melissa had for Greenie went unanswered.
This wasn't particularly surprising, given that Greenie
was probably in transit. But his other contact information, including an e-mail address, came back unknown
or disconnected. Doc tried calling the security firm
that Greenie was working for, but got no cooperation;

they refused even to confirm that he was an employee, apparently for security reasons.

Finally, Doc did what all good navy sea dogs would do in that situation: he started calling other chiefs.

If you've been in the navy, then you know that chief petty officer is more than just a rank. Becoming chief confers a certain ageless wisdom to a man, and now a woman as well. A chief—one seldom uses the full title—may not be able to walk on water, but he knows where all the rocks are, generally because he put them there. No ship in the navy could ever sail without the efforts and energy of its chiefs. You could replace a captain, and the boat would go on. Leave a dozen ensigns—*please!*—at the dock and no one will notice. But if a single chief has so much as a head cold at the wrong time, the entire ship's company can be in mortal peril.

At least that's *their* version of reality. And I'm too smart to disagree with it.

Doc started working the old chiefs' network, plumbing for information about Greenie and his ship. He tracked down the ship, and even got a satellite phone number for the chief mate. (Aboard the freighter, the chief mate headed the deck department, making him second in command.) At first he had a bit of trouble getting him because of the time difference, but Doc naturally persevered, and eventually he managed to get the chief mate.

"Dee security team hiss very good," said the chief mate, who spoke with a heavy Egyptian accent. "You speak to who?"

"Bill Reynolds."

"Do we have one by dat name? I check."

Reynolds was eventually found and brought to the chief mate's cabin, where the sat phone was handed over.

"What are you doing aboard the ship?" Doc asked, after greeting him with the usual warm regards SEALs show for each other. (It's a surprise the phones didn't break with all that cursing.)

"We're protecting the tub from Somalian pirates. The damn bastards have been going a couple hundred miles out to sea. This ship's so old I'd be surprised if they'd even want it. Got more rust on it than paint, I'll tell you that."

"Aren't you coming back to Texas?"

"Why would I do that?"

"For Melissa."

"What? Why? Is she in trouble? What's going on?"

"She's been kidnapped."

"Holy shit!"

"Relax. She's OK. Dick Marcinko rescued her."

"That ol' son of a bitch? You tell him to keep his hands off her! If he even looks at her crooked, I'm calling up the ex. She'll come after him with a shotgun and a pitchfork."

My reputation preceded me.

Doc straightened out the confusion, then let Melissa talk to her father. Once they caught up, he got back on the line and tried pumping Reynolds for information about Macleish. Reynolds knew absolutely nothing.

"But when I get back, I'll break every bone in his goddamn body," added Reynolds. "Mother-sucking predator scumbag rich bastard shithead."

"Your call," said Doc.

"Tell Marcinko I owe him one," said Reynolds. "Hey, I gotta go. Take care of my kid, all right?"

"Not a problem, Greenie."

"Greenie's my dad?" said Melissa after Doc hung up. "That's his nickname? Greenie?"

"You didn't know that?"

"My father keeps a lot to himself. What's it mean?"

"Who?"

"Greenie. How did he get it?"

"Can't tell you that. He's got to tell you himself. SEAL code."

"What? For real?"

"Yup."

Actually, I think it was Doc's code, but she let it drop.

As I understand it, the name was either a flattering reference to Reynolds's activity level when he first joined the Teams — "greenies" being a slang term for amphetamines back in the day — or a description of his face the first time he went out in an assault boat. We report, you decide.

BY THIS POINT, nothing surprised me. I told Doc to check in with our Mr. Macleish: find out where he was and what he was up to.

"But don't tell him that we have Melissa yet," I added. "Let's see how this thing unfolds first."

"Smells to you, huh?"

"Worse than donkey barn on a 120-degree day."

"Reminds me of the admiral's garage on Sicily, was it?"

"As bad as that."

RABBIT HOLE, ARIZONA, is located a few miles east of Bisbee. Like Bisbee and a lot of the other settlements nearby, the place was first discovered by miners, and went through the usual boom and bust cycles associated with mining. It never grew anywhere near as big as some of its neighbors, let alone Bisbee, but it did have a brief heyday around 1917. With World War I going strong and the U.S. just about to get involved, the price of copper started going up. A small vein at the edge of the town brought workers and an influx of cash. The copper quickly played out, but enough people had come to the area to establish a stable if small economy.

Not as well known as Bisbee, its Main Street has a well-polished sleepy town veneer. The out of the way location a few miles off the state highway adds to the hideaway allure for Grade C celebrities who can't afford to jet off overseas. Their presence entices a somewhat larger circle of hangers-on and wannabes. They, in turn, support the twenty-first century's standard tourist amenities: nice restaurants, overpriced souvenir stands, and local branches of international banks catering to the obscenely rich.

If you read the news stories, the record of economic success, campaign fund-raising power, and out-of-state connections made James Vincent a potent comer. But driving toward this burp of a town analyzing the data Junior and Shunt had gathered, I came to a much different conclusion. It was certainly true that James Vincent had connections and was getting donations from the tourists and second-homers who lived in the lavish adobe houses dotting the hills above his town. But those donations were nearly all under a hundred bucks a pop. Vincent had risen in state politics because he could raise big money for his party's candidates in elections around the state. He sponsored lavish dinners at big ticket prices, with the profits going to the party nominees. The dinners always sold out. He rounded up marks for "Hundred Circles"—a group of donors who each kicked in a hundred thousand dollars to the party. He found groups who could donate in-kind services like telephone banks and billboard space for candidates' use.

Granted, the candidates he backed had often lost, but that just endeared him even more to the hierarchy. Anyone who could raise money for these losers would surely be able to raise money for himself.

Maybe that wasn't the *exact* way they looked at it, but I'd guess it was pretty close.

So how had he raised this money?

The records mandated by election law were more confusing than the statements my publisher sends me documenting my book royalties—which is saying quite a lot. The big donations were barely mentioned, generally scraping around the regs because of some loophole inserted by the pols to keep their money suppliers clear. Meanwhile, there were thousands and thousands of pages listing small donations:

A. Able: $20.
A. B. Able: $20.
B. Able: $20.

You get the picture.

The mayor seemed extremely adept at passing the hat and picking up small bills.

"Or laundering money," commented Veronica, looking over my shoulder in the backseat of the rented Chevy Impala as we drove to Rabbit Hole. "These names appear over and over. They look like they were taken out of a telephone book."

"Could be."

"A Mexican cartel buying its own U.S. senator?" she asked, putting two and two together.

"Why not? Doesn't everyone?"

We drove on in silence after that, the only sounds the crunch of potato chips in Shotgun's mouth, and Mongoose's occasional grunt as he adjusted the cruise control. He found the turnoff for the county road that led into town. We drove past dusty brown hilltops ringed by green, then came up over a rise and looked out on a valley of every shade of yellow and brown, with a few speckles of red thrown in. A blue-tinted stream coursed down the side of a steep rock-faced hill, evidence of copper somewhere beneath the stone.

"There's the town," said Veronica, pointing out the window as we came around the bend. "Lot smaller than I thought."

Rabbit Hole's main street was a stretch of county highway not more than a quarter mile long. Most of the city's buildings were on the side streets, poking into the hills that parted in the center of town. We passed a cemetery, and when I saw some fresh mounds at the back, I couldn't help wondering if that's where her grandparents really were.

"Better watch it," Shotgun told Mongoose between chips. "Little place like this gonna be a speed trap."

"I'll do the drivin', asshole," snapped Mongoose.

Not two seconds later, a police car pulled out from

behind a dilapidated building on the other side of the road, lights flashing, siren wailing.

"Told ya," said Shotgun.

Mongoose shot him an evil eye, but said nothing.

"Best behavior, boys," I said, settling back in the seat. "We don't need to boost the fine by being jack-offs."

"License and registration," said the policeman when Mongoose rolled down the window.

"Mornin', officer," answered Mongoose in his sweet-est voice. You'd have thought he was asking for a date. "What seems to be the problem?"

"License and registration," repeated the cop, this time with attitude. "And it's well past noon, *son*."

Mongoose dug into his back pocket for his wallet. "This is a rental," he said, taking out his license.

"I see." The cop bent at the waist, getting a better look in the car. "And you're visitors?"

"Yes, sir."

"You have business in Rabbit Hole?"

"We're scouting for a movie," said Mongoose. It was our preagreed cover.

The cop wasn't impressed. He took the license and went back to his cruiser.

"Good morning," mocked Shotgun in a soft and sac-charine voice.

"Shut the hell up or I'll tell him your potato chips are laced with LSD," countered Mongoose.

"Hey, no sweat. They use that stuff for religion out here. Not against the law." Shotgun's laughter shook the car.

"How much you figure the fine's gonna be, Dick?" asked Mongoose.

"No way of knowing."

"Will the company pay?"

Shotgun's laughter doubled.

"I was talkin' to the boss," said Mongoose. "Dick?"

"I think it would probably be bad policy to pay for your speeding tickets," I told him.

"And expensive," put in Shotgun.

"Jeez. It was a speed trap. You saw. I wasn't going very fast."

"Yeah, eighty-five's standing still for Mongoose," said Shotgun.

"I'm gonna pop you, jackass."

"Gentlemen, there's a lady present," I said.

Mongoose lowered his head and gripped the steering wheel. I'm not saying his hands were tight, but his knuckles turned white.

"You can pay this at the courthouse in town," said the policeman, returning with a ticket. "I wouldn't let it go, because they'll start charging you interest. That's what gets a lot of people. That and the fees. If they have to come after you, they charge you. Then you're talking big money."

"Yeah," muttered Mongoose.

"What movie are you making?" said the cop, all friendly now.

"It's a western," grumbled Mongoose.

"Good place for it."

"Is it?" I leaned forward from the backseat. "Wide open spaces around?"

"Puhl-lenty of wide open spaces." The cop smiled, then gave me a quizzical look. "Have I seen you in something? Are you famous?"

"Not famous," I said.

"I know I've seen you somewhere." He scratched his chin. "Pro wrestling?"

I shook my head.

"My kid's got a video game," he said. "What do they call that—capture or something. Where they take a picture and put it into the game?"

"Not me," I told him.

"You have to be in pictures," he told Veronica, catching a good glimpse of her for the first time. "You're an actress—have I seen you in something?"

"We're just back lot people," she insisted. "Working for the producers. Have to find a good place to shoot. Small town, that sort of thing."

"You came to the right place."

"Any place we ought to stay away from?" I asked.

"How's that?"

"Dangerous or anything like that?"

"In Rabbit Hole? Nah."

"Old mine shafts? Hazardous waste?"

He laughed. "All the mines were dug up, mister, back in the early 1900s. They started doing strip-mining. As for hazardous waste, the only hazardous waste around these parts is the county jail about two miles out of town. There, they're under lock and key. Otherwise, this is God's country. Beautiful and clean."

"Where's there a good place to eat?" asked Shotgun, just as the cop was going to leave. "And get snacks?"

"Snacks? Best place is the grocer, center of town. That or Exxon. As for restaurants, take your pick. There are a dozen, one better than another. Tell 'em Charlie sent you."

I thought for sure Shotgun would ask if any gave a discount if you'd been ticketed by the police, but he didn't.

"Sorry about the ticket. Have a good day." He went off singing a little tune.

Mongoose stewed in the front seat as he pulled out.

"Aw come on, Mongoose, how bad can it be?" said Shotgun, trying to cheer him up. "Place out here in the wilderness like this, they probably aren't going to charge much. I'll bet you that ticket's like ten dollars."

"FIVE HUNDRED DOLLARS! Five hundred dollars! Shit." Mongoose shook his head so violently I thought it was going to fly off. "I don't have no five hundred dollars on me. For a traffic ticket? Five hundred dollars?"

"That's what the fine is, if you plead guilty," said the clerk. She was a shortish woman with bleached white hair held back in a tight ponytail. I'd guess she was only in her late twenties, but her face and arms were leathery from being out in the sun. "Now, you could plead *not* guilty and have a court date set. If you're going to be in town awhile."

"How long?"

She leaned over behind the window where she was standing and pulled up a binder. The Rabbit Hole courthouse was a two-story building at the far end of the Main Street stretch, painted bright white and constructed to look as if it had been there since the town's incorporation in 1830 or thereabouts. But it was actually all prefab metal and vinyl stucco not three years old.

"We have an opening November."

"November?"

"That's right. November, two years from now."

She said this with a straight face. Shotgun and I were practically doubled over, trying to keep from laughing out loud a few feet away.

"We do take credit cards," said the young woman.

"What if I don't have a credit card?" said Mongoose.

"Then I guess you'd have to just do it by mail. I can give you a form," she said, reaching back under the window. Mongoose was in such a bad mood he didn't even try to steal a glimpse of cleavage, which was ample and sunburned. "There will be a fifty-dollar posting fee, and then there's interest. We compound every twelve hours. I think it's quite fair."

"Damn."

She gave him her best school marm expression. I walked over.

"How much did you say it would cost him to plead guilty here and now?" I asked.

"Five hundred. Plus the processing fee."

"And how much is that?"

"Fifty dollars for a credit card."

"How about cash?" I asked, taking out my wallet.

"Oh, that's different. Then it's just the cash processing fee. Fifty dollars."

"So they're both fifty dollars," I said. "What's the difference?"

"Well, one's the credit card processing fee, and one's the cash fee."

I counted out six big ones[30] and handed them over. She smiled and put the money away in a drawer.

---

[30] Rumor has it this was from the stash of money I'd borrowed from de Sarcina. I plead ignorance; accounting is not my thing.

"Anything else?" she asked.

"Well I was expecting my change," I told her.

"But you gave me six hundred dollars."

"You said the fine was five hundred and the cash fee was fifty dollars. That makes $550."

"And then there's the clerk fee. That's another fifty. Do you want a receipt?"

"How much is the fee for that?" I asked.

"Fifty dollars."

"I think we'll live without it."

THE CLERK WAS quite friendly now that we were all on the right side of the law, and gave us all sorts of tips about where to eat and what to do. She also gave us a Chamber of Commerce map of the local sights, such as they were. We split up—Mongoose and Shotgun went off to check out the restaurants, while Veronica and I took a stroll down Main Street.

"Maybe they're prisoners in one of these basements," said Veronica. "Someplace we wouldn't suspect."

"Might be," I said, not bothering to point out that it would be the rare house with a basement in this area.

"Nice little town," she said.

"It's pretty."

"Shame about the ticket."

"Mongoose shouldn't have been going so fast."

The grocery store was about half the size of a chain drugstore back east, with a large plate-glass window and a decor that reminded me of the 1950s. A pair of choppers rode up the street, driven by older men whose long gray hair flowed back behind the motorcycles as they passed. The store across the way sold Native American art and artifacts; there were arrowheads in the window, along with stone knives and a snakeskin purse. I liked the knives and would have gone in to have a look, but the place was closed.

"Sleepy little place," said Veronica. "I wonder if de Sarcena gave us a bad steer."

"It's possible."

We turned up the last road before Main became a highway again. There were a variety of small gift shops and boutiques stuffed into very small buildings. We walked slowly past, playing tourist. When the boutiques ended, we kept up our stroll, pretending to admire the fancy tiles and the carefully arranged cacti in the gardens.

The mayor's house was on the right at the very end of the road. I had thought it would be a big place, an estate with a large iron fence surrounding it—I'd seen the fence in the Google Earth image we'd checked out before leaving. But what looked like a tall fence on the two-dimensional Google Earth turned out to be only a small rail and shadow in real life. Take away the overhang and the porch, and the house was very small, not much bigger than the shotgun shacks across from it. There were no guards, and not much pretense. You'd never know the guy was running for Senate, let alone sucking the teat of the most powerful drug cartel in Mexico.

"Doesn't look like anyone's home," said Veronica as we continued past.

"That can be deceiving."

The hard-packed road continued into a curve to the left, fading out in some rocks and scrub. I got the impression it had been created by a bulldozer some seventy or eighty years before, then completely forgotten.

"Security system?" Veronica asked when we were out of sight.

"Nothing elaborate. I think there may have been one of those Internet cameras stuck on the windowsill. If so, Shunt should be able to track it down. Might just be a local system though."

"You think my grandparents are dead?" Veronica stopped and grabbed my arm. Her fingers were trembling.

"It doesn't look all that good, to be honest."

"I saw the cemetery."

I shrugged. Neither of us spoke for a moment. When Veronica broke the silence, she had regained her composure.

"Should we start asking people about Mayor Vincent?" she asked, loosening her grip.

"I don't think we'll get too much out of them in a small town like this. There's a place I want to look at first."

"The cemetery?"

"The prison."

[VIII]

ARIZONA IS ONE of several states that contract with private companies to run prisons, or as we say in PC land, "Detention Facilities." Most of these facilities are run by fairly large corporations with a good deal of experience and an extensive staff of experts. The one outside of Rabbit Hole was not.

According to the public filings that Junior turned up on the Internet, the Copper Mine Correction and Re-education Complex was run by a privately held company of the same name. The contact person was a secretary at a law firm in Delaware, who told Junior when he called that he was welcome to send a letter with any questions he might have.

"I'm sure it will be answered within the time period allocated by law," she told him, before hanging up.

Junior went to work seeing what he could find out about the officers named in the paperwork. He discovered a remarkable coincidence. All were dead. And, in fact, had been practically since the company was started. But that's what often happened when you were well into your nineties and a resident of a nursing home.

All four were residents of the same nursing home in Arizona, though surely that, too, was a coincidence.

While relatively close to the town as the bird flew, to get to the prison by car we had to drive three miles up the county highway, then find a much smaller road to the northwest. Though paved, this road was only wide enough for a single car to pass. There was quite a drop-off from the pavement in a few places. I'm not sure what the locals did when there was two-way traffic.

Then again, that didn't seem to be a common occurrence. The road was deserted, flanked by empty fields where even the scrub seemed lonely. I'd left Mongoose and Shotgun in town—Shotgun was in the process of bankrupting a restaurant owner who foolishly ran an all-you-can-eat special on Wednesdays. Veronica didn't seem much in the mood for talking, so I put on the radio and listened to a little old school country and western as we drove.

The turnoff to the jail was marked by a single sign. It wasn't a big sign either—the nameplate on my agent's door is twice the size. I passed it before I realized what it said.

"Damn," I said, slapping on the brakes.

"Maybe we should just give up the whole thing," said Veronica before I could back up.

"What?"

"I know they're dead, Dick. You don't have to pretend. I've been in denial. Now I have to face it."

"It's not time to give up," I told her.

"I'm not. I'm facing reality."

I reached my hand over to comfort her. As I did, I noticed a set of tire tracks running off into the desert.

"What are you staring at?" Veronica asked.

"Tire tracks."

We got out to have a look. The tracks were wide and thick. They belonged to a tractor-trailer.

"Let's follow them," I told Veronica. "And see where they go."

"But the road's only ten yards away. Not even."

"I know. That's why I'm curious."

THE TRACKS STARTED parallel to the other road, then curved sharply to the north. A quick S and we were going up the side of a hill. We came to a narrow ledge overlooking a steep drop.

"Crap, don't fall off the side," said Veronica.

"If the truck could make it, I can," I told her. "Just don't look down."

I followed the tracks to a gentle bend and found myself at the entrance to a large open mining pit. From the looks of it, it hadn't been used in years; there was a defunct bulldozer, a Caterpillar from the early fifties, sitting in the dust at the south. The side of the hill to our left had been removed in flat, triangular-shaped wedges; the dirt floors of each level looked like neatly sliced pieces of cake.

Stopping the car just past the center of the pit, I got out and stretched my legs. Then I began looking in the dirt to see if I could spot tire tracks — I couldn't — then at the sliced hillside above me.

"Were we following a dump-truck trail?" asked Veronica.

"An old trail, maybe. But the mine hasn't been used for years, it looks like."

"Maybe they took a few loads of the ore out."

"It could be." The place did look level and clear; maybe that was why.

"A lot of minerals are pretty expensive now," added Veronica. "Something that wasn't worth using forty or fifty years ago might be pretty valuable now."

It was certainly possible, though I couldn't see any evidence of recent work. I looked at the side of the hill where the mining had been. There were no caves or other hiding places — it was just a carved pit.

Veronica walked to the far side of the mine and pointed down the hill. "Is that the jail?"

It certainly looked like it was — a double-fence topped by razor wire, towers in two corners. There was a cluster of buildings in the center, some open fields.

"The main entrance must be over there," said Veronica, pointing. "Behind that hill. I can see the road over there — they paved it."

There was another road, this one hard-packed dirt, that came to a side entrance on the west. The road swung around and met the same road that the main entrance used.

But neither of those roads connected in any way to the mine where we were standing. We got the binoculars out of the car, and began looking for tire tracks. Veronica finally spotted them in the back.

"There, making that curlicue down. See them?" she said, pointing.

"Yeah."

"They can't go to the front because of the rocks," she added. "Do they hook up with the side entrance?"

I took the glasses and looked. The terrain between the back of the prison and the side was fairly rough. It wouldn't be easy for a tractor-trailer to get down it, but if it did, it would tear up the brush lining the side road.

"I don't think anything's been through there," I told her, handing the binos back. "The truck went down, stopped, then did a U-turn over there. You can see the marks."

"OK. But why? There's no opening to the gate there."

I started walking to the extreme northeastern end of the pit. There was a narrow dirt road with recent tire tracks from the truck.

"Let's go for a walk," I told Veronica. "It's a lovely day."

"If you're a lizard."

The trail came down the hill at a gentle angle, curved to the left, and then turned back in the direction of the prison. We stopped when we could just see the guard tower at the corner. The tower was part of the fence line, and there was a door at the base. The door was wide, though not nearly big enough for a tractor-trailer.

Still, you could drive a truck up through the gravel pit, down the hill, and park right in front of the tower.

Why, though?

Trace's marvelous adventure sprang to mind. But I couldn't quite see how that might work, and more importantly, why.

Then I had another thought. If I wanted to kidnap someone and keep them prisoner, what better place to put them than a jail? The facility housed a few hundred people, according to what Junior had discovered; who would notice if a few were seniors?

It seemed like a stretch. But de Sarcena had said they weren't dead.

The only way to figure it all out, I thought, was to get thrown in jail.

[IX]

THERE'S A COMMON myth that SEALs, when they're not fighting terrorists and other enemies of the state, spend most of their time fighting in bars. In my experience, that's absolutely not true — SEALs fight on streets, in hotels, shopping malls, even bowling alleys. And one of the best SEAL fights I've ever heard about took place at the White House.

But with limited time and even more limited possibilities, we decided to stick to expectations. So the fight that landed Mongoose and Shotgun in the pokey took place in a bar. Or rather "club," as the neon sign in the window they broke declared it to be.

The Miners Club was a high-class tourist joint, done up in fake mining style, with faux timbers and pseudo dirt walls. Rusty lanterns hung from the ceiling, and an assortment of antique mining equipment was strategically scattered around the room. The menu featured drinks with names riffing off mining themes, and the waitstaff wore helmets with little lanterns on them.

The kind of place that deserves to be trashed, when you come right down to it.

Shotgun started the fight by slapping down his beer glass on the bar and declared in a loud voice that Mexicans were slimy pieces of walking shit. Mongoose, speaking Spanish, took exception. A loud disagreement ensued. The bartender attempted to intervene. Mongoose threw him to the floor. Shotgun tossed a bar stool through the mirror behind the bar, insuring seven years bad luck.

The bouncer attempted to intervene. He was thrown into the bartender. Furniture was broken. Bottles smashed. By the time the police finally arrived, the place looked considerably more authentic.

I WASN'T AT the bar myself, but I watched a good part of the proceedings thanks to a video camera Tex planted in one of the goofy mining props near that bar. We'd also planted bugs on Mongoose and Shotgun, hoping they would give us audio throughout the night. Unfortunately, both units stopped working soon after the fight began—clearly, the boys had taken their role playing a little too seriously.

Tex and Veronica were outside the bar for most of the fight, acting as close backup in case things got out of hand. Trace, Stoneman, and I were sitting on the hill at the top of the mining pit, watching the jail with night binos and a telescope Trace bought at one of the tourist shops in town. The video was being piped to one of our laptops over an encrypted Internet channel.

(The video camera in the bar was making use of an unprotected WiFi connection nearby. Let that be a lesson to you: you never know what's going to show up on your network if you don't protect it. The bugs were more traditional, working on a short-range radio network that transmitted to Tex and Veronica in the car. Well, they *would* have been working on a radio network if the boneheads hadn't broken them.)

Trace, Tex, and Stoneman had arrived in town a few hours before; Trace had only just finished filling me in on her adventures with the Garcias and the tractor-trailer. For the record, she wasn't entirely convinced that sending Shotgun and Mongoose into the jail was a good idea; she'd seen *The Big House* with Wallace Beery recently, and came away scarred.

Everyone else thought it was a great gig, and offered to change places.

"Man, that is so cool," said Stoneman as we watched the fight. "Look at what they did to that ice machine."

Have I talked about Stoneman yet? This was one of his first real assignments with us. He worked for the Christians In Action as a NOC. Some people claim the abbreviation stands for "non-official cover," meaning that the agent has an "outside" identity or cover—your basic spy. Of course, we know it *really* stands for Not Overly Conceited, which is meant sarcastically, since to even be a member of the CIA you have to have a head so big you have to go sideways through doors.

Having it up your ass is optional, though it helps if you want to be promoted.

Stoneman supposedly got his nickname because he was "Stoned, man." That's one of those stories that can neither be confirmed nor denied. He spent a lot of time in Thailand and environs while he was in the agency. But while he occasionally talks like a doper straight out of a Cheech and Chong sketch, he's not old enough to have experienced the sixties. He's also aced all of the drug tests we've ever administered—but then so has Lance Armstrong.

It may be a coincidence, but his favorite weapon happens to be a Stoner Rifle—an SR-25 manufacturer by Knights Armament Company. Aficionados will recognize the SR-25 as the basis for the Mk 11 Sniper Rifle, a weapon favored by many SEAL snipers. Stoneman's version is outfitted with a twenty-inch barrel, which frankly isn't practical in a lot of situations. Since joining us, he's taken to supplementing it with an Uzi, possibly under Mongoose's influence.

Stoneman is skinnier than a string bean. His face—well, about the best thing you can say is that you can't quite tell his chin was broken when he played wide receiver in college. He's always fidgeting with his hands, and he has a tendency to wear his clothes so long they could stand up without him. But he's a hell of an expert in *Luta Livre*, which is free-form Brazilian kick-the-shit-out-of-your-enemy martial art. He claims to know fifty-seven ways to choke a man to death.

Fifty-eight for a woman.

"Who do you think would win a real fight between those guys?" Stoneman asked when the police finally managed to handcuff them.

"Be pretty close," said Trace.

"Trace would kick both their asses," I said, leaning

toward the telescope. "And yours. All at the same time."

Stoneman nodded. He knew I was right—Brazilian martial arts was no match for Apache fury.

I went over to the telescope, examining the interior of the prison compound. Floodlights illuminated every inch, including the two exercise yards and the parking area near the front entrance. The prison was classified as a minimum security facility, with most of its prisoners within a year of being released; the rest were awaiting trial on minor charges, such as those that were about to be hurled at Shotgun and Mongoose. This meant that none of the inmates was considered a serious escape risk, which in turn explained why security was so light—there was one guard in each tower, and a pair of men near the front gate, but otherwise I could see no one.

There were other possible explanations—such as understaffing to save money and increase profits by a private company more interested in protecting stockholders than the citizenry. But that couldn't be the case here, right?

"Say, Dick, there's a truck coming up the county road," said Trace. "Take a look."

She gave me the night binoculars and pointed out the tractor-trailer.

I glanced at my watch as the truck slowed as it neared the turnoff for the prison. It was ten minutes past twelve. Pretty late for a delivery.

"Is it going on the trail, or the road?" asked Trace.

The vehicle slowed for the road, but then continued a few more yards and made the turn onto the trail Veronica and I had spotted earlier in the day.

"Change of plan," I told the others. "Listen up. We have about sixty seconds to get this together."

TRUCK DRIVERS ALWAYS stop for beautiful women. Especially when they are standing in front of a broken-down car and showing plenty of leg and cleavage.

The fact that they're blocking the way on the narrowest part of a treacherous trail doesn't hurt either.

The truck jerked to a stop as Trace stepped away from the rental we'd put on the trail. She began waving wildly, doing her best frantic female imitation, rubbing her forehead and thrusting her pelvis in a way guaranteed to hobble any male over the age of seven. She ran to the truck, waving her hands, and saying in Spanish that she was lost and her car had overheated.

"Why are you out here?" said the driver, rolling down the window as she hopped up on the running board next to him.

"To rob you," she said, pulling out her pistol.

The driver hit the gas. Trace grabbed the mirror bar with her left hand. With the other hand, she smacked the driver with her pistol, knocking him in the head as the truck bolted forward.

Unfortunately, he had a thick head. He swatted back, trying to knock her off with his forearm and elbow. He jerked the truck left and right, but the vehicle was in first gear and it drove extremely slowly.

Thank God. I was already in the cab, sliding across the seat toward him.

"You stop now or I put a hole in the side of your head big enough to run a fist through." I pressed my pistol into his temple.

He took his foot off the gas and raised his arms.

"Take us farther," I said. "Keep it in first."

We inched ahead to a wider spot in the road. Trace opened the door and hauled him out onto the ground. She took it as a personal insult that he had stepped on the gas and tried to brush her off. Such intransigence needed to be corrected.

While he howled, I went to the back of the truck. Stoneman, who'd been backstopping us from above, came down to cover me.

The rear door was locked. I could have picked it, or better yet let Stoneman do it, since he's supposed to be such a whiz at spy craft. But I was tired—I shot the damn thing off.

When I rolled the door up, the smell almost knocked me over.

"Shit—are they all dead?" said Stoneman.

The blinking eyes inside showed they weren't. But some of the people jammed into the back of the truck may have wished they were. All were soaked with sweat. More than a few had either vomited or lost other body fluids.

"This is a lot like what we found in Mexico," Trace told me after we'd helped them from the truck. "Even worse—there are more people here. The truck must get to a hundred and twenty degrees. They've probably been driving for days."

We culled the weakest from the group, taking them a short distance from the truck and helping them sit and lie down. We hadn't planned on doing any of this, and so we had nothing for them to eat or drink. I called Veronica, and told her to get some drinking water and come up to the pit.

"How much water?"

"Buy out the store. Leave Tex to shadow Shotgun and Mongoose. They're not going anywhere they haven't been."

TEN MINUTES LATER, I held my breath against the stench as Stoneman ground through the gears and wended his way to the prison. We weren't exactly sure what was supposed to happen once we got there, but we figured the guard would know.

Stoneman pulled in front of the tower and stopped. When no one appeared after a few seconds, he tapped his horn a few times. The door at the base of the building opened, and a guard came rushing out to scold him.

"What the hell do you think you're doing, you stupid ass bean eater," yelled the guard. "Shit for brains, you greaseball."

Stoneman rolled down the window and leaned out of the cab.

"Excuse me?"

"You're not Pedro," said the guard. "You're not even fuckin' Mexican."

"I'm fillin' in."

"You stupid shit. Why did you beep the horn?"

"So you could yell at me, asshole."

They exchanged a few more insults back and forth, with appropriate profanity and good doses of ethnic insults. Though he had seen that Stoneman was an American, the guard continued to hurl curses at him as if he were Mexican. It was almost as if he had been preprogrammed and couldn't change the script.

Inside the truck, I was sorely tempted to yell at them to get on with it. I leaned against the side wall and did my best not to become asphyxiated. It was pitch-black—a good thing, since I couldn't see that I was standing in a pool of pee.

The men around me—I'd insisted on leaving all the women behind, along with men Trace judged too sickly to continue—began mumbling.

I'd considered threatening them, telling them that they weren't to say anything about stopping, or give me away. But they all had a blank look in their eyes—faraway zone, as Stoneman called it. I felt it was better just leaving them be.

Now I wasn't so sure. They suddenly seemed a hell of a lot more alive than just a few minutes earlier.

The rear of the truck flew open. The guard who had accosted Stoneman now began yelling at us in heavily accented Spanish, saying that we were worthless pieces of putrid shit, and that we should get out of the truck before he hosed us out.

The men started to file out. One of the older men put his hand out to the guard, hoping for help down. Instead, the guard stepped back, shooting him a look of disdain. I went and helped him down, then started helping others.

"Get your ass inside the building," the guard snarled. *"Get."*

It took every ounce of self-restraint not to smack him. I waited until two Mexicans came over to help the last stragglers before shambling over in the direction of the building.

I expected that we would be greeted by guards with shotguns and dogs. Instead, there was a single grandfather type in an orange prison coverall standing near the threshold, waving his hand to urge everyone inside.

Mr. Cortina, Veronica's grandfather.

He looked a little trimmer than the photos she'd showed me, but it was definitely him. He even smiled the same.

I sidled up next to him. A liver mark made a large teardrop at the corner of his temple; he had a full head of white hair and very tired eyes.

"Mr. Cortina, my name is Richard Marcinko," I whispered. "Your granddaughter sent me. I'm here to get you out."

He looked at me for a moment. I thought he was going to cry. Then his eyes narrowed.

"Mr. Cortina?" I asked. "Did you hear me?"

"Get back in line," he snapped. "Go."

[H]

I DID AS he said, joining the rest of the men walking through the tower into the exercise yard beyond. A few of the men had bags of clothes and other belongings, but most were as empty-handed as I was. I didn't have a weapon, or a radio. I didn't even have my trick shoe.

Two more prisoner trustees were instructing the new arrivals to stand in lines ten people across by four deep. I managed to get a spot in the third line back. I slumped a little, making myself as inconspicuous as possible.

As the last stragglers filed in, a woman in her mid-twenties came out of the building across from us. Dressed in jeans and a light blue Polo shirt. The shirt had a small crest above the pocket; this was apparently the prison company's logo. It took a few seconds of staring before I realized it was an outstretched hand.

Handcuffs would have been more appropriate, no?

"Quiet now, quiet," she said in Spanish, though no one was talking. "I am Serena Gomez, the assistant director at our facility. You will all get some food and water in a minute. First, let me tell you that your journey is almost over. Your next stop will be in America. We will take you there a few at a time starting tomorrow. Have some water, and rest."

She turned around and went back to the building. As she had been speaking, two more trustees had come out with chests of ice and water bottles. They set them down, then stepped back.

A good thing. They would have been trampled in the slow-motion stampede that followed.

I joined the group. There were two trustees watching us. Neither looked particularly interested. One of the men I'd come in with approached one of them, but backed off when the trustee put up his hand and shook his head.

It had been clever of Gomez to tell them they were still in Mexico. It lessened the possibility that they would try to escape on their own.

The people running the operation had plans to extract more money from them. Each person had already ponied up a considerable sum[31] to get this far; now they would be taken to supposed safe houses where

---

[31] The payments varied slightly, but were between $9,000 and $11,000. Typically, smugglers are said to get anywhere from $7,000 to $30,000. I'm somewhat skeptical of the higher numbers, unless they include money paid after being transported. That can actually add up to considerable pocket change.

they would be made to pay exorbitant rents from low wages at menial jobs. Any who escaped without paying would find their families back home in Mexico threatened—or might not find their families at all.

One of the trustees blew a whistle and pointed at the door of a building behind him. We started walking in that direction. I put my head down, doing my best to blend in.

The building was a single-story barracks. Beds lined both sides of the room. An air conditioner at the far end made the temperature surprisingly cool. There were stands with hangers next to each bed, but no clothes. Most likely they'd have a chance to buy some in the morning.

I found a bunk and plopped down, watching the others and at the same time trying to decide how I was going to find Mr. Cortina and what to do once I did. The small, skeleton staff they had here made it easy to move around, but Cortina's apparent attitude toward me was a complication.

I hadn't considered the possibility that he had gone to work for the cartel, accepting Veronica's view of her grandparents uncritically. But now that I thought about it, I realized it might make a lot of sense: why not work for the cartel?

Maybe they thought America had screwed them in their golden days, forcing them to live south of the border to stretch their retirement dollars. Maybe they'd been corrupt all along. Or maybe they just decided to go with the flow—it was a lot easier than resisting.

I picked out a cot and sat on it, watching the others. A few went to the shower room, but most were so exhausted they just lay back on the beds and went right to sleep. After we'd been in the room about ten minutes, the overhead lights began blinking on and off. Finally they dimmed, leaving the three or four night-lights scattered around the room to provide light.

I rolled out of bed and made my way to the door. As I reached for the knob, it started to turn. I slipped back behind it, waiting as the dark shadow of a man filled the space. He stepped inside and the door closed.

I grabbed him around the neck.

"*¿Quién eres?*" I whispered. "Who are you?"

"Marcinko?" said the man in English. It was Mr. Cortina.

"What are you doing here?"

"I was coming to talk to you. You know my grand daughter?"

"Yes, I know Veronica well." I released him.

"We can't talk here," he whispered. "Sometimes they put in spies. Follow me."

I let him lead me back outside and around the building, into the side yard. Every shadow I saw tightened my short hairs—he could easily be leading me into a trap.

"Can't they see us from the tower?" I asked when we stopped outside.

"There's no one in the back tower," said Mr. Cortina. "Only the front tower is manned at night. Once the new ones come, the guard leaves."

"There's no one watching the back?"

"No. Never."

"Why doesn't anyone escape?"

The corner of his mouth edged upward, and I saw the same twinkle that animated Veronica. "We're working on it," he told me. "We have a plan. Come with me."

We walked along the side of the building, pausing

when we came to the corner. He leaned out from the wall, glancing in the direction of the front tower. He waited for a few moments, then walked very quickly across. I followed at his heels.

We crossed behind another building, then came to a squat, square building with a tin roof that edged against the exercise yard. He went to a door, knocked, then opened it. The heavy aroma of bleach nearly knocked me over as I went in behind him.

The short corridor opened into a larger room. Dozens of bedsheets were hung from the ceilings.

"Marianna," he hissed. "I have news. *Good* news."

He lifted some of the sheets and slipped past others, wending his way to a corner of the room. I followed tentatively. The fluorescents on the ceiling were off, but a dim blue light filtered through the wall-length windows and their blinds at the far end of the room.

"Marianna, this man was sent by Veronica," said Mr. Cortina as he reached his destination. "Mr. Marsinkoo."

I parted a pair of sheets and found myself standing in front of a cluster of men and women. There was an even dozen. None looked to be under seventy.

"You know Veronica?" said a woman in the corner, rising from her chair. I recognized her, just as I had her husband, from the photos Veronica had shown us. She was an inch or two taller than her husband and a lot wider. She gripped my arm like a marine.

"She sent me to find you," I told her. "Are you all alright? Why are you in jail?"

"It's a long story," said her husband. "Tonight we have planned our escape. They will be busy with the illegals they brought in and unable to go after us. We have been thinking about this for a while. Will you join us?"

"How can I refuse?"

"Good."

"I don't think we should trust him," said one of the others. "What if he's another spy?"

"What did you say your name was?" asked a small, frail looking woman who walked up close and put her face practically in my chin.

"I didn't. It's Richard Marcinko."

"I thought so," she said with a self-satisfied nod. She turned to the others. "I've read all his books in the library. We can trust him." She turned back to me. "You really should clean up your language, you know. You use an awful amount of four-letter words. Do you kiss Karen Fairchild with that mouth?"

THE PAIR HAD realized they made a mistake very soon after arriving. There were a number of things wrong with the condo, shoddy construction, wires unconnected, misaligned plumbing, molding that kept falling off the walls — all the sorts of things you get when you hire cheap unskilled labor. Within days, they also realized that the developers were having serious money problems. New units were left half built, roads unpaved.

"They were having definite cash-flow problems," said Mr. Cortina. "Everything I'd already seen in the U.S. at the start of the housing bust."

"I'm surprised that they lasted as long as they did," said his wife.

"Probably they had some cartel money all along," said Mr. Cortina. "And at some point the cartel decided to pull the plug. Maybe that was the plan from the start."

"Then they wouldn't have sold us that house, would they have?" said his wife. "Not that house. Because it ran right along their tunnel."

"You wanted that house. You insisted on that lot."

"Big mistake," admitted Mrs. Cortina.

Largely out of pride, they pretended they were happy when Veronica visited. They weren't very good actors, but vanity kept them from admitting they had made a big mistake.

The development stopped deteriorating when the cartel itself moved in, though by then the Cortinas were extremely dubious about what was going on. One day, Mrs. Cortina heard banging in the basement. Mr. Cortina went to investigate, but of course couldn't see anything. He walked around outside, but naturally there was nothing to see.

"I went up the hill to have a look and to stretch my legs," said Mr. Cortina. "My wife likes to watch her stories in the afternoon and I get bored."

"Soap operas," said Mrs. Cortina. "Never miss them."

Mr. Cortina noticed large tire tracks in the area near the community center. It was obvious that there had been earth-moving machines there recently, yet there were now none to be seen. He walked around some more without finding any. Finally he went home, confused.

He took another walk the next day. Again, he spotted tire tracks; again he saw nothing that might have left them.

"Tread marks, too. Like from a D7 dozer. You know what a D7 is?"

"Bulldozer," I said. "Sure."

Now any work going on in the condo development would be pretty big news — positive news, Mr. Cortina thought. So he started asking his neighbors if anyone had seen earth-moving machines or any activity at the development.

"A lot of people had already moved out, or never moved in," said Mr. Cortina.

"You can blame them?" said his wife.

"I don't blame them. I'm just explaining."

"You have a funny way of telling a story. Always stopping and starting."

"Always being interrupted."

Mr. Cortina decided that whatever was going on must be going on at night. So he took an early nap — during the soap operas — and after his wife had gone to bed, went out to find out what was going on.

"They were working near the community center," said Mr. Cortina. "And inside it. They were bringing out loads of dirt through the garage door at the base."

"There's no garage door there now," I said.

"Exactly. They were very careful not to be seen, and then covering up their tracks. They had an army of people working. At some sort of hidden signal, they all ran inside the building."

Probably to escape aerial surveillance, I thought. Someone must have been watching the drones employed along the border, or maybe timing the satellites.

"I watched from the backyard of one of the neighboring units, for a few nights in a row," continued

Mr. Cortina. "I wasn't sure what was going on. But I didn't think it would be a good idea to be seen. Someone digging in the ground? What I thought was—they were digging for some sort of mineral. That maybe gold was buried beneath the development."

"Always with gold on his mind," said his wife, shaking her head.

Mr. Cortina liked the mystery. It gave him something more exciting to do than watch Mexican soap operas.

"I didn't think it could be a tunnel, though," he told me. "It was too far from the border, I thought."

Then one day, two young men in suits knocked on the door and asked to talk to him. They said they were engineers and had plans to do work on the sewer system. They unfurled plans showing that the line was going to run very close to the Cortinas' house.

"You'll have to move," said one of the men. While both were Mexican, they spoke perfect English, with only the vaguest hint of an accent.

"We don't want to move," said Mr. Cortina.

The two men looked at each other. Mr. Cortina thought they were going to offer him a bargain—a new unit and some cash, maybe.

Instead, they took out pistols.

Mr. Cortina apparently had been spotted the night before; management had also heard that he was going around making inquiries. And so, they made the pair an offer they couldn't refuse. They were tied and bound, then locked in the garage. Later that night, a group of men came and got them, carrying them out to a van.

"They were very careful with us, very gentle," said Mr. Cortina. "But still I thought we were going to die."

Why they weren't killed was a bit of a mystery. It may have been because they were more valuable alive than dead: their Social Security checks were routed to the cartel, and new credit card accounts opened and quickly drained. Most of that could have been done with them dead, however; maybe whoever was supposed to kill them got cold feet.

The Cortinas were taken to a pair of Mexican prisons and kept in custody there. But they stuck out there, clearly Anglos in a Mexican prison. The afternoon of the second day, Mr. Cortina started making friends with the common criminals around him; his age gave him a certain status, though it's doubtful it would have lasted very long.

It didn't have to. His fluent Spanish made him a real risk, and someone apparently realized this wasn't a good place to keep him. That night he was packed up again and taken to a location that sounded very much like the barn where I rescued Melissa Reynolds. There he was reunited with his wife, and another couple from Angel Hills who also had been a little too nosy about the goings-on there. The next night they were packed into a van and shipped off to the Arizona prison where I found them. Like the illegals, they had been told they were still in Mexico, and in fact didn't realize they were across the border until a few weeks before. Until then, escape had seemed futile; Mr. Cortina figured they'd never make it out of Mexico.

At first, the Cortinas and the other couple were kept with the illegals, segregated from the handful of legitimate American prisoners. With the exception of a man who was clearly a schizophrenic — and was kept locked in a special cell — the Americans were all short-timers who were bused into town every day for various municipal work projects.

One by one, the legitimate prisoners were released. A few other Americans, apparently also prisoners of the cartel, were brought in, but the place was basically a ghost town. One day, Serena Gomez, the assistant prison director, came into the barracks and had a talk with them.

"Bitch Serena," snarled Mrs. Cortina.

"Oh, she's not that bad," said her husband.

"You think anything in a skirt isn't that bad."

"She wasn't wearing a skirt," he retorted. "She had those nice tight khakis that showed off her pert derriere."

"I'll give you a pert derriere, right where it'll do some good."

Gomez — there didn't appear to be an actual director above her, or at least they had never seen one — told the prisoners that they were now the trustees of the jail. As such, they had two choices: cooperate, or be sent back to the jails where they'd started.

"If you cooperate, you will have the run of the place," she said. "We are getting new prisoners in very soon. You can boss them around and instruct them. You will be treated well — your own food, baths every night, television — every privilege we can provide. If, however, you break any of our rules, you're out of here. Understood?"

"When are we being released?" asked one of the men.

Gomez smirked and walked away.

After that, inmates began arriving every week or so, maybe a hundred at a time. With rare exceptions, they were quickly shipped out. It soon became obvious to the Cortinas and others that it was useless to try to make contact with them.

"Scared of their own shadows," said Mr. Cortina. "Not that I blame them."

Eventually, the trustees began realizing what was going on. Finally convinced that they were in the U.S., Mr. Cortina and some of the others began looking for a way to escape. They studied the prison routines, taking advantage of the small security staff. They learned when to expect shipments of illegals. They gathered intelligence from the administrator's office, working there as janitors. Holding down all the jobs, they gradually came to control enough of the routine to prepare their escape.

And now, they were ready to go.

WHILE I WAS in the prison waiting for H hour, Shotgun and Mongoose were having their own encounter with justice. Grabbed by the police, they were brought before the local magistrate for arraignment. He took one look at Mongoose and stopped the proceedings.

"Is your name Thomas Yamya?" asked the judge.

"Uh, yessir."

"Were you in Iraq?"

"Uh—"

"You were, goddamnit. You're the SEAL that saved my kid in Ramadi."

Mongoose shifted around uneasily.

"You're next to him in the photo. My God, I'd know you anywhere."

"I, uh—"

"Release them," ordered the judge. "Both of them.

Mr. Yamya, I never want you to darken the streets of my town again. Now come here and let me shake your hand."

MR. CORTINA LED the small group of escapees around the back of the building to a shed. Two large garbage bins sat at the side. He went over to the first and pulled up the cover.

"Let's go," he said. "We have ten minutes before the truck arrives."

Compared to everything else I'd smelled over the past twenty-four hours, the garbage bin was . . . even worse.

I'm afraid if I describe it accurately you won't be able to go on reading. Even thinking about it now makes me a little queasy.

We hunkered down in the bins, gagging as the tops were closed. It seemed like an eternity before I heard the sound of a large truck pulling up nearby. The jaws of the lift mechanism clanked against the side, and we were lifted into the back of a large truck. We waited while the second bin was lifted and slapped down next to us.

"Won't be long now," whispered Mr. Cortina.

Just then there was a loud clank on the side of the bin. We were lifted up, then deposited back down. I slipped the lid upward to see what was going on.

Serena Gomez was standing a few feet away, grinning. She was flanked by two guards with shotguns.

"Going somewhere?" she said. "Or just nostalgic for the smell of Mexican jails?"

[XI]

Mathematically, there was no way the two guards and their shotguns could take out all thirteen of us if we spread out and then attacked together. The problem was, when you're in a situation like that, you tend not to think mathematically.

I climbed out of the garbage bin with the others and shuffled to the right, trying to look inconspicuous while figuring out a plan. Unfortunately, I was about as inconspicuous in that group as a polar bear at a wedding.

"Who are you?" demanded Ms. Gomez.

"¿Que?" I asked, pretending I didn't understand English.

"Come on, you're an American." It wasn't a question. "But you must have come in with the Mexicans, didn't you? Did you arrange this?"

She stepped toward me. My mind quickly flicked through the options. It was very quick, since there weren't many:

a) grab Gomez and use her as a shield while leaping at one of the guards,

b) fold my head into my knees and kiss my ass good-bye.

Neither was particularly inviting. But before I made up my mind, I discovered there was another option — grab the shotgun as it flew from the guard's hands as he pirouetted to the ground.

I took the gun and spun toward the second guard. But he, too, was falling to the ground, a massive hole where his right eye had been. Stoneman, watching from the summit of the pit, had shot both of the guards with the Stoner.

I turned to Gomez. She had a stunned expression on her face. She kept it just long enough for me to whack her in the temple with the shotgun.

Meanwhile, Mr. Cortina grabbed the other shotgun and pointed it at the driver of the garbage truck. The man pleaded for his life in rapid Spanish.

"You'll live as long as you do what we tell you," I said. "Hook the gear up to that garbage bin."

We took the belts from the guards and bound Serena's hands and feet, then threw her and the dead men into one of the Dumpsters. The rest of the escapees stuffed themselves into the second one; I went up front with the driver.

"Take us out of here, and don't stop," I told him. I put the shotgun in my lap, my finger on its trigger.

The guard at the gate didn't even stop us. He'd never heard the commotion, let alone the rifle shots, over his blaring iPod.

I'M NOT EXACTLY known for being teary-eyed, but even I grabbed for a hankie when Veronica and her grandparents reunited just outside of Rabbit Hole.

"You stink," she said, folding her arms around her grandmother. "You stink, too," she added, pulling her grandfather close to her.

I'm not sure I've ever heard more touching words.

[XII]

THE CORTINAS' RESCUE brought closure to *that* little sidebar of our adventures, but we were still left with the prospect of doing something about the prison and its enabler, mayor/Senate candidate James Vincent. I could of course simply alert the Border Patrol to the smuggling operation (something I intended on doing anyway), and hope they could trace back the line to Vincent.

Right. Anyone want to give me odds on that?

THE SUN ROSE bright and strong a few hours later, shining in all its God-given glory over the rugged Arizona hills. The scent of coffee and breakfast tortillas hung in the crisp desert air as a pair of black SUVs drove down the county highway to Rabbit Hole, turned up the first street at the start of Main, and pulled in front of the low fence that surrounded the mayor's house.

It happened that the mayor was inside drinking coffee and fiddling with his laptop, which for reasons unknown (to him) was not able to connect to the Internet that morning.

His phones were out as well, though as he hadn't tried to make a phone call, he didn't realize it.

A pair of burly bodyguards got out of the first SUV. Two rather shapely women — Veronica and Trace — got out of the second. The bodyguards checked the area, then escorted the women to the front of the house.

Veronica rang the bell. She had a small valise in her hand. It was lime-green, which clashed terribly with the black jeans and white blouse she was wearing. Louis Vuitton would have been scandalized.

We'd wanted a real attaché case, but couldn't come up with one in time for our little op. I'd left a bunch back at the ranch with the weapons we'd stolen from de Sarcena, but they were miles and miles away. We needed to complete our mission before the mayor found out what had happened at the prison; we calculated word would get out shortly after the shift change, which according to Mr. Cortina happened at eight.

Reynolds answered the door himself.

"Mr. Vincent," said Veronica. "We need to talk. I was sent by Senor de Sarcena."

The mayor's face turned several shades of color, briefly matching the hue of Veronica's bag before settling on red.

"I'm afraid I don't know who that is," he said finally.

"I'm sure you do. Please, we'll all feel much more comfortable discussing this matter inside."

"I don't know a Mr. de Sarcena," insisted the mayor. "I have a full slate of appointments this morning."

"Our business won't take long," said Veronica. She shifted to Spanish. "Please. Senor de Sarcena would only have sent me if it was truly important. And I'm sure you wouldn't want him to come himself."

"Honey, who is it?" asked Vincent's wife, coming into the kitchen behind him. She was a tall, thin woman, noticeably pretty and even more noticeably pregnant. She wore a long white bathrobe made of silk; she had matching pajamas under it.

"Political consultants," Vincent told his wife.

"This early? Don't these people have private lives?"

"I don't know."

She sighed. "Have them come in and get some coffee."

The mayor pushed open the screen door. Trace noticed that the house was only sparsely furnished, a bit of a surprise after Junior had told her how much Vincent had stashed away in secret accounts overseas. But his wealth had come relatively recently, and besides, it wouldn't do for a politician who was supposedly representing the "common man" to be living in a Mc-Mansion with marble coffee tables and thick leather couches.

Even if almost all of them do.

"Let's talk in here." He led Veronica and Trace to a small dining room off the side of the kitchen. Shotgun and Mongoose—wearing sunglasses to hide their bruises—stood off to the side as Trace and Veronica took seats at the table. Vincent's wife stayed in the kitchen, fussing over the coffeemaker.

"What is it you want?" the mayor asked.

"We need to get two people from the prison," said Veronica.

"What? I have nothing to do with that."

"Please, Mr. Vincent. Señor de Sarcena appreciates your help."

"Who are you even talking about?"

Veronica glanced at Trace. This was the first time the two women were working together, but they already had a simpatico rhythm.

"Maybe you should call him," Trace suggested to Vincent.

"I don't think so."

Trace reached into her hip pocket and took out a satellite phone. She turned it on, then selected a contact number.

"Call this number," she said, holding out the phone. "Hang up after the second ring. He'll call back."

"I don't think so," the mayor repeated.

Trace stared at him so hard her eyes practically drilled holes in his head. Veronica reached over, took the phone herself, and pressed the button to send. She listened a moment, made sure it rang, then hit end.

It rang thirty seconds later.

"Here," she told Vincent, handing it over.

Vincent frowned, but took the phone.

"What is the problem?" said a heavily accented voice on the other end of the line.

De Sarcena.

No, actually, it was me, pretending to be de Sarcena. I was sitting in a motel a few miles away, soaking my feet in a tub of hot water. I would have preferred a more comprehensive cure administered under Dr. Bombay's direction, but there was much work to be done over the next few hours; extensive treatment would have to wait.

"Who is this?" said Vincent.

"James. You know who this is. Is my money now not good for you?"

Vincent hung up. He slid the phone onto the table and rose, quickly leaving the room and disappearing into the back of the house. A few moments later his wife came in with a tray of cups and a coffeepot.

"First child?" asked Trace.

"Yes." She smiled faintly. It was clear she was still slightly confused and struggling to be hospitable.

"I'll do that for you," said Trace, getting up.

"Oh, it's all right. It's no bother. How would you like it?"

She even gave coffee to Shotgun, who when asked how much sugar he wanted, replied by asking how much she had.

He showed great restraint, settling for only four spoonfuls.

Vincent returned to the room with a cell phone and a small notebook. He glanced alternately at Veronica, the pad, and the phone as he dialed a phone number.

It was a number he'd been given for de Sarcena, to be used only in emergencies and alleged to be impossible to tap.

I picked it up on the second ring. (I know Shunt is a genius, but some of the things he's capable of scare even me.)

"¿Quién?" I said sharply. "Who?"

Vincent took a breath. Then another.

"We met three weeks ago at your house," he said in English. "What room?"

A damn good question, I thought.

"Is this James?" I said in English, stalling. "James, why are you using this line? We just spoke."

"What room did we meet in?"

My cell phone buzzed. I glanced down—I had an incoming text from Veronica.

Peace.

"What room?" demanded Vincent.

"We discussed matters in the Salon of Peace. Now—why are you quizzing me like a child? Do as my people ask, or there will be grave consequences. My friendship should not be taken for granted."

I hung up.

Veronica slipped her phone back into the valise on her lap. Vincent's head looked like it was about to explode.

"Mr. Vincent, I realize this is a difficult situation for you," said Veronica, using her softest, most understanding voice. "It's a difficult situation for Senor de Sarcena as well. He needs us to retrieve someone from the prison. They were accidentally placed there. They're not criminals. We tried to do this ourselves. Unfortunately, for reasons known only to them, they will release the person only on your orders."

"Those people all work for you. I have no connection with the jail."

Trace cleared her throat, rather unsubtly implying that was a lie.

"I didn't say it was logical," said Veronica quickly. "We were quite surprised by it ourselves."

"I barely know the people there."

"You know Serena Gomez."

His face changed in a way that convinced both Veronica and Trace that he knew her a little too well.

"I'll call her on the phone," said Vincent, lowering his voice.

"All of the calls to the prison are taped," said Veronica, shaking her head. "We don't need a record of this."

Vincent frowned. Veronica unzipped the valise and took out a packet of bills . . . more of those ill-gotten *dineros* lifted from de Sarcena's mansion.

"Your time is valuable, I know," she told him, sliding over a packet. "More will be waiting when you return."

Vincent stared at the money on the table for a moment.

"James?" called his wife from inside the kitchen.

He grabbed the pile. "I have to go out. I'll be back."

VERONICA TRIED GENTLY pumping him for information on the ride up to the prison. Both she and Trace were wired; the idea was to get him to say as much as possible to incriminate himself in the cartel's dealings. But Vincent was in no mood to talk.

Maybe he was having second thoughts about being involved with the cartel. Maybe he realized criminals, especially foreign ones, shouldn't have a say in American government. Maybe he was finally realizing what a tangled mess he had gotten himself into.

Or maybe he just had a lot of things to do and didn't feel like wasting his time running errands for his paymaster.

He had the bills in his pocket, which was terribly convenient of him. We'd marked them, but having them physically in his custody when he was arrested would avoid quite a lot of bother and needless testimony.

Tex and Stoneman were following the two SUVs, providing a little extra security. I was up on the cliff with phones, binoculars, and a large thermos of some of the best coffee I've ever tasted.

The guards' day shift was just coming in. That amounted to six people. The staff, once about a hundred strong, had been let go in a series of layoffs over the past year.

Not that I could blame them, really. Why pay for guards when they really aren't guarding anyone?

DOES THIS SOUND like a metaphor for many international businesses? Businesses that were *once* American?

Companies that *once* made products you could use? Companies that *once* employed Americans in real jobs? Companies that were *once* loyal to employees and customers?

Companies that now could give a hoot about anything and anyone except profits? Companies now willing to go to the slimiest corner of the world to save a half penny on a widget? Companies now taken over by people who are little more than criminals?

Oops, excuse me. Stepped onto my soapbox there for a second.

VINCENT'S ANNOYANCE BEGAN boiling over as they neared the prison. He became more and more agitated, shaking his head, folding and unfolding his arms. Finally, he began berating Veronica.

"I have a lot on my plate today," he told her. He was sitting next to her in the back; Trace was up front in the passenger seat, with Shotgun as the driver. "A lot."

"Such as what?" asked Trace. "What else do you have to do today?"

"There's a press conference, for one thing. We're unveiling a new Web site. And I have some sort of bullshit position paper to approve on bringing more jobs to the economy. Important things. This kind of crap I shouldn't be involved in."

"We're sorry that we had to talk to you personally," said Veronica. "Do you come up to the prison a lot?"

"I'm too busy. I was here a few times in the beginning."

"I was under the impression that you and Ms. Gomez were . . . friends."

"That's history."

"But you do own the prison," said Veronica. Actually, this was just a guess, but it turned out to be a good one.

"A piece," he admitted. "Through a cousin of my wife. She doesn't know it, by the way."

"Your wife or your cousin?" asked Veronica.

"Either one. Her cousin is batty. She's in an institution."

"That's convenient," said Veronica.

Vincent put his hand on Veronica's knee. Veronica looked at it for a second, then gently moved it off. She wanted information, but not *that* badly.

Vincent took the rejection well. But that made sense—he undoubtedly interpreted it to mean "not now" rather than "not ever." His ego wouldn't allow him to see it any other way.

"There's a lot more to a Senate campaign than meets the eye," he told Veronica. "It's ridiculously expensive. And it's go-go-go, all the time."

"I'm sure it is expensive," said Veronica. "Do you need more help?"

"I do have a dinner coming up in Flagstaff. We have a lot of tickets left."

"I'm sure Mr. de Sarcena would buy all of them," said Veronica. "What else do you need?"

"We've given you plenty of cash already," snapped Trace.

Vincent made a face at her.

"We can arrange more," said Veronica, "if it's important."

"It might be useful," said Vincent. He almost sounded reluctant to take it.

"If there is something else Mr. de Sarcena can do

for you, please let me know," said Veronica. "He's always eager to help. Especially good friends who help him."

"I don't know. I'll have to think. I already appreciate his assistance so far. It's been valuable. It adds up."

Veronica tried prodding him a bit more, hoping for a more explicit quid pro quo indicating a bribe; there's nothing like a long confession to make a policeman's day. Vincent groused a little more about the great burdens he was under, but never got more explicit.

THE GUARD AT the front gate was wary when they pulled up. He had a sense something was going on—the "trustees" hadn't appeared for their morning constitutional, a stroll around the inner perimeter of the prison. The shifts were due to change in a few minutes, though, which meant he was looking forward to going home and wasn't likely to make too many waves.

He walked up to the first SUV. Mongoose rolled down the driver's side window and thumbed behind him. As the guard approached the second vehicle, Vincent opened the window and stuck out his head.

"Fredrico, how are you?" said Vincent.

"Mr. Mayor? Good morning."

"I have to see Serena. Is she here?"

"Hasn't left that I know. In her office or her apartment."

"Very good. These people are all with me."

The gate was opened. The two SUVs passed through, heading for the administration building.

Not more than two minutes later, a pickup drove up. The guard went over to see what the driver wanted.

"I don't want nothin' from y'all," said Tex, turning

on his drawl for maximum effect. "But my friend here, he's a greedy sumofabitch. But I reckon I'd say that of all Yankees."

The guard looked up. Stoneman had scooted off the back of the pickup and snuck behind him. He nudged his Uzi into his ribs.

"I'm thinking that you might find it convenient to do as my friend asks," added Tex. "I just don't trust Yankees with guns."

THE ADMINISTRATION OFFICE was empty. Vincent may have claimed that he was rarely here, but he knew the layout well enough to lead Veronica, Trace, and the boys down the hall to the private entrance of Serena Gomez's apartment.

There was a bell. He rang it.

No answer.

"She's probably sleeping," said Vincent.

He rang again. Trace slipped back to the office and planted a pair of video bugs. I saw them come online and settled in for a good show.

"Damn. She must be doing an inspection or something," said Vincent. "Or maybe she went into town."

Vincent rang again.

In case you're wondering, at that very moment, Gomez was in the back of a garbage truck parked on the sidewalk in front of a U.S. Marshal's office in Bisbee. She was screaming her head off, though there wouldn't be a soul close enough to hear until nine A.M.

The mayor rang the bell a third time, waited another ten seconds, then knocked as hard as he could.

"I'm damn busy," he said when no one answered. "Really."

"Maybe we should check with her assistant?" said Veronica.

"She doesn't have an assistant."

"There must be another guard or something."

"Damn company managers are so frickin' cheap I'm surprised they still have Serena on the payroll."

"There's no second in command?"

"Just a guard. Aw hell, let's see if we can round him up. I gotta get out of here."

They went back to the office. The deputy guard supervisor—he was the senior man Vincent was referring to—had just arrived and was looking for his boss. He was confused by the fact that there was no guard on duty at the front gate, and wanted to know what the hell was going on.

As soon as he saw the mayor, he held his tongue—the last thing the company needed was controversy.

The mayor didn't really give him much of an opening anyway.

"Where is Ms. Gomez?" demanded Vincent as soon as he saw him in the office.

"I, I don't know, Mr. Mayor."

"Well, these people have important business. They're here to pick up some prisoners."

"Do they have paperwork?"

"There is no paperwork," said Veronica. "They're with the Mexicans who came in last night."

"Oh."

"You didn't tell me that," said Vincent.

"I thought it would be obvious," said Veronica coldly. "Why else would I be here? You don't have any real prisoners."

"I could have taken care of this with a phone call,

damn it. The Mexicans—take them all if you want. They're leaving anyway." He looked over at the guard: "Aren't they?"

"We have a schedule."

"Senor de Sarcena is very particular about these two," said Veronica. "We need to get them ourselves."

"Look, I have a press conference this morning," said Vincent. "I don't have time to screw around with the illegals."

Veronica said nothing.

"Well, go get these people for her," Vincent told the supervisor.

"Uh, who are they?"

"Jose Garcia and a man named Gutiérrez."

"That's like saying Smith and Jones. Can you identify them?"

"Yes."

"All right. Come on. We'll go over to the barracks."

Before Veronica could tell him he would have to figure out who they were and bring them to her, Vincent spoke up.

"I'll go, too," he said. "I need two people to work in my garden."

"You trust illegal immigrants to work for you?" said Trace.

Vincent shrugged. "Most of them work pretty hard. And they work for peanuts. Why not? As long as they know their place."

"They work for minimum wage?" asked Trace.

"Yeah, right," said Vincent. "I don't pay more than I have to. Why would I pay them minimum wage? Are you nuts?"

"You pay them in cash?"

"Don't be stupid. God. As if I'd leave a paper trail."

He walked toward the door. Veronica started to follow. Trace held her back.

"Listen," said Trace.

There was a siren in the distance. Actually a pair of sirens. The country sheriff was escorting a task force of Border Patrol guards, assorted Customs agents, and a stray FBI supervisor on a raid.

"What the hell is going on out there?" said the guard supervisor, stopping at the door. Vincent practically ran into him. "Hey, what's going on here?"

"Sit down, junior," said Trace, slamming the guard supervisor into a nearby seat. He tried to get up; the next thing he knew he was lying on his back, his own gun pressed to his head. "You don't really want to mess with me."

Vincent looked on in disbelief.

"I think you may want to reschedule that press conference about your Web site," Veronica said. "You'll be too busy to deal with it."

[XIII]

HAVING RAMBLED FAR and wide, we now lay back and enjoyed the fruits of our various labors.

Not.

I would have been very glad to. But there were still plenty of loose ends to wrap up, starting with the questioning of Ms. Reynolds's lover. I also had to figure out the best way of providing the secretary of State with my report on the nonexistence — *cough-cough* — of terror camps on the other side of the border.

Actually, I was looking forward to writing that report. Shunt was busy pulling out goodies from the hard drives we'd purloined from the terror farm, doing whatever voodoo it is he does to extract data. And there were going to be plenty of photos of guns and dead bodies. Frankly, it was an embarrassment of riches. And telling the secretary of State about it — that was something I just had to arrange in person. It would be like my birthday, only better.

Work before pleasure, they say, and cash before government checks. So I decided to give Mr. Macleish higher priority. The best way of dealing with him, surely, was for me to pay a visit with the lovely Ms. Reynolds and ask him, *WTF?*

The first step was calling Doc.

"How's Texas?" I asked Doc.

"We're not in Texas."

"Why aren't you in Texas? Where the hell are you?"

"On our way to Michigan. Here's the thing, Dick. Macleish isn't in Texas. He's up in Michigan. He owns an auto parts manufacturing place up there. They concluded some big man bites dog deal with a Chinese auto company about a month ago and they have a big ceremony set for this evening. It's a big deal."

"How big?"

"Big. President's supposed to be there. And the secretary of State."

TWO BIRDS WITH one stone? Who says God doesn't like me?

"WHAT TIME ARE you due into Detroit?" I asked Doc.

"Around four."

"I want you to wait for me at the airport. Do you understand? I do *not* want you to talk to Macleish. Keep Melissa far away."

"Something up?"

"Just do it."

"Aye, aye, skipper."

"Don't give me that aye, aye bullshit. If Melissa gives you any trouble, you put her over your knee and spank her," I added.

"I don't know that I'd get away with that."

"You outweigh her."

"It's not her I'm worried about," Doc said. "It's my wife, Donna."

Junior called just as I hung up.

"I was just about to call you," I told him.

"Dad, did you check those briefcases?" he asked. He had the tone of someone who'd just won a horse race betting on a horse you declared a nag.

"Which ones? You mean from the barn?"

"Those are the ones. Did you check them?"

"There wasn't time. Why? Are they filled with money?"

"No. Semtex. They're wired to explode."

Semtex is plastic explosive.

"Here's something else you don't know," said Junior. "Shunt just broke into one of the e-mail accounts their computer accessed regularly and found e-mails with information on a presidential event set for tonight. And a bunch of, uh, background dossiers on your friend Jordan Macleish."

"That part I did know," I told him. "Listen, I need you to get me a flight up to Detroit."

"Way ahead of you. You have to get over to the airport in a half hour. Secret Service won't hold the plane for you past that."

[XIV]

THE SECRET SERVICE as your private travel agent?

It pays to have friends in low places.

I have to skip some of the details of what happened next. To summarize, there was a debate en route to Detroit about how precisely to move ahead. The Service already had people swarming over the camp south of the border. I had not only turned over the hard drives we'd taken, but had also authorized Shunt to give them full access to the data he'd already deciphered.

Still, it wasn't exactly clear if anyone was still around to carry out the assassination. There was a good argument to be made that I had already killed all of the plotters.

Or as one Secret Service agent put it, "You just killed a shitload of bad shit, which personally I'm glad for."

But how much of a risk do you take with the president of the United States? Do you let him walk into a place where he may be targeted for assassination?

Don't answer that.

AT ROUGHLY FIVE P.M., a Secret Service team swept the premises of the JPM Electronic Auto Control Factory in Riverview, Michigan. From the outside, at least, the factory was not the kind of building you would associate with cutting edge auto electronics. It was about as attractive as a pile of cement blocks painted a fairly disgusting shade of pinkish red. Which pretty much describes the one-story bunker wannabe that housed JPM.

Inside, it had a little more going for it—assuming you were a robot. The entire assembly line was run by robots, with exactly one person supervising. There were two other employees, both part-time custodians.

But times being what they were, JPM represented an important cog in the American industrial universe. The firm had just landed a major contract to supply small electronic doodads controlling brakes to a Chinese company. Rumor has it that the Chinese were already reverse-engineering that doodad, but it's not my place to speculate.

JPM was a proud member of the local community, though they weren't actually adding to the tax base, having been granted a hundred percent abatement of all property taxes for the next fifteen years.

At least the only human full-timer was paying income taxes, right?

He was . . . but to Canada, which was a short drive (but generally long commute in rush-hour traffic) across the river.

The Secret Service completed its sweep with its normal anal-retentive efficiency and began allowing the invited guests back into the building. All the usual suspects were there—two or three dozen UAW poohbahs, vice presidents of all three U.S. (or quasi-U.S.) automakers, a few bank vice presidents, and politicians of every stripe, including a skinny vegan who had run on the Green Party line the year before, but was now in favor of what she called "high-tech mod-u-als." Maybe she thought this kept dolphins from dying.

I was there too, nodding to her mindless chatter as the crowd filed inside. I had been given credentials as an independent investor, of which there were about half a dozen invited. It wasn't really a cover; if anyone asked, I would admit to being myself and supply a story about always being on the lookout for a good investment. This is true, though my investments tend to be made at the local discount beer and soda distributor.

I spotted Macleish huddling with the mayor and one of the bank VPs. His face blanched when he saw me. He raised his hand and motioned for me to come over through the crowd and talk.

Smiling, I stayed where I was.

Doc and Melissa were outside, in the crowd beyond the security cordon. So were Trace, Shotgun, Mongoose, and Veronica. We were all hooked together by radio. I won't say my guys were looking over the crowd for the Secret Service—the Service needs no help from the likes of me. They were, however, taking in the sights. And I don't mean the river, though it was a spectacular sight from the city's nearby riverside park.

Veronica came north with us. She'd insisted, and frankly I didn't try very hard to argue her out of it. For one thing, she had many police connections in town, which might make her useful. For another, she was a good cop, and when a good cop gets a whiff of a case, they don't let it go until it's completely solved.

Last but not least, she was the most beautiful woman this side of Karen Fairchild. No way I was getting rid of her before I had to.

Just as the place filled with local dignitaries, a high school band began playing "Hail to the Chief." Everyone looked expectantly toward the front door. A pair of Secret Service agents came in through the side door and forced the crowd to move back.

They were followed by the secretary of State, who strode to the center of the room. The squirrelly aide who'd met me in Texas was in her entourage, carrying a thick loose-leaf binder. Two Chinese gentlemen in dark suits followed a respectful distance behind.

"Ladies and gentlemen, thank you for coming," the secretary of State began. "First, let me deliver some bad news. The president extends his regrets, but pressing business in Washington required his immediate attention, and he had to return to the White House."

The air in the room, what little there was of it, suddenly whooshed away.

The secretary of State gave a brief speech, then one of the Chinese gentlemen said a few words in his native language. I have no idea exactly what those words were, as no one translated them, and none of the dozen menu items or 752 curse words I know were included.

"I hope you'll all join us at the Sky Building downtown for a reception," announced Macleish when the Chinese businessman finished. "We have hors d'oeuvres and a bar."

Now there's a man who knows how to give a speech.

I clicked my radio and checked in with Doc, outside looking over the crowd.

"Nothing going on," he told me. "No one suspicious, nothing."

"All right. Keep watching."

I ADMIT IT: I was disappointed.

I was sure Hezbollah was aiming at a huge hit for its first appearance in America. Taking out the president of the United States was about as huge as these assholes would ever be able to get. The cancellation couldn't possibly have changed their plans — it had happened far too late.

Maybe I *had* gotten all of them at the farm. Or maybe we'd misread the evidence.

There's always a temptation to fit conspiracies neatly together, to connect the dots in exactly the shape you think should be there. Maybe I had jumped to conclusions. Maybe I was so eager to get these Hezbollah scumbags, and punish the cartel, that I had assumed they were a lot more competent than they were in real life.

Another common mistake in counterterror. Better than underestimating the enemy, though.

As for Macleish — I had realized he was a bit of a snake from the beginning. The fact that he hadn't told me everything that was going on — lying about contacting Melissa's father was a no-no, even if it hadn't caused any harm — meant he was going to get a good butt kicking.

But it didn't make him a terrorist. And up to now not even Shunt had found evidence at all that he was involved in the plot.

This could easily all be a coincidence. Assuming you believe in those.

"MR. MARCINKO. DICK, how are you?" Macleish held out his hand, ever so hesitantly.

I grabbed it firmly. "Mr. Macleish."

"Jordan, please. Do you have news?"

"Yes, as a matter of fact I do. We've secured Ms. Reynolds."

"You did—great."

He was relieved. It wasn't an act either. He nearly melted on the spot.

"I'm grateful. When? Where? Where is she?"

"She'll join us at the Sky Towers," I told him.

"Mr. Marcinko, you seem to be everywhere these days," said the secretary of State, joining us. The crowd had begun filtering out.

"Madam Secretary." I gave her a little bit of bow to impress the Chinese. "I hope you're well."

"And what brings you to Detroit? Looking for a new car?"

"As a matter of fact, I've taken care of that little matter Poindexter wanted me to look into for you," I said, nodding at her aide. He smiled awkwardly.

"His name isn't Poindexter, Dick."

"Don't you think it ought to be?" I smiled, then bowed again. "He kind of looks like one."

"Richard—"

"We're just spell checking the report for you. We'll present it to you in time for the hearing. I do hope my check will be as quick."

"I'll authorize it this afternoon. Will I like the report?"

"Is that a requirement for my bill to be paid?"

"No. Certainly not."

"In that case, you will absolutely adore it."

One of the Secret Service agents tugged at her sleeve, and she followed him out. I turned back to Macleish.

"Give me a ride to the reception?" I asked.

"Gladly."

By now the crowd had mostly filtered out. Macleish's limo was parked a few yards from the front door. We got into the back, settling into the thick leather seats.

"Take us over to Sky," he told the driver.

"Yes, sir," said the driver.

Macleish leaned forward. "Are you the driver I had earlier?"

"He wasn't feeling well."

"I see. What's your name?"

"You can call me Doc. Everybody does."

Macleish glanced at me, smiling. "Good nickname," he said.

"Thank you, sir."

"So when can I see Melissa?" said Macleish.

"We can arrange that pretty soon," I told him. "Any moment, actually."

Right on cue, the door on Macleish's side opened.

"Melissa!" he said, reaching out his hands.

She hit him square in the face with her fist. He jerked back, stunned. Melissa grabbed his legs and pulled him out of the car. His head bounced on the sidewalk. He started to get up, but stopped when she delivered a heel to his jaw.

The kick looked suspiciously like something Trace often taught new recruits and women in her self-defense classes.

"Whoa, whoa, that's enough," I said, jumping out of the car.

Trace ran up from nearby and grabbed her from behind before she could deliver another blow.

"Take it easy now," she said. "Easy."

"God," Macleish moaned from the ground. "God. You could have killed me."

"I *will* kill you," she said. "You had me kidnapped, you scumbag."

"No," he said. He was bleeding from his nose and his mouth. Doc unfolded himself from the car and knelt down next to him. "No. It wasn't me. They kidnapped you to get at me, so I would cooperate. They had people in the agencies—that's why I went to Marcinko. I knew he'd be able to handle it. It's what your father would have done."

"But you never told him," said Doc. "Greenie didn't even know his daughter was kidnapped."

"I couldn't get him. I'm sure he would have hired Marcinko. And—look. It worked."

"What did the cartel want from you?" I asked.

"Just for me to hire someone as my events director."

"What?"

"I told them I had people, then they kidnapped Melissa and said I'd cooperate or else."

"You need some X-rays," said Doc.

"I think my jaw is broken. It feels broken."

"Maybe," said Doc. "But your ankle is definitely broken. Look at it this way: you're still breathing. That's a good sign."

Doc glanced at me and nodded. I stepped back and took out my cell phone to call for an ambulance.

"I didn't have you kidnapped," Macleish managed. "Honest, I didn't."

It was only at that moment that I realized what the plot was.

What was it my mom used to say? A day late and a dollar short.

"Doc, stay here and get him to the hospital," I yelled, hopping in the town car. "Everybody else, with me."

[XV]

WHY WOULD A Mexican drug cartel blackmail a dopey rich guy to get an events coordinator hired?

Makes about as much sense as some of the economic forecasts coming out of Washington these days.

Unless you were looking for a way to get some of your people — or friends of your people — hired to a very specific event.

Macleish had planned a very fancy reception in downtown Detroit. Until a half hour before, the president of the United States was supposed to be the guest of honor — a fact that had been known in the right circles for roughly two months, well in advance of Melissa's kidnapping.

Traffic in Detroit doesn't approach the epic levels of L.A. or D.C., but it can still be a bitch. Coming up from the south and having just missed rush hour, it looked for a few moments that we had escaped the worst of it. I was able to get onto Biddle Avenue and, with some judicious use of the passing lane, make it north of Wyndotte inside of a minute or two. But at Goddard Street, Murphy intervened: a sea of red taillights appeared before me, the result of a backup that extended more than a mile north.

Murphy had seen fit to nudge a gasoline tanker into a tour bus up on West Outer Drive. There was no fire, but the wreck blocked traffic in both directions. Within seconds I was hemmed in on all sides, not that there was much alternative on the nearby roads anyway.

"Lots of boats in that marina, Dick," suggested Mongoose.

"Good thinking," I said. I threw the car into re-verse—possibly I nudged the bumper of the vehicle behind me—angled to the right, then hit the gas and bounded up over the sidewalk. I shot between a pair of trees—maybe I scraped the doors on the bark—and drove into a parking lot.

Veering out of the way of an oncoming truck, I steered over a railroad crossing and found myself in an industrial yard with pipes running overhead and large tanks of gas marked "DANGER" dead ahead. The Lincoln fishtailed on me as I swung to the right; about midskid I saw an alleyway between the nearest tanks and cranked the wheel back. We got through the alley and flew over another set of tracks, this time without the benefit of a crossing. One of the tires blew as the hub cracked, and I lost the tailpipe. But momentum is a stubborn thing, and I managed to get the car up over the tracks and onto an asphalt lot. I fought it straight for about twenty or thirty yards, until finally the town car just decided enough was enough.

"First one to the docks, grab the fastest boat you can find," I yelled as everyone leapt from the car.

I did my best to keep up with the others as they raced through the next lot, ducked between a pair of sewage treatment lagoons, and hopped a fence onto a long cement pier. A middle-aged black man with a trim goatee was just tying up his speedboat as Trace and Mongoose—running nearly neck to neck—reached his slip.

"Need your boat," yelled Mongoose, gasping for breath.

"Emergency downtown," said Trace.

"I'm with the police," said Veronica, fishing out a badge as she ran up behind them.

I don't know what the poor guy thought was going on, but by the time I reached them—a few steps behind Shotgun, and practically hyperventilating—the boat owner had the vessel revving along the riverside pier.

The good news was that the boat was a Magnum Maltese in close to museum shape, with a pair of upgraded 350 engines, both freshly tuned. It would have been hard to find a faster boat on that stretch of the river.

The bad news was that the boat was a Magnum Maltese, designed for speed, not passenger capacity or comfort.

We crammed six people into a space that might generously be said to handle four, then sped northward on water that turned out to be choppier than the Snake River just below the rapids. The boat bucked over the waves like a bull trying to get rid of its rider. I had to hold onto the ladies to keep them from falling out.

That's my excuse, anyway.

We tore past River Rouge and Zug Island, speeding toward the downtown area as if the devil were on our heels.

"Name's Dave," yelled the boat's owner. "Where do you need to go?"

"A place called Sky Towers," I yelled back. He was maybe two feet from me, but it was hard to hear him over the wind and surf.

"Sky Towers? That's that fancy new office building just beyond Renaissance Center, right?"

"If you say so."

"They took part of the park to build it, the bastards. Nice building, though—right on the water."

"Can you get us there?"

"I can sail you right into the lobby if you want."

"Do it."

Dave thought I was joking. But the truth is I probably would have had him jam his boat into the side of the building if it was possible. But Sky Towers turned out to be about eighty-five yards from the shoreline, sandwiched between two parking lots and the riverside park.

Throttling back, Dave fought the current as he took us into the Riverwalk pier. We leapt up onto the concrete and hopped the metal barrier, racing across the boardwalk and through the park. Once more I ended up at the back of the train, struggling to keep up as Trace, Victoria, Shotgun, and Mongoose ran to the building.

While nowhere near as high as the seventy-three-story centerpiece of the nearby Renaissance Center, Sky was no slacker. The office building counted some forty-two stories above its lobby, which was itself three normal stories high. The thick smell of drywall mud stung my nose as I came in through the river lobby door. The building was only about a third occupied, with the interiors of several floors not yet completed. The lobby itself wasn't even completed, the bare walls near the rear door contrasting sharply with the finely dressed surfaces near the elevators and main security desk not far away.

Trace had already found building security and one of the Secret Service coordinators. (Even though the president had canceled, the team stayed in place due to the earlier threat.) The coordinator's first name was Rose; she was all thorns and no flower. With thick sunglasses and massive shoulders, she looked like she could wrestle for WWE and I don't mean as a diva. A big black woman with a booming voice, she stood with her arms folded blocking the elevators, a phalanx of security and Secret Service agents looking on behind her.

"We need to get upstairs to the reception," Trace told her. "They're going to make an attempt on the secretary of State's life."

"Who's *they*?"

"Hezbollah."

"Right. This is the same bullshit rumor that sent a hundred of our best agents down to Riverview, right?" The woman glanced in my direction before Trace could answer. "Who are you?"

"Dick Marcinko," I managed. "We need to talk to the secretary of State's security team."

"You can talk to me."

"I told her what's going on," said Trace. "She doesn't believe me."

I could tell from the way Trace moved her left foot that she was planning to do a step and jump-kick that would put her left foot shoe into Rose's throat and take her down. It would undoubtedly give us enough of a diversion to reach the stairway to my right. But the last thing I wanted was a pack of Secret Service agents chasing us up the stairs.

Well, maybe as a last resort.

I raised my left hand, warning Trace off.

"The catering company," I told Rose. "How thoroughly were they checked?"

"Who the hell are you again?"

"Dick Marcinko with Red Cell International. I've

been working with one of the D.C. supervisors. We all came up to Riverview together."

"I saw that intel you developed," she said, in a voice that indicated *exactly* what she thought of it . . . not much. "Look, Dick Marcinko, I'm with the Secret Service. We're not rent-a-cops. You think we haven't checked every dish going into the building, let alone going onto the penthouse floor?"

"You check all the workers?" said Trace. "How many are undocumented?"

"We check *all* the workers."

"You just run the Social Security numbers through the computer and see what comes up," said Veronica. "That's not much of a check."

"This discussion is over, missy," said Rose.

I put up my hand again, this time to stop Veronica from taking a swing.

"Call up to the secretary's assistant," I said, pulling out my cell phone. "Here's his number."

"That could be anyone's number, on any cell phone around."

I dug out my wallet and took out the *ass*-istant's card, which by some stroke of luck I hadn't torn into little tiny pieces or shoved back down his throat. Rose gave it such a dubious look I would have sworn she knew him.

Finally she reached for her radio and called one of her people upstairs. She took a few steps away so I couldn't hear.

"Dick," said Mongoose in a stage whisper from across the room. "You know Johnny?"

Mongoose was standing with a tall man in a blue pin-striped suit and a tiny little pin in his lapel—Secret Service.

"Johnny was a detailer for the SEALs," said Mongoose. "He's part of the Filipino mafia."

I went over and introduced myself.

"Washed out of BUDS, to my everlasting shame," admitted Johnny, lowering his gaze as we shook.

"It's not a shame. Being a SEAL is not for everyone."

He made a little bit of a grimace. "Thanks."

"Johnny says they checked the food crew really carefully," said Mongoose. "No Arabs. No Mexicans."

"No Mexicans on a food crew?" I asked. "That's suspicious in itself."

"Tough to believe, huh?" Johnny nodded. "But we went through it real careful. Whole kitchen staff had to strip down. I'm not kidding. Guests are going through X-ray machines, whole nine yards."

"You have a bomb sniffer up there?"

"No. But we have the one here in the lobby. Nobody gets upstairs without going past it."

"When did it get here?"

"Yesterday."

So the bombs were brought in before the sniffer came.

"We had a sniffer upstairs. The place was clean," added the exdetailer.

The *floor* was clean. The rest of the building *might* be clean. Or it might not. No one was really in a position to say.

"What sort of tenants are in the building?" I asked.

"I can get a list," said Johnny. "But there's a directory right there."

Duh.

I went over and looked at the shallow glass case hanging on the wall, your standard list of who's who and the floor they were whooing on.

There were a bunch of marketing firms, a game development company, a suite of doctors, and an outfit that offered "therapeutic massage."

"I'll check the massages," volunteered Shotgun.

"Canceled all their appointments today, because they figured the security hassle would be too much," said Johnny. He grinned. "Pretty much the whole team volunteered ahead of you."

"How about the doctors," I asked. "They cancel their appointments?"

"Not that I know of."

"Don't they have patients? The lobby looks empty."

"Come to think of it, no. They were all let in earlier this morning."

"You sure they're doctors?"

"Uh—"

"Have there been many patients in and out?" asked Mongoose. "You just said hardly anyone came in all day except for the party."

"That's right. We had two lines."

"So were there patients?" I asked.

"Um, I don't remember any."

"You sure these guys are doctors?" asked Mongoose.

"Well, I mean, I don't know that we asked for medical licenses."

"All right, you can go up," called Rose. "No weapons. No phones. No radios."

"No phones?" said Trace. "No radios?"

"You want to argue for the next half hour, or you want to go up?"

I guess she thought we were there for the cocktails. Given all the Secret Service agents and the State

Department security people up there, our weapons were probably . . . twice as necessary. But let's not quibble.

Unarmed and without any practical means of communicating to each other, we headed for the elevator.

"Goose, you and Shotgun check out the doctors' clinic," I said. "The ladies and I will go all the way upstairs."

"What exactly should we look for?" asked Mongoose.

"Anything suspicious," said Trace.

"Frickin' Shotgun's suspicious," said Mongoose. "We need something better than that."

They all looked at me. Mongoose had an excellent point—what exactly were we looking for?

"The tango is probably going to be Middle Eastern," I told them. "If he's with Hezbollah. Heavy odds. They had the briefcases made up, so look for those. But don't let that narrow your thinking."

"In other words, suspect everything," said Mongoose.

"Yup."

"I can tell you were an officer."

The doors opened on the doctors' floor. Mongoose and Shotgun jumped out.

I pressed P for penthouse and stepped back as the doors closed.

WHAT WAS THAT from the peanut gallery? You there, in the back of the room. You have a question?

Was I *profiling* in saying that the most likely suspect was an Arab?

Was *that* your question?

It was?

Hell no, we're not profiling. We're using our COM-MON SENSE.

Which I capitalize here, because it is in such SHORT SUPPLY.

THE SECRETARY OF State's ass-istant met us in the lobby of the penthouse level. The lobby was decked out with large pieces of slate on the walls, and somewhat smaller ones on the floor. A waterfall flowed down the wall in front of us, cascading neatly into a rectangular copper base, where shards of slate deflected it before it could splatter on the floor.

Pretty. It would make excellent shrapnel if someone exploded a bomb next to it.

"Dick, so good of you to come," said the secretary of State's weasel-faced assistant. He had a phony smile to match his phony voice. "The secretary of State was just asking about you. Care for a drink? I think they have bourbon—"

"See anybody with a briefcase?" I asked.

"Briefcase?" He shook his head. "I left mine in the SUV. This is a social occasion. Have you seen Mr. Mac-leish? I thought he'd be here by now."

"He's been detained," I told him, starting into the crowd.

"The bar's that way," said the ass-istant. "Help your-self. I know you're a big whiskey lover."

I always admire someone who does his research.

Veronica and Trace were already working their way through the crowd. Though called the penthouse, the space was actually a large, open reception room, with three levels separated by a pair of steps. The walls were glass on three sides; the fourth walled off an area for a kitchen, a service elevator, and a staff room. There was an outdoor patio on the west side of the room. A handful of guests were out there, mingling beneath the fake trees.

After spotting the secretary of State in almost the exact epicenter of the room, I quickly surveyed the rest of the place without coming up with a likely suspect. So I detoured over to the bar—drinks always provide a plausible cover—where I discovered, much to my surprise and approval, that the bartender had a full bottle of Bombay Sapphire on call.

I took mine on the rocks, then began working my way over to the secretary of State, listening as she held forth on a theory of constructive engagement. I kept glancing around, but didn't see anyone who looked even half Arab.

"Constructive engagement is the way of the future," said the secretary of State just as I drew close. She paused to take a sip of her drink, a Shirley Temple from the looks of it.

"Constructive engagement," I echoed. "That means holding them very close while pounding the crap out of them, right?"

"Mr. Marcinko, I'm so glad you could make it. I so rarely see you at an event when there's a cash bar."

"I told them to add this drink to your bill." I raised the glass in salute.

"I'm sure the auditor will have no trouble approving it," she said.

"Tell me. Do you still think there's no truth at all to those rumors that Hezbollah is working with the Mexican drug cartels?"

"I think that's pure speculation," she said frostily. "But I believe that's your job, isn't it? Weren't you retained to look into that?"

"I was indeed."

"Excuse me, Madam Secretary," said one of the men nearby. "I wonder if we could get your picture."

She was only too happy to find an excuse to get away from me, of course. I stayed put, sipping my drink and studying the crowd.

Had I just been wrong?

It's been known to happen. Once, I think. Maybe twice.

The plot did lay out neatly, perhaps too neatly: come in with the briefcases a few days before, stow them in the fake doctors' offices (or somewhere nearby), then come up to the party. Controlling the caterer was either gravy, or perhaps part of the plot to escape.

One of the advantages of Detroit was that Arabs would blend in easily; a good portion of the city's population—and hardworking taxpayers, let it be said—are of Middle Eastern extraction. Terrorists would blend right in, at least for a short while.

But the briefcases wouldn't. They would stick out like sore thumbs.

That must be my mistake, I thought. The fact that we had found a bunch was an argument that I was barking at the wrong tree—if the plot was already under way, wouldn't they have brought them with them?

I leaned back against the glass that separated the room from the exterior patio. The odds were that I had already broken up the plot. Why couldn't I just accept success?

Because it didn't feel right. Like the Bombay — I think someone had watered it down.

A hanging offense.

I glanced around, still unwilling to let go of the notion that Hezbollah was targeting the building. Ideas, even when wrong, are stubborn things.

Nobody had briefcases.

Well, actually, the Secret Service guys tasked to hold the Uzis did so in a sleek and discreet case.

I started across the room, looking for the agent in charge on the floor. He was instantly recognizable by the curl of his radio wire and the color of his lapel pin. As I walked, I drained my glass and handed it to the first person I passed, a banker type who took it, then frowned at the fact that it was empty.

"Dick Marcinko," I told the Secret Service agent.

"I know who you are," said the agent.

"All of the guys with the Uzis, they're all yours?"

"What?"

"The briefcases. Does State have any gunners up here?"

He frowned. I guess it was supposed to be a big secret that the agents were carrying their heavier weaponry in discreet cases. "One, I think."

Two little words you never want to hear in a security situation: *I think*.

I might have started quizzing him, but out of the corner of my eye I saw the secretary of State go out the door to the patio. A tall man who'd been watching her from across the room followed.

He had a briefcase in his hand.

I rushed toward the door, hurrying outside. The man with the briefcase had sidled up next to the knot of well-wishers around the secretary of State, who was chatting with the man who had wanted to take her picture.

The man was tall, blond, and very Nordic-looking.

"You, move away from the secretary of State!" I yelled.

Everyone turned around.

"You with the briefcase!" I shouted.

"Are you pointing at me?" said the man, incredulous. Rather than taking a step away from her, he moved closer. "Are you saying I'm an assassin?"

"No, he is," I said, grabbing the squirrelly man in a suit who'd been standing near the door.

He, too, had a briefcase, was wearing a dark suit, and had a lapel pin IDing him as part of the security team.

He started to object, trying to duck out of my grip. I leaned into him, putting him on my waist and pivoting as I threw him over the rail opposite me.

There was a loud, collective gasp. Then silence. I walked over to the rail.

"Dick!" yelled the secretary of State. "Now you've really done it."

She literally shook with fury as she joined me at the rail, looking down toward the ground.

"There." I pointed to where he had landed, some forty-two stories below.

"Where?"

"There," I said as the man and his briefcase blew up.

[XUI]

YOU CAN INTERPRET *some* of that to good luck, as I never would have figured out where the bogus security person was until I discovered and followed the *actual* State Department agent, who had moved to be close to the secretary. From there, it was relatively easy to figure out that the guy who actually looked like a Hezbollah recruit—accepting that he had trimmed his beard for the job—was the bomber. His reaction certainly helped—no self-respecting Secret Service or even State Department security person would have tried to break my hold. They would have reversed it and put me over their shoulder. So I knew as soon as he did that I was right.

What if he'd been better trained in martial arts?

Impossible!

Plus, Trace was right behind me.

MONGOOSE AND SHOTGUN appeared a few seconds after the excitement, reporting that the doctors' office was empty of patients and doctors. But beyond the reception area in what was supposed to be an X-ray room, they had found a cache of weapons and a small stack of money, several changes of clothes, and a box of phony IDs. A raid by the police later that night would turn up evidence that the place had been rented by associates of Hezbollah. Unfortunately, the timing was bad. A raid on an apartment in Detroit a few hours later failed to net the two suspects the FBI traced to the little camp we'd crashed in Mexico. But some papers there implicated a local imam, who it appeared had provided aid and comfort to the visitors.

The imam also couldn't be found. Rumor has it he's been spotted sightseeing in Yemen, which is a lovely place this time of year.

SUFFICE TO SAY my report to the State Department was received with great huzzahs and hurrahs. Aides and analysts literally did cartwheels down the aisles.

Heh.

I did, however, get paid quite handsomely. I received the full price agreed upon, along with expenses, which I swear to you as a fellow taxpayer I did not pad. And to top it off, the secretary of State wrote me a very nice, personal thank-you card, which accompanied a bouquet of flowers.

I had both thoroughly checked for poison and explosives before opening, of course.

Though documented, the connection between Hezbollah and the Mexican cartel failed to get much play in the media, mainstream and otherwise. Homeland Insecurity released some sort of press statement making a vague reference to the camp being discovered; if you read the report quickly, you might think they were the ones responsible.

If you read it slowly, you'd be positive they were.

Junior missed out on all the excitement because he had to stay around and wait for the U.S. Marshal's office to show up and take full custody of de Sarcena, who by that point was pretty well addicted to painkillers. I understand he went cold turkey while waiting in prison to face trial on a record-setting 537 felonies. The cases haven't begun yet, but I'm guessing at least one of the charges will stick, as long as they don't pick a jury from South Florida.

Another dozen arrests were made of cartel associates in the States, due to evidence we provided. Said evidence included taped ramblings of things de Sarcena said while under the influence of Percocet—not admissible in court, perhaps, but vivid nonetheless.

As for the cartel: de Sarcena's absence set the stage for a power struggle that is still going on. The result has been to split the cartel back into its "traditional" parts; how long that lasts is anyone's guess.

The fallout can be measured unfortunately, in the rise of violence along the border. Literally hundreds of people have died on the Mexican side in the past year due to cartel infighting. Juarez, never a pleasant place to begin with, is now the murder capital of the world.

The Mexican government has responded; some Mexican army units and the Mexican attorney general are waging a valiant fight. I can't see far enough into the future to call a winner.

The tunnel under the border was shut down. I just read in the paper the other day about several similar ones being discovered in San Diego, so I'm guessing there was no real resolution or progress there.

Organized crime continues to smuggle people as well as drugs and everything else the banditos can think of across the border, in a variety of ways. But here's a positive sign—the Mexicans who lived in the hamlet near Angel Hills are all still there, and say they're doing well. A new factory making ceramic goods is locating nearby—another plus, I guess.

As for the Americans who opted to stay in Angel Hills: at last report, they're still doing well. Rumor has it they tell of their exploits every afternoon around the pool, with the aid of a few cold ones. A number of people who'd left returned, but most of the complex is still unoccupied.

Melissa Reynolds got a good scolding from her dad. I'm sure it went in one ear and out the other. On the other hand, her sugar daddy, Jordan Macleish, tried to make up with her but failed, so obviously there is still some hope for the child.

Macleish at least put his money where his mouth was—our fee hit the bank account the next day, just in time to pay for our party.

There's one other string that needs to be tied here. Remember that attack that opened the book? The kidnapping that wasn't a kidnapping?

Apparently it had to do with a grudge I'd earned in North Korea sometime back. The dictator's son put a price on my head, and thanks to some of his long-armed connections, was able to track me to the mixed-martial arts world and then figured out that I was in Mexico. My suspicion is that he had help from friends in Venezuela, though I haven't been able to flesh that out yet. When I do, there will be hell to pay.

WE BOOKED A few rooms at the nearby Marriott, and after two solid days of sleep, had a party to wrap up our operation. I'm happy to report that there was no damage to the Marriott guest rooms or its lounge.

"I really enjoyed working with you," Veronica told me toward the end of the evening. "I really appreciate everything you've done for my grandparents."

"We were lucky," I admitted. "Very lucky."

"Maybe your famous Mr. Murphy does good as well as evil."

"Murph is an equal opportunity son of a bitch. He

doesn't really care about good and bad. All he wants to do is throw a monkey wrench in somewhere."

She smiled, took another sip of her white wine, then put it down.

"I feel like kissing you," she said.

"You could do that."

She did. It was long, sweet, and deep.

"I'm going to go upstairs now," she said. "Are you?"

She was beautiful. In that light, every bit as beautiful as Karen Fairchild.

And Karen wasn't here.

"I'm afraid I'm not going to make it," I told her.

There was just the vaguest hint of regret on her face before she vanished it with a smile.

"I'm sure she's a wonderful woman," Veronica told me. "I'm jealous."

I watched her walk away. I was sorely tempted to join her.

Just a few years before, I would have. Maybe you *can* teach an old Rogue new tricks.